the NIGHT RAID

Clare Harvey is a former army wife. Her mother-in-law's experiences during WWII inspired her novel, *The Gunner Girl*, which won both The Exeter Novel Prize and The Joan Hessayon Award for debut fiction. Clare lives in Nottingham with her family. Find out more about Clare on her website: http://clareharvey.net or catch up with her on Twitter: @ClareHarveyauth or Facebook: ClareHarvey13.

Also by Clare Harvey:

The English Agent
The Gunner Girl

Praise for Clare Harvey:

'Will delight all those who love a good wartime story'
Dilly Court

'Brilliant. I was swept away by this unforgettably powerful tale of love and courage in the face of war. This beautifully written, pacy and impressively researched story binds together a group of flawed individuals in an intricate and fascinating drama, full of heart-stopping moments. Clare Harvey writes with a directness and an honesty that pins you to the page' **Kate Furnivall**

'The sense of period, the descriptive prose and the superb writing make *The English Agent* a real page-turner. Clare is certainly a gifted storyteller' **Ellie Dean**

Clare Harvey

the NIGHT RAID

SIMON & SCHUSTER

London · New York · Sydney · Toronto · New Delhi

A CBS COMPANY

First published in Great Britain by Simon & Schuster UK Ltd, 2017
A CBS COMPANY

This paperback edition, 2017

1 3 5 7 9 10 8 6 4 2

Simon & Schuster UK Ltd
1st Floor
222 Gray's Inn Road
London WC1X 8HB

Simon & Schuster Australia, Sydney
Simon & Schuster India, New Delhi

www.simonandschuster.co.uk
www.simonandschuster.com.au
www.simonandschuster.co.in

A CIP catalogue record for this book is available from the British Library

Paperback ISBN: 978-1-4711-7699-9
eBook ISBN: 978-1-4711-6185-8

Typeset in the UK by M Rules
Printed and bound by CPI Group (UK) Ltd, Croydon, CR0 4YY

Simon & Schuster UK Ltd are committed to sourcing paper that is made
from wood grown in sustainable forests and support the Forest Stewardship
Council, the leading international forest certification organisation. Our
books displaying the FSC logo are printed on FSC certified paper.

For Chris, because

'To my shame, I must admit many are
the corners of my life into which I dare not peep.'

Dame Laura Knight
(from her autobiography, *The Magic of a Line*)

Prologue

She groped, unseeing, until her fingers connected with something soft. 'I've got you,' she said, tugging at the cloth, but there was no answer from the lumpen mass of overall-covered limbs.

Her eyes were streaming, the smoke hot-acrid in her nostrils. Coughs razored up her parched throat.

The site of the fire was further in. Through squinted lashes she could make out the orange glow at ground level. If the flames reached the gas cylinders they'd be done for, but the flames hadn't reached the cylinders – not yet – and there was still a chance she could pull the woman to safety.

She wedged her clog against the edge of a lathe base for leverage, and heaved at the sleeve cuff she held. The body shifted an inch or two, but didn't pull free. She yanked, harder this time, but the body was heavy as a wet sandbag, caught on something. If only she could see – but the smoke was hot-thick. She slid down onto the concrete floor. She'd have to feel her way. She could hear sirens, and shouts calling her away, but the sounds were muffled as birdsong beyond a window pane, as she focused on her task.

She crouched low, feeling her way down the length of the overalls: strap, waist button, side pocket, trouser leg – nudging and shoving at the inert form as she went – all the way down. Here it was: a foot caught up in one of the twirling gas hoses.

Her fingers twisted the looping rubber, unhooking it from the woman's foot, tugging her leg free. At last.

The boiling air was quicksand, pooling and sucking and swallowing them up. She had to get them both out, fast. She had to get them down to the shelter, in case the fire spread and the whole thing blew.

She shuffled back, following the line of the overalls with her fingertips. She grabbed at the shoulder straps, and pushed her foot again against the lathe. She strained and wrenched, the cloth cutting into her palms.

This time the body moved, and she followed the momentum, jerking and tugging and pulling it out, along the factory floor, away from the flames. Her breath came in grunting gasps, painful, as the heat seared her lungs. There was sweat and tears in her eyes, and a metallic taste in her mouth. The woman's head jolted awkwardly over the concrete floor, but there was no time to take care. There was no time.

Suddenly there were hands at her shoulders, shouting voices, and the woman's body was pulled away, backwards, towards the shelter door: *We've got her, now get inside, for God's sake.*

No, wait.

She saw the easel, the canvas pale against the orange-grey of the growing fire. The painting was so close to completion: those butter-smooth faces that had taken weeks to create. She broke free of the hands that grabbed her.

It will only take a second to get the painting.

She turned and ran back towards the flames.

Three months earlier

Chapter 1

Laura

'What do you say, Harold?' Laura said.

'Hmm?' Harold looked up from the crossword.

'About Nottingham,' she continued.

'What about Nottingham?'

He hadn't listened to a word she'd said. She'd come straight in here after the telephone call from Ken Clark to tell him all about it and he simply hadn't listened. Laura narrowed her eyes, sucked in a breath and repeated herself: 'They want me to do another one like "Ruby Loftus". They loved it, Harold, and they say they want more. This time they said to have two women, to show team spirit and all that. Of course I said it would cost more – a double portrait, twice as long, six weeks' sitting at least, I said. I asked for double and they've gone away to discuss figures. I suspect I won't get double, but K will have to more than match what they gave me for the Ruby Loftus one, which would certainly keep the wolf from the door.'

Harold put down his pencil and stroked his chin, regarding her through his pebble glasses. The light from the hearth highlighted the defined lines of his head, edging his skull green-gold. How she'd love to paint him just like that, contained in firelight. If only he'd let her. Her husband had never once let her produce even so much as a sketch of him, although he'd painted her portrait when she was no older than the young waitress who was wobbling towards them through the cluttered tea room.

'You've only just got back from Wales,' Harold said. His face betrayed no emotion, features barely moving as the words emerged. And yet it felt – it always felt – like a kind of rebuke.

'I thought you could come with me this time,' Laura said, as the girl arrived at their table with her teetering tray. 'Revisit some of our old haunts; what do you say?'

The tea things clattered onto the polished table: cups, saucers, teaspoons, teapot, milk jug, saccharine tablets in a condiment dish. 'I'll be back with the scones presently,' the girl said, head-bobbing, fair hair escaping from the hair roll. She couldn't be much more than fourteen, dear thing, Laura thought. Wonderful clear skin, the colour of – the colour of Sennen sand at sunset. Yes, that was it: a particular shade between oyster and ivory, overlaid with a rose wash. Delicious.

'Thunder and lightning,' Laura said, remembering, as the girl turned away.

'I beg your pardon, Missus Knight?'

'Be a dear and bring the black treacle when you come back. I like my cream tea the Cornish way.'

The girl nodded and was gone. Harold had picked up his pencil again and was staring down at the crossword.

'Harold!'

He looked up. 'I was just letting it brew a while. Terribly weak, the tea, recently – beginning to wonder if they're re-using the leaves,' he said.

'We were discussing the Nottingham commission,' Laura said. 'Guns again – Royal Ordnance Factory down near the Trent somewhere – Bofors and suchlike. Remember how everyone used to say that the lace-making girls were the prettiest in England? They'll all be on munitions now – there'll be no shortage of faces to paint. What do you think?'

'Does it matter what I think?'

Laura tutted. 'Don't be like that. You could come with me. After all, it's not as if you've anything else to occupy yourself with.'

She saw him stiffen, grasp the pencil and lower his gaze. She'd gone too far. She always went too far, never seemed to know how to keep it buttoned. A better wife wouldn't hurt her husband's pride by making reference to his lack of employment, she supposed. But she wasn't a good wife, never had felt good enough for Harold. And in any case, was it her fault the blasted war meant all the usual portrait work he did for the great and the good had effectively dried up? And the War Artists' Advisory Committee would never offer him work – Harold wouldn't have accepted, even if they had.

Laura sighed and looked out of the window. The telephone wire cut through the westering sky, down towards the fields, where a herd of cows coming home was a rub of charcoal against the dun-mauve backdrop. She put out her fingertip and pulled it across the wet mist condensation on the bottom of the pane. 'I thought you'd like to come,' she said, turning away from the fading light to face her husband.

'Why?' he said, still staring down at his paper.

'Nostalgia. A trip down memory lane – a trip down Waverley Street, Noel Street and onto the Boulevard, for that matter. Oh, Harold, remember all that?'

'It was a very long time ago,' Harold said, putting his newspaper and pencil on the windowsill and picking up the teapot.

'Milk first!' Laura said, snatching up the jug as he began to pour the tea. They ended up pouring at the same time, brown and cream liquids splashing together into beige whirlpools in their cups. A storm in a teacup, Laura thought.

They picked up their cups and lifted them to their lips at the same time. It often happened like that: years of togetherness had synchronised their movements. Years of togetherness – but so often apart, since that first time in November 1916:

'Must you go?' he said. And she'd had to strain to catch his voice, because of the wind and the gulls and the distant waves breaking on the shore. She didn't reply.

He was in three-quarter profile, and she couldn't make out his expression from where she stood. All she could see was the edge of his face: features like one of the wind-gnarled hawthorns in the Cornish hedgerows, moulded from resistance to the whipping breeze. If only she could paint him here, right now, Laura thought. He looked so solid and unyielding, a wonderful contrast to the translucent sweep of Sennen Cove, with its sequinned waves and mother-of-pearl morning skies. For a moment she began a mental composition: the crescent bay curling, and Harold in the chair, looking out to sea. She thought how she could use the two gulls and the skeins of high cloud to draw the eye around, through the silver-blue sky. And Harold himself – her eyes darted over his form, sketching him in her mind's eye: the strong line of his chin, the plane of his brow – etched against the liquid light. How she longed to paint her husband, but how stubbornly he had always refused.

She was roused by the clop of hooves from the lane beyond the cottage. Mr Trevallion was here with the dog cart to take her to the station. To take her to the station, to chug away on the train, all the way to London, and then to change onto another train to Surrey. She wouldn't reach Witley Camp until tonight. She wouldn't see another Sennen morning for weeks, months maybe. 'Mr Trevallion's here,' she called out, but still he didn't turn to face her, remained staring out to sea, muffled in his coat and the tartan travel rug on his lap. His sketchbook lay unopened on the rattan table next to him, with one long, unused pencil on top.

'Be sure he always has his sketchbook and pencil nearby,' Laura told the girl, when she was packing her things last night. 'We don't know when he'll be ready to start drawing again. We must be prepared for when he does.' But the sketchbook had remained closed for almost two years now, and Laura was beginning to wonder if Harold would ever work again. Wondering, too, if he'd ever claw his way out of the hole he'd disappeared into and emerge as the real Harold, the talented, clever, wonderful artist she'd married.

Three steps cleared the distance between them across the frosted grass. She could taste the salt in the air, and hear the kettle whistling in the kitchen, as she leant over to say goodbye.

'I'll write,' she said, feeling the sand-smooth rub of his freshly shaved cheek against hers, smelling his familiar, woody scent.

He grabbed her hand, then clutched her fingers so tight it hurt. 'What do they think about your husband being a conchie?'

'We've been over this, Harold.'

'Why must you go off and paint soldiers?'

'Harold, we are at war, like it or not. Nobody will pay me to paint children flying kites at the seaside or pretty women on the clifftops any more.'

'But soldiers, Laura, training for war. If you leave now, you're a part of that, you know, a part of that whole machine of death. You're as much a part of it as I would have been if I'd let myself be conscripted.' Her wedding ring cut painfully into her flesh as he grasped her hand, tighter still. 'Don't you see? Laura, can't you see what you're doing?' She looked into his face: the strong features she'd always so admired, his serious eyes. Harold was holding her hand, looking into her eyes, and talking to her again, after all these months of silence and dislocation. Unbearable.

Dimly she heard Mr Trevallion calling her from in front of the cottage. 'Harold, we have no money,' she said, slowly, as if talking to a child. 'We cannot eat your principles. We cannot put your principles on the fire to warm the cottage. We cannot use your principles to pay the maid, or to pay for your medication or the visits from Doctor Nightingale.' She tore her hand from his. 'I'm leaving now, Harold.'

She half-ran towards the gate. From the corner of her eye she could see the girl coming out of the back door with Harold's hot water bottle and medicines, her yellow dress like an upside-down daffodil, swaying as she walked along the path. Ahead, in the lane, Mr Trevallion was heaving her trunk into the cart. He looked over at her and grinned his gap-toothed grin. She paused at the gate, fumbling with the latch, turning back to take one last look at her husband. But the girl was fussing with his rug, and from here all she could see was the back of his head, as the girl flurried and chafed him like a nervous pastry cook around a plate of petits fours.

She yanked the gate and pushed through, turning her back on the glorious Sennen morning.

*

'Do say yes, Harold. Come with me to Nottingham and we can stay in an hotel and peek at the ghosts of our former selves, chasing helter-skelter through the Lace Market,' Laura said now, replacing her cup in its saucer.

'Laura, stop exaggerating. Never once did we play tag in the marketplace. The tales you tell make it sound as if we were street urchins together.'

'We weren't much more than that, Harold. I was just fourteen when you painted my portrait, remember?'

It was Harold's turn to sigh.

Laura heard the kitchen door slam and saw the girl struggle in with the tray of scones. She had to dodge and weave through the other tables to reach them. The Petersons' terrier, Kipper, yapped at her heels as she passed, and she had to step over Mr Jones's awkwardly angled leg, which jutted out between the honeymooners' table and the fireplace. The honeymooners were touching toes beneath the table and shovelling buttered crumpets into their mouths. Ravenous, poor things – the exertions of love do seem to make young people terribly hungry, Laura thought. The girl finally arrived, apologising for the delay. Laura shifted the teapot onto the windowsill, next to the ashtray, to make room for the plate of scones. 'Not much cream, I'm afraid, Missus Knight, but I found your special treacle. Mr Peterson has been keeping it back for you,' the girl said.

'Marvellous! How very sweet,' Laura said. The girl gave a flustered smile. 'And you're doing a wonderful job, too. What's your name, dear?'

'Rosie.'

'Lovely name. It suits you. You're new, aren't you?'

'Started last week, Missus Knight.'

'I only got back today. What happened to Marjorie?'

'Her papers came. She went to join the Wrens.'

'Really? She'll look awfully good in that uniform with a figure like hers, won't she? Well, I have to say, I think you're doing very well, Rosie. Keep it up!'

The girl thanked her and left. Laura watched her threading back towards the kitchen. Dear thing. She turned her attention back to her husband, who was already biting into a scone topped with clotted cream and black treacle – her treacle.

'Harold, that's my treacle. Mr Peterson has been saving it for me.'

'Oh, for heaven's sake, Laura,' Harold said, shaking his head and reaching for his teacup.

It was stuffy in the hotel tea room, with the fire and the tightly packed clientele: small movements, small conversations, a small palette of colours: green-grey-brown, and the dull amber of the fire in the hearth. Dear Lord, where was the life in it all?

'You still haven't answered my question about Nottingham,' Laura said, taking a scone and smothering it with the remains of the cream.

Harold swallowed and wiped his lips with a napkin. 'I really don't see why you feel the need to go through the pantomime of getting my permission, Laura. When has it ever mattered what I think?'

15

Chapter 2

George

'Ey up, purple warning's just come through, boss.' The skinny lad placed the intercom receiver back in its cradle and reached for his helmet. George closed the doorway behind him, cutting off the light from the stairwell. He could see well enough; it was a clear night, with a gibbous moon sinking towards the western horizon. Searchlights sprang up, tickling the underbelly of the skies.

The planes were just a faraway buzz, almost drowned out by the clunk and hum of the factory below them. 'Don't worry about that, Alfie,' said George, reaching out for the helmet. Distant sirens yowled like feral tomcats. He raised his voice a notch. 'You get yourself downstairs and get some dinner down you. I hear it's jam roly-poly for pudding.'

'But if there's a raid, Mr Handford?' The lad's eyes were large in his pale face, his still-breaking voice stumbling over the words. 'I d-don't mind staying until the all-clear.'

The buzz was louder, more definite now. George turned

towards the sound. 'They picked a nice night for it,' he said, listening for the sonic trajectory. 'Sounds like they're headed west,' he said. 'Business over Derby again, I'll wager – poor blighters. Now, you get yourself downstairs.'

'If you're sure?' Alfie let go of the helmet.

'Go on, before I change my mind.'

The young fire watcher gave a nervous smile and bobbed back down the stairwell. The door banged shut behind him. George fitted on the helmet. The strap dug in under his chin. He fiddled with it, but couldn't loosen it, so took it off again and hung it on the hook next to the intercom. He shouldn't be up here at all, really. He could easily send someone else up to cover Alfie's break. The Board thought that the duty manager should be present at mealtimes, to show a friendly side to management and boost morale. But George had no need for chit-chat over lumpy custard, or – God forbid – someone suggesting a sing-along.

He walked over to the parapet and leant his hands on the rough-cool concrete, looking out over the rooftops to where the Trent curved like a silver necklace. The factory building was higher than the surrounding terraced houses, but still not high enough for a chap to do away with himself, if he were so inclined. It had crossed his mind once, George remembered, just after he'd started at the factory, with everything that happened back in '22. But he'd been too much of a coward to follow through. Later, he'd read that death was only a certainty if one jumped from higher than one hundred and fifty feet, and the factory roof was only around half of that.

If he'd jumped, he would have only half-killed himself. He'd felt just half-dead since what happened then, in any case, so it really made no difference, he thought, leaning out a little, letting the blue-black chasm shimmy below him. Here he was, still at the factory, living half a life, more than twenty years later.

The sirens stopped and the sound of the planes was louder, a dull, distant drone. He straightened up. They were definitely heading west, as if the fat-faced moon were a plughole, sucking them in. He could just make out his watch in the moonlight: five past twelve – halfway through the night shift. Halfway through his life. He took his hands off the parapet and rubbed them together. It was still cold at night, even though spring was on its way.

He breathed in the chill air, and reached into his pocket for his pipe, as the flares began to fall over Derby, lighting the way for the incoming bombers. 'Poor blighters,' he repeated, thinking of all the individual instances of tragedy and chance that were about to happen: loves lost and lives ruined. What was the point of loving someone, of living with them, if it could all be destroyed in a moment, like that? He exhaled and shook his head. It was better – safer – to exist alone.

Chapter 3

Violet

'Marry me,' he said, hoiking up her skirt.

'Oh, give over,' she replied, shoving the cloth back down over her thighs. But his lips were at her throat and his breath was warm and wet. The rooftops of the houses on either side almost touched above their heads – if she looked up she could see a sliver of star-specked sky between the two lines of guttering.

'Frank Timpson, what are you like?' She pulled up his head and placed her lips on his, pressing into the soft beer-smoke-sweet taste of him. She let herself sink into the kiss. Mrs Frank Timpson – could she do it? She stroked the back of his neck, where the hairline bristled into the skin of his neck. She felt his hands snake down, unbuttoning her blouse. There was no one about. Nobody used this alley any more, not since the street at the far end had been blitzed out; it was a rubble-strewn dead-end further in.

'I can't do this, Frank,' she said, pulling her mouth from his.

'I mean it, Vi. Let me, and I'll marry you. I'll marry you tomorrow if you want. Just say yes.' His breath hot against her skin, his fingers kneading and stroking. And then he slid down, the brush of cloth against cloth as he went all the way down onto one knee. His head was right by her groin, his hands pushing up her skirt, his fingers against her thighs. She let her legs relax, begin to part, as his thumbs looped under her knicker elastic and tugged them down. He pulled away from her and began to unbutton his fly.

The edge of the drainpipe bit into her back below the straps of her brassiere, and her hair snagged on the brickwork, as Frank's body nudged and butted. Vi thought, this is it, I'm a woman now, and it hurt a bit, but it wasn't as bad as they said. And it was all right, because she and Frank had been secretly meeting like this for months now, and he'd asked her to marry him, hadn't he?

And in any case, everyone knew you couldn't fall pregnant if it was your first time and you did it standing up.

I've lost my cherry! I've done it with Frank Timpson and he wants to marry me. It was a delicious secret. She thought they'd somehow be able to tell, but when she slipped into bed with Rita and May, they just complained about her cold feet, as per usual; nobody seemed to notice that she was different at all. Baby Val woke with a yowl at six in the morning, and Vi fell out of bed and down the stairs to warm her a bottle, even though she hadn't gone to bed until past midnight and everyone kept telling her that Baby Val was too old to have a bottle in the mornings these days. Vi felt sorry for the motherless mite, sent back here when her dad got rheumatic fever last month.

Nothing had changed except her. Everything was just the same: national loaf and marge for breakfast, and weak tea with the thrice-used leaves (at least the little ones went to school with something hot inside, which was more than some others got). Ma was wheezing worse than usual, and had to be helped to the privy. One of the boys barrelled into Baby Val's full potty before Vi had a chance to empty it, so there was that to clear up, and all. Vi wondered when the right time would be to tell them. Should she wait until it was official, she'd got a ring and that?

Ma was on her way back from the lav when the postman came; she pulled the brown envelope that poked through the slot like a paper tongue. She ripped it open and peered down at the typed sheet. 'Thought this would come any day,' she said, holding the paper out to Vi. 'It's been two weeks since your birthday already – they'll be wanting you for war work, girl.' She started coughing then, and Vi took the letter from her and helped her back into bed.

Vi felt the sheet of paper crackle in her pocket. The clock tower chimed the half-hour. The sun was cloud-stabbing, not quite breaking through, turning the morning street yellow-grey and bruised-looking. A poster on the bus stop opposite told her to join the ATS. Not bleeding likely, she thought, with a sudden twinge of grief, remembering her big sister, Bea.

It was a pain that the Labour Exchange was right over the other side of town, but she needed to get this out of the way as soon as. She was going to go right in there and tell them that she was engaged to be married. They couldn't send her away for war work then, could they?

A window cleaner was soaping up the windows of the Labour Exchange, his arm sudding and wiping with the practised rhythm of a machine. Vi wondered why he hadn't been conscripted – flat feet, bad teeth, infected lungs? He looked healthy enough to her, rubbing away at the glass like that. She began to walk along the pavement and he broke off his tune to give a lack-lustre wolf-whistle as she passed by. As she turned to give him a piece of her mind she could have sworn she saw Frank, coming down the street opposite. She could tell from his messy blond hair – he never wore a hat – and the slouchy way he walked with his hands in his pockets.

She paused with her hand on the Labour Exchange door. It was him, walking down the street opposite. Vi thought it was a happy coincidence. Frank could come into the Labour Exchange with her, and confirm their engagement, because there wasn't even a ring yet, was there, and they might not believe her.

She was about to call out to him when she saw him stop at the doorway next to the bus stop and take a key out of his pocket. She hadn't known he lived all the way over this side of town. He'd never said – she'd never asked, she realised – they always had other things to occupy themselves with, in the alley, after hours, when he walked her home from work.

As he got his key out, the door opened and a huge pram bumped down the front step, pushed by a dumpy woman in a floral turban and navy-blue coat. Vi hesitated: it could be his sister? That was when the bus drew up at the stop, obscuring her view.

Vi went inside the Labour Exchange and shut the door, but stopped just inside to look out of the window at the far end – the cleaner hadn't reached that one, yet. She looked outside. Frank had disappeared, the bus was pulling away, and the woman with the pram was crossing the road towards her. Just then there was the clatter of a bucket on the pavement outside and a disembodied arm began to wipe sudsy water over the windowpane. She heard voices from outside, muffled by the glass.

'Morning, Missus T!'

'Morning, Jack.'

'How's Frank Junior doing today?'

'I think his fever is getting worse, Jack. I've been up with him all night. Frank says if he won't settle in his pram then I'm to take him to the doctor.'

'Well, I hope he feels better soon.'

'Lord, so do I! Good morning, Jack.'

'Morning, Missus Timpson.'

Something gave inside Vi, then. Like an old piece of knicker elastic pulled tight until it snaps, then hanging useless-loose. She put a hand out onto the dusty windowsill, feeling it smooth and hard beneath her fingertips. Up and down the wet cloth wiped, in front of her eyes (*up and down like a barmaid's knickers*, that was how the saying went, wasn't it?).

She drew breath and tilted up her chin, watching the water run in foamy rivulets down the glass. The cheating spiv. Marry me, he'd said. And he was already married, with a sick baby, too. He must only have said it – she knew why he'd said it. She turned away from the window. There was an empty chair behind a file-covered desk. Posters for the Land Army, WAAF, ATS, and the Wrens papered the shiny cream walls. The window cleaner's shammy squeaked against the glass behind her. There was another poster above the desk: an orange one with a painting of a blonde woman with her arms flung high into the air, making a 'V' shape. *Come into the factories*, it said.

Vi walked over to the desk and banged the silver bell that lay next to the blotter. When nobody appeared she banged it again. 'All right, I'm coming!' A mousey-looking woman with buck teeth appeared from a side door.

'What pays best?' Vi said.

'I beg your pardon?' the woman said, sitting down, chair scraping the lino.

'Forces, land or industry, what pays best?' Vi said.

The woman pulled her chin into her neck and tapped her fingertips together. 'I think the factory girls are getting a shilling an hour, these days,' she said.

'Good,' Vi nodded, pulling her registration letter from

her pocket and slamming it down on the desk. 'How soon can I start?'

'Are you quite sure, dear?' the woman said, looking up. 'Because once you've made your decision, you don't get a second bite of the cherry.'

'Don't you?' Vi said. 'Says who? Churchill? Who says you can't change your mind about something, if it turns out all wrong?'

The woman sucked at her overbite and began to fill in a form. 'Industry it is,' she said. 'Probably the best place for a girl like you.'

Chapter 4

Zelah

The train was late. Zelah sat down on the hard wooden bench and looked out of the waiting-room window, watching the grey jostle of figures and the swirls of smoke and hearing the muffled chug of engines, rattle of luggage trolley, occasional shout. The dehumanising mix of people and machine reminded her of starting at the gun factory. She could see past the platform to where the ironwork on the station footbridge made criss-cross patterns, like someone ticking off the days on a calendar, and remembered how it felt, that first day in Nottingham, almost two years ago already:

The sound is like a muted air raid, but contained and syncopated, a rhythmic thud-roar, just at the level where the vibrations fill her body and push out thought. How can something be so vast and be so cluttered at the same time, she thinks, looking round at the huge space, filled with gantries, cranes, pistons, and blocks of moving metal, all slick-grey and solid.

There is a metallic taste on her tongue, the air peppery-hot in her nostrils, as a man gestures to her, and leads her to an incomprehensible piece of machinery. To her it looks like a sewing machine, but much, much larger: silver-black and dangerous-looking. She puts out her right index finger and touches it: warm and smooth.

Nobody talks – voices would be shouted down by the man-made thunder of the factory floor. And it is bright-dark: long electric strips illuminate the equipment, but there is no daylight, not a single window anywhere.

Once she starts here she'll become part of the machinery itself, Zelah thinks, a fleshy cog in the factory, not a real person at all.

It is perfect.

Now Zelah gripped the edges of the plywood sign she held in her lap. ROF hostel, it said in large, black printed lettering. As soon as the London train came in, she'd go out onto the platform and hold it high up, so the newest batch of industrial recruits could see it. Many of them would never have been away from home before. For some it might even be their first time on a train. It was important for the welfare supervisor to guide them to their new home. It was one of the reasons Zelah had been offered the role, because she'd been through it herself, and management thought she'd have an understanding of the women's concerns. That was what Mr Simmons had said, anyway.

The lady next to her shuffled in her seat and sneezed, saying 'I do beg my pardon', dabbing at her nose with a monogrammed handkerchief before turning her attention back to a feature in her magazine about creative uses of dried egg. And Zelah wished she'd brought something to distract herself with: knitting or crochet or something to read – not just because of the wait, but because of the feeling she got every time she had to do a station pick-up and bring the new girls back to the ordnance factory hostel.

The waiting-room door banged open, bringing with it the smoky dampness of the platform, and a young couple, holding hands and laughing as they barged inside. They sat down opposite Zelah, chattering loudly about what a good spread there'd been at the wedding breakfast and how Aunty Enid should never have been allowed near the sherry bottle. The young man was in army uniform, and the woman in a grey coat with huge shoulder pads, and a red hat perched on top of her golden curls. She laughed at something he said, opening her red lips wide, showing off a mouthful of perfect teeth, and resting a red-nailed hand on the thigh of his khaki trousers. The gold band on her ring finger gleamed in the waiting-room lights.

The couple turned and gazed at each other. Zelah thought they were about to kiss, but the woman glanced over at Zelah, muttered 'Not here, darling' to the man, and pulled her hand from his knee. Zelah flushed and looked down at the sign in her lap. She shouldn't have stared, but it was hard not to. She thought about the young couple's wedding: the church, the flowers, the happy grief of the bride's mother, prayer books, lace, and tiny white-edged cubes of fruit cake. She'd like to have had a wedding like that, Zelah thought, running her fingers over the roughly painted sign. But it wouldn't happen, would it? Twenty-five wasn't old, not really, but she'd almost given up hope of having a second chance, now.

The woman next to her sneezed again, and the pages of her magazine fluttered. Zelah checked her watch. Would the train come in time for them to make it back to the hostel for tea? Matron would be unhappy if she had to miss out her introductory chat to the girls. Matron was unhappy about a lot of things, Zelah thought, suppressing a sigh.

From out on the platform came a muted roar: the London train arriving. Zelah was at the door with her sign before any of the other passengers had even gathered up their things. Carriage doors swung open and people stepped out onto the damp platform before the train had even come to a halt. Zelah stood underneath the moon-faced clock, holding her sign up high, and putting on a smile, watching the passengers tumble-jumble towards her. She was expecting ten, this time. There had been twenty come down on the Manchester train earlier. This would bring the hostel to capacity.

There was a knot of three, who'd found and introduced themselves to each other on the train. That was good, Zelah thought, they'd settle easily if they already had friends. She asked them to wait for a moment for the others, and held her sign higher, lifted her smile wider, looking hopefully at the bobbing heads of the alighting throng. One-by-one, six other girls joined the group, some smiling nervously, others silent and wide-eyed.

Zelah put her sign down, pulled her list from her pocket and double checked. Had she counted correctly? She asked their names and ticked them off. The crowds were thinning out, and the passengers for Grantham had all got on. The guard was walking along the train, helping stragglers with luggage, slamming doors shut. What if a girl had fallen asleep on the train? She checked her list. Who was missing?

The guard was just about to slam the final door when a young woman stepped off, ignoring his frown. Zelah saw the red flag wave, heard the shriek of the guard's whistle, watched the brunette in the beige coat saunter towards them through the steam.

'Excuse me, are you Violet Smith?' Zelah had to shout to be heard above the sound of the train pulling out.

The girl smiled, and her left cheek dimpled. 'Depends who's asking,' she said.

Violet

'In here. The bell will go for blackout, and breakfast is at six in the canteen downstairs.' The door to room 179 was flung open, and Vi stepped inside. She heard Matron clattering off down the corridor with the remainder of the intake. She put down her case and closed the door behind her. It was posh – like she imagined a hotel would be.

There was an electric light with a flowered shade and a switch hanging down on a little gold chain, and beyond that a window that looked out onto flat fields, brown-green and endless, stretching away towards the pale grey skies. To the left of the window was a white basin with two taps – hot and cold running water, in her own bedroom! There was a glass tumbler with a toothbrush in it and a grey flannel draped over the edge – the factory even provided wash kit? Nobody had mentioned that at the Labour Exchange. Vi blinked and let her eyes take in the rest of the room: a utility wardrobe on the other side of the window, opposite the sink, and a chest of drawers to her left, with a hairbrush on top (was that part of it too? She half-expected to open the drawers and find them stocked with brand-new cami-knickers and silk stockings). It wasn't half bad for twenty-two shillings a week, she thought.

'Are you Violet Smith?' The voice came, inexplicably, from high up behind her right ear.

Vi sighed. 'Depends who's asking.' She looked up and saw a triangular face peering down, catlike, from the top bunk. Bunk beds – of course – how stupid of her to think she'd have a room to herself. That explained the wash kit and the hairbrush, then. Vi, you silly mare.

'Matron said I'd be sharing with someone called Violet Smith,' said the dark-haired girl. 'You must be her.'

'Oh, must I?' said Vi, unbuttoning her coat. 'And who are you? Gert or Daisy?'

'Mary McLaughlin,' said the girl, missing the joke. 'I came this morning.'

Funny accent, Vi thought. Irish? But she didn't sound like the Irishmen who worked at the docks and used to come into the pub. 'Come far?' Vi said, heaving her suitcase onto the lower bunk and clicking it open.

'It's a long way from Crumlin to here, so it is,' came the reply. The bedstead swayed and two bare feet swung down next to Vi's face. 'You'll be wanting help unpacking.' Mary thudded softly down next to her, reached into the old cardboard case and made a grab for her things. 'Where d'you get these?' She dangled Vi's only pair of nylons in front of her face.

'My fella,' Vi replied (Frank said they'd fallen off the back of a lorry, when he'd slipped them into her gas-mask case). She watched as Mary opened the bottom drawer in the chest and chucked them in.

'Is he a Yank?' Mary said, plucking out Vi's woollen vest and inspecting both sides before throwing it in with the stockings.

'No. Not that it's any business of yours,' Vi said, shovelling up the remainder of her clothes in an armful, shoving them in the drawer and slamming it shut before Mary could 'help' any more. 'Anyway, I've thrown him over,' Vi said.

She tipped up the case to empty her remaining things: comb, rollers, Vaseline, soap, flannel and the red-beaded rosary that Ma had insisted she take.

'Funny that they should put you in here with me,' Mary said, reaching down and prodding the rosary as if it were something slimy, 'what with you being one of them.'

'One of what?'

'A Taig.'

'What?'

'You're a Catholic, aren't you? You'd have thought they'd be worried about us being in the same room together.' Mary straightened up. She was quite short. Vi noticed flecks of dandruff in the parting of her dark hair. 'And I'm a Protestant,' Mary said, narrowing her eyes and jutting her sharp little chin forward.

Vi heard the flush of the toilet from the bathroom across the way, and the sound of someone starting to sing through the thin wall between their room and next door's. Sweet Mary Mother of Jesus, am I really going to be spending the rest of the war in this glorified chicken coop? Vi dug in her coat pocket for her fags – a whole packet of Capstan, a leaving present from her old boss at the King's Arms. 'Smoke?' she said, holding out the cigarettes.

'Sure, why not?' They sat down on the bottom bunk together. 'I suppose I don't need to tell Mammy I'm sharing with a Taig,' Mary said, holding her fag between thumb and forefinger. Vi shrugged, and took another drag, looking at her new room-mate. For such a petite thing, Mary was a little plump, she thought, the way her belly pushed out the fabric at the front of her brown woollen frock, she almost looked ... a bell rang, a tinny drilling sound, that pushed the thought from her head. 'Time to draw the blackouts,' said Mary.

Later, in bed, Vi stared up at the slats of the bunk above her, and felt the bed creak and sway as Mary tossed in her sleep. It was strange to have a whole bed to herself, strange not to be annoyed with Rita's elbows or May's cold toes

36

or the sound of John and David snoring on the floor. She wouldn't have to do the pre-dawn stumble for the baby bottle, because there was no Baby Val here to worry about and no twins to bother her when she was trying to do her hair in the morning, and no Ma to yell at her for not getting the washing inside before the rain started. No angry landlord to deal with, no nagging bills to worry about, no tea to make, no front step to scrub, and no Frank Timpson in the alley, after dark.

She clenched and unclenched her fists beneath the smooth, freshly laundered sheets, feeling empty. She missed them all so much it felt as if her heart were being wrung through the Monday morning mangle. But she'd be damned if she ever let on.

Laura

In the darkness the unsynchronised bomber engines sounded from either side of the Malvern Hills. Laura stood outside the hotel with some of the other guests, smoking and holding muttered conversations, as if they were waiting for a show to start. And in a sense they were, Laura thought. Harold had already made his excuses and gone upstairs. Laura imagined him, head hidden under the covers, long body a rigid lump, willing it all to stop.

She inhaled smoke and cool night air, watching as the searchlights sprang up like wigwams. The lights wavered upwards and it felt as if they were under a huge black-and-white tent, like a monochrome circus top. She could make out the twinkle of a companion's earring, the dark mauve of a loosened tie, as the searchlights played across the sky.

Laura had things she needed to get on with: she had to write to K, for starters, accept the Nottingham job, think about packing. But not just yet – it could wait until morning. There was time to watch the night raid first.

The German bombers' engines were getting louder, now, but the guests continued their anodyne chatter. They were discussing cats: some admired their looks, the way they hunted vermin; others hated their arrogance, the killing of songbirds. Laura exhaled, spewing smoke across their silly words. Then, 'I killed a man once,' said Mr Peterson, standing next to her on the terrace. Laura turned towards him as he spoke. Behind him, in the distance, brilliant clusters of light hung and slowly dropped to reveal a target on the ground below. 'The Dardanelles,' he continued. 'I was doing a recce for my unit, coming out of a hollow in some uneven ground, and I found myself staring into two very black eyes. Then the training kicked in, and I shot him. I remember he had a long black beard. I often wonder, did he have a family? I should like to have said sorry, told them I had no choice . . .' His voice trailed off at the first thud-crash.

The show had begun: the flare of flames, crackle of flack, splayed searchlights, boom of the anti-aircraft guns. Nobody spoke now, enraptured by the spectacle unfolding below. And Laura had a memory, of the upstairs room at

Ethel Villas: Mother waking her up in the middle of the night, dragging her over to the window and lifting the heavy sash – she couldn't have been more than six or seven years old – *Look, Laura, look! Look at the colours! Aren't they glorious?* – In the distance, orange flames licked the navy sky and smoke blanked out the starlight. Years later, when she mentioned it to Harold, he recalled a catastrophic factory fire at the time – he would have been about eleven or twelve, he said, and read about it in his father's newspaper. It must have been the same one, Laura thought. Yet mother had never mentioned the ruination or the loss of life, just the colours, the beautiful fury of it.

There was a gasp from the huddle of guests. The ack-ack guns had caught a plane. It came screaming, twisting down and down. Everyone clapped, some even cheered. Laura had had enough of it. She ran inside, storming upstairs, banging open the bedroom door, flicking on the light: everything a sudden white-yellow, Harold a hump under the eiderdown.

'I'm not going, Harold,' she said, slamming the door behind her. 'It's unbearable. I'm not going to paint anything more of these murder machines, or the business of war, no matter how much they offer me. I'm not going to Nottingham. I'm going to stay here with you. Harold – Harold?'

Why didn't he answer?

She went over to the bed and pulled back the covers. He was lying on one side, sweat plastering his white hair oil-grey against his scalp, skin strangely pale, eyes wide and unseeing.

'Harold?'

Chapter 5

Zelah

'Tickets, please.'

Zelah looks up, surprised she's heard him. Ever since that night everything has been a muffled jumble — she'd wondered if she'd ever get her hearing back — but that part of her was recovering, at least. She takes her ticket from her coat pocket. There is nothing else in there, not even a hanky.

The inspector's black trousers make an 'A' shape, as he steadies his bulk against the sway of the railway carriage. The woman with the baby in the blue shawl can't find her ticket. The inspector tuts and shakes his jowls, his scowling chops the same grey-red as the ploughed Devon fields that race past in the half-light outside the train windows. It is jam-packed already, and they've only just passed Newton Abbot. Luckily she got on at Plymouth, lucky to get a seat.

Luck clings to me like a curse, she thinks.

She can hear again, but everything is still overlaid with a metallic buzz, as if the sound comes through layers of wire mesh. The inspector turns his attention to the three sleeping sailors at the far end, who nudge *each other into brief wakefulness and wave travel warrants, before lolling back against the plush. The man with the bandaged head lowers his copy of* The Times *long enough to hand over two tickets. His birdlike wife continues to worry at her knitting.*

The man raises The Times *again:* Hundreds feared dead in direct hit on Plymouth shelter, *says the headline.* One lucky survivor cheats death. *Zelah shudders and looks away. The baby starts to mewl, and the mother's face is pale and pinched as she rocks it against herself.*

The inspector holds out his hand for Zelah's ticket, rolls his eyes down at her as he checks the destination, and clips it. He is saying something. To her damaged ears his words sound like wasps spitting from his fleshy lips. She strains to hear. He says she has to change at Derby, something about a UXB on the line near Birmingham.

Zelah says thank you and he nods and lumbers out of the compartment. The baby's foot kicks her side as it squirms against its mother. There is no room on the seat for Zelah to move away.

At Teignmouth more people pour into the train. A troop of soldiers fill the corridor. An old woman with a checked shawl gets on last. The soldiers part like a khaki sea to let her through. Zelah pushes herself up from her seat and opens the carriage door. 'There's space in here,' she says, her voice sounding muzzy and strange. The woman says something, but Zelah can't hear, so she just gestures to her empty seat, and holds the door open. The woman's face creases into a smile. As she enters the compartment she shakes her grey curls at the baby's mother, and Zelah sees the mother hand her baby over to be dandled and cosseted.

Zelah goes out into the corridor. The soldiers shift to give her space, and she wedges herself between two of them as the train pulls out of the station. Like them, she rests her exhausted face against the cool glass window, looking through the smutted pane across the sweep of estuary, smooth as pewter. She can't see the sun, yet, but evidence of sunrise is all across the southern skies, towards the Dorset coast and beyond: orange-red rising up from the horizon into the grey-sopped morning clouds. Behind them, down the tracks to the west, the night still claws. It was blue-black and freezing when she waited on the platform at Plymouth. Whatever is left of the city would be coming to life now, she supposes. Whatever is left. She blinks, and lets Plymouth go, erased like yesterday's sums on the blackboard.

She can feel the heft of the soldiers' torsos on either side of her. They sway and judder as one, caught in the motion of the train as it curves inland, away from the sea and northwards, towards her new life.

'Tickets, please!' Zelah blinked her eyes open. No, she wasn't on the train from Plymouth. That was two years ago now. This was a different train – a different life. She must have drifted off, lulled by the warmth and rhythmic rattle of it. She fumbled in her coat pocket and pulled out the two tickets, for herself and the young woman opposite who was biting her lip and looking out through the smeared carriage window.

'This'll be you, m'duck.' The skinny ticket inspector passed back the tickets and nodded out towards the dripping greyness. Zelah thanked her and put the tickets away as the train began to slow.

'We're nearly there,' Zelah said to the young woman who frowned and pulled her coat across her body without doing up the buttons.

'I don't know why we're here. The nurse said it was just my glands,' the girl said, crossly.

'Come on,' Zelah said, flicking her head in the direction of the carriage door. 'Or we'll miss it.'

The woman narrowed her eyes, but she got up as the train ground to a halt. Zelah opened the carriage window and leant out to grab the handle, her sleeve soaked in seconds from the downpour. She got out and held the door open for Mary McLaughlin. 'But the nurse said it was just my glands,' Mary repeated as she stepped off the train.

'I'm afraid Dr Gibbs has another opinion and – well – here we are,' Zelah said, slamming the train door behind them. 'Attenborough' said the sign above the platform. ('I'll get the girl booked into the one at Attenborough village,' Dr Gibbs had said, frowning over her spectacles. 'Of course they're terrifically busy these days, what with the ATS girls stationed in Chetwynd Barracks . . .' She raised knowing brows before continuing, 'But it's better than the alternatives.') The guard blew his whistle and the train juddered noisily away towards Derby.

So here they were. Dr Gibbs said Cloud House was in the middle of the village, just a couple of hundred yards up the road from the station. Zelah squinted into the rain and struggled to unfurl her umbrella. 'Squash in with me, or you'll be drenched,' she said, and they began to walk up the road together, huddled under the flapping brolly, neither in a particular rush to reach their destination, despite the weather.

'Sorry,' said Mary, accidentally splashing her with puddle water.

'It's fine,' Zelah said.

'No, it's sodding well not!' Mary suddenly stopped. 'He said my hand would look prettier with a ring on my finger, and I thought he meant—' She burst into huge, heaving sobs.

Zelah struggled to get her arms round Mary and hold on to the slippery umbrella handle. 'There, there,' she said, patting ineffectually, as Mary shuddered against her raincoat. Bareheaded, the girl's black curls barely reached Zelah's chin. It was like hugging a child. Poor thing. She hadn't even known she was pregnant. It was only when Zelah measured her for her overalls and discovered she was a size thirteen – rather large for a girl of her height – that she'd asked Nurse to take a look at her. Nurse said, with a snap of her fingers and a cursory glance, that it was nothing more than her glands. Whatever that meant. Luckily Dr Gibbs happened to have her weekly surgery that day, took one look at Mary and said she'd eat her hat if that little chit had any kind of a thyroid complaint. So now here they were, on the way to the Home for Unmarried Mothers, in the pouring rain.

'You'll feel better once we get there,' Zelah said.

'How?' Mary's voice snuffled against her chest. 'How will I feel better?'

'Well, at least you'll be in the dry,' Zelah said. Mary pulled herself away from Zelah and they began to walk again.

Mary sniffed and wiped her nose on the sleeve of her coat. 'Mammy will kill me,' she said.

'She doesn't need to know,' Zelah said.

'But surely they'll tell her.'

'Not if I tell them not to.'

'You can do that?'

'My job is your welfare,' Zelah said.

'But what about the money? If I'm not sending me wages home, she'll know something, she'll ask. Lord, the shame of it.'

They'd reached the village now, a scattering of turn-of-the-century villas, and a grey church crouched like a giant toad behind the rowan trees. And here was Cloud House: a symmetrical three-storey red-brick edifice, with the square front garden turned over to vegetables and a paved pathway from the gate to the front door. There were net curtains at every window.

Zelah paused at the gate. 'You haven't said what your plan is, Mary.'

'I don't have a plan, Miss Fitzlord.'

'You don't intend to keep your baby? Your mother wouldn't want to help?'

Sometimes they did, Zelah knew. Some mothers would pass off the illegitimate baby as merely a younger sibling, brazen it out.

'Mammy will kill me,' Mary repeated.

'So you will definitely be giving up your child for adoption?' Zelah said. She had to be sure, before they went in.

46

There would no doubt be paperwork, forms to sign and so forth. 'Mary?'

The girl just nodded, staring down at the puddled pavement.

'And what are your plans for afterwards?'

'Afterwards?' Mary said, looking up at her.

'After they've found a home for the baby, what will you do?'

'I can't go home.' Panic in her sharp little eyes. 'Mammy will kill me.'

'Do you – would you like to come back to work?'

'Can I?'

'I don't see why not.' Zelah stared past the girl to the blank façade of Cloud House in the sheeting rain, imagining how the well-meaning ladies inside would make Mary feel as if her life was over before it had even begun. The girl was one of the night shift. She hadn't had to deal with the night-shift boss to date – although she'd heard all about him, of course. 'I'll ask Mr Handford to keep your job open, if you'd like.'

'You can do that?'

'Yes.' Could she? She wasn't sure, but she had to offer the poor girl some kind of hope. 'I'll write to your mother that Nurse thinks you have a problem with your glands, and that you're going to be off work until it's sorted out – that's not really a lie, is it?' Raindrops bounced off Mary's curls as she shook her head. 'Once the adoption is complete – and you feel well enough – you can come back to work.'

'You can do that for me, Miss Fitzlord?'

Zelah nodded, biting her lip, hoping she could. She could try, at least. She had to try. 'Right then. Ready?' Zelah gestured towards the big house. Mary nodded. Zelah lifted the latch on the gate and they walked together up the path. As they approached, the front door opened.

A woman in a white apron and netted hair stood waiting in the entrance. 'Miss Mary McLaughlin?' she said, ushering them inside, where it was dark and the air smelled of floor polish and antiseptic. From upstairs there was the sound of a crying baby.

After the forms and the obligatory cup of tea, the woman in the apron said Mary could go on up, tutting over Mary's lack of personal belongings (not even a nightdress and clean underwear, dear?) and rolling her eyes at Zelah, as Mary trudged up the wooden staircase to her room. Halfway up the stairs, Mary turned, hand on banister, and looked down at Zelah. 'You will talk to Mr Handford so I can come back to work, won't you, Miss Fitzlord?' she said.

'Yes,' Zelah said, a tightness in her chest at the thought of it. 'I'll talk to him as soon as I get back, Mary.'

He had his back to her. His white coat was like a blank sheet of paper. She noticed the way his dark hair was oiled down and how the coat pulled across his shoulder blades. He had more hair and was of broader build than his day-shift counterpart, Mr Simmons, who was bald and pudgy. He hadn't heard her come in, engrossed as he was with rearranging a system of index cards that fitted in racks on the wall next to the output chart. He was shaking his head and plucking cards from their slots, swapping, and replacing them.

Zelah closed the door behind her and cleared her throat. He turned. From what everyone said, she'd expected him to look like a headmaster. Stern, they'd said. Stern and picky (those were the polite versions). It was a shock to see that he wasn't old. There was hardly any grey in his thick hair, although a frown cut his wide forehead.

'Good evening?' He made it sound like a question.

'Good evening, Mr Handford.'

He strode towards her, holding out a hand. His handshake was dry and firm. 'I don't believe we've met.'

'Miss Fitzlord,' she said. 'You don't know me, but—'

'Wait, yes I do.' He went back over to his card system and plucked one from the rack near the end. '*Zelah Fitzlord, 25, from Plymouth,*' he read from the card. 'You've been with us two years already – you must have arrived during the Blitz? I heard it was so bad down there that the authorities were handing out free train tickets just to get people out.'

'Yes,' Zelah said, remembering. 'They did.' She found herself pulled back again to that time:

It isn't safe. She knows that, inching along the floor to the place against the far wall where the bed had been. She can make it out, far below, a smash-jumble of linen and splinters. Halfway across the floor, the lino swings down to reveal the hole, the heart blasted out of the house: ripped open and shredded. But here, right against the wall, there is still a blackout curtain hanging at the one remaining window. *She yanks it down, pulling at the drawing pins that tack it in place. She wraps herself, shrouding in the coarse, dark cloth, not caring about the stray pins that scrape her flesh. She keeps on sitting, huddled into the corner, from where she can see right down to the Hoe, in the bright moonlight. So many buildings bombed – the sea view that she had always dreamed of. Eyelids gritted, mouth dry, shivering cold, splinter-sore knees, and waking dreams of a flaming vortex. Dawn turns it all rose quartz beyond the smoke, but the sounds are muffled, as if inside a jar. Seagulls fight over scraps of meat. Is it meat? She doesn't want to think.*

As the sun rises higher she sees a trail of people on what is left of the road, meagre belongings bundled in pillowcases and baskets, shoulders slumped, trudging, away towards the moors. Should she join them? She has to get out somehow. There is nothing left for her here.

'. . . quite an expert by now, I'd imagine – it says here that you cover for staff sickness and you're the welfare officer for the girls.' She'd missed half of what he said, but he didn't seem to have noticed. He slotted the card back in place and came back towards her. 'What can I do for you, Miss Fitzlord?'

She found herself looking up into his eyes: hazel-grey under thick brows. Deep breath, Zelah. No need to be nervous. Try not to think about what people say about him; it's just gossip, he's probably perfectly reasonable. 'It's about the manning, Mr Handford. One of the recruits was due to start on the lathe tonight – she's just finished her training – but I've had to send her away.'

'Send her away? Why would you do that? Have you seen the production targets for this month, and we're under-manned as it is.' He took a pipe from his pocket and jammed it between his teeth, not bothering to fill it with tobacco or light it.

'I'm sorry, I think you misunderstand. What I mean is, she had to be sent away.' Did he want her to spell it out?

'But why? We can't just go excluding good workers for petty misdemeanours, whatever Matron says.' Oh dear. He hadn't understood at all. But how to tell him, without making him feel stupid, without embarrassing herself, too? 'What did the girl do? Entertain a man in her room? Pilfer Spam from the canteen? Be late for a shift?' Zelah opened her mouth to respond, but he wouldn't let her, had taken his pipe out of his mouth and was jabbing the air as he continued. 'Actually, I couldn't be less interested in what the silly girl has or hasn't done. I need her on that lathe and I need her on it tonight. Please see that it's done, Miss Fitzlord.'

'You don't understand—' Zelah began.

'No, you don't understand,' he interrupted, now. 'The quotas have been upped. There are new targets. You've heard what's been going on in North Africa, I take it?' Zelah flushed and nodded. No wonder the night-shift girls said those things about him. 'We cannot afford to lose anyone right now. Is that clear, Miss Fitzlord?' He put his pipe back in his mouth and clamped his jaws tight on the stem.

'She's having a baby,' Zelah said, and watched his eye-brows shift up as she spoke. 'That's why we've had to send the new lathe operator away. She's gone to a home for unmarried mothers.' Here we go, Zelah thought. Here's where the tirade comes about it being downright impossible to run a factory staffed by tarts and flibbertigibbets who would be better placed in the nursery or at the kitchen sink. Here's where he goes red in the face and starts shouting and I'll just have to keep quiet and take it. She waited.

'I see,' he said. He took the pipe from his mouth and shoved it in his pocket. Then he ran a hand slowly over his face, drawing thumb and forefinger along the line of his jaw and letting out an audible breath as he did so. 'I see,' he repeated and walked over to the rack of index cards. 'What's her name?'

'Mary McLaughlin.'

His fingers brushed a row of cards until he located the right one. 'Mary McLaughlin, 18, from County Antrim, joined last month.' He shook his head. 'What the heck were they thinking of, letting a girl come here in her condition?'

'They didn't know – she didn't even know herself.'

'Didn't know, or didn't want to know?' he said, turning to look at Zelah. And he just looked sad, not judgemental at all. Not stern or picky or arrogant or patronising or any of the other things people said. His eyes – his eyes looked sad, and kind.

'I only discovered by chance when I was measuring up the new recruits for their overalls. We managed to find her a decent place for her confinement. I took her there this afternoon.'

He frowned. 'Isn't it your day off, Miss Fitzlord?'

'I thought it better to get her there as soon as we could, just in case. Anyway, time off is a bit of an overrated luxury these days.' What made her say that? She would never have made that kind of flippant remark to Mr Simmons.

'Indeed it is.' He nodded and looked as if he were about to tear up Mary McLaughlin's card.

'No,' Zelah said, putting out a hand to stop him. 'She's coming back.'

'Is she?' he said.

Zelah could feel his forearm through the layers of cloth. She took her hand away. 'What I mean is, she's asked if she can come back.'

'But we have no way of knowing how long she will be away, or if she'll change her mind.'

'She was very clear about wanting to return to work, Mr Handford.'

His eyes were scanning the rack and the chart. He rubbed at a temple with his finger. 'No, I can't risk it. It's too imprecise. We could be talking about anything from a few weeks to several months. Telephone the home and let Miss McLaughlin know that she need not return. I'll work something out in the meantime.' He dropped Mary's card in the waste-paper bin.

'You can't do that,' Zelah said.

'And your experience in ordnance factory management is what, Miss Fitzlord?' Such sarcasm. No wonder everyone hated him.

'It's all she's got,' Zelah said, pushing past him and kneeling down next to the bin. She reached in to take out the neatly printed card with its colour-coded symbols. 'They're going to take away her baby, and now you want to take away her job. You'll be leaving her with nothing. Without this place' – she gestured in the air with the stupid card – 'she's got nothing.' And even as she said it, she wondered if it was Mary McLaughlin or herself she was talking about.

There was a hand at her elbow, lifting her to her feet. That's torn it, she thought, I've probably gone and got myself the sack, too. 'That's all well and good, Miss Fitzlord,' he said, looking down at her. He was so close she could smell the soapy scent of his shaving foam and see a small crescent-shaped star on his left cheekbone. 'But what do you propose I do? Who can I put on the lathe in the meantime?'

'I'll do it,' Zelah said. 'I'm lathe-trained. I'll cover for her until she gets back.'

'And who will look after the welfare issues with you on the tools?' He still had his hand under her elbow, supporting her.

'I can do both, fit the welfare work around the shifts.'

He let go of her arm, then, and took Mary's card from her. 'All right. You win. Miss McLaughlin can have her job back, if you keep it open for her.'

'Thank you, Mr Handford.' She could feel the spot under her arm where his hand had been. He placed Mary's card in a file on his desk, and went over to the wall rack, moving

Zelah's card into the empty spot. 'I'd better get going then,' Zelah said.

'Yes, you better had,' Mr Handford replied. 'I hear there's an empty lathe in Bay Six.' He looked directly at her. Was that the hint of a smile? She couldn't be sure. 'Good evening, Miss Fitzlord.'

'Good evening, Mr Handford.'

Chapter 6

Violet

'Cor, struth, it's packed in there!' The man next to her wiped his forehead with the sleeve of his jacket.

'Lemonade or tea, Mr Tonks?' said Matron from behind the counter.

'Nothing stronger?'

'You're not at the White Hart now, Mr Tonks,' said Matron, pursing her lips and pouring a ladleful of cloudy liquid into a beaker.

The band music muffle-blared as the double doors swung open and shut. Mr Tonks downed the lemonade. 'Not much lemon and very little aid,' he said. It was meant to be a joke, so Vi smiled. Matron frowned at her. He was right, though. Citric acid and saccharine stirred up in a bucket was hardly lemonade. The lemons were a fantasy, as pretend as the air men they'd been promised for this dance.

People were bumbling in and out of the assembly hall. The music jam-banged as they came and went. Was this their idea of a good time, rattling about with a load of void coupons? She'd had more fun on a wet Sunday afternoon.

'It's a Paul Jones,' Matron said, nodding in the direction of the doors. 'You won't want to miss that, dear.'

Violet said she had a bit of a headache actually, and made for the stairs before fat, old Mr Tonks could pull her off to the dance floor.

It was odd being upstairs with the rooms all empty. Everyone else was at the hostel hop – it was practically obligatory (our way of welcoming you new girls, Matron had said, with a tight smile). Her feet tapped along the lino. The corridor was an endless tunnel of beige – not actually endless, there was a fire escape at the far end. She'd written home already, enclosing a postal order with her first week's wages (minus the twenty-two shillings for her bed and board at the hostel), telling them about her training, and the fact that she now had a room to herself on account of Mary having to go off to have a baby. She reminded them that most of the money had to go straight to Doctor Tennant, because there was still so much owing from Ma's illness, and she told them all she loved them and sprinkled the paper with kisses. Vi sighed. Well, the food was good – at least she didn't have to worry about the ration, at least she didn't have to share her food, her bed, her clothes with half a dozen others.

'Peace and bloody quiet,' she said aloud, opening the door to room 179 and going over to the window. What would she be doing back home if she were still there? On her way to the evening shift in the pub probably, tripping along the broken pavement past the hot-vinegar rush of air at the chippy door, and past the dark, cold steps down to the shelter. She felt again the hollow squeeze inside, every time she thought of home. Silly girl. Silly woman – she was a 'mobile woman' now, wasn't she? Stupid to be feeling homesick.

Outside the window she saw a bus on the distant road, then it dipped out of sight, where the road wound round to the main entrance. Could that be the coachload of airmen they'd been promised?

She checked her watch, wondering what would be happening at home now. She thought of them all, yelling and laughing and being shouted at by Ma. She thought of Baby Val, toddling about, saying 'me help' whenever anything was going on. She remembered the time Baby Val had tried to 'help' with the twins' game of marbles, how Vi had found her choking on a marble, blue-faced, and had had to hold her upside down by her fat little ankles and shake her until the bloody thing fell out, plopping wetly onto the edge of the hearth rug. How she'd screamed at Bertie for leaving his marbles out, screamed at Baby Val for being silly enough to mistake a marble for a sweetie, screamed and yelled and slapped her plump legs, then burst into tears. Because for a moment, she thought she'd lost Baby Val, lost her like they'd lost Bea. Who was looking out for Baby Val now, she wondered, who'd get her morning bottle and check for scattered marbles? Oh, heck.

Vi turned away from the window. She couldn't just mope around here worrying about things. In any case, what if that bus really had been full of airmen?

She looked in the little mirror above the sink and pushed her hair away from her eyes. She pinched her cheeks to redden them up a bit, bit her lips to do the same, and dabbed on a smear of Vaseline from the little tin in her pocket. Then she went out of her room and made her way back along the corridor towards the stairs.

He stood at the top of the steps. 'You're in the wrong place. The dance floor's that way, pal,' she said.

He turned and shrugged. 'I don't dance.'

'Everyone dances. You mean you don't want to dance? Come on, you'll enjoy it once you're there.' She'd levelled with him, at the top of the stairs, opposite the big window. He shook his head, blond hair shiny-dark with Brylcreem. 'Why did you come, if you don't want to dance?' she said.

'Leave me alone.'

'You can't stay here – you're not allowed upstairs. Anyway, why aren't you with your pals?'

'Why aren't you?'

'I had to go up to my room for something.'

'Of course you did.' He held out an open packet of Craven A. She said, 'I don't mind if I do,' and took one. He clicked open his Zippo. She looked through the flame at his face: grey eyes, long nose. He looked very young. Once he'd lit his own cigarette he sat down on the top step. She felt awkward

60

standing up beside him, so she sat down too. The metal stair riser bit into the top of her thigh.

'You been to one of these before?' she said. He shook his head. 'Why d'you come tonight, then?'

'We're celebrating.' He shifted as he spoke, and their knees touched. She pulled hers away.

'Celebrating what?'

'The end of the course.'

'What course?' Honestly, it was like pulling teeth; she didn't know why she was bothering, when she could be down there on the dance floor with some of his pals.

'Pilot training.'

'A pilot!' Well, that was a turn-up, at least. She took another drag and tapped ash out through the banisters.

'So, how many sorties have you done?'

'None, I told you, I've just finished training.' He had an odd accent – she couldn't place it. 'We passed out today.'

'You should be having fun, then.'

'I am – you want to join me?' He passed her his half-smoked cigarette and pulled a flask from his inside pocket, untwisted the little metal cap and took a swig. He screwed up his eyes. Vi could hear the double doors thudding downstairs, intermittent bursts of music and laughter.

He passed the silver flask over to her, swapping it for the remains of his cigarette. Their fingers touched. Vi put the flask to her lips. The metal rim was cool and hard as she took a gulp. It felt as if a fire were ripping down her throat and into her stomach.

'Strong stuff,' she said, managing not to choke.

'Polish vodka,' he said. 'The best.' Was that his accent? Polish?

'What's your name?' he asked, watching as she wiped her lips with the back of her hand.

'Violet Smith. Yours?'

'Jacky Symanski.'

'Symanski,' she repeated the unfamiliar surname. 'Where are you from?' she said, handing the flask back and taking a drag on her fag. The smoke soothed the place where the alcohol had burned.

'Birmingham,' he said, taking another gulp.

'No, I mean, really,' she said.

'I'm really from Birmingham. That's where my family live.'

'But you're not English?'

'No, I'm Polish.' He gestured at some badge on his RAF uniform, as if she were stupid. He handed her back the flask and she took another swig. It must have been very strong, because she was already beginning to feel pleasantly hazy, despite his rudeness.

'Flying tomorrow?' she said. He shook his head, taking the flask back from her.

'Not until I'm posted,' he said, and when she asked him where he was off to, he said he probably shouldn't be telling her, but it was RAF Northolt. He looked proud when he said it, as if it meant something important, but when she said she had no idea where Northolt was, he laughed, and admitted he didn't know either. They passed the flask again between them.

'And then you'll start flying sorties?' she said. He nodded. 'You must be looking forward to it.' He didn't answer.

Her cigarette was almost finished now, so she supposed she should go down to join the others. She stubbed it out between the banisters.

'I should get back,' she said, standing up. 'And you should come, too. Won't your pals be missing you?' She held out a hand to help him up. He took it, and his palm was warm and soft.

'I'm scared as hell,' he said, then, in a low voice. She watched his still-lit fag roll off the edge of the step, where he'd dropped it.

She squeezed his hand. 'You're trained. You know what you're doing. You'll be fine.' He kept holding her hand, not looking at her. He shook his head, but he didn't say anything. 'You'll be fine,' she repeated.

'Fifty-fifty,' he said, now, looking up at her, eyes red-rimmed, mouth cutting strange shapes as he spoke in a hoarse mutter. 'Those are the odds. I'd be better off playing Russian roulette.'

Then he started to sob, shoulders heaving, tears falling like the large drops of rain before a thunderstorm – except there was no sound, just the pat-pat of those fat drops on the stair. 'Come on,' she said, pulling him upwards. 'Come to my room. You can have a glass of water and wash your face. You'll feel better then.'

He let himself be tugged up, and she began to lead him back along the long corridor to room 179, right at the far end, by the fire escape. Her room, where they wouldn't be disturbed.

George

'Good evening, Mr Handford.' The voice broke him from his reverie. He'd been watching the glitter ball rotating in the ceiling, noticing how the spangles of light fanned out. It reminded him of the sunlight on the water at Trent Lock. He'd been thinking that soon it would be warm enough to get the dinghy out on the river again.

He turned to acknowledge the greeting. It took him a moment to register the face. Without the workplace headgear her hair fell in dark waves, softening her angular features. 'Good evening, Miss Fitzlord,' he replied. He waited for her to start a conversation, the way women seemed to feel the need to – something about the weather, how the new recruits were settling in, or the good news about Tunisia – but she simply sipped her glass of lemonade and stood next to him, looking out onto the half-empty dance floor, where dancers twirled lazily, whilst the band's string section sawed out a waltz. Old Harry Tonks had some poor woman grasped up against his beer belly, but the couples were mostly girl-girl pairings due to the lack of men. They wafted the combined scent of Woolworth's perfume and desperation into the air as they shuffled past.

George cleared his throat and pulled his pipe from his pocket as the music came to a close. At least he didn't smoke cigarettes, wouldn't be expected to offer Miss Fitzlord one, light it for her, all that nonsense. He pulled out his tobacco tin and began to stuff the pipe bowl. The double doors at the far end of the hall stuttered open-close as people pushed their way through to the refreshment table in the lobby.

'Poor things. Matron promised them airmen, and all they've got is Mr Tonks, and ...' She paused. He thought she was going to say 'and you' and start to berate him for not asking a single one of the girls to dance. '... and that must be a little disappointing,' she said. He put the pipe stem in his mouth as she continued. 'Perhaps they'll perk up when the coach arrives from Hucknall.' He nodded and clicked his lighter. He glimpsed her through the flame as he sucked the tobacco alight. Her features were very definite: sharp nose, dark brows – not what you'd call feminine, but interesting. He pulled the fragrant smoke into his lungs and felt the warmth in his chest. The band leader was taking his time about announcing the next number, and Miss Fitzlord didn't show any signs of moving away.

'What brings you here, Miss Fitzlord?' A foolish thing to say. He wished he'd kept his mouth shut.

'Matron likes me to attend,' she said. 'In any case, it doesn't do any harm for the welfare supervisor to be visible at these events. It helps them to know my face, know who to come to if they have any concerns.'

'Indeed.' He nodded.

'And you, Mr Handford? I don't believe we've had the pleasure of your company at a hostel hop before?' What was that? A slight tilt of her head, the upward inflection of her voice – could it be sarcasm?

'The new initiative. At the last Board meeting it was decided that having a member of senior management attend staff functions would foster team spirit, boost morale, and so forth.'

'Doing your bit for the war effort, then?'

'Something like that.' He chewed on his pipe stem. Up on the dais the band leader was approaching the microphone. At long last – some music to fill the uncomfortable silence. But would Miss Fitzlord expect him to ask her to dance? He hoped to God not. His neck seemed to be swelling under the starched collar. He jutted out his chin to try to ease the sensation.

Just then there was a sound of male voices in the lobby, scuffling footsteps, an excited female squeal. The band leader paused, baton raised, as the hall doors flung open and a blue-grey tidal wave of airmen engulfed the dance floor, and along with them the swirling frocks of the girls, like multi-coloured flotsam. The band leader grinned, cleared his throat and announced a foxtrot. George clenched his pipe stem between his teeth, and the band started up.

The dance floor was full now: twirling bodies, smiling faces. George took a step back to avoid the worst of the crush, but as he did so he was shunted backwards by a couple who'd broken into an impromptu jitterbug, and he accidentally shoved Miss Fitzlord, causing her to tip the lemonade glass that was halfway to her lips. 'I'm terribly sorry,' he said, mortified at the sight of the spillage, a port-coloured damp-patch on the wine-red dress. He couldn't even offer to wipe it up – it had spilled just where her left breast swelled against the cloth. The jitterbugging couple hadn't even noticed.

'It's fine.' She'd put down her glass and was mopping herself with a handkerchief.

'The very least I can do is buy you a replacement.' He had to raise his voice above the din.

'How kind.'

'Not at all.'

They began to nudge their way round the edge of the hall to the double doors. Once they'd reached the lobby he went to the refreshment table and asked Matron for two lemonades. He tapped the remaining ash from his pipe in the metal ashtray on the counter and put his pipe back in his pocket.

'Blue uniforms causing the usual hysteria?' Matron nodded her grey curls in the direction of the hall as she ladled out the lemonade.

'Bedlam.' He handed over tuppence for the drinks. Airmen were still trickling in through the front door, some already with their arms round the factory girls. They had the glazed-eyed, ruddy-faced look of lads who'd been in the pub all afternoon. 'Still, if it keeps the workforce happy. Happy workers are productive workers, so they keep telling me. Thank you, Matron.'

He picked up the glasses and turned. Miss Fitzlord was just beside him. 'Thank you for the replacement,' she said.

'The very least I could do, and I'm sorry again.'

'Not at all – it wasn't your fault, was it?' She smiled as she took the glass from him. And when she smiled her eyes glinted. How dark they were, like chips of onyx. You could barely tell where the pupil ended and the iris began. He looked away, took a sip of lemonade, shifted sideways so that other people could get their drinks.

He noticed a couple stealing a kiss, behind one of the concrete pillars that supported the stairwell.

There was a sensation inside him, like mercury rising up a barometer. 'I say, I'm feeling rather warm. I think I'll head outside for some fresh air.'

'Good idea.'

He hadn't asked her to join him, and yet here she was, sat with him on the bench, looking out over the shadowy fields. She'd put down her glass and taken out a packet of cigarettes and offered them to him. And he found himself taking one, in preference to his pipe. She'd struck a match before he had a chance to get out his lighter, so he leant into the flame. He tried to remember the last time he'd had a cigarette: not since his army days, probably. The smoke was different – lighter – and the cigarette butt was soft against his lips.

'How is it, being back on the tools?' he said, breaking the silence, remembering how she'd taken the place of the girl who'd gone off to have a baby.

She exhaled before replying. 'Hard work, if I'm honest, with the welfare supervisor role as well.'

'I can get someone else in, you know.'

'And keep the job open for Miss McLaughlin?'

'That's not possible, I'm afraid.'

'Then I'll stick with it, if it's all the same to you.'

'So long as we meet our production targets, that's my only concern.'

'Yes, that's what I heard.' She spoke in a low voice, almost a mutter, her head turned away as she exhaled.

'I'm sorry, I'm not sure what you mean?'

'Oh, nothing.'

He looked out to the flat farmland and spiky telegraph poles. The sun had already set, but it wasn't quite dark: a hint of purplish red at the horizon. Her red dress was a burgundy in the twilight. He noticed her shiver. 'Would you like my jacket?'

'That's kind of you, but no, thank you. I should be getting back inside, anyway. Matron likes to have me on hand, just in case.' She stood up, picking up her lemonade, leaving empty air in the space beside him on the bench.

'In case of what?' He stood up, too.

'Moral issues.' She raised an eyebrow. He thought of the airmen with their arms round the factory girls, the stolen kiss he'd glimpsed in the lobby. And that feeling came again, like an upward trickle of quicksilver.

'I think I'll stay out here a while longer,' he said, realising as he did so that she hadn't asked him to join her back indoors.

'Perhaps I'll see you later, then, Mr Handford,' she said.

'George,' he said. 'You can call me George, if you like, outside work, of course.'

'But I thought we'd established that this is work. You said yourself, you're only here to boost staff morale in an attempt to hit production targets.' She flicked ash from her cigarette and looked at him. She was tall, her eyes almost on a level with his.

He cleared his throat. 'Quite so. Good evening, Miss Fitzlord.'

She turned away and he watched her walk back to the hostel, heard a faint blast of band music as the door opened and closed, and she was swallowed up inside. He checked his watch, dropped the remains of the cigarette and ground it out on the kerb. He drained the last of the tepid lemonade from the glass. He should return it, really, but to go back inside, now? No, he'd made his presence known, that was good enough. There were plenty of men there now; nobody would miss him. He thought for a moment of Miss Fitzlord's face, tilted questioningly towards him.

No, nobody would notice him gone.

He went over to his car and slid inside. Thank God for his extra petrol coupon allocation; he could come and go to work events almost as he chose. He turned the key in the ignition and flicked on the blinkered headlights. As he pulled away he noticed one light on in an upstairs hostel window. Some girl had ignored blackout. Well, that wasn't on. He'd have to have a word with Matron. Perhaps he could ask Miss

Fitzlord to pass a message, catch her after her shift? No, silly idea. He drove on. There was no need for him to have anything more to do with Miss Fitzlord, was there?

Violet

'Cigarette?' she said. He nodded, looking up at her from the bottom bunk where he sat, dry-eyed now. She'd managed to get two packets of Player's before they sold out in the hostel shop on wages day. She lit one and passed it down to him, noticing how his hand shook as he took it. His hair was mussed up from where he'd had his head in his hands, and there were teardrops, like rain spatters, on the thighs of his trousers. He'd finished the water already, and put the glass down on the floor beside him.

'Feel any better?' She watched him inhale. The room dipped and slid in her peripheral vision, like when you've just got off a fairground ride. It was strong, that vodka of his. She slumped down next to him on the bed.

'You must think I'm a coward,' he muttered, not looking at her.

'Don't be daft. I bet the others feel the same as you.' He smelled nice, she thought, feeling his thigh, warm against hers. Close up, there were the scents of smoke and laundry soap and Brylcreem and maleness, all mixed up. She took a long drag. It made her feel even more muzzy round the edges.

'I don't want to die.'

'Of course you don't.'

'No, I mean I don't want to die like this, without having a girlfriend. I'm not even a man.'

'Course you are – you're old enough to fly a plane, right?' She exhaled.

'You know what I mean.'

He turned to face her, then, and although his eyes were still red-rimmed from crying there was something else there, a hardness. She knew that look. The same look Frank had had, that night. She sucked in some smoke, shifted a quarter-inch away from him so their thighs no longer touched. 'Don't worry, pal, you'll soon have plenty of girlfriends. All the girls are after a pilot!' She laughed, a funny kind of high-pitched laugh, and smoke came out in puffs. But he was still looking at her in that way. And then he took her fag and tossed it, with his own, into the tumbler. The still-lit butts fizzed and smouldered together in the dregs of water, turning it brown.

Vi knew how it looked. She'd accepted a drink and a smoke from him, and invited him back to her room. But she'd only done it because she felt sorry for him, not because – but now his lips were on hers, his wet tongue shoving into her mouth, and he tasted of smoke and vodka and toothpaste. And it was like at the fair, when you're on the waltzers, and everything spins, and you want to scream and you don't know if it's because you're having fun or because you're scared witless, but you just know that it's fast and urgent and it's too late to get off.

Too late to get off.

His hands pushed her back onto the mattress, pulled up her skirt. His mouth was on hers, stopping her from making a sound. His tongue inside her mouth, a hand up past her garter belt, shoving at her knickers. She felt him – there, inside, suddenly: a swish of cloth, a rhythmic thud-thud of the bedstead against the wall. She pulled her mouth from his and his lips worked their way down one side of her neck. She could have screamed, then, pushed him off. But she didn't. She arched her back and let him plunge deeper into her. Because in that moment – only in that moment – it felt good, and right, and better than anything else. 'Don't let the kettle boil,' she gasped, because he'd know what she meant, wouldn't he? But he carried on, and the thuds got quicker and she looked up at him, rearing above her, eyes narrowed, hair falling forward, pushing himself into her. 'For God's sake, don't go all the way to Blackpool!' she said. But as she did so, he grunted, heaved forwards onto her, and she knew it was too late.

Afterwards, she made him leave by the fire exit so nobody would know. He gave her a clumsy kiss before he went, but neither of them suggested exchanging addresses or becoming pen pals.

'Good luck,' she said, as he closed the door on his way out. But she didn't say it very loudly, and she doubted he'd heard.

The room was still shifting, and she felt a faint nausea rising as she tossed the brown-drowned fag ends from the tumbler out of the window. She could hear the airman clanging down the fire escape. A car growled up the road away from the hostel, headlights flickering over the countryside: flat and empty, the same as she felt.

She shut the window and fastened the blackouts. Then she rinsed the glass again and again under the tap, even though she knew she'd always get a sour taste in her mouth from that glass, no matter how many times she cleaned it.

Because the kettle had boiled, and the train had gone all the way to Blackpool. Oh heck.

Chapter 7

Zelah

The peas were hard and the gravy was burnt. Zelah put down her knife and fork. No point complaining. Like it or lump it, Mrs Hoyden would say, standing behind the canteen, brandishing her ladle like a policeman's truncheon. In any case, she hadn't the energy, Zelah thought, yawning.

She was back on nights, covering Mary McLaughlin's shift pattern, but she'd been up earlier in the afternoon because Agnes Donoghue got a telegram about her ill mother and there were telephone calls to make, compassionate leave forms to fill in and train tickets to sort out. She couldn't have had more than five hours' sleep, at most.

Zelah could hear the scrape of metal against china and the murmur of voices. The big hand on the clock above the canteen jerked forwards. Quarter past already. She'd have to be back on her lathe at half past. Pale faces masticated, smoke drifted ceilingwards, a group at the next table began a half-hearted game of rummy – they'd never finish before the bell went. Someone waved a packet of Player's in her direction. Zelah smiled but shook her head. In the time it took to smoke a cigarette she could grab a few minutes of shut-eye.

She pushed her greasy plate to one side and laid a head on her arm, letting the muted clatter-chatter of the night-shift dinner cocoon her. 'The Gestapo's on the prowl,' she heard Mary McLaughlin's room-mate (Violet Smith, wasn't it?) mutter, but Zelah took no notice. She closed her eyes and immediately her thoughts swirled, images chasing each other in the race to unconsciousness. There was the shattering sound of the cutlery tray being tipped over, and the thudding sound of Mrs Hoyden's ladle on the soup tureen, and Zelah was transported back to that night, just before it happened:

They pound their fists on the metal door, shouting to be let in, as the skies crack orange-white and the air thumps and screams. The shelter door begins to open and he tugs her hand, pulling her inside, into the safe darkness. But just then she notices two spots of light by the top step and catches the edge of a howling sound. A dog, left out in this raid. Hang on a sec. She twists away, lets go of his hand, starts up the steps. It will only take a moment to rescue the poor thing.

As she does so the night rips open with a monstrous roar.

'Miss Fitzlord?' A voice loud and sudden in her right ear. She opened her eyes and jerked up her head. 'Yes. How can I help, Mr Handford?'

'A waste of decent steel,' he said, placing the motor housing she'd been working on upon the table in front of her, crouching next to her uneaten dinner.

'They've all come back from the inspectors as substandard.'

She pushed her palms over her eyelids, feeling the warmth, and pulled them away. He was still there. 'I followed the drawing,' was all she said.

'You can't have done, or they wouldn't have been picked up by quality control.' He was standing next to her. She couldn't see his face without craning her neck up and around. But she could sense him: the air warmer down the right-hand side of her, the faint scent of his maleness: pipe smoke and sweat and shaving cream. Violet Smith was staring across the table at them, blowing smoke through her little rounded nostrils.

Zelah was so tired. She knew she'd followed the drawing, but was it worth the argument? Wouldn't it be easier just to say sorry, it won't happen again, and accept the dock in her pay packet for spoiling precious material and factory time?

Violet Smith was watching, waiting, and so were the group of card players at the next table. I'm the welfare officer, Zelah thought. I'm covering for Mary McLaughlin, but I'm still the welfare officer, and if I roll over and let myself be bullied by management then the other girls will think they have to do the same. She reached for the housing. It was still warm from where he'd carried it from the shop floor in his hands. She picked it up and stood up, chair legs dragging on the tiles. 'Perhaps there could be an error in the drawing?'

she said, turning to face Mr Handford. She saw the muscles in his jaw twitch before he responded.

'Are you saying I'm wrong?'

'I'm saying it could be my fault, but it could equally be something missing from the technical drawing, and perhaps we should check?' she said. Check our facts before barging in on someone's dinner and making accusations in front of their colleagues, she added, silently. 'As soon as my break is over I shall be more than happy to come to your office, and hopefully we can sort this out,' she said.

He gave the briefest of nods, his brows making a deep 'V' in his forehead. 'Very well, Miss Fitzlord. I shall expect you in my office at half past.' And he was gone.

Zelah ignored the gawping and the gossip that erupted as soon as the canteen door shut behind him. She sat down and laid her head back on her arm. Ten precious minutes left. She closed her eyes again, and her mind drifted back to the minutes before the Plymouth raid began:

At that moment she has never felt so alive. The waxing moon spreads a milky pathway right across Plymouth Sound. Her hand is in his and her head on his shoulder, and the stars seem to sway like the hips of the singer in the restaurant. It feels as if they've known each other half a lifetime, instead of just a few short hours. How serendipitous it seems that they've met, like that, today of all days, as she is starting her new life in Plymouth. There is an exquisite pause and she knows he is going to turn and kiss her and she will let him, in the moonlight, with the gentle lapping of the waves.

But instead, he tenses, draws breath. 'Can you hear that?'

She listens. A sound, far away, beyond Drake's Island, out towards the southern horizon, like a distant drill.

The drilling clang of the bell announced the end of the meal break. She lifted a leaden head and pushed herself out of her chair, dropping off her dirty plates on the trolley by the door and heading along the corridor to the stairs.

'They'll all have to be scrapped,' he said, not even looking up at her as she entered his office. He had the housing holding down the technical drawing like a paperweight. His dark hair fell forward, like a crow's wing. He could pass for someone younger than – she realised she had no idea how old he was.

'Can I look?' she said as she reached the desk. He straightened up. His unlit pipe was clenched between his teeth. She caught his eye. What was that expression? Irritation or hostility? She'd begun to think that people were unfair about him after the hostel hop, that he wasn't arrogant, just awkward. But perhaps she was wrong to have given him the benefit of the doubt.

'See?' His forefinger jabbed at a point on the drawing. She looked from the thin black lines to the cylinder of tooled metal that lay on top of it. Zelah had made fifteen of them tonight already. Surely they couldn't all be wrong?

'I don't understand,' she said, moving in for a closer look. The air was thick with the thrumming vibrations of the factory floor. The electric strip light was hot-yellow above

79

them. She was certain she'd followed the drawing correctly. But she'd almost been late clocking on, because of the Agnes Donoghue issue. Had she double-checked that the lathe was calibrated? The musty smell of the paper mingled with the scent of him as she leant in, and her forehead grazed his.

'I'm sorry,' they said in unison, springing apart.

Zelah felt herself flush, brushed her hands against her overalls and looked out through the glass office window to the open mezzanine beyond. A clerk with victory-rolled hair and smudged lipstick swayed past, carrying a stack of files. Zelah inhaled and turned back to face Mr Handford. He'd removed his pipe and thrust his hands into his pockets.

'It's because you're overtired,' he said. 'You're working too hard. Let me find someone else to do the McLaughlin girl's work now she's gone.'

'But she's coming back.'

'Is she really?'

'I promised I'd keep her job open for her.'

'Has nobody ever told you that you shouldn't make promises you can't keep, Miss Fitzlord?'

'But I can keep this promise. We discussed it. You agreed that I could cover her shifts until she's able to return.'

'Well, I shouldn't have agreed.'

Zelah put her hands on her hips 'Mr Handford—' she began.

'You're clearly suffering from overwork and I expect you to take tomorrow night off,' he interrupted.

'I can't possibly.'

'I insist.'

'I have too much to do.'

'I'm afraid it's not your decision. This is a management edict.'

'But what about your production targets, Mr Handford? You need one hundred of these by Tuesday. Who's going to do them if I don't?'

He looked so angry she thought for a moment he was going to lob the motor housing at her head. 'You need a break, Miss Fitzlord. You're taking the night off and I'm taking you to the cinema,' he said.

'Oh, are you, Mr Handford?' she said. 'Is that some kind of management edict, too?'

Laura

The air tasted damp. Clouds were scudding white-grey like herded sheep across the skies. The weather could come in suddenly, up here on the hills. Laura glanced at the paper she had taped to the board on her lightweight easel. She hoped it wouldn't rain, not now she'd lugged everything up here. It was the first time she'd dared leave the hotel since Harold was taken ill. But he was on the mend, now, the doctor said. His fever was coming down.

She looked down at the British Camp Hotel, below her in the dip in the ridge line. She'd already drawn in the outline of the buildings in the faintest of soft pencil, with the waving hills ribboning away beyond. How much of the detail to include, though? The cars parked outside looked like stag beetles, shiny and black – how to get that effect in watercolour without drawing the eye away from the nuanced wash of the landscape backdrop?

She unscrewed the lid on the water-filled jam jar and opened her paintbox. Apart from those cars, which she might very well leave out, everything else fitted perfectly: an easy composition for a morning sketch. Landscapes, that was the answer, she'd decided. She could stay here with Harold for the remainder of the war and paint landscapes and she'd written to K to say as much the other day.

Laura prepared her brush with a wash of primrose yellow, which would capture perfectly the sunshine on the white-washed walls of the hotel buildings far below. But just as she did so, the sun dipped behind a cloud, and the wall colour was suddenly pale mauve. It was most irritating. She waited, paintbrush poised, for the sun to emerge, hearing the occasional twitters of birds and smelling the spritz of greenness of the hillside. Was spring on the way?

The hotel bill would be due soon. But Laura thought perhaps the hotel would be happy to have a beautiful watercolour in lieu of payment, for the time being. After all, that was what Munnings used to do, in Cornwall, before the last war. The sun was still behind that blasted cloud. Laura waited, recalling their Cornish days. Before the last war she and Harold had had many happy years in Newlyn. She'd painted tramps and children, in the garden, and by the sea.

She remembered the golden sun-kissed skin of girls draped on clifftops, and nights singing sea shanties in public houses with Munnings and his entourage. What larks! The last war had ruined it, of course. In point of fact, things had started to turn sour even before that, when Munnings persuaded the delectable Flora to marry him – the foolish old goat. Laura shook her head at the memory, calling out to the swirling spring winds: 'Terrible, just terrible!' Before Flora's suicide and the Great War, Cornwall had been pure as the primrose yellow she held on her dripping brush. Afterwards it was purple-grey and red at the edges, like the pulped eye of a boxer.

And her marriage had been like that, too, after the last war: inflamed and wounded, she remembered. Was it really all my fault for going away? Laura thought, watching the yellow droplets from her brush spray into the wind. We had no money. What choice did I have but to accept the commission to paint those soldiers in their Surrey barracks?

As she watched and waited, Laura noticed the hotel's front door open, and insect-small figures emerge, and get into the black-beetle cars. She heard the faint, faraway growl of engines starting, and saw the cars move off, turn out of the hotel car park and roll down the hill.

The cars had all gone now, but still the sun would not come out. And Laura thought that maybe she should give in and paint the blasted hotel in shadow. It would have an altogether more brooding feel, not at all the sunshine-and-optimism chocolate-box feel she was aiming for, but still.

Laura sighed and dipped the brush in the jar, watching the yellow paint swirl away like a wish. She shivered. The wind was getting up. She could hear it rush through the trees that bordered the twisting path that led downhill to the hotel, branches jostling like a crowd on race day.

She wiped the brush on her work apron and looked at the palette. A mauve wash for the wall instead. She wiped the brush over the watercolour tablet and shivered again. The wind really was picking up now. Never mind. She'd painted in worse weather than this. The trick was to keep your eyes looking and your hand moving and simply not to dwell on the physical discomfort of it.

She swept her brush over the paper – a beginning, at least – but even as she did so, she felt the wetness hit the back of her neck like sea spray and heard a rumble of thunder coming in from behind her, beyond Giant's Cave. Raindrops spattered against her just-started sketch. Damnation. She snapped the watercolour box shut, screwed the lid back on the jam jar and set about removing herself from the hillside before the storm struck in full.

She was panting as she lugged her easel through the front door and into the lobby, nearly bumping into Rosie, who was carrying a cup of beef tea. 'I'm so sorry, dear,' Laura said. 'Is that for Harold?'

'Yes, Missus Knight, but don't trouble yourself—'

'No trouble. I have a free hand.' Laura wedged the easel under one armpit.

'Well, if you're sure?' Rosie said, smiling.

'Quite. I'm sure you have plenty of other things to be getting on with.' The cup wobbled on the saucer as she took it.

'Thank you, Missus Knight.' She turned to go. 'And I nearly forgot to say, there's been a telephone call for you, whilst you were out.'

'Was it the doctor?'

Rosie shrugged. 'Mr Peterson said that if I saw you to tell you there was a telephone call and he's taken a message.'

'Thank you, Rosie, dear.'

The girl bobbed her head and walked back along the corridor. There was the steamy rush and the smell of old bleach and burnt toast as the kitchen door opened and closed, and the girl disappeared inside. Laura continued across towards the reception desk where Mr Peterson was half-hidden behind a copy of *The Citizen*: 'Simultaneous RAF Attack on Three Countries', said the headline. He hadn't seemed to notice Laura's presence, even though the cup and saucer clinked as she set them down on the high counter in front of him. She cleared her throat.

'Oh, I am sorry,' Mr Peterson said, lowering the paper. 'Sounds like we've got Adolf on the back foot. Have you heard?'

'Yes, good news,' Laura said. 'But Rosie just mentioned something about a telephone call?'

'Ah, yes, didn't know where you were.' Mr Peterson's bulbous nose wobbled as he spoke, making his wire-rimmed spectacles bounce up and down. His moustache twitched like a rabbit's whiskers. 'It was that Clark fellow again, I took a message.' He put the paper down and rootled about behind the counter. 'Here we are.' He sniffed and pushed the spectacles back up to the bridge of his nose with a nicotine-stained forefinger. He held out an index card with scratchy writing on it. Laura asked if he could possibly read it out – his writing was hopeless. 'He says to tell you that landscapes are out because he's got Nash on those for the foreseeable, so it's the Nottingham gig or nothing and could you let him know at your earliest convenience because there's another artist in the frame.'

'Thank you, Mr Peterson,' Laura said. She pursed her lips and tapped the edge of the saucer. Why Nash? Why not her? And who else could possibly be in the running for the Nottingham job? She sucked her teeth and watched the surface of the tea ripple as she tapped. There was the sound of a vehicle drawing up outside the hotel, then, and Kipper rushed out from behind reception, yapping wildly.

'Ah, yes, he's a terror for the postman,' Mr Peterson said, pushing himself up. 'Enough, boy, shush now.' He came out from behind the counter and picked up the dog. 'I meant to mention,' he said, holding the struggling mutt at arm's length as if it were a filthy dishcloth, 'your last two months' bills are overdue.'

'It had completely slipped my mind, what with Harold's illness; I'm so sorry,' Laura said, even though she knew fine well what the date was and had been hoping Mr Peterson might have forgotten.

86

'Ah yes,' Mr Peterson said, bending down to put Kipper behind the counter and clicking the latch shut behind them both. 'Can't afford to let matters slip, I'm afraid. Not with things being the way they are.'

The front door opened then, a damp blast at Laura's back. She turned. The postman, cocooned in an endless brown scarf, held out a stack of mail. Laura left the tea on the counter and took it from him. Right on top was a large cream envelope addressed to Mr and Mrs Knight. Laura left the rest of the post to Mr Peterson and plucked that one off the pile. The postman gave a muffled 'Good morning' and the front door slammed shut.

Laura tore open the envelope. But there was no comfort to be had. It was a bill from the doctor, for Harold's treatment, plus the call-out fees. How much? For a moment she thought she must have misread. Her mind whirred with arithmetic: the doctor's bill, plus the two months' hotel bill, and there were the burst pipes in the St John's Wood house to fix, too. There wouldn't even be enough money left for paint, at this rate. Dear Lord, what a start to the day.

Laura sighed, slipped the bill in her pocket, grabbed the easel, and picked up Harold's tea. It would be cold, now, and he'd complain. She sighed again and walked off down the dark corridor towards the stairwell. Her feet tramped on the floorboards and her mind questioned itself: well, what are you going to do now, Laura?

Chapter 8

Violet

'Hurry up!' The banging on the bathroom door came again. Violet couldn't quite recognise the voice, it sounded cockney though – could be Edna – someone waiting to come in and beautify themselves ready for the weekly hop. They'd been promised airmen, again. Did they always promise airmen? Vi wondered, letting her big toe inch out of the scalding water and touch the blessed chill of the cold tap. She took another swig from the bottle of gin as she did so. 'What the heck are you doing in there, anyway?'

'Getting clean!' Vi yelled back. The half-empty gin bottle clinked against the side of the bathtub. 'Getting clean,' she repeated in a lower voice, taking another mouthful of gin and wincing.

Hot baths and 'mother's ruin'. Perhaps it was just an old wives' tale. But what else could she do – sit around pretending the problem didn't exist? If she did that, she'd end up like her big sister Bea had, having to pretend the baby was just another younger sibling – and who'd buy that story, with Ma sick in bed and Pa still away in North Africa? – or worse, having to go to the sluts' home and give the damn thing up, like Mary McLaughlin. No. No. No. She swilled the gin around in the bottle.

The gin had cost her all her bonuses, and been a bugger to get hold of. She'd been in the bath almost an hour already, constantly refilling the hot tap, but still no reassuring swirl of red had appeared between her submerged legs.

The banging at the door came again. More muffled shouts.

'All right,' Vi called out. 'Keep your hair on.'

She lay back in the boiling water. Should she have shoved something up there to dislodge it? Was that how it worked? A crochet hook or a knitting needle. But that was how girls ended up with 'appendicitis complications', wasn't it? Oh heck. She lifted the bottle to her lips again.

The gin was acid-sweet in her mouth, her throat almost closing up as she forced herself to swallow it down, drink it all up. What else could she do? She was hardly likely to hang about for the next eight months just to end up with a bastard. No. No. No.

'For Gawd's sake, you taking swimming lessons in there?' the voice squawked from the other side of the locked door. Vi waved the bottle in front of her face. Not much more to go now, a couple more swallows and she'd be good. *Bang-bang-bang* at the door again.

She remembered how the bunk beds had banged, when

they did it, *bang-bang* against the thin walls, just like the stud press on a sheet of mild steel. And she'd thought, good job everyone else is at the hop and can't hear us, as she threw her neck back and twined her legs round his back and let him carry on while the bang-banging got faster and she remembered telling him, she'd tried to tell him, she'd said, 'Don't let the kettle boil.' And he'd smothered her words with a hard kiss, pulling her arched back up from the mattress, pushing himself even deeper inside her, and collapsing forward – too late. Now she was late, too (and it couldn't have been because of Frank, in the alley, before she left, because everyone knew you couldn't fall pregnant if it was your first time, and you did it standing up).

'If you don't come out, I'm calling Matron!'

'Call her, for all I care,' Vi said, turning the hot tap on again with her toes. She drained the bottle and let it fall with a splash into the churning water.

George

He checked his watch. He could hear the faint strains of the organ from upstairs. The woman in the ticket kiosk had begun to read her magazine. On the cover a girl in a turban with factory machinery in the background was applying powder. 'The Canadians are coming', shrieked the headline. The organ music stopped. The main programme was about to start.

Miss Fitzlord might have missed her bus, he thought. She might be running up from Market Square and along Angel Row. He imagined her, dark curls flying off her forehead as she sped up past the library, lips parted, face spangled with raindrops. She could be here any moment now.

The Ritz doors slammed open and he turned with a start, but it was only a couple of screeching girls with canary-coloured hair, shaking umbrellas and leaving damp splatters on the red plush carpet.

He recalled the spilled drink at the hostel hop, how her red dress had blotted the moisture, a claret-coloured corsage against the swell of her breast. He'd hoped she'd wear that dress tonight. He'd hoped she'd be here when they'd agreed, so that there would be time to get a drink before the film. He fingered the tickets in his pockets – he'd arrived early to get them, to avoid being stuck in a queue. If it went well then perhaps he might ask her out to dinner? It would be the first time he'd taken a woman out in over twenty years – but she wasn't to know that, was she? She wouldn't have known the plummeting terror of asking her to the cinema, and the slap of panic when she actually agreed.

He checked his watch again. No, she obviously wasn't coming. He let out a breath. It was a relief, actually.

The blonde girls were making their way towards the ticket kiosk, nudging and giggling over some shared joke. 'Excuse me, ladies,' he said. They looked up, still smirking. 'Could you use these?'

'How much d'you want for 'em, duck?' the girl on the left said.

'Nothing, I – I find I have no use for them.' Their smiling faces had slipped into pity. Sympathy – God, not that – he'd had a bellyful of cloying concern in '22. 'Take them, please. My friend has been unavoidably delayed and I would rather not see them go to waste.'

'If you're sure?'

He nodded.

'Then I don't mind if I do.' The tickets were taken. 'Thank you, you're a gent.'

They scurried up the stairs. The grey-haired woman in the kiosk had lowered her magazine. She caught his eye and he saw her draw breath as if about to speak, but evidently thought better of it and lifted the magazine again, blanking him out. He headed for the door.

Outside, the rain had slowed to a drizzle, but the puddled gutters meant he was sluiced every time a bus passed. He headed up Derby Road until he got to the tunnel. Word was that rich Victorians had blasted through the rock so that their carriages had clear passage between their mansions and the theatre. There were no carriages of nouveau riche industrialists these days though, he thought, ducking out of the drizzle and into the dry. Nothing but pigeons and the smell of stale urine in the clammy darkness.

He was about a quarter of the way through when he heard the noise, thought he saw a shadow shift in the gloom. He hadn't noticed until he was almost upon them: the couple in a clinging embrace – the man's khaki uniform and the woman's black dress camouflaged them against the limestone wall. The man grunted, shunting upwards. The pale curve of a bare leg held high, a slice of exposed throat, the twin white swivel of eyes as he hurried past. 'What the hell are you looking at?' The woman's voice was throaty-loud in the enclosed space as the man continued his noisy jerking. George hurried on, eyes downcast.

He stopped to catch his breath at the tunnel exit, looking out to where the Park Estate flung across the valley, like welcoming arms. The houses were all blacked out, but there was the sudden sense of space – paler grey slabs in the darkness where the tennis courts and croquet lawns were. The clouds had begun to pull apart overhead, revealing a sprinkle of stars. It was quieter here, away from the city centre traffic, and the air tasted cleaner. George inhaled, taking his pipe and tobacco tin from his pocket.

He should never have invited Miss Fitzlord out in the first place, should he? Silly notion. What had he been thinking of? It wasn't safe to risk all that again. He'd had his chance – he was too old now. He would pause here a while longer before heading home, relish the solitude, forget all about being stood up by Zelah Fitzlord.

Chapter 9

Laura

Why did he have to make it so difficult for her? Behind his spectacles, Harold's eyes had looked old and sad when he implored her to stay. But Laura could find no sympathy, this time. They had said an awkward farewell in the tea room, earlier, in part because the doctor had advised against him going out in the cold air just yet, but also because Laura was still too angry with him to endure the kind of tender, emotional parting that any kind of privacy would demand.

Someone had to earn a living, pay the bills. She'd refused fifty guineas to paint the blitzed-out Londoners in the Tube stations at the start of the war, but she couldn't keep on refusing, could she? Where was the money to come from? Someone had to keep going, keep on going. Why could Harold never understand?

She stamped her feet against the cold. The sky was clear and the shrouded moon had begun to rise. There would be frost later, and maybe another night raid over the Midlands.

Not Nottingham, though. Nottingham was safe. There had been no raids there in nearly two years now. 'You'll be safe as houses, Laura,' K had said on the telephone, and Laura had reminded him archly that houses weren't safe at all these days.

Mr Peterson had phoned for her taxi some time ago. It should have arrived by now. How she hated just waiting in the car park like this. She looked round, eyes taking in the final straggling string of conscripts in training, threading along the ridge line, and the planes that spliced the empty sky. The war was all around them, locking them in, even up here in the middle of the Malvern Hills.

A thrush perched on a tree close to the hotel tea room was sharply outlined against the fading light. Laura thought then about the birds on the runway at RAF Mildenhall, when she'd been painting the Stirling crews last year. How infinitely lovely was the upright spread of light fainting into the dusk above. From a distance it seemed as if the air were filled with sparks, but it was birds caught in the stationary beam – when one came closer you could see its wings beating frantically in the brilliance.

A bird can scupper a plane just as surely as a German gun, they told her. Sometimes the most beautiful things are the most deadly, Laura thought.

She heard the cab, then, drawling round the corner on the long hill up from Malvern. She turned back to give Harold a final goodbye wave – why leave on a sour note, after all? – but the girl was closing the blackouts and he was lost from view.

Laura picked up her bag as the car drew close and took in a deep breath. Keep going, Laura. Keep on going.

Zelah

Zelah jumped at the touch – she hadn't heard anyone approach; it was so loud up this end, with the grinder and the lathes. 'I'm sorry.' A voice in her ear, a white coat stark against the muddle of machinery. 'Can I have a word?'

It was him. She'd been up to his office at dinner break to try to find him, discreetly, explain about what had happened. But his office had been empty, so she thought she'd try again at the end of her shift. It seemed he'd beaten her to it.

Zelah moved away from the lathe, wiping oily hands on her overalls. Mr Handford indicated with his head to the doorway at the far end and disappeared off, a ghost in the machine. Girls on equipment lowered their heads as he passed, making sure they looked as if they were concentrating on the task in hand, but they looked up as soon as he'd gone, and stared at her. Zelah could imagine the gossip in the canteen: Why did he drag her away from her station? What's going on? If the production targets are down because of her, we're all in the muck . . . 'War effort's caught it in the neck!' shouted one, and Zelah heard cackles over the sound of the equipment. She remembered to sidestep over the gas tube by the cylinders: dark in that corner, easy to trip if you weren't careful. She passed a shower of sparks with a face silhouetted in front, like a cameo brooch, and crossed the end of the swarf-strewn factory floor, the taste of metal and dirty oil hot on her tongue.

Outside in the corridor the sound was muted a little. 'Miss Fitzlord ...' He started speaking before the door had even banged shut, before she had a chance to open her mouth. Behind him was one of the posters: a dartboard painted in black and red – 'Help your shop hit the bull', it said, urging them all to work harder, faster, longer, to help win the war.

'About the other night—' She just wanted to apologise, to explain.

He made a chopping gesture with one hand, cutting her off. 'Dame Laura Knight is on her way and I need some help with hosting her visit. She's going to paint the night shift. She'll be here a few weeks. Can you find her a room in the girls' hostel?'

Zelah shook her head. 'The last batch of recruits filled us up completely,' she said. Mr Handford frowned and took his pipe from his pocket. 'Apparently, she wants to be "in with the workers" to get a feel for the camaraderie or something.' He put the pipe in his mouth and chewed on the stem, the muscles in his jaw working like a pump. 'Frankly, I could do without this. But what the War Box wants, the War Box gets.'

'She'll have to get outside digs,' Zelah said. 'I'm sorry not to be able to help you out. But about the other night, I feel I owe you—'

'Damned nuisance.'

'I'm sorry, but the bathroom was flooded and Matron was frantic—'

'What are you talking about?'

'The other night.'

He took the pipe out of his mouth and made that chopping gesture again. 'I'm talking about Dame Laura's visit, Miss Fitzlord. I urgently need to find somewhere for her to stay. Is there absolutely nowhere in the hostel?'

Zelah shook her head. 'No. Nowhere. Unless—'

'Unless?'

'She could have my room, if that would help?'

'But where would you go?'

'Me?' Zelah bit the inside of her lip. 'I suppose I could always take Miss McLaughlin's place.'

Mr Handford stared at her, not making the link. She noticed the frown that creased his brow. 'The girl I told you about – the one whose shift I'm covering. Her bed is empty for the next few weeks.' How could he have forgotten so quickly?

'But don't you mind?'

It would mean moving in with Violet Smith. It was one thing having to work with her – but another thing to be sharing a room with the same girl who'd ruined her date with Mr Handford by getting drunk and flooding the bathroom. Zelah sighed. 'No – in any case, there's nowhere else to put her.'

'Are you quite sure, Miss Fitzlord? It does seem an imposition.'

'It's fine,' Zelah said.

'Good, that's settled, then. She's arriving tomorrow.' He turned to go. He had begun to walk away, already out of reach.

'I owe you an apology,' she called out to his departing back. He paused, but didn't turn.

'No, I think it is I who owe you an apology, Miss Fitzlord. It was foolish of me to suggest . . . let's just say it never happened.' His voice was low, just audible above the factory noise. She couldn't see his face, just the way his broad shoulders seemed to have stooped slightly, as he answered.

And then he walked away, swallowed up by the yellow–beige corridor, and she was left with an inexplicable mixture of sadness and anger. You're being silly, she berated herself. Why should it matter that the date hadn't happened, in any case? She'd only agreed to it in the first place because – well, why had she agreed to it? She wondered for a moment if she should go after him, try to explain about the overflowing bath, Violet Smith drunk as a lord, and Matron having kittens about it all, and how by the time she'd finally made it into town the main picture had already begun and the woman in the ticket office told her that the man in the trilby was long gone. Shouldn't she tell him that, at least?

But just as she began to follow him along the corridor, the bell went for the end of the shift, and it was too late.

Perhaps she should just forget about it, like he said.

Violet

'Is that it?' She looked at the small pile of coins in her hand. She tried shaking the envelope upside down, but all that fell out was her wage slip. The pay clerk tutted as Vi scrabbled to pick it up. Other workers were nudging forwards and the clerk continued to dole out the brown envelopes, as if she begrudged every penny.

Vi squinted down at the slip of paper. It looked yellowish in the harsh lights of the pay office. The words and figures seemed to jiggle about in the too-bright light. Twenty-two shillings for bed and board, and then there was the health insurance payment (compulsory these days, ever since a woman called Mabel Jones had got herself half-scalped when her hair got caught up in a reamer the other week – word was that there was to be a whip-round because the hospital bills were crippling her family). But that still didn't explain why all she had to show for a week's worth of night shifts was a pile of coppers. Her eyes scanned the sheet. What was that? Damages. Emergency plumber call-out, locksmith, painter and decorator. The bathroom: thirty shillings damages payment – what the heck?

All at once the air felt hot and fuzzy – it was like when she'd had that vodka, a sick-spinning feeling, everything blurring at the edges. She gulped and put out a hand to steady herself, but there was nothing there. 'Move along.' The narky voice of the pay clerk. 'You're causing a bottle neck!' And Vi tried to say, all right, give over, I'm on my way, sweetheart, but all that came out was a strange choking sound and she couldn't see properly because everything was shifting sideways.

'I've got you.' A hand under her elbow, then, steering her out with staggering steps. 'Sit down, head between your knees. That's it. Deep breaths.' The corridor floor hard and slippery under her buttocks. The hand, on her shoulder now, and the voice again. 'Stay like that, don't you dare move. I'm going to get you a glass of water.'

She heard footsteps pattering away, swallowed down the sick feeling and opened her eyes. The first thing that came into focus was the God-awful clogs: coupon-free? Fashion-free, more like. What had just happened there? Odd, she'd never been one to have funny turns like that. Could it be – Jesus, she didn't even want to think of it – could it be because of the baby? Wasn't that what happened, in the early days, when you were up the duff? Fainting and morning sickness and all. And who'd helped her? She hadn't even seen who her Good Samaritan was.

The footsteps returned and she looked up. It was Miss Fitzlord, the welfare supervisor – the same woman who'd met her from the station the day she arrived, who'd taken Mary McLaughlin off to the sluts' home, and who'd broken the lock on the bathroom door and held her hair off her face as she vomited down the lavvy the other night. Dear God, what a mucking muddle. She carried a tin mug of water.

'Here, drink it down. Small sips, mind, or it might set you off.' Vi took it from her and did as she was told. The water was tepid and tasted metallic. But then, everything seemed to taste metallic these days. Was that another sign of being in the family way?

'I'm sorry,' Vi said between sips, wishing she weren't having to apologise, yet again, to Miss Fitzlord.

'It's not your fault. It's always rather oppressive in there, isn't it? How are you feeling, now?'

'Better,' Violet lied. The only thing that would make her feel better would be getting rid of this baby and getting on with her life. But to do that she'd need cash. And how could she possibly even think about doing that without two pennies to rub together?

'Good, well, just stay sitting a little longer – keep your head low, that's the ticket.' Violet looked up at the welfare officer. Even in work clothes she managed to look well put together: red lipstick, plucked brows, hair tucked neatly in a hairnet – elegant, somehow, despite the overalls. 'I was hoping to find you, anyway – lucky I caught you when I did,' she said. 'The thing is—'

'I can't afford it,' Vi interrupted.

'I beg your pardon?'

'I know you're doing a whip-round for Mabel Jones, but I haven't even got enough left to buy a packet of fags, so you can't expect any more from me this week, Miss Fitzlord, I'm sorry.'

'I'm afraid I don't quite follow?'

'They've taken thirty shillings out of my wages for the bathroom damages, and then on top of that there's the deduction for the hostel and the medical scheme and there's not much left, see?'

'How much?'

'Elevenpence.'

'Well, that's ridiculous. They can't possibly expect you to survive on that – you send money home, too, don't you?'

Vi nodded.

'They should be deducting your damages incrementally. I'm sure we can have that altered for you, have the payments spread out over a period of weeks.'

'Can you do it today?'

'No, not today, I'm afraid, but—'

'I need the money urgently.'

'What for?'

'Oh, nothing.' Violet took a gulp of the dank-tasting water. 'It doesn't matter.'

'It's obviously not nothing, and I shall try my best to get things rectified as soon as practicable, but I can't promise anything today, I'm afraid. But the reason I needed to find you was—'

'Pardon me for asking, Miss Fitzlord, but why are you here on the night shift anyway? I thought you were the welfare supervisor?'

'I am, but I occasionally cover for sickness, should the need arise.'

'You covering for Mabel Jones?'

'No, I'm on the capstan lathe at the moment, taking your old room-mate's workload.'

'Mary McLaughlin? But she's not off sick, she's—'

'And talking of which,' Miss Fitzlord interrupted before Violet could finish her sentence, 'I'm going to need her bed, I'm afraid.'

'You what?'

'There's a famous artist called Dame Laura Knight who's arriving to paint the night shift, and she needs a single room in the hostel. And as it's only myself and Matron who have singles at the moment, and there's a spare bunk in your room – well, I took a guess that you'd rather share with me than Matron?'

Vi thought of the night of the bathroom hullabaloo and nodded. So, the welfare supervisor was moving in with her? Oh, heck.

Chapter 10

Laura

It had gone. As if it had never existed. Number 33 was still standing, just about, roof gable toppled sideways, doorway gaping, windows caved in – like a Whiteface clown after a tumble. But number 35 Noel Street had completely disappeared: the house where they'd had so much bad luck and the doctor had said they never should have moved to in the first place, as it had been built on an old cess pit. Laura sighed. Perhaps it was for the best that the place had been bombed to oblivion in the Nottingham Blitz.

Laura walked on to where Noel Street crossed the 'Bully-vard' as they'd called it: Gregory Boulevard, cutting a dash between Hyson Green and the race track (gone now, replaced by a football stadium), empty except for a distant rag-and-bone cart clopping up past Forest Fields. Here was the church on the corner. She remembered those endless Sundays: dying a slow death to the tolling of church bells – she hadn't even been allowed to draw, let alone go out to play. She wondered what that bored little girl would think of the woman she'd become?

As she crossed the wide street, wind whipped dust into her mouth. She coughed and wiped her lips on her sleeve. Eastwards, the small sun was rising higher behind streaks of cloud: white-mauve-grey-blue, pulling sideways as if the sky were shot silk cut on the bias. She strode on up the hill, struggling to breathe a little: she hadn't remembered it being so steep – but then, how long since she'd walked up this road? Fifty years?

She stomped on, striving upwards, to the bigger houses with better views and cleaner air: onwards and upwards. Here it was: Ethel Villas, number 9 Noel Street. There were better memories from here: leaning out of the bedroom window to watch the crowds at the race track, Mother's studio upstairs, gas jets in their round opal globes, and the attic crammed with the lumber of past generations. She remembered walking all the way from here to Wilford on painting expeditions with Mother, Nellie and Sis. But all that had been before Mother's illness, and the money problems at the lace factory, when they'd had to move down the street, to the wrong side of the Boulevard.

Laura looked down the hill to the empty space where 35 Noel Street had stood. There were a few other bombed-out buildings, too. Nottingham hadn't had it nearly as bad as London or Plymouth, they said, but it hadn't escaped unscathed. The city was pockmarked: empty spaces in familiar places, like an old woman's failing memory. And she should know about that, Laura thought, starting to walk on up the hill: keep on going, Laura, no matter the rumbling stomach or the gasping breathlessness. Keep on going, because that's what you do. Plenty of time for rest when it's all over, when there will be endless rest. But now is the time for toil, honest sweat, come on, Laura. She crossed the road and cut through the top of the recreation ground: trees with bulged trunks, scabbed bark, half-clothed branches poking skywards, and underfoot the damp, muddy grass.

At the top of the hill, Noel Street joined Waverley Street and here at the junction was Brincliffe School, where she'd had to take over Mother's classes when Mother got ill. She'd been no older than the girls she was supposed to instruct: too young to be a teacher, even though she looked older than she was, even though she had talent, even though her struggling family were desperate for the money. No wonder they hadn't asked her back for another term. No, there were no good memories from Brincliffe School.

Laura hurried on down Waverley Street, legs snap-snapping under her skirt, winding the pavement in towards her like a skein of wool. She smiled to herself. Hadn't she always had excellent endurance: strong limbs and good lungs? She remembered the time she and Harold had had to run miles through a rainstorm to catch the London train for their first show at the Leicester Galleries.

She was at the arboretum already, little pond like a chamber pot, still the same. Funny how in her memory the arboretum was always bathed in sunshine. It couldn't have been sunny every day, could it? Perhaps it was just the patina of happiness. She had been so happy, strolling here with Harold, after classes. 'I do wish you were here to share this with me, Harold,' she said aloud. But the only response she got was the coo of a wood pigeon in the arboretum and the far-distant rumble of a goods train.

She was worried that the College of Art might have caught it in a raid. The man on the train had said that the University buildings in Shakespeare Street had gone. But look, the College was still here, just as it was, the stern faces of Wren, Hogarth, Titian and the others glowering down from the beige stonework. Here was where she'd met Harold: slender and dark with his *pince-nez* and aristocratic nose. She was just fourteen and he was seventeen, and already the most precociously talented artist the College had ever had. Here was where he'd painted her portrait, in the studio upstairs. She still had it: her apple-cheeked, frizzy-haired fourteen-year-old self, prepared to sit still for-ever if it meant that she had Harold's gaze fixed on her. She remembered how those long afternoons in the studio were punctuated by the grunts and yells of labouring women and the siren-screams of newborns from the maternity hospital next door. Was that why they'd never had a family, she and Harold? Had hearing the agony of childbirth in her forma-tive years put her off for good?

No, Laura, stop deceiving yourself. You know fine well why you and Harold did not have children.

For a moment Laura thought she could smell oil paint and

hear the mewling wail of a newborn. But then the smell and sound were gone, and Laura thought she must have imagined them.

The clouds were ripping apart now, the sunshine breaking through yellow-gold on her lifted face. It was time to move on. Time to get back to the present. There was work to be done.

Zelah

Zelah looked out of the grimy bus window onto the industrial landscape: smokestacks and brickwork. She thought about the conversation she'd just had with Mr Handford. He was not at all the man she'd been led to believe he was. Arrogant, they said. Stern, impatient, caring only about targets and output – no, they had him wrong. She wiped a finger over the condensation and it made a faint squeaking noise. Or at least, she thought they had him wrong. She was hardly likely to find out the truth, not now.

They said it used to be fields round here: the Meadows. The bus wound through rows and rows of tiny terraced houses. Her top-deck window was on a level with the chimneys and broken roof slates. She heard the murmur of voices from the other girls on their way back to the hostel, the fug from their cigarettes rising to the bus roof and sitting like low cloud above their nodding heads.

The girl next to her was reading a magazine. The pages

flapped every time they hit a pothole, which was often, and the girl kept snuffling and pushing her spectacles up her crooked nose. Zelah took out one of her Senior Service and offered the packet, but the girl flushed and mumbled, 'No, thank you,' holding her magazine up high to her face, like a shield. Zelah struck a match and inhaled, glancing at the magazine. It was an old copy of *Woman*. On the cover a dark-haired girl leant against the shoulder of a fair-haired man. In the background were rocks, the sea and a swooping gull. In the bottom right-hand corner you could just make out the dark blue of the man's navy uniform. It could almost have been a picture of me, Zelah thought, if things had turned out differently. She carried on smoking as the bus trundled through the dirty streets, letting her mind drift back to how it had been, that day, before the raid, when happenstance had collided, briefly, with happiness:

She is walking down Union Street in the hazy sunshine, looking for somewhere that sells camping stoves, because there is nothing to cook on in the new place. Just then a doorway opens in front of her and a woman in a peach silk frock with a fur bolero rushes out and bumps into her. 'I do beg your pardon,' the woman says, looking accusingly at Zelah, and then storming off across the road, causing a bus to swerve out of her way.

The door is still open, seeping band music out into the street, and Zelah is about to walk on when a man appears from inside. He sighs and shrugs. 'Apparently I'm the type who won't amount to anything and she wishes she'd never laid eyes on me.'

'You don't seem all that bothered,' Zelah says, looking over at him. He is in naval uniform, blue bell bottoms smartly creased.

'I would never have passed muster with her parents. A girl like that needs a chap with land, and preferably a peerage to boot.' He pushes wavy blond hair off his face and shakes his head. 'I don't suppose you fancy a tipple? They've just popped the cork and it'll only go to waste otherwise. The band aren't half bad, either.'

Zelah hears the music drifting out across the pavement, laughter from down the stairwell. She ought to be sensible, she tells herself, be buying the camping stove and some food whilst the shops are still open, as well as registering at the Labour Exchange and getting on with the business of sorting her life out. 'A glass of bubbly? At this time of day?' she says. He nods and she glances into his eyes: pale blue, with fine lines cobwebbing the corners. A girl could drown in those eyes, she thinks, and smiles, despite herself. 'I don't mind if I do.'

It is like a knife, she thought, now, as the bus pulled in to the hostel entrance. This war is a sharpened blade, with love on one side and tragedy on the other, and all of us just balanced on the slim edge in between. The naval officer – James Astley, his name was – was lost to her before their romance even had the chance to begin. And she hadn't agreed to go out with a man since – until George Handford had asked the other day. But that had been a mistake, hadn't it? She sucked in the last of the fag and ground out the butt on the floor.

Zelah waited. The snuffly girl was stuffing her magazine into her handbag and the queue for the stairs caterpillared all the way back along the aisle. When she finally got off, she noticed that the sun had gone in and the clouds had started to thicken, piling up like the coils of swarf on the factory floor. She followed the other girls in through the double doors and up the stairwell to the first floor. She put the key in the lock of room 102, the second door along. Sandwiched between the cleaning store and the bathroom, it was barely bigger than a broom cupboard, but it was hers, had been hers alone, ever since she arrived in '41.

She pushed open the door and went inside, remembering how the builders were finishing off the building when she first moved in, the road still a rutted farm track, and the air heady with wet-paint fumes. She'd picked the room to be alone, justifying it to herself as not being able to hear properly and so being no good at chit-chat with room-mates. But her hearing had almost recovered by the time she arrived at the hostel. The truth was she'd felt incapable of social contact. It was all she could do to get up, get dressed and do her shifts. The anaesthesia of factory work was a relief: a numbing privacy found amongst the noise and the boredom of it all.

Zelah went across to the window and opened the blackout curtains. The rectangle of brown earth and grey skies was just the same as it had been the day she arrived, all the way from Plymouth, with nothing but her ID card and the clothes she had on. I'll do anything, she'd told the woman in the Labour Exchange, any kind of war work you have, anywhere in the country. And she hadn't heard the woman's reply because her ears were still ringing and her head throbbing, but it said Royal Ordnance Factory, Nottingham, on the travel warrant. She didn't even know where Nottingham was, but it didn't matter – so long as it wasn't Plymouth.

Her eyes scanned the room, taking it all in. It wasn't much: cream gloss paint on the lower half of the walls like a half-drunk glass of milk, the bed with its grey blanket, the wardrobe so slim that the hangers had to be angled sideways or the door wouldn't shut properly, the small sink with her glass and toothbrush. It wasn't much, but it was everything; all she had in the world was here.

She'd been one of the first to arrive at the hostel. There were still mostly men on the tools, back then. But as more girls arrived, the men were conscripted into the forces, the hostel filled up, and the shop floor, too. She began just by helping out, because she'd been there the longest, meeting the girls when they arrived, showing them the ropes. She was older than most – an old maid by their standards. Someone must have seen on her file that she had some relevant experience. When they created the job of welfare supervisor for her, she could hardly refuse.

And now she had to move out of the room that had been her sanctuary all this time. She tossed her handbag onto the bed and went to get the bleach and a rag from the cleaning cupboard next door. But she paused, just before opening the cupboard door, and instead turned on her heel and walked back downstairs into the foyer. She would clean the room and move out to make space for Dame Laura Knight, but there was something she urgently needed to do, first.

George

The bus had already gone – he'd missed her. He'd felt bad about the way he'd been with her earlier, wanted to apologise, but by the time he'd got away, the transport had left. She'd go back to the hostel thinking him a discourteous oaf. And that wasn't what he wanted. Even though there wouldn't – couldn't – be anything between them, he found that he didn't want Miss Fitzlord to think badly of him. So he'd raced out through the shift-change crush. But too late. Dammit.

George strode back into the factory, taking no notice of the sloe-eyed girls who turned from the queue to gawk as he pushed past. The clocking-in machine was a slack-jawed mouth and they knocked the knob like a blow to the teeth as they punched their cards. George knew there would be eye-rolling and titters-behind-hands as soon as his back was turned. Those silly, silly girls. Why had they been allowed into the factory, gossiping and ruining everything? Why couldn't it just have stayed as it was, as it had been since he joined, a male preserve, where everyone knew their place, and there were no distractions? He knew why. Of course he knew why: the war effort, releasing men for front-line work, all of that, but even so . . .

He stomped up the stairs, banging open the corridor door and cutting along the open mezzanine, hearing the familiar orchestra of sound: the whine of the reamer, drone of drills, *thunk* of the stud-press and hiss of the steam-cleaning jets.

Then, a sudden clatter, like a percussionist losing the beat. He paused and looked down. Someone had tripped on a pile of dirty rags and swarf and dropped a tray of casings, scattered like beads. 'Clean that lot up! Get that swarf in the salvage bin!' Nobody looked up. No one had heard him above the din. The girl who'd dropped the tray was on her hands and knees but not one of her colleagues had bothered to pause to help her. It was a disgrace.

'All right, George?' Bill Simmons, the day-shift manager, was on his way out of the office, mug of Bovril and half-smoked fag in his right hand.

'Incident in Bay Three.'

'I'll take a look. I'm on my way out to supervise the testing, any road. You get off. Looks like you could use a bit of shut-eye. Busy night?'

'Not nearly busy enough. We'll never meet the new production targets at this rate.'

'What's the worst they can do? Send Winnie up with a big stick to chivvy us along? Anyway, now we're fully manned, things will pick up.'

They both looked down at the girl, who seemed to have retrieved the casings and had begun wandering back to her work station, leaving swarf strewn like hay on a barn floor.

'But it feels like they don't care. I mean, look at that, looks like a bomb's hit it down there.'

'Working with these girls is like herding ruddy cats,' Bill said, giving him a pat on the shoulder. 'I'll sort it, though. Go home and rest, man.'

George nodded his thanks and turned away. He went into the office and closed the door. A sheaf of papers slewed across the desk. It looked like Bill had just emptied a whole file and immediately lost interest. He was a good man, but administration was hardly his strong point. Sharing an office, sharing a job, could be barely tolerable at times. Today felt like one of those days, George thought, staring at the muddled mess of paperwork.

And there, holding down the edge of an order form, was the motor housing he'd hauled Miss Fitzlord in about, that night. He picked it up, remembering her face when he asked her to go to the flicks with him. Which he should never have done. He'd take the ruined housing with him and toss it in salvage on his way out.

A thud, then, and a sudden concussion that shook the piece of worked aluminium from his hand and back onto the desk. They must have started the gun testing already. The windows of all the terraced houses in the Meadows would be shuddering in response.

He paused and drew breath.

No, he couldn't go home. Bill said he needed rest, but how could he sleep in this state, not with this spark-fizz of humiliation inside, white-hot as an oxyacetylene jet. Why did he feel like this? He clenched his fist and banged it down onto the mess of papers. The housing jumped. Sheets of paper shifted off like blown leaves and landed on the floor. His fist hurt, but not badly enough. He should have hit the wall instead – a rush of pain to slake his embarrassment.

He wiped a palm over his face and let out a sigh. 'There's no fool like an old fool,' he said aloud. He thought of the new shell-filling factory that was being set up in Ruddington. He had an extra petrol coupon allocation to enable him to liaise with the contractors and advise on the work. That's what he should do this morning. The drive, at least, might help clear his head. Ignoring the scattered papers, he picked up his briefcase from beside the filing cabinet, pulled open a drawer, plucked out a file, and stashed it inside.

He was just about to leave when he remembered Dame Laura Knight. He put down his briefcase, found the memo pad and scrawled a note: *Bill, please phone Matron at the hostel and advise her of Dame Laura's arrival, etc. Thank you, George.* Let Bill phone the hostel. George certainly wouldn't be making the call himself. And he'd be damned if he went to any more of their dance evenings either, no matter what the Board said. He used the faulty housing to hold the memo next to the telephone, where Bill would see it.

He picked up his briefcase and headed towards the door. Through the window he could see Miss Ridley, the pay clerk, waddling along, carrying a box of envelopes. He paused. If he left the office now he'd be forced to pass the time of day with her; he couldn't face it, not today. There was another thud of a gun being tested. Miss Ridley faltered and her stack of envelopes wobbled, then she carried on. George cast a final eye round the office. He'd apologise to Bill later, give the place a good tidy up. But not now. After he'd calmed down.

He was halfway through the door when he heard the telephone. He was in no mood to talk to anyone. In any case, it would be a call for Bill, not him, at this time in the morning. The phone continued its shrill nag. But – but what if it were Dame Laura? He should really answer it. He walked back over to the desk, leaving the door ajar.

'ROF Nottingham, manager's office, who's speaking please?'

'Oh, hello, I was wondering if I could leave a message for the night-shift manager?' It was a woman's voice, but it didn't sound like an old woman's voice. Not Dame Laura, then. Damn, he could have ignored it, after all. The line was terrible. Between the hissing phone and the racket coming through the open door he could barely hear.

'Speaking.'

'I beg your pardon?'

'This is the night-shift manager. How can I help?'

'Oh, it's you.'

An unravelling feeling, like watching the coils of metal uncurl from a spinning drill-bit. 'Miss Fitzlord?'

'I just wanted to say sorry.' Her voice was scratchy and distant. He put the phone back to his ear. 'I tried to get away in time, but there was an emergency at the hostel and by the time I made it to the Ritz you'd already gone. I'm so sorry.'

Hot-forged metal plunged into the cooling tank. The hiss of steam. Frustration evaporated in an instant.

'Not at all. I'm sorry, too. Perhaps I should have waited longer.'

'No, no, you weren't to know. I mean, how could you have?' There was a pause. 'Well, that's all I wanted to say. Goodbye, George.'

She was going to hang up. No. Wait.

'Zelah.'

'Yes?'

'I was wondering if – if you'd consider a "re-calibration" of our friendship, as it were?'

She laughed, then, sounding like the notes of a glocken-spiel down the muzzy telephone line. 'Re-calibrate? George, a re-calibration sounds like an excellent plan. I wouldn't want our friendship to end up in the salvage bin.'

Zelah

She sloshed bleach into the sink and wiped the cool ceramic with the cloth, then rinsed it out and ran it over the win-dowsill. Next, she began to strip the bed, disembowelling the warm cocoon that looked so inviting. Not yet. She had to get this room ready for Dame Laura, and check with Matron that there were no urgent welfare issues this morning. Then she had to move all her things. Only then would there be time for sleep. She heaved the feather pillow out of its case, and thought about George Handford. What would he be doing now? Did he go straight to bed after his shift, or did he like to pause a while, wind down first? She thought about him in just his shirtsleeves, turning on the wireless, waiting for the kettle's whistle. She imagined herself next to him, spooning tea into the pot, him coming round behind her, lifting up her hair and kissing the nape of her neck . . .

'Glad I caught you.'

Zelah started. The pillow slipped from her fingers and slumped on the lino.

'I assumed, as your door was ajar?'

'Matron. Good morning. How can I help?'

'There's just been a call from Mr Simmons.'

'Really?' Zelah's face felt hot. She bent down to pick up the pillow.

'He says Dame Laura Knight is arriving today! She's coming to paint the night-shift girls, apparently. Do you know anything of this?'

'Mr Handford mentioned it, yes. I'm just moving my things so she can have this room.'

'He's making you move out? Honestly, that man.' Matron shook her head and pursed her lips. 'I'm not a judgemental woman, but the things I hear!'

'I offered. There's no other space – I'll just move into 179 whilst Laura Knight is here.'

'With that Smith girl? Well, good luck with that, dear.'

'I'll be fine. I'm sure that incident with the bathroom was just a one-off. Talking of which, is there anything urgent for me to deal with this morning? Have we heard anything more about Maureen White's fiancé?'

'He's been patched up and sent back on a troop ship. She won't need leave for weeks, whatever she claims. And there's nothing else that can't wait. Now then, I'll sort the bedding out. You just get your stuff moved and get your head down for a couple of hours. I'll hold the fort.' Matron leant over and began to tug at the bed covers.

'Thank you. It's very kind of you.'

'Well, you must be shattered, what with working the night shift and your welfare duties. I can't imagine what that Mr Handford was thinking, making you take on all that extra work.'

'He didn't make me. In point of fact, he tried to stop me.'

'What on earth did you do it for, then?'

'Mary McLaughlin said she wanted to come back, and it was the only way to keep her job open for her.' Zelah went to the wardrobe and began to take out her clothes, such as they were: the cream blouse, the black suit, and the red crepe dress she'd saved all her spare wages and coupons to buy, even though it had meant going without new shoes for a year.

Matron tutted, ripping the sheets from the mattress. 'If Mary McLaughlin comes back – and it's a big if, mind – it'll only be a matter of weeks before she gets herself into the same situation, and skips off for another skive, offloading another little bastard as she goes.' She kicked the sheets into a lumpen mess on the floor.

Zelah turned with her armful of clothes, waiting as Matron shook out the blanket and folded it into a neat block. 'I know Mary might not come back,' she began.

'I'll eat my hat if she does,' Matron interrupted, dumping

the folded blanket on top of the chest of drawers with a soft thud. 'I've come across her sort before.'

'But if she does come back,' Zelah carried on, opening the top drawer with her free hand and pulling out stockings and vests, 'well, don't you think she should have a second chance?'

'No,' Matron said, fixing Zelah with her gimlet gaze. 'No, I'm sorry, but I don't. Girls like that, spreading diseases, not caring that they're bringing bad blood into the world with their ways. It's unchristian and it's wrong, and I'm surprised at you, Miss Fitzlord, for taking the side of immorality, really I am, you being such a decent young lady.' Matron shook her head, and the wattle of skin on her neck wobbled in outrage.

Zelah blinked. 'Well, I'll just be getting along with my things,' she said. 'Thank you again for doing the bed for me.'

'You're welcome, Miss Fitzlord,' Matron said, bending down to an armful of dirty laundry.

Zelah knocked on the door of room 179 and waited. When there was no answer, she tried the handle. It was unlocked. She pushed open the door. Inside, the room was warm and dark. She could hear the slow breathing of someone asleep, and make out a hump in the covers on the top bunk. She closed the door as softly as she could. It clicked shut. She put her bundle of clothes on the end of the bed. Later, once Violet was awake, she'd put away her things – there was no need to disturb her now. Zelah pulled off her shoes and fell into the lower bunk, not even bothering to undress, and her mind slipped back to the last time she'd been forced out of her own space and into the lives of strangers:

Zelah pushes the door open and steps inside. 'You wanted to see me, Miss Orton?'

The older woman blots the paper she's been writing on and takes off her horn-rimmed spectacles before looking up. 'Miss Fitzlord. Good of you to pop up. I know evenings are busy for you, but there's something—' The telephone interrupts with its shrill ring. Miss Orton picks up the receiver, motioning with her free hand for Zelah to come in and sit down. 'Yes, this is the headmistress . . .' She speaks into the mouthpiece and smiles an apology at Zelah.

Zelah closes the door behind her and walks across the dark red rug with its complicated patterns, and sits down on one of the leather-seated chairs in front of the headmistress's desk. She hears the buzzing squiggle of the voice in the phone, sees Miss Orton frown and rub at the point on her temple where a grey streak snakes into her mid-brown bun. 'Indeed, but it is rather late in the day, Major . . .' she says.

Zelah folds her hands in her lap and waits, taking in the familiar shelves of books, and the timetables tacked to the wood panelling. She can still taste sugar on her lips from the top of the glazed bun Cook saved for her. Zelah always has her supper whilst the girls are in prep, and they often have a natter, down in the warm kitchen, whilst Cook is giving the work surfaces a final wipe. There were rumours, Cook said — an open secret, really — that the army was on the brink of requisitioning the school buildings. In which case the whole school would have to move. Cook said she'd heard Miss Orton was 'very pally' with the headmistress of The Mount School in Crediton. (Cook somehow hears many things, from cleaners and delivery boys, and the plump school secretary who has a weakness for shortbread.) She said odds were on The Grange joining The Mount for the duration of the war. Zelah thinks about this as she waits for Miss Orton to finish her phone call.

'I daresay, but I would rather not, at this late hour,' Miss Orton continues into the phone. There are more muffled tinny voices from the other end of the line, and Zelah sees the headmistress shake her head. 'Well, if that's your tone, I'm afraid I'm going to have to bid you good evening, Major.' She pushes the receiver hard onto its cradle. It makes a small chiming sound. Miss Orton sucks in a breath. 'I'm so sorry, Miss Fitzlord, where were we?'

'You wanted to see me?' Zelah says.

'Yes.' Miss Orton clasps her hands together on top of the blotter. 'You have been such a wonderful housemistress to the girls over these past few years since your mother passed . . .' The phone rings again. 'Dash it – sorry.' Miss Orton's liver-spotted jowls quiver as she picks up.

'Yes, speaking. How can I help? Oh, hello, Colonel.' She listens with her head on one side. 'I believe I already discussed this with a Major Bottomly-Finch, just a few moments ago, so perhaps if you have a word with him?' She shoots Zelah a bear-with-me expression as the voice at the other end of the line carries on. Zelah fiddles with a loose thread on the button of her cuff, resolving to fix it straight after she's done lights out and locked the front doors.

'I'm afraid it will have to wait, Colonel,' Miss Orton says, hanging the phone up with a chiming thump. She leans forward over the

126

desk. 'The thing is, Miss Fitzlord,' she begins, but before continuing she takes the phone off the hook. It lies buzzing on the desk between them like a dying bee.

'If this is about the move?' Zelah says.

'You know about the move?'

Zelah looks down at the phone. Miss Orton gives a small smile. 'Yes, I suppose I haven't been terribly hush-hush about it. These army chaps are so very insistent. They want everything doing yesterday, and there's no appreciation of the time it takes to relocate an entire girls' school halfway across the county. But anyway, that's not important. What's important is you, Miss Fitzlord.'

'I'm fine with it,' Zelah says, knowing that all the practical details of the move will be left to her, as Miss Orton will be busy liaising with parents and army officers. She wonders what amount of bedding, towels, cutlery, etc. they'll have to take with them to the new place. She will need to hire a van.

'Well, I have to say, you seem to be taking this very well.'

'I think I'll be fine organising the move,' Zelah says. 'If you can hold off the army until the next exeat weekend it should be a piece of cake. We're joining The Mount in Crediton, I take it?'

'We?' says Miss Orton, opening her eyes wide and pushing her face forward towards Zelah. She reaches out a hand and touches Zelah's shirtsleeve. 'There is no "we", dear. I don't know what you've heard from elsewhere, but I think your source might be mistaken. There's no easy way to say this. You see, The Mount already has two live-in housemistresses. So I'm afraid there's no longer a position for you with us, Miss Fitzlord.'

Zelah looks down at the short, clean nails and feels the

headmistress's fingertips on her arm as the older woman speaks of providing excellent references, two months' severance pay, and a friend of hers who has a room to rent in Plymouth. Zelah nods, swallowing the musty office air, feeling like a fish that's just been hooked and hauled out of water: drowning. Finally Miss Orton lifts her hand from Zelah's sleeve.

'Shall I go and pack my things?' Zelah says.

'Jump into my grave as quick, would you?' Awake. Eyes open. A pair of stockinged feet hanging down by her face.

Zelah sat up and the world shifted into focus. She wasn't sure how long she'd slept for. Her mouth was dry, and she was hot from going to bed fully clothed. 'Sorry. Sorry. You were on the top bunk, though.'

'Top bunk's Mary's. I just fancied a change.' Violet jumped down, feet slipping a little on the lino as she landed.

'So which bunk do you want me to take?'

'Stay where you are, makes no odds to me. I was only pulling your leg.' Violet's dimpled face appeared where her feet had been.

Zelah pushed back the covers, watching Violet go over to the mirror and slick her lips with pink lipstick. The sun slanted low through the window, and she heard footsteps running along the corridor, a shriek of laughter, a door banging shut. The air smelled different from her old room. 'What time is it?' Zelah said.

'Time you got yourself a watch, sweetheart,' Vi said, smacking her lips at her reflection. She turned. 'Don't worry, you haven't overslept. I'm up early, is all. Got somewhere I need to be.'

'Sorry to have to foist myself on you,' Zelah said. 'I'll go back to my own room as soon as Dame Laura has finished her painting.'

'Stay as long as you like. Mary McLaughlin's not going to be coming back any time soon.'

'Oh, I don't know. She seemed very keen to return to work.'

Vi turned, then. 'My big sister went into the ATS after she had her little one. Ma told us to pretend the baby was our sister, so's nobody would know. The shame, see? But it was the worst thing she could have done. Giving up your baby never works out, even if it is a bastard. Here ...' Vi had taken her packet of Player's from the top of the chest of drawers. She took out two, and flicked her lighter, lighting them both at once, and handing one to Zelah. 'Don't tell anyone, will you?'

'Of course I won't.'

'I know you won't.' A smile passed quickly across Violet's face. 'You're not like the others, are you, Miss Fitzlord?'

'Oh, I don't know, I—' Zelah began.

'Trust me, you're not,' Violet said. 'You're the only one who hasn't given me a hard time over the bathroom thing. Matron was a right cow about it.' She tapped ash into the sink, then walked back to the bunk beds. 'Hang on to this a sec, will you?' She passed her cigarette to Zelah, sat on the edge of Zelah's bunk and put her shoes on. 'Thanks, sweetheart.' She took back her fag, took a drag, and stood up. 'Right then.' She grabbed her coat off the hook behind the door. 'Better get going. Make yourself at home and I'll see you at work.'

'See you,' said Zelah. The door slammed and Violet was gone.

Chapter 11

Violet

Icy puddle water splashed up her legs, but she took no notice, striding on along the pavement as the bus drove off past Market Square. The bell in the domed town hall chimed the half-hour. Shops were beginning to lower their shutters for the night, and coated figures scurried homewards in the drizzle.

There it was, up ahead. Vi crossed over, clogs sliding on the wet cobbles. It was like a squashed layer cake: cream plaster walls slouching streetwards. The first floor hung out over the pavement, supported by a row of stubby columns like liquorice sticks. Vi stopped under the colonnade, took off her headscarf and ran her fingers over her waves, pinching the ends back into place and patting off the damp. There were cigarette butts all over the pavement, and the water gurgling in the drain had a dank-sweet smell. She took out her lipstick, clicked off the lid and scraped a baby fingernail round the inside, before wiping it over her lips. There wasn't much left, but she hadn't any spare money for lipstick – it had all gone on the bottle of gin, and a fat lot of good that had done, Vi thought, pressing her lips together to get an even coverage.

Vi heard music and laughter from inside the pub. Through the leaded pebble-glass she glimpsed smoky figures, a lit fire, lamps like puffballs. Then a hand pulled the blackout curtains across and everything disappeared. She hesitated just a second longer, tidying a brow with her ring finger before taking two steps to the crooked wooden door and pushing it open.

She walked into a sea of voices, all foreign-sounding, full of zeds, zigzagging through the warm-sweet air. The pub was almost full already, although it was barely evening. She'd prepared herself for her entrance: a young woman, alone, in a pub like this. She lifted her chin, hearing the pub door bang shut behind her, the tide of voices shift and swirl, as they noticed her.

She had prepared herself for the inevitable pause in their conversation, a moment where she would be stared at with that mixture of hostility and lechery. Then there'd be a ribald comment from some joker, beery breath on her neck, a slap on her arse as she made her way to the bar. Because that was what you expected as a single girl in a pub full of men. But none of that happened. There was a pause, but someone called out 'Hello, beautiful!' in cracked English, and the blue-grey uniforms of the Polish RAF rippled gently away from her as she headed across the room. Someone with dark, floppy hair blew a kiss as she passed, that was all. At the bar they made space for her to stand, without commenting or smirking at the temerity of it.

The landlady was busy serving, filling the foaming pint pots, pouring the thimble-sized shot glasses, smiling and nodding and counting out change into outstretched hands, her large breasts swaying under her cream blouse, grey hair dark on her hairline where she was beginning to sweat. She wiped a swift hand over her brow and nodded at Vi. 'What'll it be, mi duck?'

'I'm looking for Jacky Symanski,' she said. The landlady's eyes flicked over her, as if checking for a rank badge, but then she just shrugged and turned away to take another order.

'I buy you drink, beautiful?' said a short, brown-haired man standing at the bar next to her. Vi smiled and shook her head. No, she didn't want to accept a drink from a charming young Polish pilot, thank you very much. (It was precisely that which had got her into this pickle in the first place.) She could hear the pub door opening and closing, more people coming in, English voices mixing with Polish. She tapped her fingers on the varnished wood of the bar, trying to think what to do.

'Been stood up, luv?' A local voice in her right ear. She shook her head but – 'C'mon, there are worse places to be jilted. Lemme buy you a gin and lime, that'll put a smile on those pretty lips.' A gin was the very last thing likely to put a smile on her lips today. She shook her head again.

Vi nudged and 'excuse-me'd her way to the far end of

133

the bar, where there was a hinged barrier that would let the bar staff out to collect glasses and empty ashtrays. She lifted it up and stepped onto the sticky lino behind the bar. Arms reached across, waving notes, as people called for drinks, assuming her to be a barmaid. She felt her shoulders relax, on familiar territory, this side of the bar. The landlady hadn't even noticed, dealing with a tangle of lads at the far end, who'd just tumbled in off the street. The noise was like the spring tide on the estuary back home, rising up and up: 'Hey, beautiful'; 'Over here, duck'; 'When you've got a moment, sweetheart'. She ignored them all and reached up to where the chain dangled from the brass bell, the one they'd use to call 'time' at the end of the evening. She grabbed it and pulled, hard. The bell clanged and everyone looked at her and in the sudden silence she shouted out: 'I need to find Jacky Symanski!'

Vi leant against one of the squat columns and tried not to shake as she struck a match to light her last fag. The flame wobbled. She pulled in the smoke and flicked the match into the gutter, wishing her heart would ruddy well slow down. The landlady had screeched for her chubby husband, who'd thudded out from the saloon and man-handled her outside with a 'what-the-hell-d'you-think-you're-playing-at-missy' as they dodgemed through the punters and a 'get-out-and-stay-out' as he shoved her outside. She couldn't really blame them. She'd probably have done the same if it had been her pub, Vi thought, staring out into the curtain of drizzle. She just hadn't known what else to do. If she could just find the airman. She wasn't going to ask for anything except the money to get the problem sorted, that was all. Pilots got paid a fortune; it was the least he could do.

She pinched the fag end hard, concentrating on not letting her trembling fingers drop it onto the damp pavement. When she heard the pub door open and footsteps approach she deliberately looked away, out into the pencil-shaded evening, pretending not to hear the 'Hello, beautiful' in thickly accented English. She took a drag on her cigarette and then began to walk away, not bothering to put her headscarf back on, not caring about how the drenching air would spoil her hairstyle, because if she hung around, he'd just think she was hoping to be picked up. And that was the last thing she wanted.

'I know Jacky,' the voice said, and she faltered.

'You do?' She turned and took a step back towards the airman, a slight young man, barely taller than she was.

'Yes, we train together. But he go.'

'He's gone?' Her mind spun back. 'But you're on the same course?'

'No, he finish. I pass out next week – I pray.' He gave a sort of shrug as she approached. He had a short nose, and square face, hair a steel slice showing beneath his cap. 'Jacky, he go to 303 Squadron in Northolt.' Vi remembered, as he said it, recalling that the vodka had been to celebrate the passing out, and how hilarious it had seemed that neither of them knew where on earth in the country his posting actually was. It wasn't funny any more. It was important, because if she could just contact him, surely he'd do the decent thing, send enough money for her to sort herself out?

'Do you know the address?'

'Yes, but—'

'I've got a pencil and paper.' She rummaged in her pocket with her free hand. 'Hang on a sec.' Where was it? She was sure she'd put it in. Maybe she'd put it in the inside pocket. 'Can you just hold my fag for me for a moment?' She held out the lit cigarette and saw the man shake his head, shuffling his feet on the paving stones. He wouldn't take the fag, didn't look at her.

'It's not possible, beautiful,' he said, and she knew what he was going to say even before he looked up and into her eyes. 'Jacky Symanski is MIA. He went down over North Sea last week.'

'But I need him.'

His face creased and he swallowed. 'I'm sorry, *moja droga,* he is gone.'

The cigarette jolted from her fingers and onto the pavement. It was her last one. She crouched down, scrabbling, to grab it up and shove it lipstick-gritty back in her mouth. When she stood up again the trainee pilot had already gone, the pub door banging closed behind him. Beyond the columns the rain had begun to fall in earnest. Vi took another drag and walked out into the watery barrage, wondering what the hell she was going to do now.

George

His shielded headlights just about picked out the figure with the thumb stuck out, as he turned right onto Wilford Road. It felt like a duty to stop for hitchhikers these days. He slowed to a halt, trying not to splash puddle water, and leant over to wind down the window.

'I'm not going far – but where do you need to be?'

A pale face at the window, dripping wet hair clinging like seaweed to a cheek. A young woman with a southern accent: 'The gun factory.'

'Me too. Hop in then.'

'Thank you.'

She slammed out the sluicing rain and wound up the window as he pushed the car into gear and drove away. His headlights stroked the rainfall, wavering like silver beaded curtains pulling apart as they drove.

The girl was drenched, the air inside the car suddenly humid with her inside. The wipers pulled blurry semi-circles on the glass. He wiped away condensation from the windscreen with the edge of his gloved hand. They'd be at the factory in five minutes or so. If he hadn't stopped to pick her up she'd have been late clocking on, he thought, turning right onto Rupert Street.

He thought, then, of Miss Fitzlord – Zelah – she'd be there already. She was probably changing into her overalls, getting ready for her shift. He found he was smiling, thinking of her pinning her hair up into her work cap, glancing across and passing the time of day with her colleagues. He was glad they'd cleared the air. There was something about her – he hadn't found himself thinking about a woman in that way since ...

'Thank you for stopping for me,' the young woman said, interrupting his thoughts.

'Not at all – couldn't have you wandering about in this downpour,' he replied, hoping she wouldn't want to engage him in small talk, when what he really wanted to do was plan his next night off with Miss Fitzlord. It was so difficult, what with the production drive – a twenty per cent increase within the current quarter was what the man from the ministry had told the Board. George knew he couldn't really afford to take the time off. But – he thought of Miss Fitzlord's face, and the sound of her laughter down the telephone line earlier on – she would only be on the night shift for a few short weeks. And once she was back to her usual job, he'd never see her again. He couldn't afford to take time off work, but could he afford to miss his chance with the only woman in twenty years who'd made him feel like this?

Outside the car windows the blurred shapes of the Rupert Street terraces slid past. It sounded as if an army of insects were swarming over the car, the raindrops making an aggressive patter as they went. The young woman was shifting in her seat. 'Nearly there,' he said, more to himself than her, thinking of how he could engineer a way to get Zelah off the tools for a few moments tonight, chisel a wedge of privacy for them somewhere on site. If he could only be alone with her, away from sharp eyes and loose tongues.

They'd reached the entrance now. The security guard, fish-eyed in the drenching night, recognised the car and waved him through. As he pulled into the usual space he noticed that Simmons' car was still there. Odd, he didn't generally hang about at the end of his shift, having a wife, supper and two school-age boys to go home to. Why was he still here, then? George turned off the ignition and pulled on the handbrake. Before he turned off the headlights he noticed another car, a Bentley – wasn't that the Chairman's?

The girl was clearing her throat and fiddling with the door handle as he pulled off his driving gloves. 'Would you mind?' she said. She was having trouble with the catch – it did tend to stick a bit in the wet – and as he reached across her he noticed his left hand and paused to pull off his wedding ring and put it safely away in his pocket. Then he undid the door for her and she thanked him again before getting out and slamming the door behind her.

And it was only then that he remembered, watching the young woman in the beige coat walking up the steps to the factory doors. He'd been so preoccupied with Miss Fitzlord that he'd damn near forgot – Dame Laura Knight was arriving this evening, preparing to paint the night-shift girls, and the whole of the Board would have turned up to welcome her. He'd have to spend all night making polite conversation with this artist woman and there'd be precious little time for work, let alone finding time to get to know Miss Zelah Fitzlord.

Damnation.

Zelah

'Here they come now,' Violet Smith said, dashing across the shop floor. She'd only just arrived, soaked through and breathless. Zelah wondered where her room-mate had been and what she'd been doing this afternoon to make her cut it so fine to start her shift. Luckily they'd all been asked to hold off starting up the machinery, to give management a chance to show Dame Laura around in relative quiet.

Zelah watched as the doors at the far end swung open and a knot of figures snagged through. Chargehands held clipboards like weaponry; setters stood to attention like corporals. It was for all the world like a military parade, Zelah thought, wiping a stray trickle of lubricant which had splashed on the lathe.

'Was it like this when the King visited?' Violet muttered.

'Worse – we had to polish the drill bits,' Zelah replied as they waited, breathing in the oily air as the party approached. Mr Handford – George – would be with them. She could see men in suits surrounding a woman in a dark green skirt, making slow progress towards them. Where was he? There, at the back – she could see the flash of his white coat. Zelah suppressed a smile and distracted herself by wiping again with the rag, even though she'd already removed the mess.

Dame Laura was jewel-bright in the centre of dun-coloured suits, with her green skirt, blue blouse and a red scarf at her neck. She reminded Zelah of an escaped parakeet she'd seen once in the rooftops: exotic and out of place. The party was pausing at various pieces of equipment, Dame Laura nodding briskly, as if she were very interested in what type of lubricant was used, or how often a machine had to be re-calibrated. Her grey hair coiled on each side of her face like earphones. Zelah wondered how interested the artist really was. She was famous for painting ballerinas and circus troupes, George said. Could she really want to paint this sweaty box full of steel, swarf and dirty oil?

Footsteps and voices got louder as Dame Laura's party approached. 'Good evening,' Dame Laura said. Her voice was quite posh, loud, too – the voice of someone who was used to being listened to. Zelah felt the urge to curtsey, just as she'd done when the King toured the factory. Zelah said good evening, and Dame Laura asked what the machine was for, but before she could respond, Charlie Norris, her setter, had leapt forward and begun to give a demonstration. Dame Laura said it looked rather more dangerous than driving a car or manning a telephone exchange, and didn't the girls ever have concerns for their safety, with an intense expression on her beaky face. Before Charlie Norris could start again, George Handford leant over and cut in.

'Perhaps Miss Fitzlord should answer this – she is also the welfare supervisor, after all,' he said.

Zelah tried not to gabble, as she spoke about how the girls wore caps or turbans to keep their hair away from the equipment, and that workers had to put their jewellery away in lockers before shifts, for the same reason. 'And management,'

Violet Smith called out, butting in. 'You take your wedding ring off before your shift, don't you, Mr Handford?'

Zelah saw George glare at Violet, but he didn't respond to her question. One of the suited men cleared his throat and suggested they move on to the oxyacetylene cutters.

Zelah felt a sudden hollowness. A wedding ring? George wore a wedding ring outside work? So he was married, then. But how would Violet know that? Unless she'd seen him outside work? But why would she? Zelah remembered Violet putting on pink lipstick, trotting out of the room earlier on. She felt a plummeting sensation as George Handford walked off with Dame Laura and the rest of the group. She saw the back of him disappear off into Bay Seven with the others.

He didn't even turn to look at her.

It was more than disappointment, more acute, watching him go. She had been on the brink of hoping for a different future, but her ridiculous optimism was entirely misplaced, she realised. She was reminded of the feeling she'd had that time after Mother's death, when she'd had to visit the funeral parlour:

It is one of those warm, still, early-autumn days outside: pale blue skies and leaves just starting to gild. Inside is airless and close. The smell of drying varnish makes her want to wrinkle her nose. Lilies droop in an urn and dust motes play in a shaft of sunlight.

'There doesn't appear to be a problem, madam,' he says at last, glasses slipping down his long nose as he scans the sheet on the counter between them.

The Night Raid

She gulps in tepid air before replying. 'But this isn't the amount your father and I agreed on.'

He sucks his teeth and looks down at the document. She can smell his cologne, overpowering the scent of the dying lilies. 'I think he gave you the quote before we had our discussion. Perhaps that's the issue,' he says, looking up at her, watery eyes large behind the spectacles.

'Our discussion?'

'You had second thoughts about some of the details, if you recall?'

Recall? No, she doesn't recall. Mother's death was sudden, and the days afterwards a blur.

'I believe you chose the cherrywood coffin with the mauve satin lining?'

She nods.

'And a wreath of pink and white roses. The headstone was marble — those were all extras, you see, madam.' His waxy face has a look of practised concern.

'I didn't know.'

'It's a difficult time. There's a lot to take in when a beloved family member passes. Please don't be embarrassed, madam.'

'Embarrassed?'

'It's easy to lose sight of the details when your mind is elsewhere, as I'm well aware, what with my own father—'

'Yes, I heard. Please wish him a speedy recovery,' she says.

They both look down at the letter, with the invoice for an amount that almost equals what she and Mother had saved for her teaching college fees.

'I just wanted to give her a decent send-off,' Zelah says at last.

'You did her proud,' he replies.

143

It is so warm. She can't think properly in this heat. Muffled sounds filter through the tight-shut window: the clop of horses' hooves, the droning zoom of a motorbike. He pushes the letter towards her across the counter.

Zelah thinks of the phone call she's had to make to the teacher training college. Yes, in view of the circumstances they can hold her place open and she can begin a week or so late. But if they do not receive their fees by the month's end they shall assume she's had second thoughts about taking up her place.

The funeral director quoted her a much lower price than the amount printed on the letter. But the old man is in hospital with pneumonia, and not expected to recover. His son manages to look both apologetic and insistent.

Once she pays for the funeral she'll have no money left for her teaching course, Zelah realises. But the funeral has to be paid for, and where else is the money to come from? She'll have to carry on working as a housemistress until she's saved up enough again, and how long will that take?

All of a sudden Zelah's dreams of a teaching career disappear, like a soap bubble on a hawthorn bush.

There was a grinding rush, then, and a roar as the machinery was turned back on. Zelah's mind whipped back to the present. She wiped her hands over her overalls and reached down to the technical drawing on the clipboard. What was it tonight? More motor housings. Right, better get back to it. No point dwelling on Mr George Handford and what might have been. He'd duped her. He was a married man, and that was that. She was stupid to think she could have had a second chance at love.

Violet

Vi grabbed the clipboard and walked out quickly before Mr Tonks noticed. They'd been talking over dinner – something that called itself chicken stew, but she was buggered if she could find a single piece of chicken in it – and one of the girls from Bay Five said she'd heard that Dame Laura Knight would pay a fee to whomever she chose to paint. Arthur Laskey grinned at that and started striking 'artful' poses, and Eva Parker said if he thought he'd get his ugly mug up on a gallery wall he had another think coming. In any case, Dame Laura was here to paint the girls, that's what Mr Handford said.

They had been watching Dame Laura, seated at the table with some of the management, had seen her stub out her cigarette and head for the door. Off to the lavvy, no doubt, Arthur Laskey said – even dames had to take a leak at some point – and she'd be using the special WC upstairs, the one they'd had installed for the King's visit. Mr Tonks said they called it the 'throne room', and it was reserved for visiting dignitaries and directors only. Arthur made a comment about the King's arse and Eva Parker said he was being a traitor to his country, but Arthur just laughed, and said he was really going to enjoy the shit-on pie they had for pudding. Eva said she hadn't realised it was chiffon pie today, that was her favourite, and Arthur laughed even harder. Then they all got up to go over for their pudding, and Mr Tonks left his clipboard on the table.

So Vi took her chance. Dame Laura would be on her way to the mezzanine level, where the offices were. Most of the staff would be on dinner break, and if someone saw Violet up there? Well, she had a clipboard, didn't she? – you could go anywhere in this place if you had a clipboard.

Out of the double doors she went, and up the stairs, following Dame Laura. Even though everyone was on dinner break, and most of the machines shut off, the factory still made a kind of low mechanical purr, like a half-sleeping house cat – not like the ginger tom that used to stalk the bombsite up their street at home, yowling for lady cats and slaughtering sparrows.

Up the stairs, past all those posters telling them to work harder to beat Hitler and to 'be like Dad, keep Mum' and all. Up to the mezzanine level where the offices cut into the side of the factory wall, and the corridor was open like a balcony, overlooking the shop floor.

She went along the open corridor, the metal fretwork floor letting up all the burnt air from below, the railing smooth under her right hand. To her left, all the offices had glass windows, looking out onto the corridor, like shop fronts. A secretary in the pay office looked up from a filing cabinet. Vi strode on, hugging the clipboard against her chest, all the way along to the far end, by Mr Handford's office, where there was a shut door with 'WC' in black lettering, at eye height.

She stopped outside the toilet door. It was a risk. She was being stupid. If it went wrong she'd be hauled up in front of the boss for accosting a famous artist. She could lose her job. And then what?

She heard a flush from inside. Vi shuffled, began to turn, clogs clomping on the ironwork. If she went back now, they'd probably only just have sat down again. Mr Tonks might not even have noticed his clipboard was missing. She could leave it by the cutlery tray and pretend he'd left it there all along.

She heard the tap turning on. She didn't have to go through with this. She began to move away, then stopped. Because here was a chance, and it could be the only chance she'd get, to do something about the trouble she'd gone and got herself into.

The door opened. What to say? How to start?

Dame Laura emerged. 'I'm sorry if I kept you waiting,' she said. She smiled, and was almost past and gone by the time Vi managed to choke the words out.

'Paint me!' Vi said.

Dame Laura stopped, turned, still smiling. 'I'm terribly sorry, but that's not how it works, dear. You see, I need to do a series of sketches of different girls at work on the machines, and find faces and equipment that will really work together for this piece. It's a question of finding the match, don't you see? The right faces, the right composition, the right context,

147

all of that. Because the painting has to tell a story. It's really not just the case of painting the first pretty face I come across.' Dame Laura reached over and touched Vi's cheek then, with the tip of her nicotine-stained forefinger, her fingernail gently scratching the skin. 'And you are a pretty girl – I'm sure you get told that all the time, don't you?'

Violet wanted to say something, but the words wouldn't come.

'Well, in any case, it was lovely to meet you, dear. I shall be sketching for the rest of the night throughout the factory, so I'm sure I'll find my way over to you at some point. And I tell you what, I'll do an extra sketch for you to keep – give it to one of your boyfriends, if you want?'

Something gave in Violet, then, and the words broke free. 'I need the money,' she said.

There was a pause, with Dame Laura looking at her, tilting her birdlike head to one side and blinking her round eyes. 'My understanding was that you factory girls were rather well paid,' she said. 'Especially the night shift.'

'I send it all home,' Vi said. 'Apart from the twenty-two shillings for board and lodging and the bit I keep back for my essentials.'

Beyond Dame Laura, at the end of the open corridor, the door was opening. Dinner time was almost over. The management would be back any moment. Vi should be on her machine, not up here ambushing a famous visiting artist on her way out of the lavvy. Oh heck. 'I'm sorry. I shouldn't have asked. It was very rude of me,' Vi said.

'What do you need the money for?' Dame Laura said.

'Beg pardon?'

'What – or who – do you need the money for?'

Violet gripped at the clipboard, digging her palms into the edges. She cleared her throat, but said nothing, looking through the metal fretting at her feet and seeing the chopped-up top of a bald head moving below, hearing the clunk-chunter as equipment was re-set for the post-dinner shift.

'I'm not likely to be persuaded if you won't give me a reason, dear,' Dame Laura said. Vi looked up at the old woman's face, but she could hear footfalls, feel the ironwork shudder as someone approached. It was almost too late.

'I've gone and got myself in trouble and I need to get out of it, is all,' Vi said.

'I see,' said Dame Laura. And there was Mr Handford, suddenly at her shoulder, coming back to his office.

'Good evening,' he said, but he paused by Dame Laura, and his expression said what-the-hell-are-you-doing-up-here?

'Evening, Mr Handford. I found this and thought I'd bring it up to see if I could find who it belonged to,' said Violet, holding out the clipboard.

Dame Laura turned and grinned as if he were the prodigal son or something. 'George!' she said, putting a hand on his white jacket. 'Marvellous to see you. I was just chatting to one of your wonderful workers!'

Mr Handford smiled at Dame Laura but his eyes flicked down to the clipboard Vi held out. 'It says Mr Tonks, there on the top line,' he said. 'And I believe he's the chargehand for Bay Six, so you'll find him down there.' He indicated with his head in the direction of the shop floor, which was now beginning to hum with activity. 'Which Bay are you in?'

'Bay Three,' Vi said.

'You can take it down to him yourself, then,' Mr Handford said. 'Now, Dame Laura, you said over dinner you had some questions about lighting and so forth. Shall we discuss it now?'

Violet realised she'd been dismissed, and nodded goodbyes to them both and began to walk away. As she pushed through the door, the bell went for the second shift, and she had to run, along the corridor, through the far door, down the stairs two-at-a-time, clogs slipping on the lino.

'Careful, duckie!' Eva Parker was passing the bottom of the stairs as Vi barrelled down, jumping the last three. And Vi half-hoped she would slip on the stairs, because that could solve her problem once and for all. But she landed upright, panting, cap skew-whiff. 'You're lucky you didn't fall,' Arthur said, slapping Eva's behind as he caught up with them.

I have already fallen, Vi thought. I'm a fallen woman, for God's sake. But she didn't say that. She smiled and shrugged and said had Mr Tonks been looking for his clipboard, because Mr Handford had just told her to give it back to him.

They pushed through the doors and into the factory and she paused for a moment, lagging behind, clutching the clipboard, looking out over the shop floor, as people started to make their way back to their machines, and the level of noise rose like an audible tide.

It had been a stupid idea to ask the artist lady to paint her. Why would a famous painter want to paint a silly little slut like her?

Laura

The half-finished guns were a row of jabbing politicians' fingers below her as she looked out over the North Shop floor. The factory reminded her a little of Aunt Thir's lace factory in St Quentin: different smells, different equipment, but a similar feel – busy feminine heads bowed over twitching machinery.

She thought about that young woman, just now, demanding to be painted – the cheek of it! But it's precisely what I would have done myself at that age, Laura thought. Paint me, pay me (ever the money-grabbing show-off, my girl), but whatever you do, don't pity me. Better to be an upstart flibbertigibbet than a victim, any day. The girl needed money – best not to ask what for – and who could blame her for taking her chance where she could?

Laura's eyes scanned the shop floor for the girl, but she couldn't work out which one of the many bent heads was hers.

Cranes swung gun barrels across. White sparks flew like fireflies. Laura breathed in the thick-hot air and heard the dark-noise of it all. What a place to paint, trapped inside with the repetitive anger of the factory. She sighed and checked her watch. What would Harold be doing now? Sleeping, unless his neuralgia was bothering him, in which case he'd be wrestling with mangled sheets and banging his head against the pillow. A good wife would be with her husband, bringing beef tea and damp washcloths and respecting his opinions. And – and providing him with a family? Shush, now, Laura. Enough of that. Too late. Move on.

'Everything all right, Dame Laura?' She started. She'd forgotten George Handford was even there. 'Yes, yes, just getting a sense of place.' She looked down again and saw a young woman in a red flowery turban, slightly taller than the others, incongruously elegant in the way she leant in towards her equipment. 'Who's that?' She pointed. 'Over there, in the red.' There was something about that young woman, the way she held herself. It was rather intriguing.

'By the capstan lathe? That's – that's Miss Fitzlord.'

Laura turned to catch George Handford's voice above the factory din, and saw the expression on his face as he spoke. There was a sort of pride in his eyes, but he hesitated, as if he wanted to keep her name a secret.

'She's quite paintable,' Laura said.

'I introduced you to her earlier.'

'So you did.' The showcase visit had all passed in a bit of a blur, being paraded around like royalty. Tiresome, in point of fact. She didn't want to be seen as a celebrity – people put up walls, presented you with something they weren't. But she remembered meeting that woman, now – good posture and bone structure. She turned back to look down at Miss Fitzlord as she worked. Yes, very paintable.

'She's actually our welfare supervisor. She's not normally on the tools.'

'Yes, I think you mentioned. But she'll do. I'll paint her.'

'A good choice. I'm sure we can arrange something.'

Laura wasn't looking at him as he spoke this time, but even above the rising noise of machinery, she heard the inflection in his voice. The man has a soft spot for that young woman, Laura thought. I wonder how that will play out?

'Indeed. And the other one, too.'

'The other one?'

'That girl who was here just now, with the clipboard.' (Well, why not? The girl had had the gumption to ask and K was adamant that it should be a double portrait, just like those WRAF women the other year.) 'Do they work on the same equipment?'

'Well, no, but—'

'But you can arrange it. I want to have them both together. Is there some piece of equipment that requires two women working together? What about that big machine over there?'

'I think you mean the central lathe?'

'Yes, that takes two, doesn't it?'

'One to work it and one to lubricate it, I suppose, but—'

'Good, good. Have them work together on the central lathe, if you would.'

'Very well. I'll change the rota and see that there is something in place for you from tomorrow night, Dame Laura.'

Laura turned back to face him. And for a moment she

thought that he was quite paintable himself, if he'd only stop frowning. She turned on her 'Dame Laura' smile. 'Oh, I'm afraid tomorrow night won't do at all, George.' She tapped him lightly on the sleeve of his white coat. 'I need to start straight away, catch the muse, as it were.' She ignored his deepening frown. 'Let's get these girls together and make a painting, shall we? There's no time to lose!'

Chapter 12

Violet

'There's no doubt about it,' said Doctor Gibbs, looking at Violet over the top of her glasses. 'You're going to have a baby.' Vi looked back at the doctor. The eyelids behind the gold-rimmed spectacles were webbed with wrinkles. Her hair, scraped back off her liver-spotted face, was streaked with grey. She was thin as a twig.

'No, I'm not,' said Vi, lowering her voice and leaning in a little over the desk. 'I want to get rid of it.'

Because she had the wherewithal now, didn't she? Dame Laura was painting her. A few weeks, she reckoned it would take, and then there'd be the generous fee – enough to sort out this problem once and for all.

The clock tick-ticked. The doctor sat up straighter, pulling off her reading glasses. They hung on a gold chain, and bumped against her meagre bosom as she spoke. 'Now, don't be a silly girl,' she said.

'I'm not being silly. And I'm not a girl, I'm a woman. I'm a mobile woman, doing essential war work.'

'Of course you are, dear. But now you're going to be a mother, and I'm afraid that's that.' She fingered her stethoscope, which lay in front of her on the polished mahogany desk, as if checking that Vi hadn't pocketed it.

'I'm not married. I can't have a baby,' said Vi.

'Well, you'd better get him to make an honest woman of you.'

'I can't. That's not possible. So I've got to get sorted, see?'

The doctor drew in an audible breath and leant forward, glasses swinging on their chain above where her stethoscope lay. 'You can perfectly well have this child. We can arrange to have it adopted.'

Violet thought of her old room-mate, Mary, being whisked off to the Home for Unmarried Mothers. She could even be pushing out her baby as they spoke, handing it over to some uniformed woman, to be passed on, re-named, to someone else, leaving Mary with a saggy stomach and heavy breasts and the memory of the pain of it all.

'No, that's not what I want,' Violet said. She watched an expression of irritation pass over the doctor's face.

The doctor cleared her throat. 'We could, I suppose, get it fostered. Then when you find yourself another man, you could get it back. It's a bit trickier to arrange, but I have some contacts – I could look into it for you.' She pulled her mouth into an expression that was meant to be a smile, except that it wasn't, and sat upright in her chair again. She made a note in pencil on Vi's file, and placed it in the filing tray at the front of her desk, signalling that it was all settled.

'But I don't want to have it at all,' Vi said. What was the point of carrying a baby for nine whole months, going through all that agony of childbirth, and then giving it away? Even if she had it fostered – how long until she found someone to marry, and anyway, what man would be prepared to take on someone else's child?

The doctor made a tutting sound. 'Well, why don't you just tell your parents, let them help?'

Vi thought of Ma, still sick, Pa away in North Africa, all the others, struggling for money as it was. She thought of what had happened when her sister Bea had got herself in the family way, how Ma had claimed Baby Val and never let Bea near her own child. 'I can't do that,' Vi said.

'Nonsense. It will do them good. A new life is always a blessing.'

What do you know about it? Vi thought. You and your sort, telling us all we should be making jam and knitting scarves for prisoners of war and doing our bit. But you don't know what it's like to have a bedridden mother, a father away with the army and seven mouths to feed. You don't know about the freezing winter nights, the doctor's bills, the overdue rent, and every evening having to smile and laugh behind the bar in the King's Arms as if life's a ruddy fairground ride because *nobody likes a misery guts, Violet Smith, it puts them off their beer.* You and your sort, you don't have a clue, Vi thought. 'I want to get rid of it,' she said again, looking directly into the doctor's squinty old eyes.

'You do know it's against the law, dear.' The doctor talked to her like a schoolmistress talking to the dullest girl in class.

'But women do it all the time; you hear about it. And I thought, because you're a doctor, and because you're a woman, you might know somewhere – someone – who was safe, who'd do it properly. You wouldn't have to write anything down. The conversation wouldn't go outside this room,' Vi said. She didn't want to end up on the sepsis ward at the hospital, because that's what had happened to Ivy Sharp, one of her old classmates, when she'd got herself in trouble. She'd only been able to get enough money to go to some old woman down by the docks – they said she shoved a rusty coat hanger up – poor Ivy. At her funeral her family told everyone she died of 'peritonitis', but they'd all known the truth.

'Very well,' Doctor Gibbs said, sliding her stethoscope very slowly from one side of the table to the other and not looking at Vi at all. Vi listened carefully, ready to commit details to memory, because surely the doctor would help her? But instead of giving her a useful name or address, Doctor Gibbs said: 'It is, of course, entirely up to you if you choose to murder your own child.'

'Yes,' Vi said, pushing herself up out of the chair, her face burning with a sudden rush of blood. The doctor did not look at her or get up out of her own chair. 'Yes, it is. Up to me. Entirely.' Vi walked over to the door. She paused and turned back, but the doctor was still staring down at her desk, not moving or speaking. 'Thank you for your time, Doctor.'

Laura

'As still as you can, dear!' Laura called out over the *chunk-thud* of the machinery. The brunette – Violet Smith – was fidgeting again, and it didn't help with the detail of their hands if she constantly twitched like that. 'Thank you!' She had finished the underpainting now, and wanted to get on with the meat of the picture.

Laura had a particular purple-grey she'd mixed whilst they'd been on their final break (using the cadmium red instead of the crimson with the ultramarine, for more depth). She wanted to use it to fill in the shadows around inner wrists and palms, as the two sets of arms twined round, soft flesh looping over the hard metal. She'd got the women to roll their sleeves right up, to make the most of the juxtaposition of skin and steel. Yes, she was very happy with the composition, Laura thought, beginning to trace the slippery shadows with her brush on the canvas, very happy indeed. She had the girls positioned so that the viewer would see along the barrel of the half-made Bofors gun, foreshortened, but drawing the eye along from the dark circle (where one day soon anti-aircraft shells would pulse out into the night skies), along to the two pale heart-shaped faces of the women working together to create it. And the vertical line of the gantry behind them would bring the gaze up and around nicely to take in the background, which she'd already begun to rough in: mottled blues of overalls and the green from the funny protective caps that most of them seemed to wear.

Oh dear, now Violet was fidgeting again. But the other one – Zelah – managed to keep perfectly still. She was an excellent model, that one, Laura thought, wiping her brush on a rag, before popping it into the jar. As good as any of the professional models she'd worked with over the years. Pity she couldn't keep her on as a life model, but the War Office would never allow her to give up essential war work, even if Laura could afford to pay for a full-time model these days, with things being the way they were. She sighed. Still, maybe after the war? Bring her to London – if there was anything left of their house in St John's Wood after all this wretched bombing. She sighed again.

Laura decided to give up on the hands and arms for now. No point forcing it with all that twiddling going on from Violet. Now, she'd need a strong yellow-white, to contrast with the purple shadows, for cheekbones and foreheads, where the light hit and spread. Laura squeezed a good dollop of titanium white onto the palette and paused. Or maybe just pure white first, and add the yellow-gold tint afterwards? She tapped the end of the paintbrush against her lip. Yes, the nuances could wait, get the highlights in first, and maybe it would work with the harshness of the electric strip lights overhead, three of them: dash-dash-dash, punctuating the grimy mishmash of joists and steel cables overhead. Yes, maybe keep it simple . . .

'Watch out!' An urgent shout, but only just audible above the factory noise. Laura sensed something near her head, ducked, swerved, slipped. Her easel clattered to the floor. Hands under her arms, lifting her to her feet. The three-and-a-half-foot Bofors barrel swinging on the sling, just inches away, head height, like the branch of a storm-lashed oak.

Laura looked up to the gantry. High up, a portly woman was mouthing an apology. Laura nodded at her, as if it were fine, just fine, that she'd been almost brained by a half-finished anti-aircraft gun. She saw her paintbrush on the floor at her feet and leant down to pick it up. One of the setters had run over and was helping Zelah and Violet re-erect the easel, which had got all tangled up with a long coil of orange hosing that snaked the floor.

The gun was still swinging at eye-height. How many thousandths of an inch had it missed her by, Laura wondered, popping the brush in the pocket of her work apron. If she'd been anywhere else she could have made more of a joke of it, regaled them all with some of her other near-death experiences: the collapsing big top at the circus, dodging the charging elephant; the drunken gypsy with his blade, furious with her for painting his new wife; the perilous walk on the stagehand's gangplank at the Regent Theatre, where she'd almost fallen fifty feet onto the stage mid-performance; not to mention the sinking boat on their return from Holland, and, when she was just a girl, the white slaver who'd tried to entrap her at the Gare du Nord in Paris. You don't notch up three score years without cheating death a fair few times, she'd say. But it was impossible to hold a proper conversation down here, what with all the noise from the machinery and the likes of Gracie Fields being continually played through the loudspeaker system on top of all that (to keep them all cheerful and productive, Laura supposed).

Her heart was still beating fast from the shock of it, as she brushed the sharp coils of swarf from her oily palms, and walked over to where her work-in-progress lay, face down like a dropped slice of buttered toast on a hearthstone. She squatted down on the greasy concrete. The jar of turps had spilled: a pungent puddle spreading towards the painting. Violet and Zelah helped her pick up the canvas. Together they placed it on the easel. Laura stepped back to look. As she feared, the grimy floor had left smuts and dirty oil all over the picture. Was it utterly ruined? She picked the paintbrush out from her pocket and chewed the end of it, noticing Zelah and Violet in her periphery, waiting to see what she'd do. She put the paintbrush back and reached in her pocket for the palette knife. If Harold were here, what would he advise? Scrape it off and start again, he'd say. There's no shame in it. If you make a mess, start afresh. Laura could sense eyes on her.

She began to scrape away at the oil paint, dragging off the blackened grittiness from all the spots that she'd been about to highlight in titanium white, but leaving behind the purple-grey shadows, and the blue-green background, leaving all that with a mucky film of factory floor, which would dry in with the oil paint, over time. Yes, the grit and grime of the factory would become a bit of real life embedded in this piece of propaganda, she thought, wiping the trowel off, and working on. She could sense an anecdote beginning to form – the press would love it: how almost dying on the factory floor saved my painting from mediocrity, something like that. She imagined being interviewed by some keen young journalist when this picture was hung in the National Gallery (something inside her made her feel quite certain that this particular painting would end up there): *I felt that this double portrait was all about the literal and metaphorical grit involved in the dangerous lives of these hard-working ordnance factory girls.* Something like that, anyway. Oh yes. The swinging gun, the slippery floor, it was all serendipitous.

'As you were, ladies,' Laura called out, wiping her trowel off and swapping it with the brush. The women re-draped themselves over the equipment, as she directed. Violet's fingers were still twitching as if an invisible thread were attached to them. Laura decided to continue to work on their faces – the hands could wait.

Violet managed to keep her head still, at least: her curved cheeks and Cupid's-bow lips made her look like one of those china figurines of milkmaids, Laura thought. And even though she'd let herself be talked into painting her, out of pity, really, her face did provide a good foil for Zelah's. Laura loved the sharp angles of Zelah's face: that strong, almost mannish jaw – lots of Plymouth girls had jaws like that,

Laura remembered – and thick brows arching up like wings. Features like that are never considered attractive, Laura thought. People always seem to prefer moderate symmetry in girls' features. But in its calm, strong way, Zelah's face was strikingly attractive, Laura thought – beautiful, even.

Laura could no longer feel her heart pounding. She even began to smile to herself as she mixed up a brown-black with a little dab of indigo. She breathed in the familiar scent of oil paint, felt the fluid stickiness of it as she dipped in her brush. There was a particular curve at the base of Zelah's skull, where tendrils of hair escaped from her turban, that Laura wanted to capture just exactly as it was. There. Yes. Brush on canvas, a curlicue smudge in the perfect spot.

And Laura wondered why she had felt so drawn to paint this particular young woman, amongst all the hundreds of young women in the factory. Her height, perhaps, her elegant neck, the angular jaw and brows. What a joy to find a muse in such a place.

Serendipity indeed!

George

Beethoven's Fifth blared tinnily from the trumpet-shaped ceiling speakers, louder even than the screeching whine of the machines. George rested his hands on the railing and looked down at the North Shop. In the control room the red bulb would be flashing, even though it was just a drill.

The music seemed to increase in volume as workers reached for 'off' switches and tools droned to a halt. Turbanned and netted heads bobbed towards the corrugated entrances to the shelters at the end of each section. Dame Laura? Yes, there she was, in her green skirt, striding past the oxyacetylene cylinders, as if she were leading a hiking trip instead of scurrying for cover. The workers eddied into the open-doored shelters and the ceiling lights began to shut down, section by section, from the farthest end, like fingers running down a scale on piano keys: dark-darker-darkest.

Beethoven came to a scratchy stop. George imagined Mr Wragg, in the control room, pulling the needle off the record and jamming on his helmet, as if it were the real thing. Which it never was – never would be. Nottingham wasn't a target. Children were even evacuated to Nottingham from other parts of the country for heaven's sake; that's why they'd situated the ROF here, because it was relatively safe (as safe as anywhere could be, nowadays). And even if the bombers were to stray this way on a sortie, the factory roof was painted to look just like all the other terraced roofs of the Meadows; it was impossible to spot from the air. Still, the man from the ministry had told the Board that drills were necessary, and Mr Wragg liked to do things properly, regardless of the disruption to production.

George saw the small creamy oblong of Dame Laura's canvas in the darkness down below. The factory seemed eerily quiet, now. The shelter doors had all shut. He should probably pop up to the roof and do a spot check on the sand bucket and stirrup pump, so Mr Wragg could tick that off his checklist. It was as he lifted his hands off the railings when George saw the movement.

He bounded down the stairs and out onto the shop floor, his eyes still adjusting to the gloom. Someone – a girl, it looked like – walking through Bay Five.

'What the hell d'you think you're playing at?' The figure stopped. 'You know the regulations. Get inside!' It was a woman. He expected her to hurry on her way, but she turned, and answered back.

'Someone left a reamer switched on.'

He recognised the voice. 'Your safety's more important than a blasted reamer, Miss Fitzlord.'

She turned away without answering him. And he realised that she hadn't spoken to him since Dame Laura's arrival, that each time he'd seen her she'd turned away, just like she was doing now. He'd put it down to her being distracted by Dame Laura – and he'd been madly busy with the production drive himself, but, 'See here, have you been avoiding me?' She began to walk off, towards the shelter. 'Have I done something to offend you, Miss Fitzlord? Zelah?'

She paused, and he took three large strides to catch her up. 'I don't know if it's me or some other woman who should be offended, Mr Handford.'

'What are you talking about?'

He moved round so that he was facing her, blocking her path. He couldn't see the expression on her face, just her lips moving, dark in her pale face as she replied.

'Mr Handford, I am flattered by your attention, but I think we should keep our relationship on a purely professional basis. Now, if you'll let me pass?'

She made a move, but he stepped across her path. 'Listen, Zelah—' he began.

'Don't,' she said, side-stepping him. 'Your wife is a lucky woman, Mr Handford. Let's just leave it at that, shall we?'

'Wife? Who told you I had a wife?' he said, reaching out to her, but just then the sound of the 'Colonel Bogey March' thumped out from the speakers – the all-clear, already: Mr Wragg wasn't hanging about tonight. The shelter doors swung open and the lights flared back on. Workers streamed from the shelter doors. She slipped from his grasp, lost in the throng, and it was too late.

Chapter 13

Zelah

'Goodbye then,' Zelah said, as Mrs Scattergood shut the front door. Zelah looked up to the upstairs window where Mary's face was just a watery blur behind the glass. She'd been knitting a yellow matinee jacket when Zelah had gone in to visit. She hadn't said much when Zelah had asked after her health, told her she could have her old job back as soon as she was ready, apologised for not having been able to visit sooner. She'd nodded and carried on working the wool. Mrs Scattergood said it was important for the girls to have something to occupy themselves with during their confinement. All the babies from Cloud House went to their homes with a full set of home-made clothes, booties, and a crocheted blanket, she said, nodding importantly at Mary's ravelling wool. Zelah waited, waved again, but Mary couldn't have seen her; she didn't wave back.

Mrs Scattergood had said it would be any day now,

gesturing at Mary's swollen belly, as Mary's needles clicked against each other.

'But will she be all right?' Zelah asked. 'I can't come and visit her for another week because we're so busy with the production drive right now.'

And the reply came that the girl was young and strong and would be back to the factory in no time, and that all the expectant mothers were sent to church every day, to repent for their sin, and that there were no reports she'd heard of any repetition of this kind of immorality. Zelah thought she saw a flush in Mary's cheek as Mrs Scattergood talked, but she couldn't be sure, because the girl was hunched over her knitting and her hair fell forwards over her face. And Zelah had wanted to say that that wasn't what she'd meant when she'd asked would Mary be all right – she'd meant would Mary be all right going through the experience of having a baby and giving it away to strangers and having nobody to support her through it all.

Of course she wouldn't be all right, Zelah thought now, turning away from Cloud House's front door and out through the gate. How could anyone be all right after going through that?

The afternoon sun shone thick and gold, but the air wasn't hot; it churned with early spring winds: the cockerel weather vane twisted on top of the church spire across the way. A thin whistle came from the station and the sound of a train pulling out. She'd just missed the Nottingham train and it would be a good half-hour until the next one. It was too far to walk back to the hostel from here, so she'd have to find something to do. She decided to go to the churchyard, find a quiet place to sit, and enjoy the feel of the breeze on her sun-starved skin.

As she walked across the dusty street, Zelah was nearly knocked over by a bike, veering round the corner. The cyclist swerved and shouted. She glimpsed his red, angry face and felt her heart beat fast as he zoomed away. He'd been going too fast. But she should have checked, heard him, not walked straight into his path. It never was just one person's fault, was it? She sighed and walked on, passing the back garden of a red-brick villa where a woman was hanging nappies on a washing line: bending, stretching, reaching, pegging, working rhythmically along, as if it were a production line. Wisps of brown hair escaped from an orange headscarf and fine droplets of water flew out from the thrashing washing, like sea foam. Zelah walked on towards the church.

At the churchyard spring was massing its forces, a vanguard of primroses and dandelions marching on the grey tombstones. The gate creaked as Zelah pushed through and began to walk along the gravel path that wound around the end of the church. Her eyes caught the names of the dead as she passed: Thomas, Leonora, Albert – beloved sons and mothers, daughters and fathers – everyone belonging to someone else, and belonging here. Sunlight was a wicked glitter on the leaded church panes.

Zelah walked further on through the graves, to the far end where the old stones jutted at angles in the long grass and the battlemented chestnuts threw volleys of green against the yellow-blue skies. She leant against a tree trunk, liking the solid hardness of it supporting her spine. She thought about Mary and offered up a silent prayer: 'Please, God, let the birth be swift and simple, let the baby be healthy, let the adoptive parents be kind, give Mary the courage to go through it all alone. Please, God.'

Zelah had her eyes closed as she prayed and didn't take any notice of the sound of a car drawing up in Church Lane, or the footfalls on the gravel pathway.

'And please, God, give Mary the strength to cope with this and move on with her life, not have the shame stick and cling like machine grease under fingernails at the end of the shift. Amen.'

She kept her eyes closed, and let her mind drift.

When Zelah opened her eyes she saw a man with a trilby, laying flowers by a white marble grave near the church entrance. She would have to walk right past him to leave. She checked her watch. She didn't want to intrude on his grief, but she should really start walking now to get to the station in time. She pushed herself away from the comfort of the tree trunk and began to walk along the winding path, hearing a solitary magpie rattle-chatter in the treetops.

She didn't even look at the man in the hat until he called out. 'Zelah?' he said, looking up at her in surprise, scuffling to his feet. And she thought how different his face looked out here in daylight, away from the muggy factory air.

'George – I'm sorry to disturb you.' He'd put a bunch of crocuses in the urn. Her eyes took in the words on the grave-stone: *In loving memory of Alexandra Handford and her daughter Dorothy. Together in the loving arms of the Lord.*

He saw her look. 'I sometimes visit my wife and daughter on my day off,' he said, following her gaze.

'I'm sorry,' Zelah said. 'I'm so sorry. I didn't know.'

'Not at all,' he replied. 'We never really got to the stage of talking about family, did we?'

'I wish I'd known,' she said, stupidly, appalled at herself. 'I thought—'

'I know what you thought.'

Guilt and anger swirled in her gut. 'Why didn't you say?'

'You didn't really give me that chance.'

Violet was right. He had a wife. But Violet was wrong, too, because he wasn't an adulterer: he was a widower. He should have told her. She should have let him. Now it was too late. 'I'm sorry,' she said, turning away from the grave to look at him. 'I'm so sorry.'

He ran a hand over his face in that way he had, and let out a breath. 'I'm sorry too, Zelah,' he said, looking back at her. She turned away from his eyes – the look in his eyes when he said it. She took in the glorious spring day: the unrelenting sunshine, the thrashing new leaves, the spinning weather vane. But it was as if someone had smeared the scene with one of the greasy old rags from the shop floor: all ruined.

'I should go,' she said, the words thick as lard. 'Otherwise I'll miss the train. Good afternoon, Mr Handford.'

'Good afternoon, Miss Fitzlord.'

Walking was all of a sudden effortful, and the sound of her shoes on the path very loud, as if the air itself had coagulated with her regret. She could feel his eyes on her as she pulled the gate open and walked out into the lane. His car was parked on the verge. She turned, then, but he was out of sight, the stone bulk of church crouching between them. She reached out a stealthy fingertip as she passed, touching the car bonnet. It felt warm and smooth and safe, just for a moment. The washing was still flapping like a row of disturbed seagulls on the line in the back garden, but the woman had disappeared inside. Cloud House's twin gables regarded her archly as she crossed the village street. She heard the chunter of a distant train as she stepped up onto the pavement, and broke into a run.

She saw the guard's red flag fall like a careless spark in the distance, heard the shrill whistle, but she was still on the wrong side of the tracks: too late now.

George

'I couldn't possibly,' she said, not looking at him and carrying on walking.

'But it will be, what, another hour until the next train?' He had the window wound down, idling the car along beside her as she walked.

'I can wait.'

'You're working tonight, aren't you? Will you be able to make it back in time?'

'I'll be fine.'

The Austin bumped across the level crossing. Zelah was about to turn, onto the Nottingham-bound platform. 'I can drop you anywhere,' he called through the open window. 'You won't have to be seen in the car with me.'

There was a sudden splatter of drops against the windshield and the sunshine was blotted out. It was just a squall, but he saw her hesitate. 'It's unprofessional,' she said.

Droplets flecked his cheek as he leant further out. 'See, here, Zelah, I'd offer a lift to any of my workers that were stranded in a rainstorm. It's not a question of professionalism, just common courtesy.'

She took a step towards the car, then, looked down at him through the open window. He pulled on the handbrake and put the car into neutral.

'Was that why you picked up Violet Smith?' she said.

Violet Smith? The pouring rain, the hitchhiker in his wavering headlights, the awkward drive through the Meadows, dropping her off at the factory steps. 'The night Dame Laura arrived?'

She nodded.

'I didn't honestly make the connection. It was dark, and we didn't chat, much. I had no idea she was your co-worker.'

'My room-mate, too.'

He tried to remember. They hadn't really talked. 'It was

175

hammering it down, and she'd have been late clocking on if I hadn't stopped. I did nothing wrong.'

'I didn't say you did.'

He couldn't work out her expression. Her eyes squinted, blinking against the rain, and her mouth was set, hardening her features. She'd come out bare-headed and the rain was flattening her hair against the side of her face. Cold, damp and spiky – not at all like the woman at the hop. 'Please get in, Zelah, if only to stay dry whilst you wait for the train.'

She gave a small nod and walked round the bonnet to the passenger door, her dark red coat like spilled paint against the watery backdrop. He wound up his window as she got in the car beside him, slamming the door and smoothing her skirt down over her knees.

'Violet saw your wedding ring when you gave her a lift,' she said, looking out through the teary glass windscreen.

'And jumped to the conclusion that I was nothing more than an adulterous philanderer. What did she tell you?'

'Only that you picked her up in your car, that you were wearing a wedding ring, and then you took it off and put it in your pocket.'

'Well, of course I did. One can't wear jewellery in the factory. It's a safety risk, you know that as well as I do.'

'Why didn't you tell me you were married?'

'I don't care to discuss my private life with work colleagues.'

'Colleagues.' She repeated it dully.

The windscreen was a blurry mess. He turned on the windscreen wipers: *tick-swoosh*, clearing the rain-muddled view – the low, white village hall and the triangle of green grass with the lime tree jerking in the wind. Clarity, that's what was needed.

'I didn't mean that you're just a colleague. What I meant was that I would, of course, have told you all about myself, but we never got to that stage, did we? You stood me up, that night at the Ritz, remember? And in any case, why didn't you come to me when your chum Violet started gossiping? Why on earth did you choose to believe her tittle-tattle instead of asking me yourself?'

She sighed. 'You're angry. I should go. Thank you for your kind offer of a lift, Mr Handford, but I think it's better if I get the train.' She carried on talking as she reached for the catch. 'I was only here to visit Mary McLaughlin at the Home for Unmarried Mothers. Remember, the one I'm covering for?' She caught his eye and he nodded. 'Apparently, the baby's due any day, so she'll be back at work in a few weeks and I can go back to my day job, keep out of your hair. We can just forget all about this – this misunderstanding, and everything can go back to normal.'

Go back to normal? Normal was the night after night in the factory, going home to his empty house, the note from the housekeeper, next-door's cat miaowing on the doorstep. Normal was the occasional day off, sailing on the Trent, alone in the sun and the wind, and uneasy male chat in the clubhouse afterwards. Normal was visiting the grave of a girl he'd loved half a lifetime ago and whose face he could barely recall. Normal was the fading clench of grief and the guilt at the long-dead flowers in the urn. That was normal.

He lifted his left hand from the steering wheel and rested it lightly on her arm. 'Is that really what you want, Zelah? To go back to normal?'

'Isn't that what you want?'

'I'm not sure I can.' He didn't look at her, but he could feel her arm through the damp wool of her coat, smell the musky scent of her, so close. The windscreen brimmed. Out with it. Spit it out, man. 'It's twenty years since I lost Lexi and the baby. You're the first woman I've felt anything for in twenty years, Zelah. I'm not angry. I'm scared.' There, it was done.

His hand was still on her sleeve. Her fingers were on the door catch. He heard her suck in a breath. And he expected her to shove him off, fling the car door open and run off into the rain. It didn't matter. At least he was free of the stoppered up feelings and the swallowed words. For a frozen moment they were still. There was just the sound of the rain and the wipers and the feel of her next to him. He let his eyes stray across and saw that she'd let go of the door catch.

'I'm sorry,' she said. 'I reacted so badly when Violet said about your wedding ring.'

'Ruddy woman. I wish you'd just come and asked me, then.'

'I wish I had, too.' The rain stopped as suddenly as it had begun, the air acid-yellow in the eager sunshine. The wipers pulled and scratched across the dry glass. He flicked the switch and they stilled. He felt her hand, over his. 'I'm scared, too. That night of the raid drill, there wasn't really a reamer left on.' He turned the key off in the ignition.

'You know I arrived in Nottingham during the Blitz. I didn't just leave Plymouth because of the free train tickets. On that first night raid in Plymouth, I'd just met someone. It sounds silly, it's nothing compared to your loss – but I honestly thought he was, I don't know, special.' He turned to look at her, then, as she swallowed and carried on. 'We had been out and the raid started so we had to just run to the nearest public shelter, but as we got there I stopped, because I noticed a stray dog on the shelter steps and I wanted to bring it inside. And then ...' She was pulling her lips together, shaking her head, as if her face didn't want to let the words out. But out they came, in a rush: 'A direct hit, they said. But because I was just outside, I was blown free. And afterwards, there was nothing. There was just nothing left. They said I was lucky. They said it was a miracle.' She bit her lip. 'But that's why I couldn't bring myself to go down into the factory shelter the other night – couldn't bear to be crushed inside with all those people, like sitting ducks.'

'And you came to Nottingham, to get away from the memory of that night?'

She nodded. 'There was nothing left for me there. And this factory was exactly the right place for me, because ...' Her voice petered out.

He recalled how, after Lexi's death, he'd thrown himself

into work, seeking refuge in the night shift. 'Because inside the factory you're just a part of the production line, as anonymous as any other piece of equipment, and the noise and exhaustion cancel out any possibility of . . .'

'Love?' It was her turn to interrupt.

'Human contact, I was going to say.'

'Isn't that the same thing?' She shrugged, dislodging his hand. He brought it up to his face and ran his thumb and forefinger along his jawline. He cleared his throat.

Had she really just intimated what he thought? He pushed his foot down on the clutch and reached out to twist the key in the ignition. The car growled to life. He put the car into gear, and began to lift his foot from the clutch. Did she feel the same way as he did? He lowered his right foot onto the accelerator.

There was only one way to find out.

Zelah

The sun was beginning to drift down behind them, beyond the River Trent, glazing the fields and houses with a barley-sugar shimmer. He cleared his throat as if he were about to speak, but instead just clicked the indicator on, turning right. 'But this isn't the way to the hostel,' Zelah said.

'It's a bit of a detour, admittedly.'

She looked at his hands on the steering wheel as the car turned: strong, dextrous fingers. 'Kidnap?'

'Something like that. Don't worry, I'll get you to work on time.'

'I wasn't worried, just curious.'

The air was sticky-warm in the car now the sun was out again. The seats smelled of saddle soap. She imagined him cleaning the car on his day off: sudsy water and rolled up sleeves, stretching out to work the smooth soap deep into the leather. What else did he do on his days off? Zelah wondered. She wound down the window a little, and smoothed her skirt over her knees.

He slowed to let a Barton bus pull out in front of them. They were driving through the village of Chilwell now: scattered cottages with blossom in the orchards between, a boxy village hall, a woman with a blue hat pushing a pram, the sound of a dog howling in a back garden – snatches of other people's lives filtering in through the passenger window. Ordinary lives: mothers and fathers and children and roast dinners and washing the car on a Saturday afternoon ready for the Sunday outing. It was the kind of life she would have wanted, if things had worked out differently. Was it too late to hope for a life like that? She stole a glance at George Handford, but his eyes were on the road ahead. Cool air slid in through the open window, grazing her cheek.

Next to some playing fields she noticed a trio of schoolgirls getting into a waiting car, and she let her mind take her back, ten years or more, to her own schooldays:

*

'*Whatever you do, don't let them score!*' *The team captain's words echo in Zelah's ears as she shifts her weight from foot to foot, seeing the players jostle and shove, the hockey ball scudding across the damp grass between them. She watches and waits, the stick firm and safe in her hands. Safe-hands-Fitzlord: the only reason she made the first team – her quick reactions; her skill in stopping the ball before it reaches the net.*

Her gymslip tickles the goosebumped flesh of her thighs. The air smells of bonfires, and clouds scrawl across the smoke-grey skies. The angry game wears on: shouts and the dull clash of wood against wood. Men and women in hats and furs watch from the sidelines, waving cigarettes and calling out, 'Well played!' It is the final match of the season and they are a goal ahead and she can still hear team captain Janey Houseman's voice: 'Whatever you do, don't let them score!'

Zelah looks across at the clock on the pavilion. It is nearly half past. It will be over at any moment. The girls in their black gymslips look like a flock of quarrelling crows: flapping and cawing and jabbing at each other out there in the middle of the pitch. Her gaze moves back to the onlookers. A man in a long coat is lighting his pipe. Someone's father, she thinks. What would it be like if she had a father to watch her play in the first team, in the final match of the season? If he'd been alive, instead of sunken deep in the mud of some Flanders Field; would he be here? Would he be the kind of father to smoke a pipe and read the newspaper and bring home a puppy for her birthday?

'*Fitzlord!*' *A ball is hurtling towards her. She reacts without thought. There is a juddering impact, up the hockey stick, into her bones. She looks down and the ball lies still on the muddy ground at her feet. There are cheers and clapping and then the shrill shriek of the final whistle. 'Good show, Fitzlord!' Janey Houseman wraps her in a sweaty embrace, then pulls away. 'What's the matter, Fitzlord? You don't seem very happy about it.'*

'We won; of course I'm happy,' Zelah says. But she finds it hard to draw the corners of her mouth into a smile, as she sees the other girls run across the pitch to the open arms of their waiting parents.

Zelah clasped her hands in her lap. The bus in front of them pulled into a stop at the end of a row of terraced houses where a stout woman with a shopping basket was waiting. George indicated to pull out past it, moving down a gear so that the engine revved. Zelah shifted in her seat. They were driving faster now they'd left the bus behind. People, bicycles, houses and shop fronts streaked past in a muddle of colour. They turned left up a hill, and then right, through an avenue of tall trees.

'Wollaton Hall, over there.' He nodded to their left, but all she could see from the window was a flash of green.

'Are you taking me on a sightseeing trip?' she said.

'I suppose I am, in a manner of speaking.'

Trees gave way to houses, as the road went over a canal, and railway lines. She glanced again at his profile, and he turned to catch her eye at the same time. 'Hope you've got enough petrol coupons,' she said.

'It's not far – we're almost there, now.'

They drove on between lines of tall red-brick houses, peering down, disapproving of the speed they sped along at. There wasn't much traffic: the odd red bus, delivery boys on bikes, a green army lorry chugging in the opposite direction. Zelah looked at George's hands as he twisted the steering wheel. He indicated right at a junction, then seemed to change his mind. 'Maybe we should take the scenic route.' She saw him smile to himself and they carried straight on when the lights turned green.

She didn't really know Nottingham at all, Zelah realised. Since she'd been here she'd used her odd days off to catch up on washing, ironing, mending and haircuts. She'd been into the town centre a few times, too, to borrow books from Boots or go to the flicks. Once another girl lent her a bicycle and she cycled along the towpath, past the canal boats, all the way to Trent Lock, where dinghies dipped and swerved across the silvery water like swallows' wings. But if George Handford were to drop her off now, she'd be completely lost, she thought, as now the car wound uphill through a collage of densely packed backstreets.

'Here we are.' He brought the car to a halt in front of a terrace of cream houses. She got out and shut the car door behind her. The sharp air ribboned round her neck and pulled hair across her face. She pushed it away and looked round. They were high up. She could see Nottingham Castle nearby, just a couple of streets away, occupied by the army now – a lacy curl of barbed wire circling the squat stonework. She couldn't see the ROF from here. It was hidden away in the valley below the castle, but she knew that down in the Meadows the gun factory would be chuntering and humming, the workers checking the clock, willing the shift to end. In the distance the sun was westering, distant furrowed fields were untangling gold chains. She heard the clunk as George shut the car door, the twist of the key in the lock. She turned to look at him. He'd put his trilby back on, but left his trench coat unbuttoned; it tugged like a sail in the breeze. His face was in shadow, but she caught a flash of white as he smiled at her.

'This way.' He pointed behind her. She spun round and saw how the terraced houses fell away to reveal a deep chasm in the limestone rock. A set of steps led downwards from the pavement where they'd parked. Where the railings had once been were snaggle-toothed stumps – perhaps they'd been melted down into one of the ingots they used to make the guns, she thought, although they could equally well have ended up as the hull of a battleship or the turret of a tank – and beyond where they would have been was a sheer drop down the seventy-odd feet to the tunnel below.

'Mind your step – they can be slippery.' He held out his left hand, and she took it. His palm was warm and dry. 'I'll go on the outside, I'm used to them.' They began to step down, away from the waning day into the dark tunnel. 'Are you nervous?'

She shook her head. 'I trust you.' It was true, she realised, as the air got darker and she could taste the stale dampness of the underground on her tongue. She trusted him. She looked up: ferns clinging to dripping rock, the edges of towering houses, a circle of yellow-grey sky. A pigeon flew across, tracing the diameter.

Once they'd made it down the steps, there was no longer a need to hold hands. But she didn't let go, and neither did he, and their palms stayed together, close as a secret.

'Come on.' A pull at her hand as he led her into the tunnel, which sloped away to their left. The walls were mustard-brown and dank smelling, but as they walked, a patch of light green grew larger and brighter. They were still holding hands, her right in his left, the dig of his wedding band as he tugged her towards the light.

'Nearly home,' he said, as they stepped out of the tunnel mouth. Spread out like an extravagant picnic was a scattering of elegant houses, tennis courts, circular parks and ponds. 'The Park Estate. You can drive in from the other side, but this is the best way to see it for the first time.'

Elm trees swayed. The air was cool on her lips. 'You live here?' she said.

'The white building, over there.' He pointed with his right hand. 'I think it was once a coachman's cottage, back when the big houses were properly staffed – they're mostly junior officers' billets these days. D'you see it?'

She squinted, but the lowering sun cast long shadows, and there was more than one white cottage on the opposite hill-side. 'I'm not sure I can make it out.' They were still holding hands. He moved in close, his whole body almost touching hers as he reached across, pointing. She looked along the length of his arm. The cloth of his coat rubbed against her. She could smell his hair oil, the scent of his skin. His face was so close she could feel the warmth of him.

The Night Raid

'Over there, on the left-hand side, halfway up. Can you see it now?' She looked where his fingertip lay: a low white house with a slate roof.

She nodded, and, as she did so, felt her cheek graze the roughness of his. 'Yes, I see it.'

Her hand was in his, his body half-shielding hers, his face so close. 'I just wanted to bring you here to prove that I'm not hiding a mad woman in the attic, that's all.' He dropped his right arm, turned towards her. His breath was warm, his lips – she couldn't help but kiss him. It was like floating and sinking at the same time. She felt his free hand circle her waist, pulling her towards him.

A loud cough, nearby. They pulled apart, turned to see a fur-coated woman with a terrier on a lead glaring at them as she crossed from the elm trees to the tennis courts.

'I'm sorry,' he said, straightening his hat and turning back to face Zelah.

'Don't be. I started it,' she replied. His eyes were grey: dark, dark grey, with flecks of amber. And there was that tiny moon-shaped scar on his cheek. When he smiled the frown line between his brows smoothed away. She checked her watch. 'But we really should be getting back. I wouldn't want to be late clocking on. I'll be in trouble with the boss.'

He swerved through the factory gates and into the space marked 'Management'.

'People will talk,' she said, noticing the turning heads.

'Let them.' He turned off the ignition and began to twist

the ring off his left hand. Zelah remembered what Violet had said, about him taking off his wedding band in the car. It had all been such a silly misunderstanding. She moved forward for the door catch. 'Wait,' he said. She turned. He held the gold ring between the thumb and forefinger of his right hand. 'Here, take it.'

'I couldn't.'

'What we talked about in the car, earlier—' He paused and cleared his throat, still holding out the ring. 'I feel like we understand each other and don't want you to doubt me, to doubt my – my sincerity. That's why I want you to have this. Please.' He placed the ring in her hand.

'Thank you.' The metal circle was hard and warm in her palm as he closed her fingers over it. 'Thank you, George.'

Chapter 14

Laura

Laura heard the sound of a piano, the trilling of the keys sounded like musical laughter. She pushed open the doors to the ladies' loos and the *plinkety-plonk* got louder and louder as she strode up the corridor towards the canteen. The warm-up had already started, and the canteen door was ajar. She slipped inside, standing at the back, hearing the jaunty tune, glimpsing the girls on the dais in their sparkly frocks and heels, wowing the lunchtime crowd with high kicks and twirls. Half the night shift had shown up, too, even though they weren't due in for a good six hours, desperate to get in on the action. There'd been talk of nothing else at break times and on the bus for the last week. You'd have thought Churchill himself was coming to visit.

As she slipped her sketchbook out of her bag she noticed George Handford, almost hidden by a pillar. She saw him whisper something into Zelah Fitzlord's ear, and saw Zelah spring back, laughing. How sweet, the pair of them – Laura hadn't realised they were a couple. The workplace flirtation added to the party atmosphere. Dinner plates discarded, everyone milling around, feeling their best selves. Really, who couldn't love a show, any show: a circus, a ballet, or an ENSA party in the lunch break. Laura smiled and pulled out a well-sharpened 6B pencil.

It was a perfect opportunity for quick life drawing: a woman with her hands on her hips, head thrown back in laughter, the man leaning in towards her, hair flopping forward. Laura smelled the smoke-gravy air and felt the warmth of hundreds of bodies piled into the dining hall. As her hand and eyes worked, Laura cast her mind back to those early days at the art college, when she'd first met Harold and fallen for his talent and his self-contained wit. It had seemed like an eternity before he'd even noticed she existed. But once she'd grabbed his attention, she had to constantly nurture it, by being more fun to be with, more humorous, more talented than anyone else he could ever hope to meet. What was that French saying? *Entre deux amants il y a toujours l'un qui baise et l'autre qui tend la joue* – between two lovers there is always one who kisses and one who offers the cheek, or some such. She looked down at the sheet and shaded the negative space between the lovers – if that's what they were – wondering who was the kisser and who was the offerer of the cheek in this particular romance? Harold had been the one offering the proverbial cheek, in their day. He had always been older, wealthier, wittier, more talented – she had never quite felt she deserved his attention.

She looked up, but George and Zelah had disappeared, and the moment was lost.

She felt a tap on her shoulder. 'Dame Laura.'

'Zelah! There you are, dear. I was just looking for you.'

'I didn't know you were coming in.'

'Wouldn't miss it for the world. Never miss a show, that's my motto!'

'You'll be exhausted later.'

'Oh, I'll have a little cat-nap and I'll be fine, dear. What about you?'

'I'll probably grab a few hours this afternoon, too. I'm expected to be here, though – management like us all on board at this kind of thing.'

'Just doing your duty, then?'

Laura looked sideways at Zelah as she nodded. 'Nice to be able to mix work and pleasure,' Laura said, noticing a rose tint wash over the pale skin of Zelah's throat as she ripped off the sketch from her notebook and presented it to the girl.

'I didn't think anyone had seen,' Zelah said.

'Your secret is safe with me – if it is a secret?'

Zelah was out of her work clothes and Laura noticed the gold ring on a red ribbon at her neck. As if sensing her gaze, Zelah touched the ring before replying. 'We haven't made it official yet. I mean, it's not been long, but ...'

'... but when you know, you know,' Laura said. She couldn't stop looking at the ring on the ribbon. Years ago, before the last war, when they'd been in Cornwall, Harold had taken to wearing a red scarf at his neck, instead of a tie or cravat, and he'd borrowed her wedding ring to thread it through to keep the ensemble in place. He was still young then – it was a gypsy fashion he'd given up when the war came. But she still remembered his long neck, the red silk scarf, the gold ring, and how he'd touched the ring with his tapered fingers sometimes, as a distraction, when he was feeling anxious about a situation. The pale skin on the throat, the red and gold, the long fingers: something so reminiscent about it.

Zelah was thanking her for the sketch, putting it inside her handbag. And Laura said, 'Not at all, my pleasure, dear, George Handford is a very lucky man,' but all the while she was thinking about the neck, the fingers, the red and gold.

The air was thick with smoke and applause as the dancing girls finished their turn, grinning and bowing and blowing kisses into the audience. Laura put away her sketchbook and pencil and pulled out her cigarettes, as the compere took to the microphone, thanking the Slattery Sisters and announcing a comfort break. It was easier to talk without the blaring music.

'How old are you, if you don't mind my asking?' Laura said, offering a cigarette to Zelah, who smiled and took one.

'Twenty-five. I know, a bit old for "love's young dream", but it feels like a second chance, for both of us.'

Laura clicked her lighter and lit their cigarettes. 'So you were born in 1917,' she said.

'That's right.' Zelah inhaled. 'I was born the year George joined up. It's a bit of an age gap, I suppose, but, honestly, it doesn't feel like it.'

'And you're from Devon, by the sounds of it,' Laura said – it was so much easier to talk without that dreadful band music blaring out, or the horrible noise they had to endure on the North Shop floor during the shift.

'I grew up in Plymouth, but I think I'm from Cornwall originally. Zelah is a little village in Cornwall, apparently.'

'Ah, Cornwall. Beautiful, wonderful Cornwall.' Laura inhaled deeply, savouring the warm smoke.

'I don't really know it. I never left Plymouth until I came here two years ago.'

'You didn't ever visit family in Cornwall?'

'I don't have family. There was only Mother. She passed away a few years ago. Nobody came to the funeral from her family, even though I put a notice in the *Western Morning News*.'

'But how dreadful for you.'

'Not really. She was well-liked, locally, so there was a good turn-out. And everyone from school came – she was a housemistress at a girls' school. I inherited her job, after she passed.' Zelah exhaled, and tapped ash into one of the metal ashtrays on the table beside them.

'Still, it must have been very hard for you,' Laura said. 'I lost my own mother young. It felt as if I became a woman, overnight, when she passed. I had to take on all her art students.' An image flicked through Laura's mind of the

193

varnished oak coffin with the brass handles, being lowered into the family grave at Nottingham General Cemetery.

She refocused her eyes on Zelah's face. Their eyes met in understanding. A fatherless girl losing her mother, becoming the breadwinner so young. Not many people knew what that was like.

She noticed Zelah fiddling with the gold ring on the red ribbon.

So Zelah was born in Cornwall in 1917?

The long neck, the tapered fingers, the red, the gold: an abandoned wartime baby; a fatherless child born in Cornwall during the last war. No, no, no, Laura. You are being over-dramatic and letting your imagination run away with you. There couldn't possibly be any connection, could there?

In the background the conductor lifted his baton like a wand, ready to conjure up more magic. He tapped the microphone and then leant towards it: 'Ladies and gentlemen, it is now my pleasure to introduce Elsie and Doris Waters, better known to you as Gert and Daisy!' The piano struck up the tune of 'Daisy, Daisy', the crowd cheered, and Laura caught sight of two portly women in sealskin coats waddling onstage.

''Ello, ladies!' The padded arms waved.

''Ere, Gert, is your face dirty, or is it my imagination?'

'My face is clean enough, Daisy, but I don't know about your imagination!'

Laughter erupted all around her, but Laura didn't join in, couldn't stop the gnawing feeling in her gut. She inhaled again, letting herself drift away from Zelah and towards the back wall as the act wore on: jokes about landlords and air-raid wardens and knitting in the shelter. Everyone was smiling and laughing as if today was the best day of the year so far. As if they were all just absolutely in the pink.

Laura sucked in the smoke, mind working. Gert and Daisy were at it again up on the stage, with their unending cheer.

'What shall we sing, Gert?'

'Let's sing 'em a song about when the war's over, Daisy!'

'Come on, girls and boys,

Whoops, let's make a noise,

Come on in and all join in the chorus ...'

And then there was that bit in the middle with the music and dancing, and everyone linked arms and jigged about, just like they'd done in Gert and Daisy's film, whatever it was called, and Laura took her chance to slip quietly away without Zelah or anyone else noticing.

Because there was something on her mind, and no amount of mindless carousing could dislodge it.

Chapter 15

Zelah

'Here's where I married Harold!' Laura said, as they rounded the line of cottages and followed the gravel path through the gate. Laura had brought them to Wilford Village, not far from the hostel. The shift finished early for the annual audit, and Laura had persuaded them to come with her on a sketching trip.

In front of them was a low, grey Norman church, boxy and castellated. Shards of gravestones were strewn between the daisies and long grass. They paused to take it in; it looked like it had been there forever, no-nonsense and matter-of-fact, bearing witness to thousands of ceremonies: churchings, christenings, confirmations, weddings, funerals – the endless spiritual production line of it all.

Laura was regaling them with stories as they walked up towards the entrance, something about chicken feathers in the bridal carriage and a whole five pounds to spend on a honeymoon in London. Zelah only half-listened, instead imagining herself and George, standing on the step right there, holding hands giddily beneath a shower of confetti. Laura went on ahead into the church, and Zelah waited in the entrance for Vi.

Laura was calling them: 'Come on now, girls. Violet! Zelah!'

Something in the way the older lady called her name reminded Zelah of another lady – a moment from childhood suddenly surfacing:

'Zelah! What a pretty name!' The woman's eyes are the colour of toffee and her skin like melted candle wax. Zelah looks past the older woman's face and up at her mother, who stands just behind. Mother raises her eyebrows and nods at Zelah.

'Thank you, Miss Orton,' Zelah says (always say please and thank you, always acknowledge a compliment). 'How very kind.'

'What beautiful manners,' the woman says, straightening up. Mother looks pleased. 'A charming daughter you have, Mrs Fitzlord. I'm sure she'll settle in nicely with the other girls, despite—' She turns to face Mother and her voice lowers a tone, but Zelah can still hear. 'We don't tolerate any snobbery or anything of that sort at The Grange,' she says, rubbing her palms together as if ridding them of dust.

Mother smiles and nods, her curls bouncing as her head bobs. Zelah turns her attention back to the pillow she's been trying to push into the candy-striped pillowcase, but it is fat and won't fit. Outside the small window is a grassy bank splattered with yellow and white flowers, and a plum tree drips purple fruit. Mother says she'll be allowed to go out and pick plums and make daisy chains later, but first they have to unpack and settle in. Their big trunk is an open-mouthed hippo filling the middle of the room.

Miss Orton is still talking to Mother. Zelah pushes at the squishy slab of pillow, and listens. 'As I mentioned at the interview, a housemistress is far more than a housekeeper. You'll find yourself becoming a bit of a mother to the girls during term-time, especially the younger ones. Homesickness . . .' Zelah stops listening to the grown-up talk. She holds the corners of the pillowcase and shakes, but still the fat heft of pillow sticks out. She throws it on the bed. Mother is still nodding and smiling at this Miss Orton woman, and twisting the gold ring on her left hand. Zelah glimpses the green line that circles the skin underneath, the one that Mother tries so hard to scrub off, but which always returns. Zelah decides to listen again. '. . . but I'm sure those kinds of pastoral issues won't be a problem, as you've clearly done wonderfully well with your own daughter, in spite of . . .' The woman clears her throat. 'I don't want to pry, but the girl's father?' She puts her head on one side as she asks the question. 'The war?'

Zelah sees her mother clutch her left hand with her right, covering the ring and the green mark. 'Yes,' Mother says. 'Sadly, Zelah's father was lost to the Great War.'

'My father?' Zelah says, more loudly than she meant to. And both women spin round to look at her.

She heard footfalls, blinked back to the present, and Vi was next to her in the doorway.

'You okay?' said Zelah, as Vi caught up.

'Course,' Vi said, biting her lip and not making eye contact. 'Why wouldn't I be?'

Eat, sleep, work, pose for Laura: that was the routine of their lives these days, slung together like twins in a crib, at the factory and in the hostel. The production drive meant they hadn't had a day off for ages. She'd expected it to be harder, sharing everything with Violet Smith, but Vi turned out to be generous and discreet, and hadn't breathed a word to anyone about Mr Handford, even though it would have been easy to gossip about Zelah's stolen moments away from the shop floor, or the lifts back to the hostel in the boss's car.

But something was bothering Violet, wasn't it? Every day she seemed to be smoking more, eating less and clenching and unclenching her fists, as if trying to grasp at something that kept slipping through her palms.

Zelah held the door open. The cool air enveloped them as they went inside. Laura strode on ahead, gesticulating with her notebook as she continued to recount her wedding day. She stopped when she reached the top of the aisle, by the altar, and stretched her arms up high. '*Oh God, our help in ages past ...*' she began to sing the hymn, her voice surprisingly low and powerful for an old woman. Zelah turned to exchange a glance with her fellow sitter, but Violet was looking in the other direction and pulling a half-empty packet of cigarettes from her skirt pocket. Zelah turned back to look at Laura who had begun to slowly twirl in the boiled-sweet-jar sunlight that came in through the stained-glass windows. '*... From everlasting Thou art God ...*' Laura sang on. Zelah could see a robed figure emerging from a side door beyond the pulpit, but Laura hadn't yet noticed him.

There was the sound of a match being struck. 'The vicar's just come in,' Zelah said, turning back to Vi, who frowned, shook the match out and put her cigarette back in the packet. The singing came to an abrupt halt, and there was a jocular exchange of voices from the far end of the church. Evidently Laura was introducing herself to the vicar.

'Are you sure you're all right?' Zelah asked. Vi wouldn't look at her. 'What is it?' But Vi didn't answer. 'Let's go over here,' Zelah said, leading Vi towards the font, which was at the opposite end of the church from where Laura and the vicar were chatting. Laura was probably telling him about the chicken feathers and the five-pound honeymoon, Zelah thought.

Zelah and Vi stood by the font. There was no stained glass in the window here, it was just plain leaded diamonds, like the taped-up plate glass in the shop windows. Sunshine puddled the flagstones. Vi dipped the tips of her red-painted fingernails in the holy water. 'You know, you can talk to me,' Zelah said now. 'Welfare is my job, after all. I might be able to help.'

'I don't think you can.' Still not making eye contact, fingers dabbling the water.

'How bad is it?'

Laura's loud laughter carried down the aisle towards them.

'Really bad.'

'But you can't tell me?'

Vi shrugged, and a small splatter of water from her pattering fingers fell on Zelah's hand.

'You don't want to tell me?'

'If I did, it wouldn't do any good.'

'How do you know that? I want to help. Please.'

Zelah glanced round. Laura had her sketchbook open to show the vicar. They were safe to talk for a while longer. 'And even if I can't do anything, sometimes just talking about a problem makes it seem, well, less troublesome.'

'You think I'm in trouble?'

'Well, are you?'

Vi nodded.

'Well, don't worry, we can talk to Dr Gibbs and—'

'I'm not having anything more to do with that old sow.'

'You've seen her already?'

'Yes, I've seen her. She told me I was in the family way, and I could have told her that myself. I'm not stupid. And I've done all I can, but I can't shift it. So, do you want to help me, Zelah?' Vi looked up now, directly into Zelah's face, her eyes wet and empty. 'Do you still want to help me, Little Miss Welfare Supervisor? Want to help me rid myself of this bastard child before I end up going the same way as Mary-sodding-McLaughlin?'

Laura

Violet was lagging behind. Laura resisted the urge to call back and tell her to stop dawdling now, there's a good girl, just like Mother used to say when she came here with Nellie and

Sis – quick sticks, and I might find enough money for ginger beer, girls. But these weren't girls, they were young women, and she wasn't their mother – she wasn't anyone's mother, was she? Oh goodness, Laura, we don't need to dwell on that now, not here, not with it being such a beautiful spring day.

Laura paused to wait for Violet, who'd been dithering since they came out of church. Zelah was walking beside her. 'Tell me more about yourself,' Laura said, as they walked towards the footbridge. The Trent swerved glassy-smooth beyond the riverbank.

'Not much to tell,' Zelah said.

'I know you say your mother lost touch with her family, but you say she was from Cornwall originally?'

'Yes, at least, I think so. I'm not sure – does it matter, Dame Laura?'

'Just Laura. Call me Laura, dear. And, yes, it does matter, to me. Because the more I know about my subject, the more the details translate through the brush and the oils and into the finished painting. It helps give the piece character, don't you see?'

Violet still hadn't caught up. She'd stopped just past the Ferry Inn to pull a packet of cigs from her pocket. Never mind, there was no hurry. Laura watched two gulls circle, stark white as they swooped down near the bottle-green river, then disappearing into nothingness as they arced against the filmy spring skies.

'All I know is that we moved to Plymouth when I was very young, not long after I was born. I never knew my father, so I can't tell you anything about his family, either. Sorry I can't be more help, Laura.'

'My own father died when I was three,' Laura said, 'so I have no memory of him whatsoever. I never felt the loss, though.' (Father had been a ne'er-do-well and a lush, to boot. Aunt Thir said it was a relief all round that he kicked the bucket when he did.)

'I don't know if my father died,' Zelah began, then stopped. 'No, he did, he must have done. I think he was a soldier in France. Mother always said he was "lost to the war" so I suppose he would have been in the trenches when I was born.'

'How very sad and difficult for your poor mother,' Laura said, wondering why the girl got confused about her father. Was he dead or wasn't he? It was the sort of thing one knew – unless he was a father who was deliberately not talked about.

'If I think of anything, I'll tell you, though,' Zelah said. 'If it will help the painting.'

'If you could, dear.' Laura put her hand over Zelah's, and Zelah twisted her wrist so they clenched hands, just briefly, before Vi caught up with them.

'We're nearly there now,' Laura said, pointing at the red-brick stanchions with the coroneted swans in plasterwork on either one. *Tenez le droit* was inscribed above: Uphold that which is right. 'I always used to pretend I was entering a castle across a moat when we came here,' Laura said, pointing at the swans. 'This way, now, follow me, girls.' She led them down a pathway that ran from the side of the bridge to the water, past the seven brick arches that supported the cast-iron structure. 'One can only imagine the kinds of shenanigans that the local boys and girls get up to under there on warm summer evenings,' Laura said, gesturing at them and laughing. 'Actually, let's go this way, further up the bank. There used to be a little beach of sorts—' She turned off to the right, leading them along a pathway that cut through the goose grass and brambles. It was still damp with dew. Laura reached out with a fingertip to glance the lace edge of some early cow parsley, catching the scent of it. She felt as if fifty or sixty years had just been spliced out of her life. She wanted to run, flop down on the shore, tease Sis with that silly ditty, what was it?

Adam and Eve and Pinch-me-tight went down to the river to bathe
Adam and Eve were drowned, and who do you think was saved?

And Sis would answer 'Pinch-me-tight', even though she knew that it would end with Laura chasing her and giving her a horse-bite pinch on her arm!

'Watch out for the nettles,' Laura called over her shoulder as they continued in single file along the path. These young nettles were the worst; she recalled red stings circling her legs like an anklet after she'd run barefoot to the shore. She was often barefoot in those days, boots slung round her neck, tied by the laces, bumping against her chest: *thud-thud* like horses' hooves. Mother hadn't cared, said it saved on shoe leather – there was precious little money to spare on trips to the cobbler's, back then.

The path opened up to reveal the river shore: brownish sand and a weeping willow over by the rocks. 'Here we are. Spread the rug just there and sit down. It's a perfect spot for sketching.' Laura ushered Zelah past her and onto the little beach. She could hear Violet sparking up – again: the girl was like a steam train today! Laura watched Zelah sink down and settle on the green tartan travel blanket, her red skirt making an uneven oval around her, like an autumn leaf. Violet was swearing, struggling to get a light. Never mind, she could capture Violet presently. She would start with a couple of warm-up sketches of Zelah, Laura thought, taking out her notebook and charcoal from her bag.

'That's it, make yourself comfortable and just look across the river for me,' Laura said. She'd get her eye in first with the charcoal, and then move on to a watercolour – it felt like a watercolour day, with the high-up, half-hidden sunshine and the fresh spring colours. At some point she would need Violet to sit down and stop fidgeting for five minutes, though – what was wrong with the girl?

Laura took in a cooling breath and began with a line: the curl and stretch of the river. Next, the weighted curve of Zelah's skull and the flowing arc of her spine. A loose scrawl for the rug and back up to describe Zelah's profile: it was almost masculine, Laura thought, with that wide brow and the definite angle of the nose. Laura continued, almost finished already, no need to overwork the thing. The sun filtered down through the high clouds, spangling the surface of the river bend. There was the sound of water lapping the shore. Gulls mewed, wheeling through the damp air.

'Sennen,' Zelah said, holding the pose and barely moving her lips. 'I remember that Mother did once mention that during the last war she was a live-in help in Sennen Cove for a while, before I was born. I found a postcard of it tucked inside her Bible, when she passed. I'll see if I can remember anything else – if you think it will help you with the portrait?'

Zelah's mother had been a live-in help in Sennen, during the last war. In Sennen. Oh, dear Lord.

Laura's charcoal snapped off in her fingers, leaving a horrible blackened scrawl in the middle of the sketch. It was ruined, utterly ruined.

Chapter 16

Violet

'Nah then. It'll take more 'n that, mi duck.' Mrs Kirk's face twisted as she looked at the handful of coins Vi held out, as if she disapproved of the paltry amount on offer. The air swirled smoky-damp as the shift-change crowds surged past them up the steps.

'A deposit was all we agreed,' Zelah said. 'You said the balance was only payable on the day.'

'It is. Only, the price has gone up.'

Vi clenched her fist back over the money, before anyone could see. Her back was being continually nudged by the disgorging day shift. 'Can't we go somewhere else to discuss this?' she said.

'I've got no time for chat. I need to get on,' Mrs Kirk said. 'Some of us have got families to go home to.' Her mouth carried on working after she finished speaking, as if she were trying to dislodge something from her teeth.

'But I don't have that kind of money, not yet.' Vi looked

away from Mrs Kirk's nodding grey curls, up beyond the saw-edged factory roof to the mackerel-patterned evening skies. Money: it all came down to money. But until Dame Laura finished the painting and paid the sitter's fee, she had none to spare. And who knew how long it would be? She seemed to have been stuck on it forever. Ever since the day she'd taken them off on that sketching trip to Wilford, she hadn't done much more than dab at the canvas and frown at them.

'That's a nice piece. Is it real?' Vi heard Mrs Kirk talking to Zelah. Vi looked across to see Mrs Kirk pointing at the gold ring that hung on the red ribbon at Zelah's neck. And Vi knew what the grasping old bag was thinking about before Zelah ever cottoned on.

'No!' Vi said at once, but at the same time Zelah answered yes, yes it was real.

Mrs Kirk's eyes narrowed and her lips twitched. 'I'd say you'd get a fair amount if you popped that,' she said, reaching out.

'No,' Vi repeated. 'No, she can't do that.' She pushed away Mrs Kirk's greedy fingers.

Mrs Kirk tutted. 'I was only thinking of you,' she said. 'If you're short of money, and you're in a hurry, you might like to think about popping it.'

Of course I'm in a hurry. Every moment this thing is getting bigger, growing inside, Vi thought. But that ring is a love token from Mr Handford to Zelah. She can't possibly pawn it.

'I could, I suppose,' Zelah said. 'Just until we get paid for the sitting.'

'You can't, Zelah. It wouldn't be right.'

'But how else are you going to get the money?'

'I have to go or I'll be late, ladies,' Mrs Kirk said. 'You know how much it is, take it or leave it. Let me know tomorrow if you're still interested.' And she was gone. Vi watched the fake cherries bobbing on her hat as she bustled down the factory steps.

Vi turned to look at Zelah, who was twisting the ring round and round on the ribbon. 'I'm not going to ask, so don't even think about it,' Vi said.

'But the longer you have to wait, the more dangerous it is,' Zelah said. 'And if something were to happen, because we'd left it too late—'

'You can't. I can't let you,' Vi said.

Zelah's eyes were so dark, they were almost black. Vi met her questioning gaze. 'But what would you do, if you were in my shoes?' Zelah said.

George

'So this is where you hide, Mr Handford?'

He looked across to where she stood in the doorway, back-lit from the stairwell lights, a slice of sluicing rain between her and the covered shelter where he sat. He could just make out her eyes in the shadow of her features. 'I wouldn't call it hiding, exactly.'

'Don't you need something to eat?' she said. The door

211

closed behind her and the voice became disembodied. He was staring into a shadow behind the falling water.

'Don't you?'

'I'm not hungry.'

She still hadn't moved from the doorway. He wasn't sure why he felt awkward. After all that had happened – had happened so naturally between them – why was he still reduced to a nervous schoolboy at these stolen moments during the night shift?

'Zelah?' he began.

'Miss Fitzlord to you, as we're on work time, Mr Handford.'

'Do you want to join me?'

In lieu of an answer, he watched how the blurred shadow behind the falling water grew larger and more focused, until here she was: Zelah Fitzlord – rain-washed cheeks, eyes midnight-dark.

And there it was again, suddenly and quite easily, without thought or overture: the warmth of her lips, the scent of her skin overlaid with the burnt-metal tang of the factory air. The rain pelted down like a curtain, sealing them off. He closed his eyes, felt her hands on his back, pulling him closer to her. The hot-forged delirium of breath-touch-taste and the sound of the falling rain. It was exquisitely unbearable, being so close, knowing that they couldn't be any closer, not here – knowing it couldn't last.

She must have heard the footsteps before he did, turned her head. He noticed the flick of her eyes and the frown that passed over her face. 'Meet me at the end of the shift,' he muttered into her hair as they pulled apart. 'Come back to mine.'

The light was already seeping from the opening door as she replied. 'I'm so sorry, I can't. I promised Violet Smith I'd do something with her first thing.'

'Later then. I know you've got a shift free and I can re-arrange my schedule. We can go to dinner.'

'It's the hostel hop, remember.'

'Damn!' he said as the door swung open.

'Everything all right, boss?' The smudged figure of Alfie Perkins appeared in the doorway. He paused, peering through the storm at them both. Zelah stepped away through the wall of water, catching the closing door and thanking Alfie for holding it open for her, as if he'd paused on the threshold out of politeness, rather than curiosity.

'I got them to save you some apple crumble,' Alfie said as he reached the shelter. George cleared his throat. It mustn't look as if he were chasing after Miss Fitzlord, but he needed to catch her, needed desperately to . . .

'Thank you, Alfie,' he said. 'Well, I'd better be off then.' He ignored Alfie's questioning stare and strode across to the door, letting it bang behind him as he took the stairs two-at-a-time, down-down-down, but it was too late. He heard the downstairs door slam. She'd be back on the factory floor already, with the noise and the nosy girls and the demands of Dame Laura. Damn. Damn. Damn. He kept running, even though he knew it was too late, swinging through the doorway and into the main corridor.

What was it Alfie had said about crumble? George wondered, passing the canteen door. No matter. He had no appetite now. He walked on down the corridor towards his office, passing all the posters about production targets and the propaganda pictures: *Factories of Freedom*, said one, with pictures of men and woman doing various ordnance roles, grouped round an anti-aircraft gun. A factory of freedom? At the moment it felt like a prison, stopping him from having the chance to spend time with Zelah. They couldn't carry on like this, furtive moments of snatched passion like swarf on the factory floor, swept to one side and forgotten.

He walked along to the mezzanine level, pausing to look down. He could see her down below, wiping the lathe down with a rag, nodding at something her co-worker was saying. He could see Dame Laura's canvas in front of them, small as a postage stamp from his vantage point, the two pinkish blobs of the girls' faces and the grey-painted gun barrel between them. He watched as Dame Laura appeared from the other end of the shop floor. How much longer would she be here, he wondered? And how long until the McLaughlin girl returned and regained her place on the night shift? Zelah had said it wouldn't be long. And then what? She'd get back to her day job as welfare supervisor, and he'd see even less of her.

As if she could sense him watching her, she looked up from the lathe, her face tiny and far below. He saw the swift flash of a smile. She lifted a hand in a half-wave, and lowered it before anyone else noticed. He lifted his hand in response, and the insufficiency of the gesture angered him. He turned away.

It wouldn't do. How often in life did one get second chances? He didn't want to let this one slip between his fingers. It was time to take charge of the situation.

Chapter 17

Zelah

'Up there,' Violet said. Zelah looked up the paved alleyway. Drizzle was damp against her cheeks, seeping through her coat. She could see the figure of a dumpy woman opening up the shop. There was a dull glitter from the shop windows as shutters lifted like eyelids, making a grinding noise as they rose. Above the door hung three brass globes.

'Ey oop,' the woman said, giving the shutters one last nudge with the pole as they approached. She turned towards them. 'Coming in, ducks?'

Zelah nodded.

'Are you sure?' Vi muttered.

'Of course. That's why we're here, isn't it?'

Zelah's shoes slithered a little on the wet flagstones as they walked up the alley. *Jeweller's*, said the faded gold writing on the peeling black paintwork on the left-hand window. *Pawnbroker's*, said the other side. The woman had gone on ahead of them into the shop. Zelah let Vi go in front of her.

Clare Harvey

It wasn't the first time she'd been to a pawnbroker's. The first time must have been before they moved to The Grange, she thought, remembering:

'It's an original,' Mother says, but after that Zelah stops listening because she and the shopkeeper are going on and on, talking about money, and Zelah is more interested in the white cat that's curled up on the red plush seat of the chair next to the grandfather clock, sleeping in the shaft of sunlight that's shining in through the shop front.

Outside, the sky is blue and the clouds are chasing each other and there will be white horses on the sea. When the weather is like this, Zelah sometimes sees other children with paper windmills on wooden sticks, twirling and whirling like dizzy flowers. Zelah wants one. More than anything. But she knows there is no money, knows better than to ask.

Above the cat the air sparkles with dust motes. Zelah thinks of the song they have to sing in Sunday school: 'A sunbeam, a sunbeam, Jesus wants me for a sunbeam . . .' Zelah thinks about the words. Why would Jesus want her to be a sunbeam? The cat stretches in the pool of light. Zelah shifts across the floorboards towards it.

The grown-ups are still talking. 'I daresay, but there's not much call for art round these parts,' the tall man says in his scratchy voice, and Mother's feet move as if they're trampling down an invisible sandcastle.

Zelah is close to the cat, now. She has always wanted a cat. She has wanted a cat even longer than she's wanted a windmill. Well, a kitten. What would be better, if there was a choice? A kitten or a windmill?

218

The air smells of spit and polish, Zelah thinks. The cat opens its eyes and they are as blue as the sky outside the shop window. Zelah knows she should ask before she pets animals. She looks across at Mother, but Mother is busy, taking a small painting out of her handbag. It is the painting of the pretty woman in the yellow dress that sits on the mantelpiece in their room. Why has Mother brought it here? Mother is saying 'renowned artist' and Zelah does not know what 'renowned' means. She has three questions for Mother now: Can I stroke the cat? Why is our picture here? What does 'renowned' mean? But Mother has that look on her face like she doesn't want to be asked anything: closed up and hard.

The tall man holds out the painting at arm's length. The woman in the painting has curly hair, like Mother's, and she's looking out of a window. Beyond the window there is a beach, and waves. Zelah thinks of another question for Mother.

Zelah moves closer to the cat. The cat blinks at her and Zelah begins to stroke his warm fur, very gently, along his flank. She sees the tip of his tail twitch.

'Mother,' Zelah says, but Mother doesn't appear to hear. 'Mother,' Zelah says in a louder voice, still stroking the cat. The fur is soft under her fingers.

'What? What is it, Zelah?'

'Who is the lady in the painting?' She looks up at Mother as she asks, and the cat suddenly hisses and claws. Zelah snatches her hand away, but the sharpness is blood-wet.

'Nobody,' Mother says. 'Nobody you know. Now will you stop bothering that poor creature. It's time we went.' Mother is nodding her thanks at the man and fiddling with something on her finger.

Zelah sucks at the place on her hand where the cat scratched. It is metal-tasting. She watches as Mother puts on her gloves, even though it's quite warm outside in the sunshine, not really a day when you need to have your hands covered, Zelah thinks.

'Come on, Zelah.' Mother reaches out. Zelah grasps the gloved hand and lets herself be pulled away from the angry cat. The shop door jangles as they leave.

The door jangled as they entered. It was darker than outside, even with the electric lamp. The woman lifted the hinged end and slipped behind the counter. 'Buying or hocking?' the woman said, plump hands spayed out on the glass.

Zelah heard a rustle as Vi pulled out a cigarette. 'Hocking,' Zelah said. Vi struck a match. The woman grunted an acknowledgement. Zelah looked at her: yellow–grey curls and face like an un–plumped cushion.

'Let's 'ave a look at what you've got me then, duck.' One of her front teeth was grey: rotten and ready to fall.

'You don't have to do this for me, Zelah,' Vi said, her smoke misting the space between them and the woman. Zelah glanced sideways at her. Vi was frowning, sucking on her fag, a chimney of ash already formed at the tip.

'But what choice do we have?' Zelah said, reaching up and feeling for the ribbon at her neck.

'There is no "we". I'm on my own in this.'

'When we were in the church I promised to help you. And I keep my promises. Besides, how else are you going to get the money?'

The woman stared on, impassive at their exchange. She must have witnessed hundreds, maybe thousands of conversations like this over the years, Zelah thought, her fingers fiddling with the slippery ribbon.

'Want some help?' The woman leant across the counter. Zelah heard her grunting breath, felt her pudgy fingertips worrying the knot free. She saw Vi's hand tipping ash into the rusty ashtray on the counter top. 'There, let's take a gander.' Zelah's neck felt empty without the circle of ribbon, with George's ring, which now swung from the pawnbroker's hand like a fortune-teller's divination pendulum. Suddenly the woman slung it up, popped it in her mouth and bit down on it. 'Feels real,' she said. 'Wedding band?'

Zelah nodded. George's wedding ring: a symbol of his commitment to her. And now here she was in a pawnbroker's on a nondescript spring morning, hocking it so she could help pay for a woman to get rid of her unwanted baby. What she was doing was wrong, wrong, wrong.

But . . . She put herself in Vi's place. An accidental pregnancy, the father dead, no money, no other means of support. The only other option was letting her go the same way as Mary McLaughlin, off to the 'sluts' home' to give up her 'bastard child' and live with the pain and shame for the rest of her life. Letting that happen would be wrong, too, wouldn't it? Zelah sighed, and looked over at Vi, who had her half-finished cigarette to her lips again.

The woman had put the ring on the jewellery scales now, made a note of the weight of it, and then taken a closer look, through some kind of magnifying monocle, her saggy face all scrunched up, breathing like a bulldog.

They had to get this money to Mrs Kirk and get Vi sorted, because if they left it too late – how many women left it too late, botched it, ended up in the sepsis ward at hospital, or worse? It was too awful to contemplate. No, she would think of George's ring not as a love token, but as a means to an end, just for now, just until Laura finished the painting and paid the sitter's fee – which must surely be any day, mustn't it? And as soon as the painting was complete, they could come straight back here and reclaim the ring.

Zelah watched the woman pop the ring back on the ribbon and put it in the till. Then she counted out the notes and coins so Zelah and Violet could see, and sealed them up inside a manila envelope, together with the hocking slip. She locked the till afterwards with a key from the bunch that she kept in the pocket of her pinny.

It was done, now.

George would never need to know.

George

It was fate. What else could it be? Usually he went straight to bed after his shift, getting up and making himself scarce for an hour or so in the afternoon, just to give Mrs Packer a chance to tidy the place up a bit. But when he arrived home today he knew the futility of attempting sleep. He'd come straight out into town, with a view to putting his plan into action.

The air was still drizzle-thick as he strode down Angel Row towards Old Market Square, his hat low over his eyes to keep out the chill dampness. A trolley-bus rattled in front of him and he paused to let it pass, shifting from foot to foot, impatient at the hold-up. He knew what he needed to do. He just wanted to get on with it.

The trolley-bus passed and the expanse of the empty market square spread out in front of him, white-grey paving slabs the same colour as the low-slung clouds. The spray from the fountain spattered his cheek as he passed and the new Town Hall building lurched up ahead like the white cliffs of Dover. Figures criss-crossed in front or behind, scurrying to work or to beat the shopping queues. Buses chugged slow circles around the marketplace. The air tasted of petrol fumes. Pigeons fluttered half-heartedly away from his stride as he began to veer to the right, just below the Town Hall steps, close enough to see the expression of disdain on the marble lions' faces.

Just before it happened, his mind was away and somewhere else, remembering the day the old Prince of Wales had come to open the Town Hall, back in '29. It had been in the papers and on the newsreels, the future King looking like a schoolboy forced into detention. Which in a sense he was, George thought. Perhaps he'd lost that petulant frown now he was able to be with the woman he loved, despite her shameful past. George didn't blame him one bit – love wasn't a rational choice, was it? Apparently it had been a shockingly poor speech, though.

It was just at that moment, striding past the imperious right-hand lion, thinking muddled thoughts about love and royal scandal, that he caught sight of a woman in a wine-coloured coat walking down Poultry Lane. He hadn't even noticed the other woman with her when he shouted her name.

'Zelah!' She looked round blindly, not seeing him at first, pausing in the middle of the pavement. It was only then that he saw the woman in beige beside her. 'Zelah!' He broke into a run. The woman in beige pointed at him. He saw Zelah's right hand fly to her lips in surprise.

It was fate, bumping into her now, at this time, in this place, with all he'd planned for today. What else could it be?

He saw her pass a brown envelope to the other young woman – Violet Smith, wasn't it? – as he approached. He wished Zelah was alone. Evidently she was of the same mind. He saw her say something to Miss Smith, who nodded and began to walk away.

'Morning, Mr Handford,' Miss Smith said, passing him on the pavement as he came to a halt in front of Zelah.

'Morning,' he replied, touching the damp felt of his hat in her direction. George saw Zelah watch her go. A frown passed over her brow, before her eyes met his.

'I'm so pleased I bumped into you,' he said, leaning forward. He meant to kiss her, but something in her expression made him stop short. Perhaps it was better not to, here, in such a public place. After all, they hadn't made their relationship official. Not yet, at least. 'Zelah, I've been think-ing,' he said. And she opened her mouth as if she were about to interrupt, but he couldn't let her, because, after all, it was serendipitous, meeting her here.

'Please let me finish,' he said, getting down on one knee, the paving slabs hard and damp through his trouser leg. He took off his hat with his left hand, and with his right took her gloved hand in his. He looked up into her face – those intelligent eyes and lips he could never tire of kissing – and before she could interrupt he said: 'Zelah Fitzlord, will you marry me?'

Odd, how she seemed to rock backwards on her heels. He grasped her hand, tethering her. She hesitated, just for a moment, biting her lip. Then, 'Yes,' she said. Relief engulfed him. He got up and they embraced, kissing again and again.

When they parted, laughing a little in embarrassed joy, he explained that he was just on his way out to get her a ring when he saw her. 'It's fate,' he said. 'Now you can choose it yourself.' She seemed to falter, so he kissed her again, then grasped her hand and began to lead her up the hill, back in the direction she'd come from. 'Come on, there's a jeweller's just up here.'

Zelah

'That one.' Zelah touched the glass with the tip of her gloved finger as she spoke. There, behind the smeared pane, in a blue velvet display box, lay the perfect ring. It was quite plain: a gold circlet with an oval stone set in a twisted setting. The stone was apricot-scarlet with rainbow flecks – the colour the dawn sky above the Exe Estuary had been as she'd seen it through the train window on the day she left Plymouth forever.

George stood close; she could feel the warmth of him beside her. 'The fire opal?' he said. Zelah hadn't known the name of the stone, just that it was beautiful. 'You're sure?'

'I'm sure.' She turned to kiss him and her chest squeezed so tight she felt she couldn't breathe. 'But we don't have to get it now. I mean, there's no rush – you could come back later.' It was one thing standing outside the jeweller's and choosing an engagement ring, but to go back inside, so soon after she'd been here with Violet – what if the woman said something? What then?

'Darling, what are you saying?' He kissed the spot just under her ear, where her hair fell to her neck. She shivered and leant in – his breath, his lips, the feel of him. But then she remembered that the red ribbon was missing from her throat; what if he noticed, asked questions? She twisted free. 'Not getting cold feet, I hope?' he said.

'Cold feet? No, of course not, but—'

'But what? Come on, let's go inside and you can try it on.' He tugged her hand, pulled her towards the shop doorway.

'Marry in haste, repent at leisure,' she said, holding back.

'You've been listening to Matron too much.' He looked at her in that way he had, his dark forelock escaping from beneath the brim of his trilby. How could she respond? She wanted him, all of him, now and forever, and she didn't want to wait one more second. Because how often in life do second chances come around?

So she laughed, then, as if she were just joking, and let herself be led through the jangling door and inside the shop.

It was empty. Zelah gulped a breath. Perhaps the woman had gone on a break and someone else would serve them. It was the best she could hope for, now. George was saying something about how he hoped they took cheques, otherwise he'd have to go to the bank. Zelah stood beside him, gripping the edge of the counter, breathing. The musty air tasted like the girls' dormitories during the school holidays.

'You'd think they didn't want the business.' George tapped his fingers on the counter top.

'Maybe we should go. Come back later.' Her voice sounded strange, wavering and worn out.

'Anyone would think you're stalling, having second thoughts, Miss Fitzlord.' George stilled his drumming fingers and took off his trilby. 'You're not, are you, darling?' He turned and looked directly at her, then: those grey eyes under their thick brows.

'Of course not. I love you.' Her first confession of love came out in a desperate rush. She realised, then, that what she'd felt for that poor naval officer had been nothing more than an unfulfilled dream. But this was real. It was now and it was real.

'I love you too, Zelah.'

They looked into each other's eyes and everything else fell away.

There was the sound of someone coughing. Zelah blinked, turned. The woman with the rotten tooth had appeared behind the counter, carrying a chipped cream mug. Tan-coloured tea sloshed over the side as she put it down by the till. She put her hands on her hips. 'Buying or hocking?' she said, and as she said it she looked quizzically at Zelah.

'We'd like to take a look at the fire opal ring in the window,' George said. The woman nodded and pulled a bunch of keys from the pocket of her pinny.

'It's a nice piece,' she said, manoeuvring out from behind the counter and over to the front of the shop. 'Some say opals are bad luck, but I reckon that's just an old wives' tale.'

It will be fine, Zelah thought. After all, discretion should be part of her business. She'll stay quiet about my coming in with Violet, and George won't notice that I'm not wearing his wedding band because I'll keep my coat buttoned up. And soon – for God's sake, soon, surely? – Dame Laura will finish the painting and pay the sitter's fee and George need never know.

Zelah watched the woman unlock the back of the window display and grapple inside, heard George say, 'Yes, that's the one.' The woman was talking about how you had to be careful with opals: 'My old mum had an opal ring – not a fire opal, mind, just a regular one – and she wore it out to Evensong one winter's night – she was very religious, my mum, liked to go to church twice of a Sunday ...'

As the woman fiddled with the ring and the keys and chattered away, Zelah peeled the glove from her left hand, wishing distractedly that she'd given her nails a better scrub after the shift. She hadn't cleaned the machine grease out from her nail beds properly: they were grime-etched, like one of Dame Laura's charcoal sketches. She stretched out her fingers. They felt cold and naked.

'. . . and when she put her hands in front of the fire, the opal crumbled, just like that, nothing left but dust. Of course Dad was livid. It was the only time I ever saw him raise a hand to her . . .' The woman gave the velvet box to George and he walked the three paces across the dusty lino towards Zelah. She watched as, for the second time that morning, he got down on one knee and asked her to marry him. She said yes, he slipped the ring onto her finger and it fitted – it fitted perfectly.

And Zelah let out a breath and smiled, because she'd got through it, and it was all going to be all right, wasn't it?

George got up off his knees and embraced her and she let herself sink into him, feeling safe. Then he pulled away and began to talk to the woman about payment because the woman had gone back behind the counter and was standing pointedly at the till. Zelah looked down at the beautiful, perfect engagement ring that she would wear forever. She heard George asking the woman if a cheque would be all right.

And the woman said: 'What, you not using the cash from hocking that other ring, then, duck?' Zelah looked up. The woman had turned, hands on hips, looking directly at Zelah, as if what she'd just said made perfect sense. As if it didn't signify the end of everything.

Zelah looked from the woman to the engagement ring, to George. 'I beg your pardon?' George said.

With horrifying slowness, the woman pulled a red ribbon from the till, let the gold band fall so it swung slow circles in the stale shop air. 'I just assumed. But no matter, don't mind me. A cheque will do fine.'

Zelah watched George's head turn towards her, saw the appalled look in his kind eyes. 'Zelah?'

She opened her mouth to reply, but no words came.

'Zelah!'

'Zelah!' The feel of Mother's sweaty hand tugging at hers as they run though the lychgate. There is the sound of the organ from inside the church: 'Praise, my soul, the King of Heaven', as they slip in through the heavy door. Heads turn, eyebrows rise, brows furrow. The suffocating sadness and the wooden box at the front and mother's face all small and tight, and kneeling down to pray – the hard stone floor hurts her wounded knee where she fell as they raced from the bus stop. Then men carry the wooden box out through the door and everyone looks, turning their heads, and follows on outside where the men put it down in a hole in the ground, like a chest of buried treasure, Zelah thinks (there is a book of pirate stories beside the bed at home). Everyone is stern-faced and there are lace-edged handkerchiefs, and the smell of mothballs. She and Mother stand at the back: a forest of legs, hundreds of black tree trunks. Nobody looks at them, except one little boy, and when his mummy sees him

staring, she grabs him, hisses something in his ear, makes him turn away. Everyone sniffs, clearing throats, as if they all have colds. The vicar's voice sounds like the sea.

Afterwards Mother touches the sleeve of a short woman with white hair and a black straw bonnet, who is walking off down the path. The woman goes red in the face, turns, wrenches her sleeve free. 'It's not the girl's fault – she's done nothing wrong!' Mother calls out, but the woman goes off without answering. Zelah sees people whisper to each other, glance in their direction and then look away.

It is as if they are stranded on a desert island, Zelah thinks, like the one in the pirate book, and the people are the ships that sail past without seeing the smoke from the bonfire, or picking up the messages floating in bottles.

Everyone leaves the churchyard except Zelah and her mother. Mother stares at the mound of earth where the chest is buried for a very long time. The sky turns from primrose to ash at a stroke, and Mother says they should get going. On the walk back to the bus stop the village green is empty. The children are inside because it is dinner time already, and the sky is purple-black over the moors. Fat drops start to fall and they wait at the bus stop in the rain.

Zelah watches the raindrops coursing down her mother's cheeks and how she doesn't even bother wiping them away.

And they carry on dribbling down her face all the way back to Plymouth, even though it isn't raining inside the bus.

The corridor was a spinning drill bit as Zelah bore down to room 179, at the far end. The door was unlocked, she noticed, as if Vi didn't care who barged in on her. Zelah pushed it open, went inside, slammed it shut behind her. The blackout blinds were drawn but she ripped them open, letting in the dirty daylight.

'Zelah? Is that you?'

'Who else did you think it was? Another one of your men?' Anger bitter as over-brewed coffee in her mouth. Violet's painted toenails hanging down from the top bunk and her sleepy drawl: 'Don't be like that, Zelah. What is it? What happened with George?'

'What happened?' A mirthless laugh escaped her lips. 'He asked me to marry him and I said yes.' Violet slid off the bunk and stood facing Zelah. Her hair was twisted into curling rags, but they'd begun to unravel. She looked like a slovenly Medusa. 'He took me back to the same shop to pick out the engagement ring,' Zelah said, and watched as Violet's sleep-heavy eyelids sprung suddenly wide.

'And the woman?' Vi said. 'Did she let on?'

'What do you think, Violet? What the hell do you think? Would I be here if the woman kept quiet?'

'Oh, God, Zelah. I'm so sorry.'

'Thank you, Violet. That makes all the difference. Because you being sorry is just going to send George running back to me and make him trust me again.' She couldn't stop the spewing words. 'Your being sorry is going to magically cancel out my betrayal of his love and trust. I'm sure he won't mind that I sold his wedding ring, now you've said sorry, Violet Smith.'

'Oh, Zelah—' Vi reached out but Zelah shoved her hand

away, noticing how her own arm was quivering with anger. It was all she could do not to slap the girl, launch herself at her, scratching and punching.

'Tell me where he is, now. Let me go and explain to him.'

'You think I didn't try? You think I didn't try to tell him that I only pawned his ring to pay for your sodding abortion?'

'Keep your voice down, Zelah.'

'Or what, Violet?'

'D'you want someone to hear, get us all in the muck?'

'There is no "us", Violet. There never was. You've ruined everything by dragging me down into your sorry mess of a life and I've had enough of it. You're on your own. Now go away and leave me alone.'

She pushed past Violet and threw herself down onto the bottom bunk, buried her face in the pillow and screamed. Not caring. Not caring about Violet or her baby or what Matron thought or who heard. Not caring about any of it. Because nothing mattered, now.

Chapter 18

Violet

'Just go away,' he said, slouched against the door jamb, not even looking at her. 'Go away, Miss Smith,' he repeated. She could smell whisky-smoke breath, see the five o'clock shadow on his unshaven cheeks as light spilled out onto the pavement. He must have been playing a record on a gramophone. From inside came the faint scratch and click of the needle, again and again, like an itch.

'It wasn't her fault. She did it for me because I needed the money. But I never meant for this to happen.' Vi held out the envelope. 'It's all there, and the slip, too. Count it, if you want. You can get the ring back first thing.'

'It's not about the money.' He waved the envelope away. 'It's about the principle.'

'But she was only trying to help me.'

'She went behind my back. She betrayed my trust. She—'

'But she only did it for my sake!'

235

Why wouldn't he take back the money? Why wouldn't he listen?

'Didn't she explain? It was a loan, that's all.'

'I would have lent her money if she'd asked. It's the deceit, don't you see?'

'But I needed money quickly for my – for my mistake.'

'Oh, *that*,' he said, running a hand over his face, then making eye contact at last.

'Yes, that,' Vi said. 'How would it look if it came out that a boss was lending out money for *that*? Zelah was protecting you.' She held his gaze. 'She was trying to help me and protect you, and between us both we've made her the most miserable woman this side of the Siegfried Line. Take the ruddy money, Mr Handford. I don't want it now I know what it's done to you two.'

He didn't answer her immediately, just kept looking at her, standing in the doorway with the proud-slump of a half-drunk man. For a moment she was reminded of Frank Timpson, at the edge of the alleyway, that time. She shivered. There were footsteps on the pavement behind her.

'Put that light out!' A man's voice in the darkness behind her.

'Why?'

'You know fine well why, Mr Handford. Hitler'll be over here.' The voice and footsteps got closer.

'No, he won't.' Mr Handford sounded bored. 'You know as well as I do, Mr Packer, that we haven't had a raid here for two years and nor are we likely to. Nottingham is not a strategic target for the Nazis. And even if it were, I hardly think the chink of light from my front door is likely to send the bombers swooping down.'

Violet turned and saw a bandy-legged man in an ARP warden helmet behind her on the street. 'You put that light out, or I'll put it out for you, Mister! And I won't have my missus coming over and doing your whatnots for you, neither.'

Mr Handford sighed. 'All right, Mr Packer. My visitor was just leaving anyway, weren't you, Miss Smith?'

The ARP warden harrumphed, but continued on his way. 'I'll be back later to check, you mark my words!'

Violet heard the footsteps stomp away. She looked back at Mr Handford. She saw him run his left hand through his hair, then shove it off his forehead, and she noticed the glint of a ring on his finger.

He saw her looking. 'I've paid back the pawnbroker's and got my ring, Miss Smith,' he said. 'You can treat what's in that envelope as an advance against your wages. Now, please, will you go away and leave me in peace?'

And before she had a chance to reply, the door slammed in her face. She hesitated, still holding the envelope, looking at the shut door. It was very quiet, just the far-distant tramp of the warden's boots on the pavement up the street. With her free hand, Vi clenched and unclenched her fist. Then she leant forwards and pushed the fat package through the brass letterbox. She had to shove, hard, to get it right inside. She thought of how she used to dose the little ones with their cod liver oil once a week, pushing the spoon in through those pursed lips. She heard the envelope fall onto the doormat, and turned to go.

Zelah

She would just carry on, she supposed. Zelah gave the ersatz lemonade a stir with the metal ladle. It made a dull *thunk* sound against the edge of the bucket. Because when things go wrong, that's what you do, just move on. After Plymouth she'd had to start again, and perhaps that was the answer now. She could approach the Board and ask for a transfer. There was a shell-filling factory being built out near Ruddington, although it was supposed to be all hush-hush. Maybe they'd need a welfare supervisor. As soon as Dame Laura had finished this portrait she should ask, move on. George Handford would never have to see her again.

The lobby was all but empty. A spot prize waltz was underway in the assembly hall, and the prize was a pair of nylons, a Cuban cigar and two grapefruits. No wonder they were all packed in there. Even Matron had allowed herself to be steered through the double doors and onto the dance floor by an over-gallant Mr Tonks. There was just one airman and a girl in a yellow dress, passion-clamped by the fire doors. If Matron were here she would probably have marched over and wrenched them apart, spitting out words like 'decorum', 'modesty' and 'diseases'. But Matron was behind the double doors, trotting a sweaty one-two-three in Harry Tonks's embrace, so Zelah ignored the kissing couple. There was precious little fun to be had. Why shouldn't they grab at love whilst they still had the opportunity?

They might not get another bite at the cherry.

Zelah continued to stir, working in the final remains of citric acid and saccharine powder into the cloudy liquid. She swallowed, her throat dry and a tightness in her jaw, thinking of all of them waltzing away in there, twirling in the darkness, hoping the spot would fall and pin their twisting bodies like a plane in a searchlight beam. If things had been different, would she have been on the dance floor with George Handford now? Zelah wondered. Would she have been laughing and showing off her engagement ring to the girls? She'd never danced with George, she realised. She was never likely to either. Not now. Not after what had happened today.

Out of the corner of her eye she saw the front door open, felt the swift draught of cold outside seep in. And she thought for a moment it might be George, because he was supposed to be at the hop tonight. But of course it wasn't him. It was just Vi coming back from dropping her deposit off with Mrs Kirk. She walked over to the stairs, sat down on the third step and took out her cigarettes. As Zelah watched, she found she held no animosity towards her colleague for what had happened, but neither did she want to speak to her. There was just this overwhelming numbness. Violet caught her eye as she put the match to her cigarette. Zelah looked away, across towards the hall doors, where the band music had just stopped and there was the sound of a muffled cheer. Some lucky couple had just won.

She heard a vehicle drawing up outside, and thought it must be more airmen arriving – the men might finally out-number the women, at this rate. The couple by the fire exit were still kissing like there was no tomorrow, and maybe there wouldn't be, for him, at least, Zelah thought sadly, wondering how many more Mary McLaughlins and Violet Smiths there were throughout the country. All those cou-ples kissing like there was no tomorrow, all those unbidden lives forged in the passion-panic of it all. Accidents of war. Civilian casualties. Collateral damage.

The murky lemonade was like breath on a cold day. She put down the ladle and began to re-arrange the tumblers. The urn was steaming at the far end of the counter, and Matron had left her plenty of change in the tin. She heard the applause from the hall and smoothed her hands down her skirt. The rush was about to begin. They'd be thirsty. She reached again for the ladle.

There was a blast of cold air as the front door banged open again, but at the same time a wave of warm air from the dance floor washed into the lobby as couples spilled in through the double doors. Zelah heard the surge of voices, watched the bodies like fairground dodgems, bouncing and laughing. She saw a puce-faced Mr Tonks peck Matron, who put a nervous hand up to a pallid cheek, as if to rub away the evidence of his kiss. Then, 'Where's the ruddy welfare supervisor?' A man's voice, louder than the others. The throng of bodies pulled apart to let him through.

It was George.

Her guts twisted like the rifling lathe, spinning hard concentric circles, boring deep inside.

'Over here.' Everyone looked and it was suddenly quiet. He was hatless, his coat buttons undone and he had no tie on. He strode over to the counter. 'How can I help you?' She struggled to make her voice rise above a whisper.

'I have an urgent welfare issue I need to discuss with you, Miss Fitzlord,' he said, his words oddly drawn out. Was that alcohol she could smell on his breath?

'I'm afraid I'm rather busy,' she said, gesturing at the tea things and the lemonade, feeling as if she were one of the gun barrels, white-hot, raised by chains, waiting. She saw George open his mouth to speak, and she thought not now, not here, not in front of all these people. Please. Feeling like she was the un-forged barrel, swinging on the gantry, about to plummet into oil and be engulfed by the rush of flames.

But then Violet was there, taking the ladle from her hand. 'I can manage here,' she said. 'Why don't you two go somewhere more private for your talk?' And Zelah allowed her legs to propel her from behind the counter to where George Handford stood.

It was too awful. She couldn't even look him in the eye. 'Shall we?' she said and led the way through the crowd to the front door, without even waiting for his response.

Outside, the cold air pinched her cheeks and stars blinked in the clear skies. She traced her way across to the bench, sat down and took out her cigarettes. She offered the packet to him but he shook his head and sat at the far end of the seat. She clicked her lighter and glanced across at him through the flame. She inhaled.

Here it comes, she thought. All the things he hadn't said in the pawnbroker's earlier. He'd talk about deceit and betrayal, and what would she say? What could she say? She couldn't possibly defend herself, because what she'd done was indefensible.

He cleared his throat. 'So, Miss Fitzlord, am I correct in thinking your job is to advise on welfare issues?'

'Yes.' She exhaled.

'Perhaps you can advise me on a welfare issue, then?'

'I can try.'

'You see, the thing is, I have fallen in love with someone and she's let me down badly, and . . .'

'George, please—'

'No, let me finish. If it's your job to advise factory staff on welfare issues, then you can advise me on my welfare issue, Miss Fitzlord.'

She inhaled, holding the smoke inside and biting her lip.

'You see, I gave this woman a love token – a gold ring – and then I discovered that she'd pawned it. She had taken my love and cashed it in. What should I do?'

It was mortifying. She deserved it. She exhaled, watching the smoke disintegrate into the blackness.

After a pause he continued. 'What, don't you know? Don't you have any advice for me, Miss Welfare Supervisor? Can't you tell me what to do for my own good?'

She tapped ash away and brought the cigarette back up to her lips. What could she say? What she'd done was wrong.

'You see, I happen to have fallen in love with this woman. I didn't mean to, but love came as suddenly as an explosion, ripping my world apart. But how can I risk forgiving her?'

The air between them on the bench was cold and empty. 'Do you know why this woman pawned the ring?' Zelah said at last.

'I heard that she did it to lend some money to a young woman – a colleague of hers – to sort out a costly mistake.'

'And what do you think of her now you know the reason behind her actions?' Let's have it. Lower that gun barrel into the oil. Wait for the inevitable surge of heat, watch the flames leap.

'I think she could be found guilty of aiding and abetting a crime. Because it is a crime, the thing she's lending the money for.' There it was, the rush of fire. He blamed her. Of course he did. What right-thinking man wouldn't?

'But I'm not convinced she's fully at fault, this girl – this woman – I find somehow that I cannot blame her,' he continued. 'She was trying to do what she always does. She was helping someone, putting their needs before her own. And that very selflessness is one of the reasons I love her.'

Zelah breathed in smoke again, not trusting herself to speak.

'So, Miss Fitzlord, as you are the welfare supervisor here, I find myself in need of your advice. This woman did the wrong thing when she pawned the ring I'd given her, but I have come to the conclusion that she did it for the right reasons. Would you agree?'

Zelah nodded. She could feel his eyes on her, but she couldn't bring herself to meet his gaze.

'Was I doing the wrong thing when I broke off my engagement to this woman? Should I have given her more of a chance to explain? You're the welfare expert. What should I do now? Miss Fitzlord?'

Zelah threw the remains of her cigarette away into the night. 'I think, if you asked her, this woman would be truly sorry for what happened today. She has been—' Zelah's voice caught as she spoke, her mouth mangling the difficult words. 'She has felt bereft since it happened and she so wishes things had been different, but she wishes that you'd known it was impossible, impossible . . .' She broke off, unable to carry on, fighting to hold in the stupid tears.

And then he was there. A solid presence next to her. A strong arm round her shoulders. 'And if – if I asked this woman again to marry me, what do you think her response would be?' He smelled of whisky and pipe smoke. He felt like home.

She sniffed, wiped the wetness from her cheeks. 'As welfare supervisor my advice is this,' she said, managing a small smile as she continued. 'If you were to ask this particular woman to marry you, then I suspect she would in all likelihood say yes. But whether or not you choose to take my advice is entirely up to you, Mr Handford.'

Laura

Laura sat down behind the desk. It was a relief just to be off her feet. An ache travelled all the way from her heels, up the back of her legs to the base of her spine, when she spent too long standing at the canvas these days. Still, it couldn't be helped. She had to finish the damn thing and move on, let the girls get back to their lives. Get back to her own life, come to that. If she could. Could she?

The office vibrated with the sound of the band from the assembly hall across the way, but with the door shut all that remained was an echoing hum, like the inside of a sea shell. The air smelled of ink and paper.

Laura reached across the blotter to the telephone. For a moment she let her hand rest on the black Bakelite. These magic little contraptions, letting you break into the lives of people far away. They hadn't been around when she was a girl. Back then they all lived as if the whole of life were contained in the streets around Forest Fields. Was it better that way, she wondered, looking round Matron's office: filing cabinets and charts and files and notebooks angled against each other – blocks of white, beige and dun layered on grey, looking like some frightful Cubist effort by that Braque fellow. Dreadful. When would someone put a stop to all this modernist nonsense? she wondered.

Enough, Laura. You're letting your mind wander. Remember why you're here.

Laura picked up the receiver, put her index finger in the '0' hole on the telephone and pulled the dial round to the metal stop, hearing it *click-whir* back into position. The disembodied voice of the operator said 'Yes, please' and Laura gave the area and number she wanted. With a click the operator put her through. Laura's hand tightened on the receiver and she wished she'd lit a cigarette before starting the call. She took in a deep breath and listened to the jangle-drill sound of the phone ringing at the other end of the line.

'Egham two-seven-eight,' came a voice. The line crackled and hissed.

'Ella?'

'Yes, speaking.'

'Ella, this is Laura, dear.'

'Laura?'

'Laura Knight.'

'Oh, Laura. I say, it's rather late. Is it urgent?'

Laura checked her watch. Was it that time already? One rather lost track.

'It's about Harold,' Laura said.

'Oh, dear God!'

'He's absolutely fine, don't worry.'

'I don't understand.'

'What can you remember from the winter of '16?'

'For heaven's sake, Laura, that's more than twenty years ago.'

'Twenty-seven, in point of fact, dear. We were renting next door to each other in Sennen when I had to head off to Witley to paint those Canadian soldiers, and I left Harold behind at the cottage. Do you remember, Ella?'

'Not really, darling. It was such a long time ago. A lot of water has gone under the bridge since then.'

What on earth was Ella talking about? Water and bridges indeed. 'Do you remember the girl?'

'What girl?'

'The girl I had in to look after Harold, after his – his illness. You found her for me, didn't you?'

'Yes, as a matter of fact I do remember her: curly hair and pink cheeks. Some distant relative of Cecily's – parents died of cholera out in India, and hadn't left enough money for her to be "finished" as I recall.'

'What was her name?'

'Her name?' There was a pause then, and Laura could imagine Ella rolling her delft-blue eyes up to the ceiling, in that way she had, when she was trying to think of something. The line fizzed between them. 'Sarah,' she said at last. 'It was Sarah, wasn't it?'

'Sarah,' Laura repeated, taking up a pencil and writing the name down on the edge of the blotter. 'What was her surname – can you remember?'

'Ah, you've got me there. I only remember her as Sarah.

Frankly, I'm amazed I remember that much. I'm not one for looking back, you know. Twenty-seven years, you say? My word. But – Laura, it is rather late. I'd love to talk but perhaps we could arrange lunch in town, next time you're up?'

Laura could hear Ella yawning loudly over the muzzy phone line, not even bothering to try to hide it – probably exaggerating it – which would be just like Ella, making a point. 'What a marvellous suggestion,' Laura said. 'Just one last thing, though. What happened to her?'

'Who, darling?' Ella drawled.

'The girl – Sarah. Because when I got back from Witley, she'd gone, and you were taking care of Harold.'

'Nothing ever happened . . .' Ella's voice was suddenly precise, and pitched a tone higher, her vowels breaking into a sprint. 'With Harold. I've been told what you thought, and I understand why that would make things cool between us, but I can assure you, you can put your mind at rest on that score. If that's what this call is all about.'

'Not at all,' Laura said. (Although it was true, she had had her suspicions about Ella, when she came back from Witley, to find things so changed. But she'd asked Mr Trevallion once, and he'd said, 'Harold and Ella? No, my lovely. Nothing went on there. It's not Ella you need to worry about.') 'I was just wondering what happened to Sarah, that's all.'

'She had to go, I'm afraid. She'd gone and got herself in trouble, so I sent her back to her relatives. By which time, you were almost due to return, so it hardly seemed worth engaging a replacement.'

'Harold never said.'

'Why would he? He's never been one to involve himself with practicalities much, has he? I thought you said this was urgent, darling?'

'Did I?'

'Yes, you did. You said it was something urgent to do with Harold.'

'Ella, I didn't quite catch that – there seems to be something wrong with the line, dear,' Laura said, even though she could hear her old friend, her voice clear as a bell.

'You said this was something about H—'

But Laura had already slammed the receiver back down in its cradle. A dalliance with Ella would have been bad enough. But this was awful. And no less terrible for being precisely what she'd most feared.

Zelah

'We can't get married, you know,' George said.

'What?' Why had he turned up at the hop, then? She didn't understand. The moonlight caught the stone in the ring on her left hand as she shifted down a gear, bumping over the rutted track towards the clubhouse. He'd insisted on bringing her here, after what had happened at the hostel – but when she'd smelled the whisky on his breath, she'd decided to drive.

'We can't get married if you haven't got a birth certificate,'

George continued. 'You said you came here with nothing. It's all very well telling me that you think you were born in Cornwall because of your unusual name, but I hardly think that's going to cut it with a registrar, darling. You'll have to apply for a copy.'

She let out a breath. 'Of course. Of course I shall. First thing.' She braked and they came to a halt in front of the clubhouse. 'So this is where you escape to when you're not holed up in your office, Mr Handford?' She turned the key in the ignition and the engine stilled.

'Sometimes.' He looked out through the windscreen to where water stretched silver-blue towards charcoal fields. 'In the summer, mostly.'

'And did you come here with—'

'Lexi? No, wasn't her thing. Tennis – we used to play mixed doubles together, before . . .' He drew breath and turned to look at Zelah. 'It was a long time ago. Shall we?' She nodded and they both got out of the car.

The wooden twin-gabled clubhouse was up on stilts, with dinghy hulls stashed underneath. More boats were hauled up on the stretch of grass beside the clubhouse. A Union Jack flapped lazily against the star-speckled sky. Zelah closed the car door.

'I used to sail a lot, as a boy – Father taught me,' George said, coming round to the front of the car to meet her. 'I stopped when I joined up. Then there was Lexi. But after-wards – afterwards it was something of a comfort, I found.'

'It stills the mind, doesn't it?' Zelah said, moving in

towards him. His coat was unbuttoned. She slipped an arm round his waist. They began to walk towards the pontoon. 'We took the girls sometimes, at weekends. There would always be one or two who couldn't go home for an exeat weekend, for some reason or other – you know, a case of measles in the house, or a newborn sibling – and so we'd take them off sailing or hiking, so they didn't feel they'd missed out too much when the rest of the dorm came back on Sunday evening with full tuck boxes and tales of days out at the seaside.'

'I didn't know you sailed. What else don't I know about you?'

'I'm not sure – plenty of time to find out, though.'

'The rest of our lives.'

They walked across the damp grass. The moon hung large and bright in the sky: a bombers' moon, shedding a strip of tinselled light on the water. 'I've been here once before, actually,' she said. 'It wasn't long after I arrived in Nottingham. I borrowed a bike and cycled all the way along the Beeston Cut until I got here. I had a cup of tea in the tea garden at the Lock tea rooms, and looked across at the dinghies on the water. It reminded me too much of Plymouth, though: the sun and the wind and the coloured sails. So I never came again, couldn't face it.'

'But you're here now.'

'With you. It's different, with you.' Zelah leant her head on George's shoulder and they looked out over the water together.

There was a beat, then, and she knew that they'd both turn and their lips would meet. But in that moment there began a tiny sound, distant and insistent, like a drill, boring a hole through the edge of the sky. She stiffened. 'Do you hear that?'

'Don't worry, darling, they're not headed this way. They never do. There's not been a night raid here for years. We're just not a target. Trust me, I'm a fire watcher.' He turned and pulled her closer to him, and she let herself fall into his embrace. Her lips met his and there was the whisky-smoke-warm taste of him and the feel of his hands stroking the curve of her back. The buzz of the planes passing overhead was nothing more than a swarm of distracted wasps. Then the air was still once more, with just the waves lapping the pontoon, and the gentle chink of halyards, and the sound of her own heartbeat.

And she knew she was the luckiest woman alive.

Chapter 19

Violet

'It's beautiful, Zelah,' Vi said, looking down at where the fire opal in her engagement ring gleamed with trapped rainbow colours as it caught the light. George Handford had gone back for the ring with the money Vi had shoved through his letterbox. And Vi had apologised to them both, said she'd decided to go through with the pregnancy, have the baby adopted, just as Doctor Gibbs suggested.

Sometimes you had to tell people what they wanted to hear, Vi thought. Even if it wasn't exactly the truth. She still wanted rid of the thing that was growing in her belly, wanted it gone before she began to think of it as a baby. Because as soon as she thought of it as a real child, as her child, she'd never be able to let go, she knew. But she couldn't say that to Zelah, not after all that had happened. No, she was on her own with this problem now.

'Thank you,' Zelah said, taking another drag of the cigarette and passing it back to her room-mate.

'When is the wedding?' Vi asked through an inhalation.

'As soon as my copy birth certificate comes through then we can apply for a licence. It could be any day!' The fields were pale lime with new growth. Yellow dandelions spotted the grass by the fire escape. In the distance she could see the green bus caterpillaring through the country roads towards the hostel. Vi passed the cigarette back and Zelah took a thoughtful drag. 'When it comes, would you be my maid of honour? It'll only be in Nottingham Registry Office, not a big "do" or anything, but—'

'I'd love to,' Vi said, and meant it. She felt Zelah's arms encircle her. She smelled of smoke and talcum powder, and for a moment it was just like sharing a hug with her big sister Bea. Vi sighed and chucked the cigarette out of the window. Just then a voice started to sing, loudly but a little flat, from the open window of the room next door. '"There'll be blue birds over, the white cliffs of Dover . . ."' Vi rolled her eyes and took out the paper packet from her overall pocket.

'Would Vera Lynn like a humbug?' she yelled, thrusting the bag of sweets outside. The singing stopped.

'Don't mind if I do. Ta, ducks.' A hand reached round from the open window, rustled in Vi's outstretched sweetie bag and disappeared.

'Never mind my sweet ration, at least that's shut her up for a bit,' Vi said under her breath, and mimed operatic hand movements and dramatic expressions in mimicry. Zelah put a hand to her mouth to stifle her laughter. 'You want one?' Vi said, and Zelah said 'Thanks', popping a striped peppermint into her mouth.

'I've not had one of these for years,' Zelah said, leaning on the windowsill and shutting her eyes.

Zelah

'Miss West gave me a humbug,' Zelah says, pulling on Mother's hand to get her attention. The street is steep and it's a long climb home from school to the top end where their room is, above Radipole's Butcher's, and underneath Madame DuBois' Dancing Studio for Girls.

'What did you get sweets for? Had you been a very good class today?'

'No, just me,' Zelah says, pausing by where Langford Alley turns off to look at the dead rat in the gutter. She looks at it every day. At first it still had fur on, and looked quite nice, apart from the slithery-worm tail, but then the eyes went sticky and sunken, and flies clustered. Then maggots came, and stuff like black treacle oozed out underneath. After a while there was no fur or flesh left. Now there are just bones.

'Come on, Zelah,' Mother says, pulling her away from the tiny skeleton by the wall. Zelah plods on up the hill beside her mother. The cobbles feel very bumpy because her shoe leather has worn through and mother has had to put cardboard inside to cover up the holes, but the cardboard is giving way because it was raining at playtime, and now she can feel the smooth pebbles underfoot as she walks.

'*Miss West said it's because I'm a poor, unfortunate girl,*' Zelah says, looking up at the long, grey-brown road and wishing home wasn't so far away. She is hungry, the humbug just a sweet echo of taste on the back of her tongue. She hopes it is toast and dripping for supper.

'*A what?*' Mother stops, loosening her grip on Zelah's hand. A door bangs open next to them and a man staggers out. The air smells smoke-sickly-sweet behind the open door. The man sways over to the wall and leans against it, resting his head against his arm.

'*A poor, unfortunate girl,*' Zelah says, pleased that she has remembered the long word: unfortunate – so difficult to say without getting your tongue tangled.

The man's body starts to jerk and heave. Sick splatters from his mouth onto the cobbles. It is orange-coloured. The smell is horrid, but watching the man is interesting, even better than the dead rat.

Mother tightens her grip again, tugs her across the street, away from the sick man. '*Don't stare, Zelah,*' Mother hisses and Zelah obediently looks ahead and trudges on. It is like climbing a mountain, this going-home business, she thinks. Seagulls swoop and scream overhead.

Zelah felt a nudge in her ribs. 'Wake up, Little Miss Head-in-the-clouds, the bus is here.'

They banged out of the room, and into the corridor, meeting Dame Laura at the bottom of the stairs. 'Are we sitting for you today, ma'am?' Vi said and Laura replied, 'Yes please, if it wouldn't be too much bother.' Just as the three of them were pushing out through the entrance with the others, Matron called out from her office, saying she had a letter for Zelah that had come second post, and held out an envelope.

Zelah took it but didn't open it straight away because the bus was waiting, engine running, and they were last on as it was.

There were two seats left, so of course Dame Laura had one, and Zelah insisted that Vi take the other. Vi didn't argue, but slumped down, looking exhausted already, even though it would be a full thirteen hours until she could get some sleep. Zelah hung on to the pole, struggling to keep upright as the bus veered off, holding the envelope in her free hand. It would be the birth certificate. She'd been expecting it for days. All she needed was the names of her parents and her place of birth, for the marriage licence. She could drop the envelope off in George's office at the first break.

The girl in the yellow headscarf two seats back was coughing uncontrollably and Zelah made a mental note to take her to one side and have her sent back to the hostel, and to have her signed off until Doctor Gibbs had taken a look at her. The last thing they needed was TB riddling the workforce.

The bus had stopped at the level crossing and Zelah had time to open the envelope, carefully lifting the gummed flap, not wanting to tear it. Inside was the cream sheet of paper with the lipstick-red lines: *Certified Copy of an Entry of Birth*, it said. The red lines contained boxes. Where and when born was filled with curly black writing: *Born in Zelah on 18th September 1917.* The paper shook in her hand as the barrier lifted and the bus juddered over the train tracks. What was the second box? She squinted down. She could still taste the sweet-mint humbug on her tongue:

*

'Miss West says it's not my fault I don't have a daddy,' Zelah carries on, panting a little because the hill is so steep that it's hard to walk and talk. And Mother suddenly lets go of her hand. Zelah feels cut adrift, watches Mother's yellow skirt swish-swish as she walks on ahead.

'She's no right to say such things!' Mother says, stopping, turning back. Her face looks very small, like a pinched-off piece of pastry dough. Mother is angry, Zelah thinks. Was it wrong to accept the humbug? Zelah runs to catch up with her mother, who has turned and started to walk again. Zelah's legs pump fast and the breath squeezes from her, but she manages to catch up with Mother at last and reaches for her hand. Mother grabs it very tight, so tight her fingers hurt, but doesn't turn her head to look at Zelah. 'That woman has no right!' she repeats, and Zelah still doesn't understand why Miss West's humbug has made Mother so very angry.

Zelah thinks about how it's all happened:

'Miss Quiss
Look at this
A pocket full of liquorice
You may have some, if you wish
But every stick will cost a kiss!'

That's what Tommy Norman sang to her at playtime, when it started to rain and they went under the big tree for shelter. She looked in his pocket but there was nothing in there but some dirty old twigs and he laughed in her face hah-hah-hah, like that, with his missing front teeth and his fishy breath and said he didn't want to kiss her anyway because she was a bastard.

And Zelah asked Miss West what a 'bastard' was? Miss West's eyes went large and blue, like marbles in a puddle of rainwater, and she said that it was a very, very bad word that some rude people used when your mummy didn't have a wedding ring and that Zelah must never, ever repeat the word to anyone.

That's when she called her a 'poor, unfortunate girl' and stroked her cheek, and gave her a humbug.

Zelah's hand was slick with sweat on the pole. It was hard to hold on as the bus swung its way towards the factory. She stared down at the fluttering sheet in her hand, willing it to be different. There must be a mistake. Mother had never said – no, Mother had never said anything, she realised, forcing herself to remember:

Zelah knows she mustn't say that word again, because Miss West said not to, and Miss West is a teacher and you have to do what teachers say. Zelah feels Mother's hand gripping hers, pulling her homewards, and she thinks that Miss West and Tommy Norman must be right, though, because there's no metal ring digging in as her mother grasps Zelah's hand in hers.

'Why don't you have a gold ring like the other mothers?' Zelah says. But Mother doesn't answer, just pulls her harder up the hill, so that in the end they are running. And when they get home, Mother locks herself in the privy in the back yard. Zelah waits, sitting on the cold stone on the back steps for what feels like forever, watching

the black cloud coming in from the sea and the rain haze down like a chiffon scarf underneath it, hoping that Mother will come out of the privy and unlock the door to their room before the rain makes it up the hill.

The next time the bus stopped at a junction, Zelah folded up the copy birth certificate and shoved it out of sight in a pocket. Something large and hard was lodged at the base of her throat, like a stone was stuck and she couldn't swallow it down. She twisted off the ring on her left hand.

As they hurried off the bus it was Dame Laura who seemed to notice, tapping her on the arm, asking her if she was quite all right, looking at her with those clever-parrot eyes of hers. But Zelah lifted up her mouth at the corners and said that she was fine. Because how could she say that b-word out loud? I'm a bastard. He won't marry me, now. I'm from bad blood.

I'm a bloody bastard and I will never marry because of it.

George

He was inching the Austin through a gaggle of workers when he saw her getting off the bus – a shade taller than the other girls, bare-headed, black hair, twist of dark red coat. It was like falling and being winded, the realisation: that's her – Zelah – my future wife.

The day shifters were heading home and the night shift arriving, the factory entrance a heaving mass, bodies eddying like a turning tide. He edged into his space, twisted off the ignition, grabbed his briefcase and pushed himself out of the car, snagging the edge of his trench coat in the door in his haste to escape.

He needed to catch her before the shift started. There were things to discuss, but more than that, he wanted to touch her, hold her, remind himself that she was real: Zelah Fitzlord, his fiancée, his future wife. But by the time he'd wrenched his coat free and locked the car door she was already hidden in the crush. Dammit. His eyes scanned the crowds. There – over there – almost at the factory steps already.

'Zelah!' There were acres of bodies between them, the workers shifting and twitter-chattering like roosting starlings as he shoved his way through.

Her foot was already on the bottom step. 'Zelah!' He saw her turn and her mouth fall open, as if it were a shock to see him there. 'Zelah, darling.' He leant over to kiss her but she flinched and pulled away. 'Zelah?'

Crowds swirled round them, a rush of black-brown-grey as he stepped towards her again. She couldn't possibly be shy. It's not as if their relationship was a secret any longer. They were engaged, and the whole night shift knew it. By this time next week they'd probably be man and wife, for goodness' sake.

'Darling?' But again she pulled away from his embrace, frowning and biting her lip. 'What on earth's the matter?'

What had happened? Had someone hurt her?

She was pushing her hair off her face as he spoke and he should have noticed then, but didn't – the missing spot on her left hand where the engagement ring should have been.

'I'm sorry, George,' she said. Some homebound worker nudged into her from behind and she stumbled forwards into him. He grasped her arm to stop her falling, but as soon as she'd found her footing she shook herself free and took something from her coat pocket: a piece of cream paper, folded up small. 'I can't marry you, George. I'm so very sorry.' She thrust the paper at him.

'What the hell are you saying?' Confusion engulfing like fumes.

'Open it and you'll understand,' she said.

He unfolded the paper. Her engagement ring was wrapped up inside her copy birth certificate, he could see that. But why? The gold circlet with the fire opal lay on top of the curly black writing. His eyes darted over the red lines and the black words, but none of it made sense.

'Look – here.' Her fingertip pointed into one of the red-lined text boxes. Where she pointed, in box number four, which listed the name and surname of father, there was nothing but a slashed line. And then again, further on, in box six, under rank or profession of father, there was just a line. And that's where the engagement ring lay, balanced on top of the copy birth certificate on his palm.

'I don't have a father. There's bad blood and shame in my

family, and you won't be wanting it in yours. I'm sorry. I'm so sorry.'

He opened his mouth to reply, but as he did so he, too, was shunted from behind, one of the night-shift workers rushing to clock on. The ring and paper slipped from his palm and landed down amongst the chaos of tramping feet. He leant over and managed to scrabble-grab the ring, but the birth certificate was trampled underfoot, a muddy clog-print across the crumpled paper. 'Now listen here,' he began, straightening up, shaking the grit off the paper.

But all he could see was the sea of bobbing heads, and the factory doors gaping open and swallowing, like Jonah's whale.

'Zelah!'

She'd gone – he'd lost her.

Laura

All you have to do is finish the damn thing and go back to Malvern, Laura told herself, nodding her thanks at the portly man who held the factory door open for her. Once inside, the switch from the dreary outdoors to the stark electric lights made her eyes ache. Overlaid above the twitter of voices and the chug-grind of machinery, Gracie Fields' voice whined with irritating cheer through the loudspeakers: '*I'm the girl that makes the thing, that drills the hole that holds the ring, that drives the rod that turns the knob, that works the thing-ummy bob . . .*' Dear Lord, she'd have that awful song as an earworm all day now, Laura thought. She waited in the bottleneck of bodies as the factory girls tapped their cards into the clocking-on machine. Looking at them, she realised she'd forgotten to put Harold's postcard in the post. Never mind, it could wait. She'd found a picture of the lions on the Town Hall steps, scrawled a lot of nothingness on the reverse, lies about how well the painting was coming along, something about how all being well she'd be home by May Day.

May Day. *M'aidez*. Wasn't that the call sinking ships put out when they were in trouble? Am I a sinking ship, Laura wondered, letting herself be carried along with the swell of young bodies towards the shop floor.

She thought of Zelah Fitzlord's dark, angular features, and the coincidence of her age and birthplace. She almost lost her footing as she was jostled from behind. Someone said 'Sorry, ma'am' and Laura muttered 'Not at all, no harm done, dear', without even turning her head to see which of the bustling youngsters it was.

Am I really adding two and two together and making five? she thought. Why would the girl's mother have kept a postcard of Sennen Cove if there weren't some kind of emotional tie to the place? Zelah was twenty-five; she was born in September 1917, which meant she would have been conceived ... Oh dear Lord, Laura, stop thinking about it, just finish the damned picture and go home to your husband.

There was so little left to do. The background was fine, and Violet's face was almost complete, but too bland – it lacked something. And then there was Zelah. She could not seem to get Zelah's face right at all. And every time she tried, the more closely she looked – it didn't bear thinking about, and yet she couldn't help herself. She needed time to compose herself. She paused, shoved and nudged from behind. Just a few moments in the ladies' loos to give herself a good talking to before getting back to work. Not procrastination, merely a question of steeling herself, she thought, heading right, across the flow of workers, towards the bathroom door.

'Dame Laura, glad I caught you!' It was Violet, tugging at her sleeve. 'Can we talk?'

'Yes, of course, dear. It will be quieter in here, if a little insalubrious,' Laura said, opening the bathroom door and ushering Violet inside.

'I just wondered how long you think it will be until the painting's ready?' Violet said.

Gracie Fields became mercifully quiet as the door clicked shut behind them.

'Hard to say, dear.'

'Only it's been a while now, and you did say . . .'

'One can't force these things,' Laura interrupted, taking in the surroundings: liver-spotted mirror, cold white porcelain, dank smell – not quite the same as the 'throne room' upstairs. 'The portrait has to have integrity – it's hard to explain.'

'You mean you don't want it to look fake?'

'I suppose so. A Laura Knight painting is a Laura Knight painting. It has to be done properly. I don't want to turn into a pale imitation of myself, just bashing things out, knowing they'll sell because I put my signature on the bottom. And this one's not right, not yet. It lacks – it lacks honesty.'

'It looks pretty good to me.'

'That's just it, dear. Pretty good isn't good enough, nowhere near. When people look at a portrait they need to feel as if they really know the subject: her secrets, dreams and history.'

'Is that all? 'Cos I'll tell you everything about me if it'll make you hurry up – if it makes the painting finish quicker.'

'Does it bore you terribly, sitting for me, Violet?' Laura put her hands on her hips. The girl's face was a sullen mask and Laura was suddenly irritated with the little chit. Violet Smith didn't care about truth or beauty. All she cared about was cash. The impertinence of it. Did she not realise that her face would in all likelihood grace the walls of the National Gallery? Most girls would give their eye teeth to have their portrait painted by Dame Laura Knight, no matter how long it took. Laura opened her mouth to say the same when there was a shuffle of feet, and the sound of a flushing toilet. Laura hadn't realised there was someone else in there with them.

An elderly woman appeared from a cubicle and stood in front of the sink. She still had her curlers in. Without bothering to wash her hands, she took a large mustard-coloured scarf from her overall pocket and began to wrap it round her hair, making faint snuffle-grunts as she reached to fasten it at the front.

'D'you need help, sweetheart?' Violet said. The woman replied that she wouldn't mind, only she'd bashed her shoulder on the reamer yesterday and it was giving her merry hell but she couldn't afford to take a day off on account of her grand-daughter needing new shoes for school. 'There you go,' Vi said, deft fingers folding the fabric and pinning it to cover the curlers. The woman said thank you and waddled out, a slice of white noise as the door opened and closed as she went through. That woman is probably older than I am, Laura thought, and coming to work even though she's hurt and in pain, because she needs the money. Laura thought of Harold, the doctor's bill, the hotel bill, and the repairs on their London home. It all needed paying for – it all came down to money in the end. Hard cash trumped truth and beauty every time.

Laura let her hands drop back down to her sides. 'I'm sorry, dear. This particular portrait is proving an unexpected challenge,' she said. 'But when I consider it finished you shall be the first to know, I promise.'

'Thank you. I know I will, Dame Laura. I'm sorry, I shouldn't have nagged.' And Violet Smith gave her a swift and unexpected hug, before banging out of the bathroom door.

Laura stood in the empty bathroom, looking at the shut door, feeling like the tugged end of a line of knitting. Unravelling.

Zelah

Zelah thought of his house, the parents she had yet to meet – would never meet, now – the army officer brother, a whole tribe of aunts, uncles and cousins: lawyers, engineers, businessmen, magistrates. How could she ever have thought the likes of her could deserve to be part of that world?

She felt tears rising, unbidden. But it wouldn't do. Not here. Not at work. But she couldn't possibly go to the changing rooms now, not with all the other girls and the gossip. They were already asking when the wedding was, who'd be maid of honour, where the honeymoon would be. How could she face them? What could she say?

The door of the loos was like a sanctuary. She pushed inside. A moment. She just needed a moment, to suck down this despair, wash her face, and paint a smile on her face. One moment alone.

The door banged open, and there, facing her, was Dame Laura. Zelah faltered, swallowing, blinking, willing the tears to stop. The door fell shut behind her.

'What is it, dear?' Dame Laura said.

Zelah shook her head. 'Nothing.'

'It doesn't look like nothing to me.'

'I can't marry George,' Zelah said, the sour pinch of withheld grief in her jaws. 'He's from a good family, and I—' She couldn't say it.

'Is it to do with your birth certificate?' Laura said, and Zelah nodded. 'Oh dear. Come here, my love.' Laura opened up her arms and Zelah let herself be enfolded. The tears came in painful jerks at first, and then in a rush. Dame Laura smelled of smoke and turps and eau de Cologne, and her bony fingers rubbed Zelah's shoulder in a slow rhythm, syncopating her despair. 'The course of true love never did run smooth,' she whispered into Zelah's hair.

'Zelah!' There came a muffled shout from outside the door.

Laura gave Zelah a gentle nudge to break free from the embrace, and passed her a piece of tissue. 'Blow,' she said, as a mother would say to a child. Zelah wiped her eyes and blew her nose.

'Zelah!' His voice again from outside the door. Zelah felt trapped, numb, incapable.

'Let's have a look at you.' Laura took out a clean handker-chief and wiped Zelah's face with it. Then she spun Zelah around so she could see her reflection in the liver-spotted mirror that was screwed to the wall above the sink. 'If you're a bastard, you're a beautiful one,' she said, standing behind Zelah with a half-smile on her face. 'And I would be the proudest mother in the world if you were my daughter. Now for God's sake, go out there and put that poor man out of his misery.'

Zelah opened the bathroom door and George was there, waiting. The birth certificate flapped like a truce from his right hand. She stepped forward and opened her mouth to say something, but before she could, his face was close, his lips on hers: soft and urgent. The taste of him. She lifted her arms up and drew him in.

Laura

Despite the heat, it made her shiver, seeing them kiss. Young love – so potent. Had it ever been like that between her and Harold, Laura wondered? There had always been admiration, loyalty, and mutual respect, but passion such as that she could not recall – had Harold ever been like that with anyone else?

Laura closed the bathroom door behind her. So Zelah was an illegitimate child, born in Cornwall in September 1917. She had grown up believing that her paternity was another casualty of the Great War, some fallen soldier in France. There had been so very many of them, after all. Laura sighed to herself and slipped away down the corridor, leaving the lovers to their embrace.

Laura knew Zelah's surname was Fitzlord. She knew the girl who'd looked after Harold was called Sarah. Did she dare ask Zelah what her mother's first name was? Laura shook her head, hurrying along. 'Oh Harold!' she said aloud, and tubby Mr Tonks, who'd just come out of the men's WC, gave her an odd look as he hoiked up his braces and started to re-button his overalls.

Laura pushed through the double doors and onto the factory floor. The thunder-heat assaulted her. A white-hot rivet arced like a spark and fizzed into a bucket of water. Gun barrels swung like ship's booms. The greasy floor was littered with the dirty rags they used to wipe down the machinery at the end of the shift. Laura thought of

Bruegel's 'Dulle Griet', a sixteenth-century painting of an army of peasant women pillaging hell: red–orange–black, and all those angry, scurrying figures. She passed the white shower of oxyacetylene sparks and remembered to step over the orange piping, coiled snakelike from the gas cylinders. Finally she made it through to the central lathe, where Vi waited, white-faced, sucking on a cigarette and leaning on a half-finished Bofors barrel.

'All right?' Violet yelled, and Laura could barely hear her voice above the machine noise.

Laura nodded and repositioned herself behind the canvas. Keep going, Laura. Come on. It won't paint itself, you know. Violet sank into position. Laura's eyes flicked from the girl herself to her painted equivalent, noticing the dark circles under Violet's eyes. Laura picked up her paintbrush. Should she paint in the evident exhaustion in the girl's face? Violet had crushed out her cigarette, and her hands lay still, exactly where they should be. But something was very wrong: the dark eye sockets, the faint mesh of frown lines over her forehead, even in repose, and the hard set of her jaw.

Laura mixed ochre with Prussian blue to create a hazy grey. The oil paint was slick as the machine grease that the girls slathered on the tools. And Laura was suddenly reminded of poor, dear Flora Munnings and how she'd looked that last time Laura had seen her alive, her beautiful face sheared with despair. Darling Flora. If only she'd realised, been able to help her, before it was too late. Was that what she was catching in Violet's eyes today? Despair?

Laura stepped back. The painting was so near to completion now. But – it was the faces; there was a hopelessness in those painted expressions. What was it Violet had said on that first day, when she'd demanded to sit for her?

Laura put down her brush.

'Can we talk?' Laura had to raise her voice to a shout to be heard above the factory noise. Violet nodded and broke out of the pose. Laura gestured towards the door.

It was time to sort a few things out.

Violet

'I'm fine,' Violet repeated.

'If you're fine, then I'm a monkey's uncle,' Dame Laura said. 'Come with me; I need to sketch you outside.'

At the top of the factory steps Dame Laura paused, looking out at the domino rows of grimy terraces. Double summertime diluted the colourless day like tea made from thrice-used leaves. 'The Meadows.' Dame Laura sighed. 'I remember when it really was all meadows round here.' And Violet thought, who cares? Some of us have got more important things to worry about than where people build houses. But she said nothing; she just let herself be led through side streets and snickets. 'The River Leen, the River Leen, not the Cut or the Trent, but something in between,' Dame Laura said, as the alleyway opened out to a patch of green dissected by a thread of water.

There was nobody about at this time in the evening, although the cigarette butts and glimmer of broken glass in the dewfall were evidence of a thousand lunch breaks for day shifters. There was a line of trees on one side, and to the other side the factory buildings blanked out half the pale grey sky. The river was a precious drizzle between steep banks, underwater weed like sopping hair.

'Where shall I stand? Or should I sit?' Vi said. There didn't seem anywhere obvious to go.

'All in good time. Walk with me a while, first. It's always good to be outside, get everything out in the open.'

There was something in the way she phrased it that pricked Vi's attention. Get everything out in the open? What did she want to find out? 'Why are we here, Dame Laura?' Vi said.

'Why do you think we're here, dear?'

'Well, if I knew, I wouldn't be asking, would I?'

'Don't take that tone. You know fine well.' Her skirts swished as she walked. 'Violet Smith, something is wrong. I cannot finish your portrait. You fidget and frown and disappear with no explanation. You look exhausted. I know you want this painting finished as quickly as I do. You told me you needed the money for something, remember?'

There was a pause. The two women continued walking along the path above the river. In the far distance, the rising prongs of the colliery chimneys coughed smoke. There was the sudden roaring shiver of a goods train passing just behind the trees.

'I cannot paint a decent portrait of you unless you give of

yourself. The painting won't work without honesty. I need you to be honest with me, Violet.'

'I am being honest.'

'No, you're not. You're not "fine" at all, are you? But whatever is bothering you, you think you can't tell an old woman like me, is that it?'

'It's not your age.'

'You can't tell a "respectable" woman like me, is that it? Worried I'll have a fit of the vapours or scurry off and tell tales to the King?' Vi shrugged. Dame Laura put a hand on Vi's arm, leant in, close enough so that Vi could feel her breath warm and moist on her cheek. 'It's a baby, isn't it, dear?' Vi nodded, and Dame Laura let go.

'Right, stand there. No, not there, over there, by the fence.' She pointed. 'That concrete is pale enough to capture the last of the light, if we're quick.'

Vi did as she was told and stood next to the fence. Wood panels were slatted in between concrete posts. The roughness snagged her coat. She stood still and looked out into the fading skies beyond the saw-edged factory rooftops.

Dame Laura put down her bag on the grass and pulled out a large notebook and a black stub of pencil. She didn't ask any more questions, but she talked as she worked, and Vi decided to listen, if only to drown out the voices inside her head – the voices that told her she was a silly tart and a slut and her life was over before it had even started.

'I knew a girl about your age called Flora,' Laura said. 'Before the last war. She had a kind of calm beauty. It was a long time ago – we were living in Cornwall, back then. We all wanted to paint her – all of us artists – and I suppose we were all a bit in love with her, too. She had this quality of lightness about her, you see? Like sunrise. You know how sunsets can be all showy and brash? But sunrise is understated and serene. Yes, that's the word: serene. She had a serenity about her.'

The drawing pad half-covered her face as she worked, hand skittering across the page, eyes flicking from the drawing to Vi, wrapping her in an invisible mesh of observation.

'This girl – Flora – she married an artist friend of mine. He was famous and wealthy, but also somewhat troubled. It's hard to explain. She should never have agreed to marry him, but a man like that can be terribly persuasive. And she was an aspiring artist herself, so she would have been in awe of his talent. But hero-worship is not necessarily a sound basis for a marriage,' Dame Laura said. She hesitated, then, cleared her throat, and her gaze shifted momentarily away from Violet and up into the darkening sky.

'Anyway, later on, after the marriage, she discovered she had fallen pregnant, which one would have supposed to be a cause for celebration. The problem was, it was not her husband's baby. The marriage had never been consummated. As I said, he was a troubled man and we were a tight-knit community, and we were all friends. Harold and I had even joined the couple on their honeymoon. We all knew that Flora and her husband were strangers, in the physical sense.'

Dame Laura paused again, pulled out a scalpel from her

bag, and sharpened the pencil with swift definite strokes. Violet kept as still as she could, although she was getting pins-and-needles in one leg. Dame Laura resumed her sketching.

'The terrible thing was that rather than endure the shame and scandal that this would have brought, the poor girl decided to end her own life. She killed herself. Arsenic poisoning. And I was the one who discovered the body. Of course I tried to revive her, but it was clearly too late – the body bloats and the stench is awful. So beautiful in life, and in death, so grotesque. And all because she was carrying a child that she didn't want. She felt she had no choice, I suppose, thought she'd squandered her one chance.'

Dame Laura looked up from the drawing. 'Do you ever feel like that, Violet?'

Violet nodded, not trusting herself to speak. Dame Laura held the drawing at arm's length and squinted at it. 'Yes, I feel I have caught you there,' she said, then closed the notebook. 'I can use that sketch to help complete the painting. There will be no further requirement for you to sit for me. I shall not need you again tonight, and I shall have the sitter's fee with you first thing in the morning. How would that suit you, Violet?'

'That would suit me very well,' Vi said, almost not believing what she'd just heard. She stamped her feet, trying to get rid of the painful tingling in her leg. 'I'd be in the pink if you could do that.' Dame Laura was going to give her the money! She could go back to Mrs Kirk. It wasn't too late. Everything would work out.

'The most tragic thing of all is that it was so needless,' Dame Laura went on, putting her pencil and notepad away in her bag. 'Dear Flora felt she had no choice. But she did have a choice. There were those very close to her who could have helped.'

'Who? You?' Violet said, walking back across the grass towards her.

'Come on, now, we should be getting back. Wasn't it good to get out into the open air?' the older woman said, not answering the question. 'Mind your step, this path will be slippery in those clogs, especially now the dew is falling. Let's get back to the night shift.'

Violet thought about the story she'd just heard. Dame Laura couldn't help that Flora girl, and she wished she had, and now she's helping me.

'Thank you,' Violet said, as they began to walk back towards the factory.

'Don't thank me, thank the War Artists' Advisory Committee, for giving us both a chance to deal with our mistakes,' Dame Laura said. And Violet didn't quite know what she meant, but she didn't care, because by this time tomorrow she'd be rid of the baby and life could get back to normal again, couldn't it?

Chapter 20

Zelah

'You'll be back for the wedding?' Zelah said, pulling away from the embrace.

'I'm only going to Malvern for the Easter weekend,' Laura replied, grappling with the heavy train door. 'I'm keen to get back as soon as possible and get the painting finished so you two lovebirds can fly off on your honeymoon.' She stepped up into the train, slammed the door shut behind her and pushed down the window, reaching out one of her bony hands for Zelah to take.

As they held hands Zelah looked into Laura's eyes and wondered how she'd managed to get so close to this old woman, whom she'd only known a few weeks. Perhaps that was why Laura was such a good portrait artist, Zelah thought, because people felt they could be their real selves when she was painting them. Perhaps all her models felt the same way. There was the sound of slamming doors and the hiss of steam from all along the platform – the train was about to leave. She gave Laura's hand a last squeeze and let her go.

Zelah followed along the platform, seeing Laura safely into her carriage. Through the glass she saw Laura smile and nod as she met her fellow passengers. An airman lifted her Gladstone bag into the netted luggage rack, two women with knitting shifted across to let her have the window seat, and a man with a newspaper lowered it half an inch and nodded as she sat down opposite him. She'll have sketched them all and heard all their life stories by the time the train reaches Birmingham, Zelah thought.

The engine growled and the train jolted forwards a notch. Laura looked out of the carriage window and, seeing Zelah, lifted a hand in farewell. Zelah put a palm onto the glass, wishing she could reach through and clasp Laura's hand again.

The guard's whistle shrieked; steam billowed. Zelah pulled her hand away and stepped back from the platform edge. The train began to move, and she watched Laura's seated figure shrink and slide from view as the train jerked and clattered out of the station. When the train had gone, the smoke and steam cleared, revealing an arch of blue sky between the two platform roofs. Zelah turned to go. The hand that had been on the carriage window was smeared with smuts. Zelah wrung her palms together, getting rid of most of the dirt, and started to walk slowly back towards the steps. A woman in a burgundy coat in front of her was tugging along a tearful little sandy-haired boy, his gulping sobs sounding loud on the empty platform. 'Nah then, you'll be all right, Teddy,' the woman said in a weary voice, but the boy continued to cry, stumbling along behind.

Zelah walked past them and started to climb the steps to the concourse. A couple coming down in the opposite direction were quarrelling openly, their bodies all sharp angles and their voices jabbing consonants: 'Dirty little slut,' the man spat out as they passed on the steps, and Zelah saw him try to grab the woman's arm, and how she wrenched herself free.

She walked out into the high-roofed concourse, where pigeons nestled and cooed in corners, and the mass of busy passengers nudged and sidestepped each other. She checked her watch as she walked. If she was quick she could catch the quarter past.

'Zelah!' She turned her head, not seeing at first.

'Zelah!' The shout came louder.

'George?' There he was, shove-running through the crowds towards her, his undone coat flapping. 'Excuse me,' she said, pushing forwards to meet him. 'I'm sorry, excuse me, could I pass, please?' shunting and apologising her way to meet him. She could see he was smiling, rushing towards her.

When they finally connected he grabbed her with both arms and swung her round: an orange-white-brown swirl of bricks and tiles and passengers – round and round and his lips on her neck and the damp-smoke swish of air and she laughed out loud, because it was madness. It was love and it was madness.

'I'm so glad I caught you! There's been a cancellation,' he said when he put her down. 'I've just been to the registry office and they can fit us in today, if we can make it there by half past.'

Zelah thought of Vi, and she thought of Laura and she held her breath and faltered. If they got married now then they'd miss having Vi and Laura there to witness it. She looked into George's face and took his hand in hers. 'George,' she began, seeing his smile start to fade at her hesitation. She started to turn away from him, towards the station's exit. 'We'll have to run pretty fast to make it there in time!'

They walked together past the tennis courts and up the hill, underneath the curly gas lights that punctuated the pavement until they reached his home – her home, now, she realised with a jolt. As he unlocked the front door, she leant across and kissed his neck, just below his earlobe, and smiled to herself as he fumbled with the key.

He held the door open and she stepped through the threshold. Once inside there was, as he'd predicted, a plate of sandwiches covered with a fly net in the centre of the polished wooden dining table. The door clicked shut behind them. 'I'll just—' He began to walk past her into the room.

She caught his coat sleeve. She didn't need to say anything. He turned. She reached her other hand up behind his neck. They twined together. Lips, skin, the taste of him, the feel of his hands against her. Sinking into the feeling, drowning in his touch. Two people with one pulse – time was away and somewhere else.

Later – afterwards – a strange feeling of being full and empty at the same time, exhausted and enervated. Her eyes scanned the bedroom: his hat on top of the chest of drawers, the clothes brush on the windowsill, pipe and ashtray on the bedside table, no pictures, just the window framing the green-terracotta-grey rectangle of the walled garden and sky. The low sun shot through the glass, and the room seemed to glow, picking out the colours: a blue dressing gown hanging from a hook on the back of the door, a book with a pale turquoise cover that had slipped off the gold eiderdown and lay half open on the sheepskin rug next to the bed. She breathed in, noticing how the pillowcase held the musky scent of him.

She heard a clock chime five times from the other room. 'I'll have to go, or I'll be late clocking on,' she said, frowning. It felt as if she were talking about someone else. Life was suddenly no longer what it was.

He leant over and kissed her bare shoulder. 'I can get to the factory in ten minutes if I put my foot down,' he said, and his lips began to move up her neck.

The sun was setting and the horizon a tarnished gleam as they stumbled up the factory steps hand-in-hand. They stopped at the top step, pausing to look out, as if the terracotta-grey evening fuddle of the Meadows was a glorious view, as if it were their joint future laid out in front of them in a golden glow. The dying light struck, flaring orange on the dirty brickwork and causing taped-up windows to diamond-flash. They hesitated, palms clenched, holding tight the secret of their togetherness. They were late – everyone else had already clocked on. She didn't care.

'When shall we tell them?'

'Tonight. I'll do an announcement at dinner break and get it over with in one go. And I'll sort out our leave – hang the production drive – our honeymoon starts from the end of this night shift.'

'I can't wait that long.'

'Just a few hours.'

'In the meantime, you may kiss the bride – again,' she said, turning to face him. As their lips touched, the night-shift bell began its drilling clang, but neither of them took any notice, as if the jarring sound was silent in the air as they kissed. And it was only when the ringing stopped that they finally, reluctantly, relinquished each other.

They turned away from the glow of the spring sunset and entered the factory. Inside, the familiar noise assaulted them. There was the usual metallic taste on her tongue and the air pepper-hot in her nostrils as they walked together under the electric strip lights and onto the shop floor.

Working here had made her part of the machinery – the thud and grind of it all – but without it she'd never have found him, her husband, her future. Still holding his hand, she leant in to give him one last kiss, not caring who saw. It was perfect.

Violet

'Have you got the money?'

'Yes.' Vi held out the fistful of notes and coins she'd been carrying. The woman put her still-lit cigarette on top of the parapet and slowly counted the money from Vi's hand into her own. As she did so, Vi looked out over the city garden, dug over, with lacy asparagus fronds and carrot tops poking out of the reddish earth. At the far end, where the vegetables petered out, a stone wall met the sky. Steel-grey clouds lifted to reveal a line of gold, where the sun had just sunk.

'You're short,' the woman said.

'What?' Vi felt as if her chest was being squeezed. It had to be enough; it was all she had. 'What about the deposit I paid Mrs Kirk already?' Vi told her the amount.

The woman sucked her teeth. 'She took that much, did she? I'll have to have words.' She tipped the money into an envelope, licked it, sealed it, shoved it down the cleavage of her sprigged day dress, and pulled her pink cardigan over the top to cover the bulge. She picked up her cigarette, knocked off the chimney of ash, took a quick drag and motioned Vi to follow her.

Inside, their shoes tapped on the tiled floor. Vi followed the woman along a corridor, past a loudly ticking grandfather clock and a wilting aspidistra and up a wide wooden-balustraded staircase that curved upwards. The woman's skinny buttocks shuddered underneath the thin cotton of her dress. Everywhere there were dark oil paintings of disapproving old men in heavy gilt frames, staring sternly down from the cream walls as they climbed the stairs. At the top they arrived at a large room shelved with dusty books.

'In there.' The woman pointed to an ante room. Behind her thick spectacles her eyes were glassy-round. 'He's ready for you.' Her pearl-drop earrings wobbled like just-shed tears as she ushered Vi into the reading room and closed the glass-panelled door behind her. Vi turned and saw her sit down at a desk opposite, stubbing out her cigarette in an ashtray and checking her watch. She'll be able to see, Vi thought. She'll be able to see everything.

The shutters were closed already, even though blackout wasn't until after nine. Vi walked into the gloom, hearing the muffled street sounds from below: the bell in the Town Hall chiming the half-hour, a burst of laughter, and the chug of a bus idling at the stop. The room was lined with books, just like the other one, only this one had a huge table in the centre, surrounded by red-seated chairs. There was an empty hearth with two green plush armchairs at the far end.

As Vi entered, a man stood up from one of the armchairs. He nodded at her, but didn't speak, just flicked a light switch, which turned on the electric chandelier, sending the room into sharp relief: the sagging bookshelves with rows of brown-spined books, like rotten smiles, and the huge plaster ceiling rose, like the top of an upside-down wedding cake.

He walked towards her, skirting the table. He was tall and thin, with dark hair plastered over his shiny skull. He held out a folded sheet. Vi helped him unfold it and flap it open so it lay on the table. He pulled some things out of a Gladstone bag: a length of orange rubber tubing that reminded her of the hose connecting the oxyacetylene cylinders on the shop floor, a piece of wire about as long as a ruler, and a metal contraption that looked a bit like two spoons fixed together. It was as if he were laying a table for a posh dinner with the cloth and the utensils: a supper for the pudding club – what's on the menu? Bun-in-the-oven! Vi felt a sound somewhere between a laugh and a scream rising in her throat. She clapped her hand over her mouth and gulped the hysterics away. Her palm was wet with sweat.

The man smoothed a wrinkle from the cloth with his long, thin fingers and cleared his throat. Then he took off his suit jacket and rolled up his shirtsleeves. He cleared his throat again and made direct eye contact with Vi. He didn't even need to speak. She knew what she had to do, to take off her knickers for the procedure.

The indecent procedure.

He turned away and she tugged her knickers down, had to hop awkwardly from one leg to the other and lean on a chair-back to get them off. She kicked them under the table, ready to pull back on afterwards.

'Shall I get up?' she said. He turned and nodded. So she climbed onto the table and lay down, on her back, with her arms crossed over her chest, hugging herself as if she were cold. The air smelled musty and old. A profile of a chubby-cheeked young woman was moulded in plasterwork on the ceiling rose, tendrils of hair playing over her plump neckline. She looks a bit like me, Vi thought, only happier.

The man tapped her legs. She knew she had to lift her knees. Her skirt fell away from her thighs, and she didn't push it back down. She closed her eyes and felt her fingertips dig into her upper arms as if they were someone else, grasping her by the shoulders, ready to give her a good shake.

She heard a soft swish as the man picked something up from the cloth. Then she felt something very cold, and hard, there, and her knees jerked inwards. The man made a kind of hissing sound as he sucked in his breath. She kept her eyes shut, but made herself open her knees again. There was the feel of cold metal, working its way up inside her. The man made a faint, audible grunt as the metal was stalled by the wall of flesh. Was that it, she thought, does he just scoop the baby out? Then there was a sharp pinch and she jerked again with the sudden shock of it. At the same time a thudding came from downstairs, a muted voice calling out from the street. 'Mrs Blair, open up. It's the fire watch! Mrs Blair! Mrs Blair!'

The metal pulled out, opening her eyes, the utensils already thrown into the bag and the bag snapped shut, the man pulling his jacket on and the woman banging open the glass door and shoving her off the table.

'Go, go! The Angel fire watch are early – you need to get out of here!' the woman hissed. She opened half a shutter and lifted the sash window, calling down onto the street, 'Hang on a sec. I'm on my way, lads.'

'Don't know why you don't let us have a key, it would be easier for you,' the voice wavered up.

'Oh, I can't be giving out keys, having all-and-sundry coming into the library,' she answered. 'I'll get the kettle on for you and I'll be right down.' She turned away from the window.

Vi was scrabbling under the table to try to find her knickers. She could hear the man's footfalls running a scale down the staircase and along the corridor. 'Get out! You want to get us all arrested, you silly tart?' The woman tugged her sleeve and shunted her away. 'Out the back, the way you came in!'

Out in the street it was twilight now, Old Market Square a monochrome smudge. Violet kept her hands pressed down the sides of her skirt. She could feel the cold air, there between the top of her thighs as she walked. What happened if it started now? She imagined blood spatters, grey-red on the paving stones.

There was a grimy pub wedged between two shops and an old feller was playing a penny whistle outside. Vi glanced apologetically at him and the empty cap open at his feet. If she'd had any change she would have shared. She had no money for a bus; she had given it all to that Blair woman, not even a soldered penny left to fool the clippie. The sound of the whistle wheedled along behind her, getting gradually fainter as she walked on.

What he'd done, that silent man in the library, had it been

enough? Was that all it was, a pinching jab up inside against the wall of flesh? Was that it? Nothing more? But then when would the bleeding begin? How long would it last? Would it hurt? Nobody had told her anything and there hadn't been a chance to ask.

She noticed a policeman, then, appearing from a side street as she walked down towards the canal. She felt as if she were sinking. But he couldn't know, could he? You couldn't tell just by looking at someone. Don't be a silly mare, Violet Smith. You're fine. You will be fine.

Except she'd just tried to kill her unborn baby and her knickers were under a table in the reading room at Bromley House Library. How is any of that fine? Oh heck. Vi faltered, scuffling her feet, waiting for the navy-blue figure to plod up the hill towards the town centre, his boots thudding at half the speed of her own sprinting heartbeat.

When he was out of earshot she started walking again, down the hill, and across the main road. The streets were almost empty already, blackouts shut, cats being kicked outdoors. She paused on the canal bridge, pulling out her fags and lighting one. The skies were clear. She sucked in smoke and put her hands on the sticky-cold metalwork of the bridge, trying to steady herself, but she couldn't stop shaking, and the cigarette slipped from her fingers into the inky gash of the canal – orange-black, then gone: extinguished.

She carried on walking, not knowing what else to do. A bus zoomed past. She didn't bother trying to hail it down. No point. No money. Shanks's pony. What if it started before she reached the hostel? Don't think about it, Vi. Keep walking. You'll be fine. It will all be fine.

She looked up at the way ahead. Some of the barrage balloons were silver, some white, like dead fish on the surface of a putrid pool. The moon shone above the rooftops the colour of amber, almost as dark as the fire opal ring that Zelah had on her left hand these days.

That's it. Think about Zelah, take your mind off it. You'll be maid of honour at the boss's wedding, Violet Smith, how very la–di–da. If – if you're not on the sepsis ward by then, you little slut. Shut up, shut up! The mess of inner voices was like the factory floor at the end of the shift: grubby and tangled.

Vi pushed her skirt down over her thighs as she walked, following the road over the railway lines. She could hear the distant rattle of stock in the factory sidings and felt a vibration in the tracks. The factory itself was somewhere up there to her right, through the terraced streets of the Meadows, huddled huge in the darkness.

If she carried on walking she could cross the Trent at the old toll bridge and get to the hostel through Wilford Village. She remembered how Dame Laura had taken them to Wilford on their day off to sketch them.

She passed a solitary ash tree that had shoved its way up between the paving slabs. *Knickerless girls should never climb trees,* that's what Pa used to say. Her throat tightened as she thought of her father. What would he say if she knew what a mucking muddle she was in? He could never know. Nobody could. The shame of it.

She reached the corner where Rupert Street joined the main road, and she paused before crossing. As she stopped, she heard the faintest tootle-whine of the penny whistle, way back behind her.

And that's when it started.

George

'What's all this?'

'Your wedding breakfast, Mrs Handford.' He looked at her face as he said it, watched her eyes widen, lips lift into a smile at the two plates of fried Spam sandwiches and two mugs of tea on the table. A lit candle in an empty beer bottle stood in between. The rest of the canteen was empty as a desert. He held her chair back and helped her into her seat. 'I thought you might be hungry, as we skipped supper.'

'Ravenous.' She took a huge bite of sandwich. He sat opposite and felt her feet slide in between his. There were two mugs and two chairs and two people with one pulse as they sat together, wolfing the food, feet in an unseen embrace beneath the table.

They hadn't told anyone about the wedding, yet. The secret lay delicious as a stolen kiss between them. But after the night shift she could come back to his bed. He'd sort out the rota, find a way of getting them away on honeymoon, take her up to Northumbria to meet his family. A fresh start. Life was suddenly no longer what it was.

From behind the distant counter came the smell of braising offal and the clatter of saucepans. The radio waltz spouted out of the trumpet-shaped speakers in the corners of the canteen like water from a rock.

'A table for two. However did you manage it?'

'I had a word with the boss.' He winked.

'I hear he's a one. All he cares about are production targets. Bit of a brute, by all accounts.' Her teasing eyes as she looked across at him. Her tongue flicked out to catch a crumb from her lip. And he couldn't help thinking of her mouth, her kiss and the sweet, sweet taste of her when they'd been together, just a few hours ago.

'I heard that too. Apparently the man's a good-for-nothing swanker.' He grinned, took a gulp of tea, watched her lick her fingers one by one.

The candle flickered between them, making the space glow. He had a strange sensation of being neither up nor down. And he knew he'd remember this moment for the rest of his life.

'Will there be speeches at this wedding reception?' she asked, tilting her head, breaking his reverie.

'Naturally.' He stood up. 'I'd like to raise a glass to my wife, Zelah, whom I love more than I can say.' He looked at her, there, with her dark, sharp eyes, arched brows and curving mouth. 'I neither wanted, nor felt I deserved, a second chance. But then you came along, and changed everything. I love you, Zelah.'

'I love you too, George.' She stood up, then, her eyes

almost on a level with his, and they stayed still, as the clock forgot them. Time was away and she was here.

'Aren't you gonna toast 'is Majesty?' A voice from the far end of the room – Mrs Hoyden, rattling out from the kitchen with the cutlery trolley.

The spell was broken. They grinned at each other. 'The King,' they said in unison, picking up their half-drunk tea mugs and chinking them.

He noticed then that the music had changed, from the waltz to something else. It was Vera Lynn's voice: *'There were angels dining at the Ritz . . .'*

Mrs Hoyden disappeared back into the kitchen. George put down his mug. The candle flame flickered as Zelah walked round, pulled him into the space between the dining tables and the counter and put her arms round him. They moved closer together – his lips on her cheek, the softness of her skin, the scent of her hair. 'I never dance,' he said, swaying in sync with her, feeling her soft curves pressing through the layers of cloth between them as they moved to the music.

'But you must have the first dance with your bride at the wedding breakfast,' she said.

'I suppose I could get used to being manhandled by you,' he muttered, his lips finding hers. He ran his hand down her spine and pulled her closer towards him. And Vera Lynn sang: *'Our homeward step was just as light as the tap dancing feet of Fred Astaire . . .'*

A sudden crash of strings. Beethoven's Fifth slamming

violently into the airwaves. She pulled away from him. 'Was a raid drill part of the wedding breakfast plan?'

'It's not a drill,' he said, loosening his arms from around her. 'You need to get down to the shelter.'

'And you?'

'I can't. I can't have young Alfie Perkins up on the roof on his own, not if it's the real thing. I'm sorry.'

She nodded and pulled away, but he caught her hand and they walked through the canteen doors together. Mrs Hoyden and the canteen staff were already clattering down the corridor.

At the stairwell they paused for a final kiss. 'You will go straight to the shelter, won't you?' She didn't answer. Beethoven's Fifth was still sawing violently out through the wall speakers. 'Promise me, Zelah?'

He saw her open her mouth to reply, but didn't hear her response because just then there was a tearing thud and all the lights went out.

Violet

In the still night air the whistle was suddenly overcome by the sound of sirens. And she realised that the humming drone she'd thought of as the sound of the distant gun factory when she crossed the railway lines was increasing in volume – not machine chatter at all, but the thrum of approaching bombers.

She hesitated on the street corner, as the siren sounds reached their aching crescendo. To go to a public shelter in this state – with no knickers on – was unthinkable. But how long would it take to get to the hostel from here? The sirens keened. A dog began to howl in a nearby backyard, underlaid by the incessant buzz of the incoming planes. If she ran to the factory now she could pull on her overalls before going down to the shelter.

Vi put a palm up against the rough brickwork of the wall beside her, below an empty hanging basket, still hesitating, even though the dark-noise was everywhere now. What to do?

Then the tear-sheet noise of the first bomb falling, the burst of light in the distance, the sound of shouting, running feet, fire watchers' whistles. They fell in a line, the incendiaries: one-two-three, like the bad fairy casting her curses at the royal baby's christening.

The sirens had stopped now the raid had started, and Violet stood transfixed, listening to the crackling-twig sound of distant machine gunfire, the boom of the ack-ack guns and the patter of shell splinters like fine rain.

And for a moment Violet was back in time, in the Blitz-months of '41, when she was still sweet-sixteen-and-never-been-kissed and lived at home and helped Ma with the washing and the little ones. She'd been hungry and tired and scared all the time. But it had been better than this: up the duff, in the pudding club, miles from home.

Another crash, closer this time. The hanging basket jerked

backwards and forwards above her and the ground shuddered. She turned, then, down Rupert Street, half-blinded by the flashing incendiaries, hearing the fire engine bells' and ambulance bells' jarring melody as the first wave of bombers zoom-droned away. But she could hear another wave already coming in. If she ran, she might make it to the factory shelter before they hit.

Her panting breath was sand-scratchy in her throat as she took the factory steps at a sprint. Her eyeballs still burnt from the on-off of bright light and darkness as the bombs fell. The security guard wasn't at his post and the lights were all off inside the building. She zigzagged along the empty blackness of the corridor, and straight to the cloakroom, ripping off her coat, slinging it on the floor, feeling her way, and pulling her overall off the peg. She struggled into the grimy cloth and pushed through the door, along the corridor and onto the shop floor. The shelter was down at the far end of Bay Three. They'd all be inside, now. The equipment was a mass of shadows in the gloomy space. She had to stop running or she'd trip, bash into something. Jesus, but those planes were loud now, even from inside the factory building, like a swarm of hornets, everywhere.

She just had to make her way across the shop floor to the shelter and she'd be safe. What was that? A figure, up ahead, near the capstan lathes? 'Hey,' Violet called out. 'Hey, you! Shouldn't you be under cover?' And the shadowy figure seemed to turn, but then there was a sudden blast of light.

A thunderclap roar and the sense of fast-moving air. Black,

then bright light, then darkness again – the ripping crash of it, then silence.

She groped, unseeing, until her fingers connected with something soft. 'I've got you,' she said, tugging at the cloth, but there was no answer from the lumpen mass of overall-covered limbs.

Her eyes were streaming; the smoke hot-acrid in her nostrils. Coughs razored up her parched throat.

The site of the fire was further in. Through squinted lashes she could make out the orange glow at ground level. If the flames reached the gas cylinders they'd be done for, but the flames hadn't reached the cylinders – not yet – and there was still a chance she could pull the woman to safety.

She wedged her clog against the edge of a lathe base for leverage, and heaved at the sleeve cuff she held. The body shifted an inch or two, but didn't pull free. She yanked, harder this time, but the body was heavy as a wet sandbag, caught on something. If only she could see – but the smoke was hot-thick. She slid down onto the concrete floor. She'd have to feel her way. She could hear sirens, and shouts calling her away, but the sounds were muffled as birdsong beyond a window pane, as she focused on her task.

She crouched low, feeling her way down the length of the overalls: strap, waist button, side pocket, trouser leg – nudging and shoving at the inert form as she went – all the way down. Here it was: a foot caught up in one of the twirling gas hoses.

Her fingers twisted the looping rubber, unhooking it from the woman's foot, tugging her leg free. At last.

The boiling air was quicksand, pooling and sucking and swallowing them up. She had to get them both out, fast. She had to get them down to the shelter, in case the fire spread and the whole thing blew.

She shuffled back, following the line of the overalls with her fingertips. She grabbed at the shoulder straps, and pushed her foot again against the lathe. She strained and wrenched, the cloth cutting into her palms.

This time the body moved, and she followed the momentum, jerking and tugging and pulling it out, along the factory floor, away from the flames. Her breath came in grunting gasps, painful, as the heat seared her lungs. There was sweat and tears in her eyes, and a metallic taste in her mouth. The woman's head jolted awkwardly over the concrete floor, but there was no time to take care. There was no time.

Suddenly there were hands at her shoulders, shouting voices, and the woman's body was pulled away, backwards, towards the shelter door: *We've got her, now get inside, for God's sake.*

No, wait.

She saw the easel, the canvas pale against the orange-grey glow of the growing fire. The painting was so close to completion: those butter-smooth faces that had taken weeks to create. She broke free of the hands that grabbed her.

It will only take a second to get the painting.

She turned and ran back towards the flames.

Chapter 21

Laura

The air tasted clean on her tongue. It reminded her of Cornwall, and she turned to say so to Harold, catching the sleeve of his tweed jacket, the wool warm in the spring sunshine.

'It's nothing like Cornwall; we're nowhere near the sea,' he said, wheezing a little after the steep climb from the hotel.

'But it feels like a cliff top, don't you think?' Laura looked at the Malvern Hills, snaking into the distance like a sleeping sea serpent, and the cloud-dappled fields below, undulating like lapping waves on a calm day. 'Don't you think, Harold?'

'Mmm,' he said, which could have meant anything. She let go of his sleeve.

'So long since our Cornwall days,' Laura continued as they gazed down at the flat farmland stretched over three counties. 'Do you ever think of them?' She turned her head so that she could see his expression as he responded, noting the strong line of his profile, his aristocratic nose – could she be mistaken about Zelah?

'Not really,' Harold said, leaning on his walking stick. 'Half a lifetime ago.'

'Remember Sennen?' Was it her imagination, or did his expression shift? 'So beautiful. I was utterly bereft when I had to leave in '16.' The air was butterscotch-scented with gorse blossom. She waited a moment, to give Harold a chance to respond, but he continued leaning on his stick, looking away. 'I missed you so dreadfully when I was at Witley Camp. It was the first time we'd been apart for any length of time. I felt utterly cut adrift and alone.'

'You had plenty of boisterous young Canadian soldiers for company, as I recall.'

'Were you jealous?'

'Not a bit.'

'Why not?'

'I trusted you. What is a marriage, without trust?'

What indeed, Laura thought. A crow cut the sky in front of them like a plummeting exclamation mark.

'Were you lonely?'

'I remember Ella swinging by to check up on me. Look here, I don't really want to rake up old coals, Laura.' He shifted, banging his stick down into the soft, mossy grass.

'Was it Ella who dismissed the girl?'

'What girl?'

'The girl I'd employed to look after you – Sarah, wasn't it?'

'I really can't recall.'

302

'Why did Ella dismiss Sarah? What had she done?'

'Nothing – I think she left of her own volition.' So he did remember Sarah. He remembered and yet he'd affected forgetfulness. 'I don't remember Ella giving her the sack. Why would she? In any case, Laura, you're talking about things that took place twenty-five years ago—'

'Twenty-seven years ago,' Laura interrupted. 'It was twenty-seven years ago that Sarah left you in Sennen.'

Harold made an impatient gesture. 'Twenty-seven, then. I really don't understand why this is so important just now, Laura. Can't we enjoy the view in peace?'

Despite the sunshine, the wind was cool on Laura's cheeks. She noted how he dug his stick further into the earth, how his brow jutted where he was frowning. 'If we'd had children they'd be grown up by now,' Laura said. 'And they'd be off doing war work of some sort. If we'd had a girl she might even be working in a factory.' She saw his fist tighten on the top of his stick, but he didn't say anything. She sighed, waited: nothing. 'Well, I think I'll head on up to the top. Are you coming?'

Harold shook his head.

Laura walked on up the path, her sturdy brogues squashing angular pebbles into the mud as she went. Onwards and upwards, Laura, just keep going on. Her chest felt tight and her breath came in bursts. Her cheeks were hot with the effort of it.

At the top, the ancient earthworks spiralled under the blue dome of sky. It was quiet, nothing but birdsong and the faint ringing in her ears, an echo of the factory machines. Here in the open air she felt alive, and free. She looked down the incline to where Harold still stood, a nub of charcoal against the sage hillside. Below him were the grey curling roads and slate rooftops of the British Camp Hotel. They looked so insignificant from up here: her husband and her wartime home. Harold was nothing more than a small and definite focal point in the green-blue vista. He seemed so far away. But hadn't he always seemed far away? Or had she herself put the distance between them?

Laura heard laughter and looked in the direction it came from. There was a couple, some five hundred yards away on the ridge line, holding hands, the woman's white skirt swirling, their mirth carried effortlessly on the blue hilltop wind. And then, from far below, church bells began to peal. Of course: it had said on the wireless that the bells were allowed to be rung for Easter Sunday. It sounded like a wedding. She looked back down at Harold, and suddenly she was certain. But she had to ask him, get it all out in the open air. Because if it were true, well, that changed everything, didn't it?

Laura saw Harold turn his back and begin to make his way down to the hotel. 'Harold, wait!' she started, stumbling down the steep path.

He turned his head, called back: 'I was getting cold waiting for you,' the wind carried his words up the hill to her – she could only just hear them above the jangling church bells.

Did Sarah keep you warm, Harold? Did Sarah keep you

warm on those cold cliff-top nights in Sennen whilst I was away in Witley? Did Sarah make sure you didn't get cold waiting for me? Her feet slip-thudded on the muddy path. It was too steep to run. She couldn't catch up. She couldn't catch up with Harold. She'd never been able to catch up with him – he'd never let her.

She finally reached him at the road junction in front of the hotel: too close. People could see and hear them from here, and she didn't want to cause a scene. No, she wasn't one for airing her dirty linen in public, no matter what anyone said. They crossed the road together. The bells were still ringing as they entered the hotel reception. The hall was crowded with suitcases and Kipper yapped, tried to bite Harold's walking stick. Upstairs, she thought. When we are in the privacy of our own top-floor room, with its thick walls, that's when I'll ask.

As they passed the reception desk, the telephone jangled and Mr Peterson answered. 'Yes, she's just here, as a matter of fact, so you can tell her yourself.' He motioned at Laura. 'Call for you, Mrs Knight.'

Laura took the receiver and held it to her ear. There was a hiss-crackle; the line was very bad and she could hardly hear. 'Laura Knight speaking,' she said, watching Harold being swallowed up by the gloomy hotel corridor, sucked up the dark wooden staircase, out of sight. She didn't want to take this call. She wanted to talk to Harold, to find out the truth. For heaven's sake, what could be so very important that it necessitated a phone call on Easter Sunday?

'Is that Mrs Knight?' the voice sounded metallic and far away.

'Yes, yes. What is it?'

'I'm afraid there's been a terrible incident at the gun factory.'

George

Fatigue fell across his mind as he roboted his way through the street of gutted houses. There was no rain, but the fogged air seeped damp and the sky was a mucky pink wound above the snaggled rooftops. A grey-faced fireman was slumped half-asleep on a pile of rubble. A fat man in a Homburg and a brown suit was heaving along the crumbled paving slabs towards him. George paused in front of the fireman, jowls wobbling as he began to talk and gesticulate. He saw the fireman nodding, opening his mouth to speak, and realised he couldn't hear the man – couldn't hear either of them – even though he couldn't have been more than a few yards away. His ears were full of a kind of muted clang, and the world was a silent film.

An old woman tottered out from the remains of a side street: black coat and the crumpled cardboard expression of someone too tired to speak. She joined the fireman and the fat man, nodding and looking at where they pointed. Then the three of them suddenly all turned at once, heads swivelling like ball bearings on a production line. George followed their gaze and saw a half-destroyed wall finally fall, with a clumsy slither and a puff of dust. But he heard nothing. He saw heads rotate in the opposite direction, felt a rush of wind at his back, and turned to see an ambulance speed past. But the ringing of the ambulance bell was silent in the morning air, drowned out by the sound inside his head.

And there was a girl running down the street, in the same direction the fat man had come from, ankles turning inwards on high heels, orange turban coming loose, one end flapping against her cheek as she ran, exposing a patch of dark hair. For a moment, just a moment, he thought it might be *her* – by some glorious divine sleight of hand – but of course it wasn't.

He watched as she joined the little group: the fireman, the old lady and the fat man. 'They got the gun factory?' He saw her mouth it, even though he couldn't hear. The others nodded and he watched as her hands slapped up to her face, covering her eyes, as if by not seeing the darkness of the smoking pile it would cease to exist.

He walked on then, trudging in the wake of the long-gone ambulance. Police were patrolling the streets, stern-faced, their navy-blue uniforms with shiny buttons looking like patches of the night sky, ripped off and left behind by the planes that had torn through in the night. The early morning fog mingled with the remains of the smoky air, drenching his face smutty-wet as he went. Even this early, cheap Union Jack flags were already appearing in the windows of half-bombed houses, and women were sweeping glass into gutters. Small shopkeepers hammered boards across broken windows. An angry robin eyed him from a cracked gatepost.

There was less bomb damage across the canal. Buses trundled and cycles wheeled as usual. He saw the puffed cheeks of a man whistling as he carried a ladder across the street, but heard nothing but the endless muffled ringing in his ears.

He followed the road round the underbelly of the castle, through the alley and into the Park Estate. By the old stables he saw the woman with the terrier. She put a hand on his sleeve and he winced at her touch. Her lips rubber-banded empty words, as she gesticulated – up at the sky, over in the direction of the Meadows, down at the ground. Her dog snuffled at the kerb. George lifted his hat and walked away, leaving her chattering dumbly to herself.

The world was a slowed-up roundabout, turning, turning. His eyes slid up and around to the Nottingham General, clinging to the near hillside, ambulances clustered like maggots feasting on decay. Everything continued its lazy spin. Eventually his feet would hit hard ground and he'd have to drop off the ride.

He was nearly home, now.

Splinters of glass in the pads of his fingers – a sharp, searing pain as he twisted the key in the lock. The cat appeared at the step. He saw it open its mouth: sharp, pink-white – but he could hear no mew. He went inside, slamming it out.

The house was as they'd left it. In the bedroom the bed was unmade, rumpled sheets like a mountain range. He threw his hat in the direction of the chest of drawers, not bothering to check where it landed, and sat down on the bed. His fingers stung as he fumbled with his laces. He kicked off his shoes, then unpeeled his clothes, suddenly aware of all the cuts and grazes that hadn't hurt, until now.

Naked, he slipped under the cold sheets.

This was where they had lain, he and his wife. His jaws felt as if they were clamped in a vice as he lay, remembering. She'd been here. They'd been together, here, not more than a dozen hours ago. He nuzzled his face in the pillow, aching for the scent of her, but smoke clogged his nostrils and all he could smell was the staleness of spent flames.

Violet

The coughing wouldn't stop: great heaves that made her feel as if her chest were being ripped open, her throat shredded. She opened her eyes. She needed something to drink, to quench the tearing roughness. She had the impression of something white and light, but with each cough her eyes screwed up again and it was hard to see. She could feel that she was in a bed, but the impression she got through her watery-eyed squint was that this was not the room in the hostel. The coughs subsided for a moment and she saw that there were other beds, white walls. Her head throbbed as she turned. A glass of water on the locker top, thank God. She reached out for it, but there was something on her hands, bound up like baby's mitts, and the glass flew from her clumsy grasp, off the locker top and onto the tiled floor, smashing.

She tried to get up, to clear up the mess, struggling against the tight constrict of bed sheets, her bandaged hands useless. As she lifted her torso upright her head thudded and the room spun and the awful coughing started again, ripping down her throat, making her whole body spasm and jack-knife.

Something was shoved behind her, hands pushing her backwards. The coughing began to lessen, but the room was a dizzying rush. Then the cool feel of a metal beaker against her lips. It hurt, bee-sting raw as the water ran down her parched throat, but thirst was stronger than pain and she drank the whole glass, wincing at each gulp. How it hurt, how it soothed. She coughed a little more, sputtering water over the tight, white sheet. A hand rubbing between her shoulders.

The coughing stopped. The world ceased turning. But there was a noise in her head like bluebottles.

She could see where she was, now. Pale, quiet and vast: a hospital ward. Motionless lumps under other beds stretched away in ranks towards double doors at the far end. She watched the figure of a nurse crouch on the floor, sweeping up the shards of glass into the dustpan, taking out the big grey-headed mop and wiping the puddle of water away. There was the sweet-acid smell of disinfectant as she pulled the stringy tendrils over the wet tiles. The woman was small and contained, her cleaning was done with swift, compact movements. She checked the watch she had clipped onto her uniform and her mouth moved, but Vi couldn't hear what was said above the buzzing sound inside her head.

The mop bucket banged against the nurse's leg as she walked off. The windows were a line of identical blue rectangles, stretching away. Vi's head felt as if it were stuck in a vice, but she found that if she moved her head whilst it still rested on the pillow, the dizziness didn't happen. When she pressed her lips together it hurt, and there was something slathered on them, glutinous and medicinal. She swallowed – her saliva tasted odd: putrid. *Where am I? What am I doing here?* The nurse had gone. There was nobody to ask. At the far end, by the double doors, someone's arms flailed, blankets jerked, and a sheet slid onto the floor. Nobody came, and the bed sheet stayed on the floor, like a white puddle.

She waited. A distant plane flew past the windows. She looked down at how her bandaged hands rested on the line where the sheet and grey blanket met. She tried to lift her knees but the bed sheets were pulled too tight for her to move properly. There was a clipboard attached to the bedstead at the far end, but she couldn't see what was written on it, couldn't reach it without risking the petrifying dizzy-rush again, probably wouldn't be able to grab it properly if she could, what with these bandaged paws.

Why was she here? Why and how? She remembered running down a dark wooden staircase. Had she fallen? No, it wasn't that. She remembered sprinting blindly in the darkness, the incandescent splashes of incendiaries. Then, nothing. And now she was here, in hospital.

The woman in the next bed rolled over and looked at her with large, sad, cow-like eyes. 'Is this the sepsis ward?' Vi said aloud, clarity like a bursting bubble. But her voice was just a vibration, even though she could feel the warm air rushing up her throat as she spoke. The woman blinked and turned away.

The double doors at the far end banged open, and the nurse came back, scurrying up towards her bed, mouthing empty words. She smiled as she got close: crooked front teeth and eyes that turned down at the corners.

'Is this the sepsis ward?' Vi said, every syllable an effortful hiss.

The nurse shook her head, made a nervous gesture and came in very close. She is younger than me, Vi thought, noticing the pimple on her chin, her unlined features. Violet lip-read: 'This is the burns unit.' The nurse bit her lip, smoothed an invisible wrinkle from the bedcovers above Vi's belly and straightened up: 'Your baby is fine, Miss Smith.'

Chapter 22

Laura

Despite it all, they carried on. Canvas had been jimmied up to cover holes in the roof and walls. Cables snaked from a buzzing generator to enormous standard lamps.

'Remarkably intact, structurally – but that's sometimes the way with the delayed devices because they come in cleanly. The machinery's all gone for a burton, of course,' Laura heard a man in a hard hat say to another with a white coat, as she passed by. Neither man seemed to notice her, and nor did anyone else, as she floated like a ghost through the rubble and debris. It was only when she perched on a pile of broken pallets and took out her sketchbook that heads turned. She glimpsed hands held up to whisper behind, nods in her direction, and, eventually, they began to approach, leaving their tasks of sweeping or wiping tools or heaving broken equipment to one side. They came to see what she was doing, and to talk.

She only had chalk, charcoal and her miniature water-colour set with her, but it was enough. Throughout the night faces swam in and out of focus, pale and weary against the backdrop of mangled metal and dust. Voices were urgent, disjointed, not seeming to match the lips that mouthed the words:

Is that you, Dame Laura?

So lucky you missed it!

I'd had to miss me shift because Jimmy was ill, thank God.

You don't expect it, do you, not here – meant to be safe – they even sent evacuees to Nottingham.

I've not seen 'owt like it since '41.

I heard she'd just married Mr Handford in secret – you know they were engaged – they were in the canteen just before, Mrs Hoyden said.

He'd taken leave for their honeymoon. Such a shame.

They said it could have been worse. If that delayed whatsit had been a few feet further over it would have had the whole shelter, not just the entrance.

It's just a shock!

The beginning of the end of the war, they said on the wireless, and now this.

Isn't it terrible?

And your painting, too. They said she was going back for it, that other girl, the one who survived.

Violet Smith, wasn't it?

Shifting in and out of her vision, faces like waxing and waning moons, the equipment silent for once, as if hibernating, the voices coming and going, lapping like waves on the shore. Laura kept her hand moving over the paper, flicking the page after each sketch and on to the next, drawing on and on, capturing the disbelief and fear: the crumpled faces, the broken machines; the crumpled machines, the broken faces. Sheet after sheet she filled, as if somehow the magic of her charcoal lines could cast a spell over the grief and destruction. But like the good fairy at the end of Sleeping Beauty's christening, there wasn't much she could do, no matter how rapidly she waved her wand, no matter how good her intentions; the damage was done, the curse was set, and the only cure would be time.

She was almost down to the last sheet in her sketchpad when a short, dark-haired girl sidled up. 'Terrible,' she said. 'I didn't know the others that died, but I knew Miss Fitzlord. She was a kind lady, so she was.' Laura began to draw the girl, almost reflexively, although by now her arm was aching and her wrist stiff.

'You knew Miss Fitzlord?'

'She was covering my shifts for me, so's I could come back to work. I was off – off sick with my glands.'

'You weren't here when it happened?' She had a sharp little face, the girl, all angles and shadows, but there was a melancholy dulling her eyes.

'No. I only came back to work tonight – to this!' She gestured around, taking in the flapping khaki canvas, the scaffolding struts, the jagged hole in the floor, cordoned off with canteen chairs, and the piles of rubble and shrapnel in the corners, waiting to be carted away. 'Though they say they want to start production again soon – for the war effort. Anyways, I only came by because I found this when I was sweeping up over there and I thought you might want it, seeing as it's yours.'

Laura put down her sketchpad and charcoal to see what the girl held out. It was a triangular scrap of canvas, no bigger than a folded napkin, rough cloth on one side and smooth, dried oil paint on the other. The edges were charred. It took a moment for Laura's eyes to re-focus as she looked: something painted pale cream and a black smudge – it was an eye, the eyebrow arching like a wing, the eye itself such a dark brown that it was hard to make out where the pupil ended and the iris began.

Zelah: all that was left of her.

Laura thanked the girl, who went back to her sweeping over the far side of the factory. Laura put the scrap of painted face in her skirt pocket. She packed her sketchbook, chalk and charcoal in her bag and prepared to leave. Nobody noticed her go.

Outside, on the factory steps, the sun had already risen, a golden ring, struggling up through the wan skies above the Meadows. It was tomorrow already, and there were things to do.

Was she in the right place? The room stretched out, vast, in front of her: lines of metal bedsteads and windows too high to see anything from except oblongs of sky – pale grey and empty. She began to walk, passing the immobile mounds under bed sheets, faces pink daubs and eyes dark dots, one after the other, after the other, as she went on. Keep on going, Laura. On, on.

The far end, they'd said, near the fire escape. The yellow heads of the daffodils trembled in her right hand and her bag dragged down her shoulder on the left-hand side. She tried not to look to the left or the right, not to catch any glimpse of raw crimson, oozing ochre, scabbed burgundy. The sharp scent of surgical spirit was in her nostrils, and something else, too, dank and sweet.

On the far right, by the wall, that would be her: brown hair spilling onto the pillow. It was impossible to see her face from here, impossible to see the extent—

See her, and then go. Do what you need to do and then get away from this tragedy, this unholy pain.

There was a wide aisle of lino between the ranks of beds, but Laura felt as if she were walking along a thin plank of wood, like she had that time at the Regent Theatre, that time when the stage manager had convinced her to climb up above the stage, to draw the performance from up high. She remembered the bare and narrow board, and just a wobbly iron rail to cling to, and then a gap in the planking a whole yard wide, right above the centre of the stage where the play was going on ('The Barretts of Wimpole Street', wasn't it?). She must have been twenty feet above the performers, in her slippery shoes. How did she ever cross that gap? How had she found the courage to step over the void?

Don't look left, don't look right, and whatever you do, don't look down, Laura.

She was close to the end of the ward now. Violet had turned on the pillow to watch her approach. Laura's chest felt tight and hard. She lifted her mouth at the corners and waved the bunch of daffodils, feeling the old newsprint they were wrapped in begin to tear soggily apart in her palm. Violet waved back. Her hands were bandaged, like boxing gloves. Laura could see that although Violet had hair on the left-hand side of her head, the right side was bald, and a huge dressing cut across her forehead. And her face, her pretty china-milkmaid's face, how had that fared?

Closer now. Almost there.

Stride out and bridge that gap, Laura.

Violet's face on the right-hand side was blush-red as a pot of rose madder pigment. But not damaged. Not disfigured, just raw. Laura let out a breath. Thank God. Her footfalls came to a halt at the bedside.

'Hello, Violet, dear.' Laura leant across and kissed the girl on her left cheek – the good cheek. There was the smell of dirty hair and disinfectant. Laura pulled away.

There was a jug on the bedside locker, so Laura put down her bag and busied herself with ripping the paper from the flowers and putting them in water, fiddling with the blooms so that they splayed out symmetrically. 'If you can't get out into the open air, then I thought I should bring some of the spring in to you.' False cheer. Distraction. But what else to do except keep going, Laura. Keep on going.

The newsprint had left inky marks on her hands so she rubbed them together. Then she took off her hat. 'Windy out,' she said, putting a hand up to her hair to check that her 'earphones' hadn't come loose. She put the hat on the bed knob by Violet's feet.

'Thank you.' Violet's voice was barely more than a whisper. Laura thought of waves raking a pebbled beach.

'Not at all, dear. How are you feeling?'

'I'm sorry, I can't hear very well. It's coming back, but you'll have to speak up.'

Laura perched on the side of the bed, taking care not to jostle any part of Violet's body. Who knew what the extent of her burns were? 'They say you're recovering well,' she said, leaning in so Violet could hear. 'They tell me that the baby is going to be fine.'

Violet didn't answer. At least the girl was alive, and she wasn't on the sepsis ward. One had to be thankful for such things.

'Has anyone visited?'

'Mr Simmons.'

'But not Mr Handford?'

Violet shook her head.

'And Mr Simmons told you—'

'About Zelah? Yes, he told me.' Violet looked away. Her voice was just a breath.

'I'm so sorry,' Laura said. She wanted to embrace the poor girl, or at least hold her hand, but everything was either red-raw or swaddled up. 'You must be gasping for a ciggie,'

Laura said, looking at Vi's bandaged fingers. 'Want me to help you with one?' Laura began to fiddle with the catch on her handbag – she had a fresh packet in there somewhere.

'Not allowed,' Violet whispered. 'My lungs.'

'I see, yes, silly me. Inhaling all that burning air must have caused some damage—' She broke off, shifted on the bed-covers. 'Still, it won't be long before that changes, I'm sure. And you'll get more visitors, during your convalescence, I shouldn't wonder.'

Fractured ribs, burns, lung damage from breathing in the boiling air and smoke. But Violet had got off lightly, all things considered. Of course if she hadn't been so late for her shift she would have been in the shelter with the others. She should have been there. So should Zelah – why hadn't she been in the shelter?

'You saved me.' Violet's hoarse voice interrupted her thoughts. Laura looked at her, the scabbed lips mouthing those words. 'I was going back for the painting when the delayed device went off. That's what saved me from going the same way as Zelah, and the others, Mr Simmons said.'

Violet started to cough, then, a hacking wheeze. And there was no water to be had, because Laura had stupidly put the daffodils in the jug. You silly old woman, Laura. It's all your fault. She tried pouring some of the daffodil water into a beaker and helping Violet to sip at it, but she must have tipped the water at too acute an angle, or the daffodil stems had tainted it, or something, because Violet choked even more, spraying water and spittle all over the bed sheets.

'Nurse,' Laura yelled, pushing herself off the bed and beginning to run back along the ward towards the nurses' station. 'Nurse!'

A scowling, angular woman emerged from the nurses' station, elbowed her aside and bustled along to Violet's bed. Laura followed on behind, and by the time she reached the bed the nurse had already done something, and Vi's coughs were subsiding. 'Who put those in there?' She waggled a skinny forefinger at the daffs.

'I'm sorry.'

The nurse tutted and scissored away up the ward.

'Are you all right?' Laura said.

'Not supposed to talk.'

'Sorry. I shouldn't have come.'

'I'm glad. Wanted to see you.'

'I'll just ask yes or no questions from now on.'

Vi nodded, and Laura sat back down on the very edge of the mattress, towards the end of the bed. 'Are you going to go back to work when you've recovered?' A nod. 'Is the factory paying all your medical bills?' Another nod. Then Laura shifted further up the bed, closer to Violet, smelling again the dirty hair, disinfectant smell and seeing the red and yellow stains on the dressing on her forehead. 'What about the baby? Will you keep it, now?' From the corner of her eye Laura could see the nurse returning, carrying a fresh water jug and a clipboard. 'Violet, are you keeping the baby?' Violet nodded, then shook her head, opened her lips and drew breath as if to speak, then closed them again.

321

The nurse's footfalls came to a halt next to them. Laura looked up. The woman made a show of looking at the upside-down watch-thing she wore. 'It's not even visiting hours. I'm afraid I'm going to have to ask you to leave,' she said. Laura sighed and took her hat off the bed knob. The nurse put the fresh jug of water on the locker and began writing something on the clipboard. Laura put on her hat, and picked her bag up off the floor.

'What about the painting?' Violet said in that painfully hoarse whisper.

'There won't be a painting.'

'So it was all for nothing?'

Laura didn't reply. What could she say? She watched the nurse frown and hang the clipboard up on the end of the bedstead.

'What are you going to do now, Dame Laura?' Violet said.

'That's quite enough chit-chat, Miss Smith,' the nurse cut in. 'You need to rest those lungs and that larynx of yours.'

'Dame Laura?' Violet said, ignoring the nurse.

Laura pushed herself up off the covers and stood. How the bag pulled on her aching shoulder. She straightened up, ignoring the pain. She looked down at Violet, lying there on the bed. Her bandaged hands lay still on the covers, and she stared straight ahead, like a marble effigy on a tombstone. Not at all like the fidgety, sparky chit who'd been almost impossible to hold in a pose, Laura thought.

Looking down at her, Laura became again the lady artist visiting the injured factory girl, nothing more. 'It was such a pleasure painting you and I do wish you a speedy recovery and a swift return to the vital work you and your colleagues are doing in the gun factory,' Laura said, painting a smile on her face. 'Goodbye, dear.' And she turned and walked away from the bed, not answering Violet's question, striding back through the lines of beds, looking neither left nor right.

But the polished lino was a river bed, and Violet's words tugged at her ankles like underwater weed:

What are you going to do now, Laura?

Try as she might, she could not get the penny in the slot. Her right hand had completely seized up from drawing all night. It was no more use than a fleshy claw.

'Hello? Hello?' The voice at the other end sounded like a tinny parrot.

One last effortful try and the penny plinked into the metal mouth. 'It's Laura here. Is that you, K?'

'Laura, where the devil are you? Gone AWOL? Harold said you were at the gun factory, but they said there was no sign of you so you must have gone home.'

'Well, I suppose I have, in a manner of speaking.'

'You're in Malvern?'

'No, Long Eaton.'

'Where's that?'

'Derbyshire. I was born here, you see.' (He'll assume I'm visiting relatives. Let him think that, if it helps.)

'I heard about the raid. Thank God you weren't there, Laura.'

'Oh, it was a dreadful business, K. I visited last night. The painting's destroyed. One of my models was killed outright, and the other's in hospital.' She felt in her right pocket for the slip of canvas and touched it with her fingertips, still holding the clammy receiver to her left ear with her other hand. The phone box air smelled of stale smoke and urine.

'I'm so sorry, Laura.'

'So am I, K.'

A pause, then, the line hissing between them. Laura imagined it as a two-headed snake: one head in central London and the other here in this nondescript Derbyshire mill town, the telephone cable coiling and slithering down the miles between them. 'Will you be all right?'

'I'm very tired, that's all – I spent the whole night in the factory and then I went on to visit the surviving girl in hospital. And now the ruddy train's delayed, so I thought I'd just stay over here for the night and then – do you have anything else for me, K? After something like this I just feel one should get back in the saddle, so to speak.'

She heard K suck in a breath. 'I thought this was to be the last one, Laura. You told me that Harold thinks—'

'Oh, when has it ever mattered what Harold thinks?' Laura interrupted. 'I need to work. I need to keep on going, don't you see?'

There was a faint scratchy sound at the far end of the line and Laura could imagine K running his manicured nails over a freshly shaven cheek. Laura looked out through the glass pane. Raindrops trickled as if the glass were melting. There was a red-brick building across the street: *Station Hotel*, the sign said in gold letters on a peeling black backdrop. The drizzle made everything smudged like an old photograph, where someone had moved too soon, leaving the moment blurred and uncaptured. 'There's not much about right now, unless you can stomach another factory?' K said at last.

'I can stomach anything. I need to work.'

'There's a ball-bearing factory in Skeffington that has been asking for an artist, and one that makes railway lines, too. And later on in the year there's talk of doing something at the tank training unit in Barnard Castle, if that suits?'

'I'll take them, and anything else that comes in, in the meantime.'

'You're sure? I thought you'd had enough of painting the mucky business of war?'

'Quite sure. How soon can I begin on the Skeffington job?'

'Almost immediately, I daresay. I'll need to make a couple of calls. But what about Harold, Laura?'

'What *about* Harold, K?' The pips went, then. 'Call me back at the Station Hotel in Long Eaton to confirm,' she managed to call out before the line went dead.

She hung the receiver back on the cradle. Her right hand was still in her skirt pocket, aching fingers pinching the edge of the torn canvas. She let go of it now, took her right hand out of her pocket and lifted it towards her left. Her painful fingers struggled to take the slippery gold band off her ring finger, twisting and pulling until it worried up the skin and wrenched away. She put it in the pocket, next to the scrap of canvas. It felt like the right place.

She splayed out the fingers of both hands. Her skin was stained with charcoal smudges, newsprint and old yellow nicotine, but there was no adornment.

They were no longer the hands of a wife; they were merely the hands of a working artist: empty and free.

Chapter 23

George

It ought to be simple, he thought, as the blue-green countryside flashed past and the open windows filled the car with the scent of hot tar. Simple enough, to end a life, in wartime. If he were in the boiler room on a convoy ship or a tail-end Charlie on a bomber – pretty much any other job except being in a senior management position in a reserved occupation.

He pushed his foot down hard on the accelerator so the car sped forward even faster, the engine making that choking whine it did when the revs got too high. The steering wheel started to judder.

Wilford Road was empty. He could see for the best part of a mile ahead and there was nothing but the poking smokestacks of the distant brickworks, and the railway line like a zip fastener, holding the yellow-green strips of farmland together.

He took a hand off the jerking steering wheel to push

his hair away from his eyes and felt the car lurch onwards, almost driving itself. There was a heat haze like machine grease on the road ahead. If there was a pothole? He imagined the vehicle pirouetting, a tumble-rush of earth and sky, then nothing.

An accident, that's what they'd say. It would save his parents the shame of suicide. He was overworked, racing between the two ordnance factory sites in Nottingham and Ruddington, pushing himself to the limit to do his best for the war effort. In a way he might be considered some kind of white-collar hero, and all this – this mess of life – would be over and done with. His breath tasted sour in his mouth. He didn't bother replacing his hand on the steering wheel, instead leant an elbow on the open window frame, feeling the warm wind through his shirtsleeve. He kept his foot pushed hard on the accelerator as the brickworks approached, chimneys like proffered cigarettes, and the car sped over the slash of railway line and on in the direction of Wilford Village.

A sprinkling of houses up ahead, distant smatters like discarded confetti on a church step. A large old oak tree was a growing green blob, on the outskirts of the village. He'd passed it many times on his way to and from the Ruddington depot over the last year or so – the trunk must be nearly two yards in diameter. Could that be big enough? If he hit it at this speed?

The tree loomed larger now as the car thundered on. If he were to do it, he should do it, without thought or hesitation.

He twisted the wheel and let the car swerve towards it. Now. He was ready.

Wait: what was that? A flash of white in his periphery – something? Someone?

He grabbed the wheel with both hands and twisted it away, hitting the brakes, forcing the car into a sideways skid: the sudden lurch, a thud, darkness, and silence.

But then, the agony of a breath, ripping open his lungs, gulping in the hot petrol fumes. Eyes opening. Everything fuzzy and half-erased. The brickworks on the wrong side of the zippered-up countryside, the tree nowhere to be seen, a pain across his forehead like a fallen axe. Blinking into focus. Hearing the car engine chugging, a slicing ache in his chest as he leant forward and fumbled with the key, turning it off. His breathing like pumping bellows. A wrenching spasm as he turned his neck. The car had skidded right round, and was now facing back towards Ruddington.

He got out of the car, slow as an old man. Everything seemed taut and stretched, like the skin over a blister. He looked round. Had he missed it? Whatever it was, that flash of white he'd seen? The road was empty, no screams of pain or running feet, no pools of accusatory blood on the hot gravel. His eyes travelled over to the oak tree, the broad trunk and the canopy of green. He could see the curlicue of tracks tracing the dust in front of it, where the car had skidded full circle. He stepped across the empty road. He had seen something, he was certain.

What was that? A noise, coming from the tree. He walked

closer, stepping slowly through curving skid marks, feeling as if a bruise were seeping upwards from his toes, all the way up his legs, until each step was a gentle agony. He looked up, and there, where the branches began to fork off from the trunk, was a white cat, miaowing. So that was it. A cat.

He walked painfully under the green-cool of the shady tree and reached up. The cat ran its nose along his forefinger, half closing its eyes as it nudged him. He stroked its soft fur and it began to purr. As he stroked, the sweat that ran between his shoulder blades began to evaporate, and his breathing slowed. It was just a cat, skinny, half-feral by the look of it. Probably nobody would even have noticed if he'd run it over, such a small, insignificant life. But it was a life, at least, and worth saving.

He heard a steam train toot and chug down the railway line, heading towards the depot. And something shifted inside him.

He walked back to the car, got back inside, turned on the ignition and shoved it into reverse, manoeuvring back in the right direction, back towards the gun factory, and home.

He'd reached the outskirts of the village when he saw her: the woman in the blue dress, beige winter coat slung over one arm. She was plodding towards him on the opposite side, head down, staring at the dusty road. He swerved slowly across the road and came to a halt in front of her, aware of the tremor in his forearms, the fogginess in his head, and the smell of scorched tyres in his nostrils. Carefully does it. The window was still wound down. He leant out and was about to call out her name, when she looked up.

'Mr Handford?'

'Miss Smith.'

There were bluebells the same colour as her dress on the verge. She stopped, looking in through the window at him. And neither of them spoke, because what was there to say? He switched off the car engine and got out. They faced each other, and he thrust out a hand, because he couldn't think what else to do – an embrace would be too much, but there had to be some contact between them, after the events of that night. When he took her hand in his it felt warm and rough-dry, and he found himself apologising: 'So sorry, is it painful?'

'No, no, they say I've healed up really well,' she said. One side of her face was slightly pinker than the other, as if she'd had a nap in the sun. A green turban covered her hair. His eyes slid inadvertently down, over her blue dress, and he saw the way the fabric gaped a little where it buttoned, over the gentle mound of her belly. She moved the arm carrying the coat across the centre of her body, covering the bump. Had she seen him notice? He hadn't meant to stare. What an oaf he was. And all these weeks she'd been in Nottingham General and he hadn't thought to visit, so wrapped up in his own selfish grief. What a heel.

'It's good to see you recovering. I didn't expect you to be out of hospital so soon,' he said.

'I was just discharged this morning. I'm on my way to the

hostel. They phoned – Matron says I can have my old bed back.'

'Good, good. That's good. I'm sorry, I didn't realise.'

'No, they weren't expecting to let me go today, so you weren't to know.'

'I would have arranged transport for you – a lift or a taxi – if I'd known, but I can drive you the rest of the way.'

'No, I'd rather walk. It's good to be outside, after all that time indoors.'

'Indeed.' He cleared his throat and ran his thumb and forefinger over his face. 'But you must be very tired, and it's really no trouble. After all, a woman in your, your—' His muzzy brain searched for an appropriate word.

'Condition?'

He felt himself redden, cleared his throat again. 'Yes. I'd feel terrible if I left you to walk, alone like this.'

She nodded. 'That's kind of you, Mr Handford.'

'It's the least I can do, under the circumstances.'

'Yes,' she said. 'The circumstances.' Her tongue darted briefly out between her lips and she drew breath as if she were about to say something more, but instead she simply walked round to the passenger door and got in. George followed her lead and got back in himself, settling into the seat and turning the key in the ignition. The engine chugged awake. 'Your car smells funny,' she said. 'Engine overheating?'

'I had to brake suddenly to avoid a cat, just now,' he said. 'Tyres and brakes, that's probably what you can smell.'

'Oh.' Her head lolled sideways against the doorframe as

he pushed the car into gear and turned it round. 'To tell the truth, I'm glad you caught up with me. It's further than I thought, and I'm out of the habit of walking, what with having been stuck in hospital all this time.' Her lids fluttered down and she closed her eyes as he drove her to the hostel. His forehead had started to throb and he felt sick. But all he needed to do was drive her the final mile or so to the hostel and drop her off. Surely he could do that? The rest – the awkward conversation about her future with the factory – that could wait.

'I know what you're thinking, but I'm coming back to the night shift,' she said. He glanced across at her as they paused at a junction. Her eyes were still closed. He could hear a distant ambulance bell, but the road was empty. He turned left down the side road.

'What about the baby?'

'A girl's got to earn a living, Mr Handford.'

He wished he could drive faster, get it over and done with, but he felt as if he had a bone-china teacup in the passenger seat, and in any case, he didn't trust himself, not with the ache in his head, the tremor in his limbs and the rising nausea. 'I'm sure we can find something that's not overly taxing for you,' he said, gripping the steering wheel and blinking in the strobing bars of light-shade as they drove through an avenue of beech trees. 'When are you planning on coming back?'

'Tonight.'

'So soon?'

'Why wait? What else am I going to do, mope around in the room and get poorer every hour?'

'You wouldn't prefer to be on days?'

'Trying to get shot of me?'

'Not at all – I'm only thinking that you might prefer days, after what happened, and with the baby on the way. It might be less tiring.'

'No, Mr H. The night shift is where I started, and that's where I'll stay, thank you.'

He clicked the indicator and turned off onto the private road that only led to the hostel, trying not to remember the last time he was here.

'You can drop me here,' she said. 'I know you won't want to go all the way to the entrance. You might end up having to talk to Matron or some other do-gooder.' She knew. How did she know? She must be feeling the same way: steeling herself for the onslaught of prurient pity. He pulled in next to a five-bar gate. They were only a couple of hundred yards from the hostel block.

As she leant over towards the door catch, he touched her lightly on the shoulder. 'I'm so glad you came through all right, Miss Smith, and the baby, too.' But she didn't answer him. She got out and slammed the door behind her and began to walk along the last bit of road towards the hostel. The hem of her beige coat dropped off her arm and trailed in the dust.

'I'll see you later, then, Miss Smith,' he called out of the car window at her.

She lifted a hand and fluttered fingers, as she carried on

walking away. 'Not if I see you first, Mr Handford,' she called back, without bothering to turn round.

He couldn't help but smile. Brave, he thought. Brave girl. Puts the rest of us to shame.

Violet

'You do know I hold a weekly surgery at the factory?' the doctor said, her head tilted to one side over Vi's bare belly, listening to the ear trumpet. The tip of her tongue was visible between her thin lips as she listened. The ear trumpet left pink circles on Vi's skin as the doctor moved it over her bump.

'But I'd rather see you here,' Vi said, feeling the flesh dip under the pressure of the metal.

'There it is,' the doctor said at last. 'Yes, that's a good steady heartbeat. How many months did you say you thought you were?' She straightened up and placed the ear trumpet on the mantelpiece, next to the carriage clock.

'Three,' said Vi.

'Oh, I shouldn't be surprised if you're further along than that,' the doctor said. 'It's rare to feel the baby move before about four months, especially if it's your first one,' the doctor said, and went over to sit behind her big desk. 'You can get up, now, dear.'

Vi heaved herself up from the chaise longue and pulled her frock down over the curve of her stomach, feeling her breasts tug, pendulous and tender, squeezed into the too-tight brassiere. She thought of the airman, the bang of the bunk beds against the dormitory wall. And she thought of Frank Timpson and the rough-rub of the bricks in the alley. Could she be more than three months gone already? But everyone knew you couldn't get pregnant if you did it standing up and it was your first time. She left one button undone – it just wouldn't stretch that far any more. It didn't matter when she was at work. Those overalls would disguise her condition for months.

As Vi walked across the rag rug towards the doctor's desk, she noticed scurrying shoes at eye level beyond the basement window. She could hear the clatter of saucepans and smell frying onions from an adjoining room. The carriage clock chimed five times. Dr Gibbs was rearranging the pen, ruler and notepad on her desk. She looked up and motioned for Vi to sit down. Vi sat, and clasped her hands on her knees. The onion smell was making her feel nauseous. Dr Gibbs glanced down at Vi's hands. 'I see you've not persuaded him to make an honest woman of you,' she said. 'But there's still time, dear. Unless you've given some thought to the alternatives.'

'About that,' Vi said. The doctor gave a slow nod, to show she was listening. 'I don't want to have it adopted.' She could see the doctor's face harden. 'But what about that other way. You said you could have a baby looked after, just until you could get it back?' The doctor pressed her thin lips together in a discouraging way. 'Because the baby's father is dead, you see.'

'Oh, I'm terribly sorry to hear that.'

'And I can't afford to stop working, not at the moment, because I have to send most of my wages home.'

'Oh dear.' Dr Gibbs shifted her pencil and ruler round on her desk, so they swapped places. She took a deep intake of breath. 'And when exactly do you think you will be able to afford to?'

'I don't know. Once Ma's medical bills are paid off, and when Rita's old enough to enlist. The twins have got paper rounds now, so that helps. Maybe in a year or so?' Her voice wavered. She sounded unconvincing, even to herself.

'Are you certain you won't consider adoption? With money so tight could you ever afford to be a good mother to this child? Wouldn't adoption be the better option?'

'Better for who?' Vi said.

'For whom,' Dr Gibbs corrected her grammar. 'Better for whom.' She smiled one of her flat-mouthed smiles that held no warmth. 'Better for the child to be brought up in an educated and nurturing environment, wouldn't you say?'

'But I want to be able to get my baby back.'

'And by the time you are able, he or she may very well not be a baby any more, and may be perfectly well settled in their foster family.'

'That's the word: foster. I want to have it fostered. You said you could do it. That's what you said before.'

The doctor sucked in a breath, paused, then picked up her pencil and opened her notebook. 'Very well. You have made your choice,' she said, writing something down. She looked up. 'My only concern now is the health of the child. Nobody will want to look after a defective baby for you. If your plan is to have it fostered, then you need to ensure its health, that's all. I'll mention it to management when I'm in on Thursday.'

'Don't,' Vi said. 'Please.'

'Well, I'm sorry, young lady, but I feel duty bound—'

'I'll do it myself. I'll tell them today.' Vi's words came out in a rush.

'Well, that's your choice, but if you don't, then I shall,' Dr Gibbs said, shutting the notebook. 'Now, if you don't mind, the surgery is closing.'

Chapter 24

Laura

'Good turn-out, wasn't it?' she said, letting her hand rest on the leather inlay of his desk and casting her eye round the room: stacks and stacks of framed artwork leaning up against the flocked wallpaper like an interrupted card game. They had just got back from the unveiling of her painting: 'Ruby Loftus Screwing a Breech Ring' at the Royal Academy. Young Ruby had come along herself, all the way from Wales, dear thing, and there'd been a whole army of journalists and photographers. Even Pathé had turned up. 'What do you think the press will say?' She leant her portfolio against the edge of the desk (he hadn't asked why she'd brought it with her, and she hadn't told him, not yet).

'They will say that Dame Laura has infused an urgency and vitality into this study, making permanent a vivid impression of how girls in the Second World War toiled to make victory certain,' K said, smoothing down his hair. Laura smiled. He knew how to play the game, all right. 'So that's what Harold will read in the papers tomorrow. Or on a newsreel, if he makes an excursion to Malvern to the flicks.' K gave her a sharp look, and Laura felt heat rising in her chest. He continued before she'd thought to respond: 'And, yes, it was a good turn-out. Everyone likes an excuse to come up to town, escape the evacuee mentality of the provinces, no?' Laura nodded.

'I say, what do you think to this?' He motioned to an unframed canvas propped against the wall behind his desk. It showed army tailors at work in a barracks. The perspective was interesting, how it looked down at the tops of their heads. 'It's by an ATS girl: Stella Schmolle. I don't think it's half bad, actually. You?'

Laura squinted at the painting with her head on one side. The composition was excellent, but the colours – she needed to work on using colour more effectively. On the other hand, it was a unique style. 'Interesting,' Laura said.

'Really?' He raised an eyebrow.

'I wasn't being catty, K, I think she shows promise.'

'Yes, I rather think so, too. Then we'll buy it, and tell her CO to make sure she gets the time to do more.' He turned away from the painting to face her, rubbing his hands together. 'So, how's tricks?' He leant against his desk, shoving one of the snowdrift piles of paperwork out of the way. His dark hair was slicked smooth against his neat skull. He was slender as a cigarillo in his brown Italian wool suit.

Laura paused before answering. 'Fine,' she said at last.

'And Harold?'

She didn't answer, and he didn't pursue it. She walked around to the other side of the desk and he rushed round to pull out the chair for her, apologising for not having offered her a seat sooner. Say what you like about K, Laura thought (and people did say things about K, and about his wife, too, if one cared to listen), he was nothing if not courteous.

There was banging from an adjoining room. 'Sorry about that. Framers – I know it's a terrible racket, but I do like to keep an eye on them,' K said, with an apologetic shrug.

Laura settled herself into the large chair with the leather-padded seat and arm rests, and took off her gloves. She took one of K's expensive cigarettes from the ivory box, and let him light it for her. She noticed him glance at her left hand as he did so, and wondered, briefly, whether she should claim rheumatism for the absence of the ring. No. She wasn't going to lie to him, or to anyone else. Besides, if he thought her fingers were seizing up, he'd think twice about offering her another commission, and she needed the work.

She looked out of K's office window to the brown-grey tumble of London rooftops and the lowering skies: smog smothering down, as usual. She leant back in his seat and looked up at K, handsome as a film star (not that it did anything for her, Laura thought, even if she had been twenty years younger).

'The Committee still owes me for the Nottingham

commission. I thought it vulgar to bring up during the press junket, but now we're in private, and there we are.'

'There we are indeed,' K said, raising those handsome brows again. 'But I never received a painting from ROF Nottingham.'

'You know fine well why not,' Laura said. 'It was in all the papers – even if you hadn't bothered to read the letter I sent.'

'Yes, it was regrettable,' he said.

'Regrettable? It was a tragedy, K. That poor woman had just got married, was due to go on her honeymoon.'

K cleared his throat. 'Yes, dreadful business. But you see, Laura, I can't pay for something I don't have. The rules are that I pay for the finished piece, not for the work that goes into it. It's taxpayers' money, old girl.'

'Show your taxpayers this, then, K.' Laura pulled the triangular scrap of charred canvas from her pocket and banged it down, causing an avalanche of paperwork to slew across the desk.

K sighed. 'I'm so sorry, but I just can't, Laura.'

'What about this, then?' She pulled at the ties on the portfolio and opened it up. 'I went back to the factory, talked to everyone who was there. I only painted it for myself, but it is something, K. There is something to show for that commission.'

'Do you mind if I—' Without waiting for her response, Sir Kenneth took it out of the portfolio and held it up.

'Laura, it's—'

'Chalk, charcoal and watercolour,' Laura said.

'That's not what I meant. What I was going to say is that it's wonderfully powerful – the burnt debris, the expressions on those people's faces.'

'It's not at all what you asked for,' Laura said. 'And I was just going to keep it for my personal collection, but—'

'We must have it,' Sir Kenneth said, holding it up, walking across the room to the window with it. 'It's perfect.'

'It's not a double Ruby Loftus, and that's what you asked for.'

'No, I'm afraid I still can't pay you for the original commission. But I can pay you for this. We can posterise it, add text, roll it out across all the munitions factories in the country, to warn of the dangers at work, factory fires and so forth. It's exactly the kind of thing the chaps at the ministry have been asking for.'

'But it's not a factory fire. It's the aftermath of a bombing raid. I only painted it as a way of making sense of the tragedy in my own mind.'

'And that's why it will work, because it is so personal. It's not some hectoring man from the ministry wagging his finger; it's a testament to the real anguish that workplace incidents can cause. If anything's going to make people clean up their rubbish and turn their machines off properly, it's something like this.' He turned back from the window and came towards the desk.

'I'm not sure I want to sell it,' Laura said. K did the eyebrow thing again and placed the painting down on the desk. He pulled a chequebook from his pocket.

'How much?'

'It's not for sale.'

'Laura, how much?'

'Four hundred pounds.'

'Two hundred?'

'I couldn't possibly part with it for less than three hundred guineas.'

'Three hundred pounds?'

'Done.'

He opened the chequebook and took a pen from his top pocket. As he unclipped the lid and reached towards the open cheque, Laura stayed his hand. 'Come on now, I'm overpaying as it is. There'll be a riot if the others find out how much you're getting for this, so keep it under your hat, won't you? Right then, three hundred pounds to Mr and Mrs Knight . . .'

She tightened her grasp, making him pause. 'It's not that. Could you, just this once, not—'

'Squirrel fund?' he interrupted, looking pointedly at the space on her finger where the ring should have been. He thought she needed the money to set herself up independently, or shack up with some lover in a seedy apartment? The impertinence!

'Not at all,' she replied, lifting her hand. 'Could you leave the cheque blank, if you would?'

'As you wish,' K said, glancing up and giving her a look. Judging her by his own low moral standards, most likely. Laura looked away. He could think what he liked. Only she would ever know where that money was destined.

Violet

'Looks like snowfall, so it does,' Mary said. They were walk-ing along Attenborough Lane. Above the charcoal outline of the church, the sky hung low and grey with pulpy cloud, and a stiff breeze shook leaves from the trees like multicoloured snowflakes.

Vi's coat buttons were undone to give her pregnant belly space. The autumn air was chill against the stretched flesh, and her swollen breasts had started to ache. A single magpie flew overhead, chuckle-chuntering as it went. 'Is it far?' Vi said.

'We're almost there, now.'

'Thank you for coming all this way with me, Mary.'

'Couldn't have you coming alone. Miss Fitzlord brought me, when it was my time.'

'She was good like that, wasn't she?'

'Aye, she was.'

They walked on in silence for a while. Vi's bag banged against her calf, and she looked down at her feet in her God-awful factory clogs trudging along the pavement: clump-clump-clump. Then she looked up again, at the swirling leaves, making a grab for one as it fell. She looked over and saw that Mary was doing the same. They caught each other's eyes and laughed out loud. Vi dropped her bag, opened her arms wide, in a huge 'V' shape like the woman in the recruitment poster, and spun slowly round, trying to catch a falling leaf. 'It's a whole month of good luck next year, for each one you catch,' she called out, still spinning, keeping her eyes fixed upwards into the yellow-brown rush of it. And she kept her head looking skywards, grabbing the falling leaves, as Mary talked about how they drifted so thick in the glen near her home that they'd sledged on them on old tin trays, like snow, and about how her brother Billy had fallen off and got a gash in his head when he whacked into a tree branch.

Vi spun and leapt, still trying to catch leaves. She had ten already – she'd always been quick with her hands. 'I used to use a tin tray, too, not on leaves though, just when it snowed,' Vi said, grinning at the memory of winters at home. There, she'd caught her eleventh. Just one left to get. 'I nicked it from the back of the school kitchen. Pa called me a tea leaf, but he never made me give it back.' She remembered the white blur, laughter bubbling up, the rush of speed. Bruised to buggery afterwards, but happy. She had had a happy childhood, despite it all, she thought, spinning even faster now, dizzy as hell. There, that was the last one. She shoved it in her coat pocket with the others.

She and Mary fell into each other, chortling like drunkards. They slumped together against the gatepost, waiting for the world to stop turning. She caught Mary's eye and they laughed afresh. What were they doing, grown, responsible women, with jobs and all, behaving like snow-struck schoolgirls? As their giggles petered out, Vi spoke: 'I'm sorry, Mary.'

'What for?'

'I wasn't very nice to you at first. I just didn't realise—'

Mary made a swiping gesture with her hand, like shooing away a fly. 'Oh, that's all in the past, so it is.' And Mary hooked her arm through Vi's and tugged her onwards, towards an orangey blur on the left-hand side, a three-storey red-brick Victorian villa: Cloud House.

Mary pecked Vi on the cheek as they parted company in the open doorway, but she turned her head and walked quickly away when the woman holding the door open tutted and said something about letting all the cold air in. 'Thank you again for bringing me,' Vi called out as the door slammed shut. She wasn't sure if Mary had heard her or not. She shoved her free hand in her pocket: twelve fallen leaves – a whole year of good luck? Fat lot of good those leaves would do her here.

It was very dark in the hallway. 'You're late,' the woman said.

'Only about nine months,' Vi said, but the woman didn't laugh. As Vi's eyes became accustomed to the darkness of the hallway, she was able to see the woman more clearly: tiny, darting eyes and oily, scraped-back hair. The woman tutted again. 'It's that kind of attitude that got you into your condition in the first place, I'll bet,' she said.

Vi sighed and picked up her bag. 'Can you show me to my room?' she said.

'I can, but don't get too comfy. All of you girls are going to church in five minutes, and after that you'll be assigned your duties.'

George

'Please tell Marjorie that it's a very kind offer, but I have other plans.' He could hardly bear to meet Bill's eyes. Again Bill Simmons had invited him over, and again he was refusing. This was the third time, now.

Bill nodded. 'Well, game birds are off-ration, so there'll be plenty to go round if you change your mind. We'd all love to see you.'

George made a non-committal grunt. The suffocating kindness of it was too much. He turned away and began checking the updated charts. Production was down again, for the third week running. Bill was still at the desk, shuffling a report into his briefcase. He looked over at George. 'Can't keep up with demand,' he said, shrugging. 'It's impossible. They will keep going off and having babies and the replacements don't come in fast enough. And when they do, they're about as much use as a chocolate teapot for the first few weeks. You know how it is. Still, girls will be girls, I suppose. What can you do?'

Indeed, what could one do? George thought of Violet Smith, who'd gone off to the Home for Unmarried Mothers, and there was still no news from the Labour Exchange about providing cover. He ran his hand over his face, feeling the rough scratch of stubble. He should have shaved before coming out, but it had slipped his mind, just as it had slipped his mind to eat Mrs Packer's sandwiches, again.

'Well, other than the woeful shortage of workers, there

are no major incidents to report.' He clicked the catch on his briefcase. It was only a quarter to six, but Bill had a reason to hurry home: a wife, supper on the table, bedtime stories for the boys.

'You get off,' George said. 'I can take it from here.'

'Wait, I'll just double-check these figures on the aluminium purchase invoice first, don't trust the buggers.' The telephone rang and Bill answered: 'Manager's office ... no, this is Bill Simmons speaking. Oh, good evening, and how are you? Good, good, what can I help with? ... I'll just see if he's arrived, yet. One moment, please.' He put a hand over the receiver. 'Are you here?'

'Who is it?'

'Dame whatsit, the one who did the painting, wants to talk. What shall I say?'

'I'm here,' George said, even though his stomach lurched at the thought of it. He stepped over to the desk, and reached to take the receiver from Bill. 'Hello?'

'George Handford, is that you?' Her voice scratchy and faint down the phone line. 'Can you hear me?'

'Yes, it's me, Dame Laura. I can hear you. How are you?'

'Well, more to the point, how are you?'

'I'm fine.' He could feel Bill looking at him. 'Fine,' he repeated. There was a pause, then. When he turned to look down, Bill was scribbling a sum in the margin of an invoice and frowning.

'It's about Zelah.'

Hearing her name was a jolt. Nobody else so much as

breathed it. Since that night it was as if even mentioning her name would cause something terrible to happen. It was like the way actors always referred to Macbeth as the 'Scottish Play'. People spoke of the 'personal tragedy' he'd suffered or his 'tragic loss'. Nobody said her name, hadn't done for months. Until now. He grasped the receiver hard, feeling it slide where his palm pricked with fresh sweat. 'What about her?'

'The painting . . .' The line went muzzy then and her voice faded into white noise. Was Dame Laura coming back? Were they sending her back to have another attempt? Her voice came again: '. . . turn it into a poster and roll it out to factories nationwide, and I just wanted to check you didn't mind, George.'

'But the painting was destroyed in the raid.'

'I know that. I'm not talking about that one, I'm talking about the other one. I was worried that you might see it as exploiting the grief surrounding Zelah's death. Do you? Because I can put the kibosh on it, if that's the case?'

'I'm sorry, Laura, I don't understand.'

'Ah, I forgot. Of course, you weren't there, that night.'

What night? What painting? He was lost. He heard her draw breath. 'After the raid I came back to Nottingham, and I sketched the night shift – all that was left of it. Afterwards I spent some time in a grubby hotel in Long Eaton and worked it up into a watercolour. I had a few days before they needed me for the Skeffington job. I only did it for myself, at the time, as a way of making sense of the senselessness, do you see?'

He did. He knew all about the senselessness of it.

'Anyway, I happened to show it to K – Ken Clark, you know – and he said he'd like to posterise it, put it up in the factories. Apparently the ministry have been asking for something suitable to warn of the dangers of factory fires.

'But it wasn't a fire,' George said. 'It was a raid.' He watched Bill shoving some purchase orders into the in-tray and taking a last swig from his Bovril mug.

He heard Laura sigh. 'I know. I think it was the expression of shock and loss on people's faces, and the backdrop of burnt equipment, which he thought he could put to good use. Listen, George, if you're not happy with it, then, as I said, I can ask them not to go ahead.'

'It makes no odds to me. Life goes on.'

'Good of you to be so understanding, George.'

He heard Bill's chair scrape on the lino as he stood up. 'Life goes on.' George repeated the empty platitude, not knowing what else to say.

'And Violet?'

'Who?'

'Violet Smith?'

'She's fine. She's out of hospital. The burns have healed up and she's been back on the tools.' He saw Bill shrugging on his coat.

'Good. Would it be too much trouble to ask to have a quick word?'

'I'm afraid she's not available. She's – she might be off for some time.'

'The baby?'

'Yes.' He hadn't known she knew. Who had told her?

'And what has she decided to do? Will she take it back to her family in Kent?'

Bill had finished buttoning up his coat and was taking his hat off the peg. 'No, that's not a feasible option, so—'

'Adoption, then?'

'I don't think so, but—' With Bill still in the room it was impossible to speak freely of such things. (Violet had told him in confidence, awkwardly, with a defiant jut to her chin, as if he'd judge. Christ. As if he had any right to judge her, after everything that had happened.)

'Ah, I think I understand,' Dame Laura said. 'Do send her my love, won't you?'

'Yes, I will, of course I will.'

Another pause, then, 'I was wondering if you'd like the painting,' she said. 'The original, I mean. I can get them to send it to you, once the print run has been set up, if you'd like?'

A painting of the aftermath of the raid, of all the trauma and disbelief – did he want it? Did he really want to hang that up in his house, a constant reminder of his loss?

'It's very kind of you, but—'

'I quite understand.' She rescued him.

'So, what are you up to, these days?' he began, but the pips went then – he hadn't realised she was in a call box – and he just about managed to say goodbye before the line went dead.

He placed the receiver back in its cradle and exhaled

slowly, taking in the messy desk: ashtray overflowing with Bill's butts, toppling in-tray. When he looked up Bill was in the doorway, about to leave.

'I'll be off then,' Bill said.

'Hang on, old man.' He walked over to where Bill stood. 'Those plans I had? I can cancel them. Please tell Marjorie I'd love to join you and the family some time.'

'If you're sure?'

George nodded.

'She'll be delighted, and so will the boys,' Bill said, and smiled.

George leant in and reached out a hand, and Bill took it. His firm clasp gripped hard. 'I'm lucky to have a colleague like you,' George said.

'Sadly, I think I'm the lucky one. But I appreciate the sentiment. And – and I'm always here, if things ever – you know.'

George's eyes stung. He forced words up his constricted throat: 'Thank you, Bill.' He couldn't trust himself to make eye contact – he'd be lost if he did. He let go of Bill's hand and turned away.

'Cheerio, then,' Bill said.

'Cheerio,' he managed, hearing the sudden thunder-blast as the office door opened and closed behind his colleague.

It was time to get on with things.

Chapter 25

Violet

'And were you thinking of the Lord when you conceived the child?' His urgent whisper made her flesh crawl.

'I don't remember, Reverend.'

His watery eyes bulged and his nostrils flared. 'Then tell me how the sin came to be committed.'

'I really can't say, Reverend.'

'But you must recall something of the event? Better that one offers up details of the sin in its fullest nature, to seek complete atonement.'

'I'm sorry, Reverend. Perhaps Lilian will be able to remember her sin better than I can.'

'Lilian?'

'The one with the blonde hair.'

'Ah, yes, yes, send her through, then.' Violet stood up, and took a pace backwards, towards the door. The vicar stood, too. 'Know that Jesus loves you, sinner though you are,' he said, arms outstretched. But Violet had already begun to open the door to the church. She was not going to enter the spiritual embrace of that man. Not on your nelly.

'Tag, you're it.' She tapped bottle-blonde-Lil on her shoulder and nodded in the direction of the vestry. Bottle-blonde-Lil rolled her eyes. Mrs Scattergood scowled at them both and bottle-blonde-Lil got up from her seat next to weepy-Jean and shuffled towards the open door. Mrs Scattergood approved of the 'individual moral guidance' that the vicar insisted on.

Violet sat down in the pew behind, next to Ivy-the-ATS-girl and daft-Sybil, who still didn't seem to understand why the 'special cuddles' she'd had when out on cycle rides with the grocer's boy had resulted in her being holed up in Cloud House. Weepy-Jean sat in the front pew, because it was her churching. Weepy-Jean's baby was already ten days old. (Violet remembered the night he was born. Lord, how Jean had yelled, you'd have thought she was birthing a chamber pot. Breech: they said she had to be sliced from arse to fanny to get him out. She'd spent half the time sitting in salt-water baths, since.)

There would have been more of them there for the service, but Iris (nose like a goose's beak, swore like a trooper) had gone last night, straight after her boy was taken. And there'd been Bella (the Spanish girl, who was only fourteen and who spoke English with such a heavy accent that nobody could understand her properly). She had been in labour for days, and they'd had to cart her off to hospital just this morning. So there weren't that many of them there to church weepy-Jean in her faded orange dress, sodden with milk and tears.

Bottle-blonde-Lil emerged from the vestry, then, red-faced, head dipped, and slipped into the pew at the front beside weepy-Jean. The vicar came out a few moments later, wiping his hands on his cassock. An organist in a mauve cardigan scurried mouselike from the shadows, blowing on her fingers before settling her haunches on the organ stool.

Violet had been to a couple of these services already since being sent to Cloud House. She guessed there'd be a few more before it was her turn. After all, her own baby wasn't due for another month or so. It was always the same: a couple of hymns, a prayer, some guff about atonement and deliverance from the snares of death, and then they'd all go back to a God-awful dinner of Oxo-and-swede casserole. Again.

They started with an autumn hymn: *'We plough the fields and scatt-er the good seed on the land . . .'* they sang, with Mrs Scattergood's voice warbling up towards the bell tower – must have been her favourite hymn because of the words, Violet thought. It was probably only chosen because of it being around harvest festival time, and the organist being used to the tune, but Vi suppressed a little smirk – hadn't anyone seen the irony of a group of unmarried mothers singing about scattering seed? Of course not, she thought. Nobody here had a sense of humour. But then, why would they, in a place like this, at a time like this?

The vicar then motioned for weepy-Jean to come and kneel in front of him. They all sat down as she bowed her head and sniffed into her hanky whilst he prayed for her sinning soul. Her sniffs got louder and her hanky wiped frantically as he droned on. Violet noticed the vicar looked pleased that she seemed suitably repentant (probably nobody had ever told him that mothers got the 'baby blues' when their milk came in). Outside the rain slewed down, and the light-deprived stained-glass windows were as dingy as one of the watercolours on the parlour wall at Cloud House.

Now the organ started and everyone stood up. She didn't recognise this one. Some of the High Anglican hymns were different, the type of service, too, she'd found out – nobody had seemed bothered that she was Catholic, hadn't even asked (perhaps in Mrs Scattergood's eyes they were all merely sinners, regardless of faith). Vi reached for the hymn book from the little shelf in front, the old leather cover reptilian dry under her fingertips. 'Two six two,' ATS-Ivy said, seeing Vi's confusion, and Vi rifled through the tissue-thin pages, as the organ droned loudly. Two six two ...

'*Oh God, our help in ages past ...*' Violet tried to lift her voice with the others and join in, but she was starting to get terrible gut-rot. It must have been that stew they had last night. Sybil had been on kitchen duty, and Violet was certain she didn't bother washing her hands very often.

She tried again: '*Under the shadow of Thy throne ...*' No, it was no good. There was a twisting ache right across her belly. Mrs Scattergood turned to glare at her, for not singing, so Vi made a show of checking the squiggly words in the hymn book and opened her mouth: '*From everlasting Thou art God, To endless years the same.*' But there it was, again, that squeezing sensation. Trapped wind, maybe. She gulped in a breath and looked down at the hymn book. '*Thy word commands our flesh to dust*,' she managed to join in, despite the discomfort: '*Be thou our guard while troubles last, And our eternal home.*'

They stayed standing as the organ music vibrated to a hush, because this was the bit where the vicar asked them to close their eyes and take a minute to reflect on their own sins, and how they could improve their moral welfare in future.

And it was in that moment, just as the tiny congregation fell silent in the vast church, closing their eyes in contemplation, that Violet felt a sudden wetness in her gusset, and liquid splashed down onto the flagstones at her feet. She opened her eyes and looked down at the small puddle on the church floor. She looked up again, unsure of what to do, and saw Mrs Scattergood's pasty features scrunched up in horror. Then the pain came: a swift, hard thump, between her chest and her guts, making her double over and grab at the pew in front.

It was like someone turning up a dial on a wireless. People began to look, and as they did, the pain rose up inside her. Then another one of those gut-punches knocked the breath clean from her; she lost her grip on the pew and landed with a bruising thud, hands and knees on the cold floor. Confusion, then: voices and faces and hands pulling her upright and as she got to her feet the relentless pummelling came again and she cried out, even though they said 'Shush, shush now, you're in a church' and she said she could just walk to Cloud House because it was only just over the way but even with all those hands and voices her knees buckled under her because the invisible fists kept coming, thumping and winding and hurting her. Lord, it hurt. She screamed and they said, 'Quiet, be quiet, don't make a fuss, this is your punishment, the pain is punishment for the sin.' And in between the pain-rush she could hear the sound of running footsteps and Jean's weeping. They slung her arms round their shoulders and she tried to make her legs move, really she did, but all of a sudden she needed the lav really bad, like her guts were about to spill out of her arse. And there were jagged spikes of pain and faces swam and faded from view, hands at her back and a cloth put under her thighs, which were naked now. Naked, and where were her knickers? And the voices told her not to worry because the vicar was fetching the midwife and she said: 'Don't be silly, I'm not having a baby, it's not due for weeks, must have been that fish stew because Sybil never washes her hands,' and Sybil said: 'I bloody do,' but then the pain was back and Mrs Scattergood said: 'We can't wait for the midwife, she's already crowning, it's time to push,' so Violet bore down, grunting, and when Mrs Scattergood said: 'That's it, good girl, Violet,' panting, in a moment of lucidity, she said: 'Don't you dare call me a good girl. I'm not a girl, I'm a woman, and here's the ruddy proof, you old cow.' And she thought she heard stifled laughter but then the grinding awful pain came again and she couldn't think, couldn't breathe, couldn't, couldn't, couldn't.

An endless tunnel of agony.

An effortful heave and something shifted.

There, on the scratchy black cloth, a small sideways head,

smooth as a boiled egg. What was that doing there? What was it? Push again, Violet. She pushed. She roared. The still church air mangled with the echoes of her pain, and out slithered a tiny body. What's that? A baby. A baby? Your baby, Violet. Hands plucked it up. Push, push again, you're not finished yet. A twisting pain, slippery rush of bloodied afterbirth. Hands and faces and footsteps on flagstones and a baby, wrapped in a woolly mauve cardigan and thrust into her arms.

She drew breath, looked down at the rose-red wrinkled little face. 'Oh,' said Violet, with a rush of recognition. 'Oh, it's *you*!'

Laura

The queue snaked back all the way to the door, which gaped open in dull surprise. Laura stood in the doorway, where fog mingled with pipe smoke from the man in front of her in the line, making Laura cough. The London fug always choked up her airways. Oh, to be away from all this, in the open air.

A woman with an elaborate yellow hat shunted past with a muttered 'Excuse me', the queue inched forwards, and at last there was space to let the door close. If only the postmistress would get a move on. She'd be lucky to make the 10.15 to Darlington, at this rate.

Laura looked round. The usual posters plastered the post office walls: *Be Like Dad, Keep Mum*, advised one; *Careless*

Talk Costs Lives, retorted another. Careless talk, Laura thought – careless talk of what, pray? Careless talk of carrot fudge and darning socks and make-do-and-mend and how many beans make five? She shifted her bag into her other hand. It was all too depressing, this war nonsense. Four years, the last one was, and that was supposed to be the war to end all wars, they said. This one had been going more than four years already, and still no end in sight, a bit like this ruddy queue for the counter. She checked her watch. How long would it take to get to the station from here? Too long, even if she ran (at your age, Laura? Don't be ridiculous). She sighed. Someone else passed by, and the queue moved forward a notch.

When she eventually reached the front, the postmistress was busy scribbling something on a form. 'Parcel post, first class,' Laura said, pulling the package from her pocket and placing it on the counter. The woman looked up with the vacant, watery-eyed look of someone who hadn't slept properly.

The postmistress reached out and squished the parcel as if it were fruit on a market stall. 'Could've fitted that in an envelope,' she said.

'I wanted to wrap it properly.'

'Fragile, is it?'

'Not exactly, no. Just precious. I need to be sure it will arrive.'

'It'll cost you extra for a signature.'

The woman said the amount and Laura said that was fine.

Just hurry up and get it done, she thought, taking out her coin purse and making sure she counted out the exact money, so there'd be no need to hang around waiting for change.

'Oh, no, that won't do, madam.' The woman's evident tiredness made her voice drawn out, like a drunk's.

'What do you mean?'

'The address is incomplete.'

'Not at all. I've written the postcode, there, see?' Laura jabbed a finger.

'But you haven't put the postal town. It's Post Office rules.'

'But if the postcode is there, then I hardly see why they need—'

'I can't send it without the postal town. It's the rules.'

Laura drew breath. 'May I borrow your pen, then, dear?'

The postmistress turned the parcel round and Laura wrote *Nottingham* in the space before the postcode. She paused, then, holding the pen and squinting down at the package: appraising it, as if she were checking a sketch of a seated nude for foreshortening of the thighs. She drew a line underneath Nottingham, put down the pen, and turned to go.

Outside the post office she hailed a cab, trying not to think of the expense – she might just make it to the station in time. She saw a red post office van approaching from the opposite direction as the taxi pulled off into the London traffic. The parcel would get in the first post, then. She settled back against the plush seat and let out a breath as they sped away.

She had drawn a line under Nottingham: it was done.

*

'Oh don't mind me, dear,' Laura said, as the young girl with the cello case elbowed her again, apologised again, shoving her ticket back into her coat pocket. The door slammed shut and there was a disembodied whistling as the inspector wandered along the corridor to the next compartment.

Laura looked out at the smudge on the glass where a hand had been. She thought then of Zelah's face, pale at the window, the grey slick of the crowded platform behind her, that last time at Nottingham Railway Station. And then she found herself recalling the urchins she used to get to pose for her all those years ago: grubby-faced and hungry, willing to sit for as long as it took to earn a penny and a cup of hot cocoa. The feeling she'd had about those children was the same feeling she had about Zelah: a tug in the chest, a tenderness – how to describe it?

Maternal?

Good God, that was it. A mother's anxiety and a mother's pride – Zelah had made her feel like a mother. Laura shook her head. Lord. What a mess.

She looked out beyond the mucky glass to the scene beyond. They were chugging through suburbia now. The train cut a swathe through urban backyards. She saw flapping washing, broken bicycles, chicken coops, and a bull terrier, chained to a gatepost, barking at the passing train, its tongue a snip of pink. Bindweed crawled over an abscess of smashed rubble.

She thought again of Zelah's face in the train window. She thought of how Harold's face looked in the bathroom mirror as he shaved in the mornings: the soot-dark eyes and angular features. The train slowed and came to a standstill at the platform.

The girl with the sharp elbows and the cello case got off, and a tall woman entered the compartment, flapping shut a large, black umbrella. Laura felt droplets spatter like spittle and reached up to wipe her cheek.

'You don't mind if I—?' the woman said, neither finishing her sentence nor waiting for a response as she parked herself in the space where the girl had sat. Laura shifted closer to the window, away from the wet brolly. 'I say,' the woman said. 'I know you, don't I?' Her voice was quite loud.

'I'm not sure,' Laura said. She didn't recognise the woman, but one could never be certain. Perhaps they'd clinked glasses at one of Barry's after-show parties? 'Are you an actress, dear?'

'Most certainly not!' The woman managed to laugh and look offended at the same time. She had bad breath and over-plucked eyebrows. 'Well, shall we get acquainted anyway, seeing as it looks like we'll be here for some time – the guard told me there's a problem with the signals so there'll be a delay.'

'What's that?' The man with the bowler sitting opposite appeared from behind his copy of the *Standard*.

'Problem with the signals, apparently,' the woman said, as if she were delighted with the opportunity to give them all the bad news. The man harrumphed and disappeared back behind his paper. The two ATS girls by the door exchanged worried glances. The woman in the far corner put down the complicated Fair Isle tank top she was halfway through, checked her watch, sighed, and picked up her wool again, knitting even faster now, as if her clicking needles could somehow speed up time.

'My name is Potts,' the woman said, holding out a hand as if they were at a dinner party, not stuck in a second-class carriage in the rain. 'Mrs Frances Potts.' Her fingers were slippery-hard, like raw chicken bones.

'Laura Knight,' Laura said. The woman – Mrs Frances Potts – let out a sound like a yelping terrier.

'Laura Knight! So that's why I recognised you!' She had the attention of the whole carriage now and she wasn't about to squander it. 'Dame Laura Knight, the famous artist – but I was only just reading about you in the paper this morning. Look!' She jumped up, knocking the umbrella sideways, and pointed a finger at the front page of the man's copy of the *Standard*. 'More Allied Successes', exclaimed the headline. Laura hadn't noticed before, but there, indeed, towards the bottom of the page and opposite an advert for a coat sale at C&A, was a picture of her. 'Ruby in canvas', it said above the portrait. Of course, it was the hoo-hah about the Ruby Loftus portrait, which had just gone up. Mrs Frances Potts was now holding up the paper for the whole compartment to see, like a schoolmistress in front of an infants' class. 'Well, how marvellous. What a very great pleasure to meet you, ma'am,' she said, before returning the *Standard* to the bowler-hatted man and sitting back down next to Laura.

'And where are you off to today, if you don't mind my asking?'

Laura reminded herself to smile. 'Not at all. I am on my way up north. I've been asked to undertake another work for the War Artists' Advisory Committee.'

'Another factory?'

'No, outdoors, this time. I'm looking forward to it.'

'Can I ask where?'

What a nosy bird this Potts woman was. 'I'm not sure I should mention – careless talk and all that.'

'Oh, quite. And your husband? It said in the paper that he wasn't well enough to attend the unveiling.'

Why did everyone keep asking her about Harold? 'A head cold, that's all. Not worth dragging him out of his sick bed to bring him to a draughty gallery, but quite well enough to cope on his own.'

'You must miss him, though?'

Laura suppressed her irritation, and folded her right hand protectively over her left, even though she was wearing gloves, and nobody would notice the missing ring. 'I do miss Harold when I have to travel away for work,' Laura said. And as she spoke she realised it wasn't a lie. She did miss him. She missed the companionship. She missed having someone to bounce ideas off, someone who understood her work. She missed the pot of tea for two, and the bickering over precious treacle. But the Harold she missed was a different Harold, wasn't he? The man she thought she was married to was different from the one she'd discovered during the

Nottingham commission. No, it was all over between them, wasn't it? It had to be.

The Potts woman was nodding, head tilted, as if she understood perfectly. Who knew, she might very well be a journalist, or married to one, Laura thought, with all these silly questions, and continued, 'It is always so hard to leave behind the ones that you hold most dear. But I remain very aware that I am far from the only woman who has to suffer the pain of separation in these trying times. And what is a few weeks away painting pictures for the War Artists' Advisory Committee, when so many of our brave young people have to face a far greater separation from the ones they cherish?' Laura said, nodding sympathetically in the direction of the two ATS girls, who smiled back at her.

There was a pause after her little speech. The Potts woman was leaning forward with a sincere look on her spiky features and the bowler-hatted man was nodding behind his paper. The elderly woman's knitting needles clicked against each other. There was a grinding jerk and the train lurched forwards a few inches then stopped again. Laura stacked up cheerful anecdotes and memories like dominoes, and prepared for the duration.

Chapter 26

George

The tired autumn air lifted his hair from his forehead. He pushed his trilby back on and turned away from the grave. He'd left a pot of chrysanthemums this time: orange and burnt-smelling. Organ music filtered out from the church, and the sound of voices: *'Praise, my soul, the King of Heaven ...'* He couldn't face church these days – all those people, the effort of it. It had been difficult enough going round to the Simmons' for dinner.

His shoes crunched on the path as he walked away. Wood smoke scented the air – a bonfire somewhere nearby. Virginia creeper twisted like flames up the rectory walls. There was the rumbling zoom of a squadron of Stirling bombers overhead. He looked up and watched them rush through the scudding clouds, like southbound geese, beyond the trees and disappear.

The package rustled in his pocket as he unlocked his car and climbed into the driver's seat. The air inside the car was still and warm. It was just a minute's drive round the corner, past a couple of houses, then he parked up again and got out. All he needed to do was to deliver the package. *Violet Smith*, it said on the front in large, looped script. *Violet Smith c/o Mr G. Handford, Esq.*

He stepped out of the car and pushed open the gate to Cloud House. There were stained-glass flowers above the red front door. But no letterbox. He cast his eye around. Why was there no letterbox? Should he wait? The church service must be nearly over. Could he catch her on her way back? He baulked at the thought of giving it to her in person. No. There would doubtless be a housemaid or someone who could pass it on to her later. He knocked on the shiny crimson paintwork, heard footsteps and the click of the catch.

The door opened inwards to reveal a woman carrying a shawl-wrapped baby. As the door opened fully, the baby began a choking mew. It sounded like a kitten. Did they all sound like that? he wondered. 'I'm sorry to bother you, but would you mind just passing this on to—' He paused and reached into his pocket and felt for the parcel as he spoke.

'Mr Handford!' the woman with the baby interrupted. He looked at her. Without the lipstick, with her hair greasy-loose and dark circles round her eyes, he simply hadn't recognised her.

'Violet?'

She nodded.

'I'm sorry, I – I assumed you'd be in church, so I simply wasn't expecting—'

'It's fine. I expect I look a little different. I haven't had much sleep, recently.'

He cleared his throat. 'I – um – thought the baby wasn't due until next month.'

'So did I.'

The baby carried on making the mewling sound, and she jigged it in her arms, saying 'Ssh–sshh, there now, little one'. Just like a real mother would, just like Lexi would have done. But she is a real mother, he inwardly berated himself. Maternal instincts trump morality, or immorality, or whatever all this sorry mess is.

'Are you well?' He didn't know what else to say.

'I suppose so.'

'And the baby?'

'Oh, she's well enough. It's just this colic. She howls every time I put her down. Mrs Scattergood said I was in no fit state for church, so I'm supposed to be helping out in the kitchen.'

'Good, good,' he said. A stupid thing to say. How was any of it 'good'? 'Will you – will you be coming back to us?'

'Of course. Any day now. As soon as they've done the medical checks and confirmed with the foster parents.'

'Then shall I tell Matron to have a bed ready?' She nodded. 'And I'll make sure you're only put on light duties in the factory for the next few weeks. How about the cranes? You'd be sitting down most of the time, then?'

'That's kind of you, Mr Handford.'

He didn't feel kind. He felt unease rising like nausea. But he looked directly at her, then, into her brown eyes with the mauve semi-circles below them, like bruises. 'I never thanked you,' he said.

'What for?'

'They said you were trying to rescue her when she – when it happened.'

'You have nothing to thank me for.' He watched her swift frown, saw her jiggle the sobbing child even faster.

'You tried.'

'I failed.' She turned away from his gaze.

It was too big. It was too big to talk about. He wondered if they ever would? Or would it become another one of those things, like Lexi's death, like Violet's baby – another one of those enormous, painful things about which one never spoke?

He could smell the scent of braising meat from inside the house, hear the sound of a clock ting-tinging the hour. 'I should probably let you get on with Sunday dinner,' he said.

'Thank you for visiting, Mr Handford,' she replied, turning back to look at him.

'George – you can call me George outside of work.'

'Thank you, George.'

'You're very welcome. I'm glad both you and the baby are well and I'll see you back at work soon, I hope.'

'Yes. Soon.'

They nodded at each other and she closed the door. In the distance was the sound of the Nottingham train chugging into the station platform.

It was only once he was already in the car, waiting at the barrier for the train to leave, that he noticed the rustle-bulge of the packet in his pocket. He hadn't even given it to her, in the end. He couldn't face going back, not now. The barriers started to lift and he released the handbrake. Never mind. It surely wouldn't be anything so important that it couldn't wait a few days until she was back at the factory, would it?

Laura

To be out in the open air again, how glorious!

The boys had driven her in their bone-shuddering tank right to the top of the hill, just so she could see the layout of the training camp and the landscape beyond. On the way they'd passed a group of swarthy-looking prisoners of war with huge red circles painted on their clothes, working the land. And Laura was reminded of the clown face she'd painted on the bomber at RAF Mildenhall. The crew had re-named it 'Circus' after she'd finished. She hoped it hadn't proved too much of a target, that big red splodge of a nose; she hoped that it had brought them luck, somehow, those dear boys. Was it still flying, her circus plane, or had it come wailing down over Europe somewhere? She hadn't heard – but then one didn't, did one?

The POWs waved their hoes in the air and cheered. 'Eye-ties,' the fair-haired gunner yelled to her over the guttural judder of the engine. 'Must've heard about Naples.' Laura smiled, and waved back.

Now they were here, up on top, the lowering sun to their right casting endless navy-blue shadows from hedgerow and armoured truck. The colours of the countryside were as concentrated as pure pigment, and the cool air sharp as lemon juice on her tongue. When they turned off the engine she could hear the rustle and twitter of sparrows in the hedge. The boys (for boys they were – the commander only just nineteen) helped her off, careful as if she were a china doll. One of them even apologised for the mud.

She walked up the hill a little further, to get a good view over the top of the tank. Down in the valley, the training camp spread out like a discarded picnic: Romney huts like sausage rolls and people scurrying ant-like. Tanks beetled a pale figure of eight on the chalky ground between the camp and the railway line. She put down her bag on one of the ice-hard ridges of mud in the shadow of the hedge, where the late autumn sun hadn't had a chance to thaw the ground – and wouldn't, until spring, in all likelihood. (She had forgotten how much colder it was here up north – it had been half a lifetime since she lived in Staithes – and she was glad of the fingerless gloves that one of the sweet WAAF girls had knitted her at the airfield last year.) Laura took her sketchbook and pencil from the bag.

Almost winter already, she thought as she drew, taking in the cool strokes of afternoon sun, threadbare trees, and empty skies.

The gunner had set up a stove near the parked-up vehicle, and began to brew up. He'd taken off his beret, and Laura noticed how his blond hair fell in a golden lick over his forehead, the way a cat's tongue curls as it yawns – such a beautiful line. Laura began to sketch, quickly, before he could notice he was being observed, and stiffen up, the way people would. There were distant growls from the tanks on the driving track, and the occasional stutter of fire from the ranges, but other than that it was peaceful up here: no horrific factory din, no roar of planes taking off or bombs dropping down, no London traffic noise. Quiet, almost. She tilted her head. Just that faint metallic whine, insistent as a mosquito. It had been with her since the Nottingham commission. Would it ever go away?

Laura flicked a page and turned her attention to the driver, a compact black-haired Welshman, who was lying on the front of the vehicle, using his folded beret as a pillow, whistling a tune she didn't recognise. She sketched his slung-out body, muscle-taut even in repose. The commander popped a head out of the hatch and called out to ask if she'd like a smoke, then, and when Laura said 'Ra-ther' he pushed himself up and out of the vehicle and lit one of his own for her, walking up the slope and popping it into her mouth as she continued to draw. They were being very kind about having her foisted on them, she thought, even though she was certain that they'd rather not have had 'Grandma' out on manoeuvres with them.

There was a chink of metal against metal, as the gunner

stirred the tea in the mess tin. Laura took a drag from the cigarette. She cross-hatched a few shadows beneath the driver's sketched body before pulling out the fag from her mouth. 'How kind of you, Corporal,' she said. He said, 'Not at all, ma'am,' and stood at her shoulder, looking out over the rolling countryside, green-gold and tapestry-rich in the late afternoon sunshine.

'God's own country,' she said. 'I tell myself that this is what we're fighting for, when I have doubts.' She sucked in more smoke, looking at the way the horizon trundled a hazy line between fields and sky.

'Doubts?'

'Forgive me. I'm an old woman. I'm not like you brave boys. I think too much, that's all. I'm sure it must all be very – very enervating for you youngsters. But for those of us who went through it last time round it's . . .' She drifted off, exhaled slowly. There were no words to describe how she felt at this moment.

'Indecent,' the tank commander said, completing her sentence. His voice was very low, not loud enough for his gunner or driver to hear. 'When I joined up it was fun,' he continued. 'I felt powerful, raging round the countryside in this thing, blowing things up. But soon – really soon – it won't be cardboard tanks, and fake buildings, it'll be the real thing, with real people on the other end of it. It plays on your mind, sometimes.' The gunner was pouring the tea into enamel mugs. Laura watched as he stabbed a hole in the evaporated milk tin.

'Why did you enlist, if you felt that way?' she said.

'What, wave the white feather? Not my style. Anyway, I didn't feel like that, not at first. It was all a bit of a rowdy game in basic training. Then you meet some of the lads who've made it back from North Africa – but it's too late to think like that, isn't it?'

'It's never too late. There's always a choice,' she said.

'If I pull out now, someone else would have to take my place, wouldn't they? In any case, I'm not a coward and I'm not going to be a deserter.' He spat, then, as he said the word, and there was a soft plop as it landed in the frozen mud at their feet.

Laura saw the gunner stir the tea in the mess tin. His face was in shadow, but a ray of sun caught his hair: perfect spun gold. Beautiful.

She and the commander carried on smoking their ciga-rettes, looking out over the rolling farmland. The driver had sat up now, knees hunched, regarding them gargoyle-like from the tank as he clutched his brew. The gunner brought two steaming mugs of tea up to them. Laura looked out at the fields through a blur of steam, sipping slowly, finishing the smoke, and letting the thoughts come:

Everyone had called Harold a conchie back in '14, Laura remembered. At first she said she understood, was steadfast and loyal. But it was so hard to stay that way, especially after his collapse. So when the offer came to leave, to go and paint young, muscular, perfect boys like this, she'd gone. She left Harold and went off with the soldiers, and then – no, it was in the past. She had nothing to feel guilty for, had she?

A sparrow-hawk was hovering in the next field, wings quivering, waiting to fall on its prey.

The gunner began to pack the stove away, and there was the tine of metal against metal. The driver turned away, sitting back on the front of the vehicle, whistling again, the tune catching the chill air. She threw her fag end to the ground, took a last gulp of tea, and thanked the commander as took her mug from her. He took a step back down the hill, then paused.

'What do you think?' he said at last. 'Do you think I should have been a conchie? Or is it better to do my bit for King and country, even if that means killing whoever I'm told to, without question or compunction?'

'What do I think?' Laura said. She drew breath. Pictures shoved through her mind as she looked back with horror over the years: a long gallery of factories and workshops where she'd been employed to picture the making of instruments to kill: sugar-coating the murderous intent of it all.

In the distance she saw the sparrow-hawk, resolute, torpedo down.

Laura looked away. 'When has it ever mattered what I think?'

The commander walked silently back to his tank. Laura tried another sketch, but it was no use. As they prepared to move out, she asked whether there were postal facilities in the NAAFI, and what time it shut. They told her they could make it back in time, if she didn't mind a bit of speed, and she said not at all, it would be fun, you'd give an old lady a bit of excitement, and they'd grinned, and laughed together as the tank bump-rushed back downhill to the training camp.

But none of them thought to ask her why she had to find a post office with such urgency, so she didn't have to tell them about the telegram that she now knew she had to send.

Chapter 27

Violet

They wouldn't tell her anything except that the foster parents would be arriving after her feed and she was to wait in the parlour.

Vi held her daughter high up against her left shoulder and swayed rhythmically from side to side, feeling the baby's warm peach-skin head against her cheek. She had a muslin cloth slung over her shoulder to protect her dress – it wouldn't do to get it dirty, not when she'd have to travel in it later. They'd already phoned the hostel to say that Violet would be back that night, and she'd be starting work again the following night.

Vi's bag was packed and ready, next to the horsehair sofa. The baby's layette was laid on top of the crocheted doily on the circular occasional table. She'd covered the box herself with scraps of nursery wallpaper that the home's staff had given her: rabbits and daffodils on a pale green background. Inside were the baby clothes she'd made: matinee jackets, caps and matching mittens and bootees laced with ribbon, in white and yellow wool – for who could tell whether her baby would be a boy or girl, they said. And when Vi had said she knew she was having a girl, and asked for some pink wool, or at least pink ribbon to lace the mitts, they'd laughed at her, said it would be asking for trouble, because what if she was wrong and had a boy? What if? Vi said. Babies didn't care what colour they wore, so long as they were warm. She'd only just finished making the blanket this morning, edging the cream and green wool squares with a line of raspberry pink. See, she said, I told you I was having a girl. The blanket was folded up on top of the clothes in the box. She'd tucked a sheet of notepaper underneath:

Dearest darling

I am sorry that I can't look after you myself just yet, but I will come and find you as soon as I am able, I promise.

Love you always, Your mummy xxx

The baby wouldn't be able to read it, but somehow it felt important to put it in. She needs to know that she is loved, Vi thought. She needs to know it deep down inside, for when someone finds out the truth – because people always do – and calls her the bastard child of a slut of a factory girl, she needs to know that she is loved more than a goddess, in this moment, and forever.

Vi hugged the warm bundle closer in, turning to kiss her head, smelling her sweet-baby scent. She was asleep already. With any luck she'll stay asleep as she's passed to the foster parents, Mrs Scattergood said. She won't even know she's been given away.

Vi continued to sway, rocking the girl, who made tiny snuffling noises in her sleep. The foster parents were prepared to look after the girl until she was school age. Vi had five years to sort herself out and the child could be reclaimed at any point during that period. And in the meantime, if she changed her mind about the arrangements, a formal adoption procedure could be started. That's what Mrs Scattergood had said this morning, looking over Vi's shoulder as she sat and signed the forms. 'Reclaimed' – Vi thought Mrs Scattergood made it sound as if her baby were lost property. In a way, she is, Vi thought, I'm sending her to the lost-and-foundling. She winced at her poor pun. When she swallowed, there was a sour taste on her tongue.

The blackout curtains were already drawn, so she couldn't see out of the parlour window, but she heard the car draw up outside Cloud House, the crunch of tyres on the icy road, the sudden silence as the engine cut out. And Vi reminded herself again that she was doing the best she could for her baby girl. Mrs Scattergood said that Cloud House only dealt with the 'right sort'. And a couple with a car, and petrol, had to be well-heeled, didn't they? Even if it were a taxi, well, that would cost a bob or two, so surely there was some comfort to be had in the fact that her baby girl was going to be looked after by a posh family, somewhere.

Vi heard one car door slam, then another, and two sets of footfalls on the front path. The doorbell drilled. Her baby shifted at the sound. 'Shh,' Vi said, hugging her tighter, seeing how her tiny fingers curled in distress at the nasty noise. She's like me, Vi thought. She balls up her fists when she's anxious. Of course she's like me. She's my baby girl. And I'm her mother.

Vi heard Mrs Scattergood's footsteps on the tiled corridor floor and the front door being opened from the inside. There were voices: a man and a woman's. They sound nice, Vi told herself. They sound well-bred. They sound like they have a wireless in the front room and a maid in the kitchen. They probably have a garden with a swing hanging from a branch of the cherry tree and rose bushes in the borders. There would always be meat on the table at dinner time and story books at bedtime and enough money to pay the doctor's bills. They can give her more than I ever had – more than I ever could.

The front door slammed shut and the voices and footsteps moved down the corridor towards the office. They'll have to sign all those forms, Vi thought. And maybe they'll be offered a cup of tea. She glanced at the clock on the mantelpiece. How long does it take to drink tea, she thought: five minutes? Ten, if they have to fill in paperwork, too.

She still had ten minutes left with her baby daughter. Vi held her close, and began to sway a faltering waltz around the room, humming loud enough to block out the sound of the ticking clock. Her jaws felt as if someone had wired them shut, aching with the premonition of grief. Oh heck.

You can get her back, Vi reminded herself. This is just until you can make enough money to support you both. She was waltzing faster now, round the little table with its gift-boxed layette. She saw the armchairs with their antimacassars, the murky watercolours of woodland scenes, the cold, empty fireplace. The clock tick-tocked like a metronome, marking time, and her baby slept soundly on, soothed by the warmth and scent of her mother, and the motion of the dance.

What if I can't earn enough money to support us both by the time she's five, what if I never can, what then?

Vi heard voices and footsteps approach the door. She looked at the clock. It hadn't been five minutes yet. They hadn't even taken tea, and she'd been cheated out of five precious minutes with her girl. 'This way, if you will.' Vi heard Mrs Scattergood's voice just outside the parlour door. She kept on waltzing.

What if I go to get her back and she's already calling these people Mummy and Daddy and doesn't know me at all? What if she's got used to the cherry tree and the bedtime stories and doesn't want me?

Vi stopped dancing as the door began to open. The baby, sensing the change, began to gripe, balling her fists and squirming. An older couple came into the parlour: grey hair and nervous smiles. They're too old to have their own, Vi thought. And once they've got my baby girl, my perfect baby girl, they'll want to keep her. They'll do all they can to keep me away. Because I'm just a good-for-nothing slut of a factory girl and I should be grateful that anyone would take on my bastard child.

Mrs Scattergood came into the room, too. She didn't even

close the door behind her. And that's when Vi realised it would just be a grab-and-go affair. She marched right over to Vi and reached out for the baby. 'Come on now,' she said. 'It's time.' Her knotted fingers grasped at the baby's torso, but Vi found she couldn't let go. The baby began to scream, her little mouth an oval of despair.

Vi saw the grey-haired woman wince, the partridge feathers quivered in her hat. 'Come on, Violet. Everything is in place. Don't be a silly girl.' Mrs Scattergood pulled again and Violet hung on tighter and the baby howled louder and Vi thought she saw the man roll his eyes at the woman.

'No,' Vi said, wrenching her child away from Mrs Scattergood's grasp. 'I've changed my mind. I'm keeping my baby.'

George

George took a card from the rack, checked the name and tossed it in the bin. Pamela Walker (née Jones), 18, from Streatham: hadn't lasted five minutes. That was happening a lot, nowadays, girls with boyfriends in the forces, married and pregnant before a forty-eight-hour leave pass was up. It was hard to retain them, at that age. He looked up at the output graph on the wall. Those blips in output could mostly be put down to sheer biology. If only there were some way of managing it, instead of losing all that expertise to maternity. He sighed.

A mental picture of a line of swaddled babies trundling along a production line like the shell casings at the Ruddington works came to mind. He shook his head and blinked the image away. He was overtired, that was all. He'd been working all hours since the raid. But what the man from the ministry didn't know, what the Chairman of the Board didn't know, was that his titanic work ethic had nothing whatsoever to do with the war effort. It was not an act of selfless commitment to the common good. Quite the reverse: he lost himself in work to try to forget about Zelah. He dreaded the day the war ended – and it would end, one day – and he'd be forced to take a holiday, visit his family, have time to sit and think.

If only the war could go on forever, he thought, and was immediately outraged at his own selfishness.

He took a deep breath in. Enough. Right, where was he? Rescheduling the night-shift rota. Then there were the purchase orders to authorise, the report for the ministry to complete, and the works council needed an answer on the proposed new health insurance scheme. With Pamela Walker off, that was five lost to maternity this month alone, so he'd need to put in a request to the Labour Exchange for cover. He put his pipe back in his pocket and ran a hand across his face. Better get on with it, man.

There was a knock at the door, then. An interruption, just as he'd got his thoughts in order. 'What is it?' he said, spinning on his heel to face the incomer.

The door opened with irritating slowness, so he couldn't

see who it was, at first, just heard a voice above the blare of the factory: 'Good evening, Mr Handford.'

'Good evening,' he said as the figure entered. He couldn't help the questioning tone of his voice. 'Violet Smith?'

'Depends who's asking,' she said, standing awkwardly, right hand still on the door handle.

And held in the crook of her left arm was a shawl-wrapped bundle: a baby.

Violet

Was it a mistake? Keeping her baby, the night-time flit to the factory —was it just another impulsive decision that would only get her into more trouble? Violet thought, as the taxi jolted them over the canal bridge.

Mr Handford had paid for the cab in advance, given her his door key, said she and the baby could sleep the night in his bed.(Their presence would not be tolerated in the hostel: Matron had been perfectly, judgementally, clear on that score.) But won't people talk? she'd asked. And he'd said about what? You'll be there and I'll be here on the night shift, what's there to say, and what do either of us care, in any case? So she'd let him call for a taxi, bundle her and the sleeping baby into the back seat and give the driver the address. So she had a bed for the night. But what about tomorrow, and the night after that, and all the other nights to come?

The stars were out, skies glitter-clear, and the moon a hazy crescent bobbing above the city centre. She held the baby tight against her, so close that she could smell the sweet-baby scent of her, even over the stale-smoke dankness of the back of the cab.

'The corner of Tunnel Road and Cavendish Crescent, is it?' The driver's jowl was a mauve oval catching the dim light from the shielded headlamps, as he half-turned towards the back seat.

Violet nodded. 'The white one with the blue door.' She spoke as if she knew, but she was just repeating what she'd heard Mr Handford say to the driver. She'd never been to this part of town before. The houses were all blacked out, but the starlight hinted at huge slabs of buildings, like a whole street full of Methodist chapels. So this was where Mr Handford lived – it was the kind of place she'd imagined the baby's foster parents would have lived: large homes with cars on driveways and a servants' entrance. Baby might even have been able to spend her childhood in a place like this, Vi thought. Baby might have had a decent start in life, if Violet hadn't stupidly, selfishly, changed her mind. And now the poor mite was saddled with a mother who had nothing: no husband, no house, no money, not even a pot to piss in. What had she done? Oh, heck.

She reached into her pocket to find the key Mr Handford had given her, and her fingers connected with the paper-wrapped package. He said it came a few days ago; he'd meant to give it to her when he visited. The car was travelling slowly now, as the driver looked out for the white house on the corner. Vi put the baby down next to her on the seat. She was fast asleep and barely stirred.

It was only a small package, hardly worth wrapping at all – whatever it contained could probably have been fitted in an envelope. Vi undid the scratchy string and the outer wrapping. Underneath was a folded sheet of paper and some-thing inside some crumpled tissue. Her fingers worried open the tissue, tearing it a little. Inside was a gold ring. Someone's wedding ring? But whose? She unfolded the sheet of paper. A cheque! She squinted down, trying to make out the letters and numbers.

The cab pulled up in front of a white cottage halfway up the hillside. 'Here you are, duck.'

Vi narrowed her eyes, trying to bring the cheque into focus. It was made out to Violet Smith, and the amount was three hundred pounds. Three hundred pounds!

'Need help?' the driver said, as the engine idled. Violet didn't answer, and he turned off the engine.

A wedding ring and about a year's wages, for her. It couldn't be true. She turned the outer sheet, to see if she could recognise the handwriting, and there, written on the reverse, a note scrawled in charcoal: *Dearest Violet. A second bite at the cherry, should you wish. All my love, Laura x*

She felt a draught of air, saw the purplish blob of the driv-er's face as he held the door open for her. 'Nah then, d'you need a hand?' he said. 'What with the baby and all?'

'No,' Violet replied, slipping the ring on her finger and

stuffing the paper deep into her pocket. 'Thank you for offering.' She picked up her sleeping baby and shunted out of the cab and into the cold night air. The driver shut the car door behind her. 'I think we'll be just fine on our own, now.'

Chapter 28

Laura

She kept her hand moving, despite the paralysing panic that threatened to halt her entirely. Oh, good Lord, Laura, what the hell are you playing at?

She tried to distract herself with the landscape, the way the headland nudged the waves like a dragon's snout, sea spray like smoke from its nostrils. Her cold, scared fingers muddled the shadows of boulders and surf as she continued to sketch. Perhaps she could work it up into a painting, later on: November in Sennen – the mauves and shades of teal of the winter skies and waves, horizon citrus-bright as lit touch paper, flashing in between as the sun westered low.

The shoreline sighed. Soon the men would be crunching down to their boats, ready to launch the first herring fleet of the season, heaving in lines and heading off into the inky night. But not quite yet. There was still daylight to be had. And the last bus from Penzance had not yet arrived.

Laura leant against the rough pebble-dash wall of the lifeboat station, in the lee of the wind, sketching, and waiting. What if he didn't come? But what if he did? The waves whispered like post office gossips and the sand shifted uneasily underfoot.

Then, a sudden screech, loud laughter, footfalls and high-pitched shouts: a swarm of children swirling down the sand towards the water's edge. Of course – school must have finished for the day. Sennen was jam-packed with evacuees, now, cockney voices twanging in the wind. As Laura looked on she saw boys 'shoot' each other with pieces of driftwood, making machine-gun noises and dropping dramatically sandwards. Some girls were searching for shells, others began making 'pies' in the damp sand by the shore. The older boys and girls were skimming ducks-and-drakes, which tilted and span out over the pewter waves. None of them so much as glanced in Laura's direction. One little girl, pixie hat tilted skew-whiff and half-unbuttoned brown coat three sizes too big, trailed along behind the others, cradling a rag doll. She looked too young to have been in school, she couldn't have been more than three or four – perhaps her mother just let her out to play with the bigger children at the end of the day whilst she was making supper, Laura thought, just as her own mother had done, sending her outside to play with Nellie and Sis, to stop her hopping on Cook's bustle, trying to ride it like a pony and getting in the way of the important meal-making business.

'Hello, dear,' Laura said. The girl looked up: huge, dark

eyes in her heart-shaped face, a crust of snot on the edge of one nostril. 'If you can stand still like that for five minutes, I'll give you a penny.' The girl blinked. Her lashes were long and curled. 'Can you do that?' The girl nodded. 'Very well.' Laura turned over a fresh sheet of her sketchbook. 'Just like musical statues, still as a statue, starting – now!'

Laura's hand gripped the pencil, swerving over the paper, taking in the diagonal of the girl's coat, which was flapping half-open in the breeze, the curl of chestnut hair across her wide forehead. Her pencil moved down, catching the jumble of clutched doll dangling down near the uneven hem of her frock.

Perhaps she could use this, Laura thought: the girl and the headland. It would be like one of her pictures from the old days, the good old Cornwall days, before there were wars, before she had to paint soldiers and airmen and factories.

She was just focusing on the way the girl's plump toddler's calves looked like stool legs pushed into the sand, when she heard it: the sound of the Penzance bus winding down the road into Sennen Cove. Laura leant over and put her pad and pencil down on the sand, then fumbled in her pocket for change. As she did so, her fingers slipped over the triangle of painted canvas that she'd kept with her all these months, since Nottingham, and she shivered.

'Here you are, dear. You did a very good job of standing still.' The girl's fingers were like peeled prawns, curling and closing over the coin. She ran off to join the others, then, shoes pad-padding on the sand, coat flying out behind her.

Laura heard the bus coming to a halt on the front. She looked over to where it idled, watching the passengers getting off, feeling the base of her throat tighten like the drawstring on an old-fashioned purse. Two women in black hats got off first, and a man with a huge sack of something. Behind them a queue of airmen and women, a grey-blue spurt of youth and vigour. There was an almost identical line of RAF men and women waiting to get on. The two cloud-coloured ribbons mingled and swirled as the colleagues exchanged greetings in passing. That was it, then: a couple of civvies and half an RAF unit, and nothing more.

So he hadn't come, despite her telegram?

No, wait.

Slowly, a tall, dark figure emerged from the doorway, uncurling a little as it went, like a flower finding sunlight. Black coat and hat: he looked like a silhouette against the bright green paintwork of the country bus – bag in one hand, hooked walking stick in the other. (A stick – did he always use a stick, nowadays? He'd used one when they went for that walk, on Easter Sunday, she remembered. But that was nearly seven months ago, now.)

Leaving her sketchbook on the sand, Laura began to walk up the beach towards him. She hadn't coiled her hair in its usual 'earphones' today, merely twisted it up into a low bun, as she used to in those early days of marriage. Now, as she strode out into the windy afternoon, it began to pull loose, hairpins scratching against her skull as the breeze tried to tug it free.

'Harold,' she called out, but her voice was whisked away, and he looked round, not seeing her, whilst the wave of air-force uniforms slid past him and onto the bus. 'Harold!' She forced her voice louder, and this time he glanced in her direction, startled. He looks like a lost old man, she thought. She stopped, then, by the path that ran up from the strand, past the sea wall and onto the road. She lifted one hand to her face. The skin was sagging, where once it had been taut and firm. And the strand of hair that had broken free and flung itself against her cheek was no longer corn-blonde, but snow-white. He is an old man, she thought. He is an old man, and I am an old woman.

Are we too old for this?

She strode up the path to the bus stop. As she arrived, the bus pulled away. Petrol fumes mingled with the salty air on her tongue. She walked straight up to him, but stopped short just a couple of feet away. '*Come-quick-to-Sennen-I-am-on-the-brink-stop-Laura*,' he said, glaring at her. 'What the hell, Laura? What the bloody hell?' He turned away, then, looking out to sea.

'We need to talk, Harold.'

'Why couldn't we talk in Malvern? I thought you were ill. I thought something was wrong!'

'Come on. I'll explain.'

He let himself be led down the path to the beach, back to her sheltered perch by the lifeboat station. She offered her arm, but he refused, instead planting his stick firmly and deeply in the sand at each step.

The sun had sunk lower now, a glowing golden ring dipping towards the edge of the sea. The wind had got up, too, white horses flecking the seascape and gulls tossed like ticker tape on a parade. The children were still playing their noisy games, but Laura had lost sight of the little girl with the doll.

They leant next to each other against the wall: dash–dash, like the start of a tally mark. Harold took out cigarettes. They were a devil to light, in the wind, and burnt fierce and quick when they did. Smoke and briny-chill Atlantic air rushed and boiled in Laura's lungs.

'Well?' Harold said, at length.

Laura sighed and tossed the remains of her ciggie down on the sand. She pushed her flapping hair off her forehead with her left hand. Out with it, Laura, get it all out into the open air. She took in a breath, ready to begin, but it was Harold who cut in: 'Where's your wedding ring? Why aren't you wearing it? Is that what this is all about? Is it over between us?'

'I think it's been over for a long time, Harold. Since the winter of '16, in point of fact.'

'You left me. Never forget that. You were the one who went off with the soldiers, with that Canadian boxer boy. Harold-the-conchie cuckolded by a soldier, that's what they were saying, remember?'

'Cuckolded? I had a commission to paint the Canadian Regiment in Surrey, that was all.'

'You shacked up with that amateur boxer boy in London. You were away for months.'

Laura didn't answer immediately, but let her gaze move to the horizon. There was that sense, as there often was on the western coastal edge, of the sea being tugged towards America, like a vast damask tablecloth about to be whisked off. She drew breath and turned back to face her husband.

'Shacked up?' she said at last. 'Who told you that? Ella? I did not "shack up" with him. I painted him.'

'Paintable, was he?'

'You don't know what you're talking about. In any case, what about the girl?'

'Who?'

'The girl. The one who "looked after" you when I was away.'

'I barely remember anything from that time, you know that.'

'How convenient.'

'What are you talking about?'

'The girl – Sarah.'

'Surely you're not suggesting?'

'Surely, you're not denying!'

'Why bring it up now?'

'What if there was a child?'

'What do you mean? Was there? Is there?'

'No! No, not any more, there isn't.' She looked back at the sea, the golden globe dipping into the dark waters. No boats out there – who would set out in this?

'I don't understand. What are you saying, Laura?'

She turned back and saw her husband's face, as if it were a

stranger's: the old man with the aristocratic nose and darkly arching brows, despite the whiteness of his hair. She cleared her throat. 'I'm saying that I will not have you thinking that I left you for a soldier, when you yourself—'

'When has it ever mattered to you what I think, Laura?' he butted in. 'After the Surrey affair, there were the circuses and the gypsies and the ballerinas and the theatre and the trip to America. Any excuse to escape me, to escape the marital bed. And you're still doing it now. I haven't seen you since April, for God's sake.'

'Yes. You have me there, Harold. I have spent the last twenty-five years avoiding married life. And you know why? Because I thought you didn't want me any more. When I came back in '17 everything had changed between us.' She could smell the dank fishy smell of low-tide weed, the rising wind was shoving it up her nostrils as she waited for his response, turning away from him again. She could hear the waves, louder now, crashing and sucking on the shoreline.

'You changed, Laura. It was you. You turned your back on our marriage. You did it then, and you're still doing it now, swanking round the country. They think I don't hear them, but I do, "Laura behaves as if she has no husband" – that's what they say. That's what they've been saying all these years.'

'Who is this "they"? Barry? Ella? K? For God's sake, I'd like to know, because all I've ever done is work damned hard to keep a roof over our heads, and you know it, Harold

Knight.' The sun had almost set. Night was coming in, bringing a gale with it. She kept looking out to sea, away from Harold, away from the schoolchildren, away from it all. Wishing she could be out there, too.

'You've been working damned hard to make sure your precious public don't forget you.'

'Oh, you think I do this to show off?' She turned back to face him.

'To a point, yes.'

'I do it to pay your ruddy doctor's bills and to put food in our mouths. That's what I did in '16, and I'm still doing it now, you foolish old man.'

'I never asked for your charity.' He couldn't even look at her as he said it, had his eyes fixed somewhere further along the shore.

'It's not charity. In sickness and in health. That's what I promised, and I kept *my* vows.'

'The implication being?'

'Oh, you know fine well what the implication is, Harold. I just want this out in the open air. I want the truth.'

'I'm going, Laura.'

'You'll do no such thing!' She put a hand out to stop him, but he wrenched free.

'No – I'm going to help those girls, see.' He flung out an arm. Laura looked to where her husband pointed. There was a gaggle of girls at the shoreline poking mittened fingers out to where a rag doll was floating, snatched and tossed by a wave. Harold began to stump across the sand.

'I'm coming, we can use my stick to hook your dolly,' he called out, and half a dozen little woolly-hatted heads turned to look.

Laura set off after him, and had almost caught up, when there was a sudden commotion from the group, a high-pitched yell as someone struggled free. 'No, let me go, I want my baby back!' And Laura watched, horrified, as the little girl she'd been sketching just a handful of minutes earlier launched herself into the roiling sea. Out she went, right into the surf, arms out to try to rescue her dolly, and Laura saw her eyes open wide, the panic in her face, as the freezing brine embraced her, grabbing her heavy coat, dragging her down. She opened her mouth to scream, but as she did so a huge wave crested and crashed, sucking her under and away from the shore. Oh, God.

'Children, quick, run for help,' Laura shouted, but the wind took her words, and the girls faltered dumbly. 'Run!' Laura screamed, catching up with the group. 'Get help, now!' and they fled as one at the urgency in her voice.

She didn't hesitate.

'Laura, no, it's too dangerous,' Harold called, trying to catch her sleeve, but she ignored him and plunged into the waves where she'd last seen the girl.

Ice cold, everywhere, heart-stopping. Don't open your mouth, Laura, don't you dare scream. Water dragging her clothes, salt in her eyes, in her mouth. Where was the girl? There, cloth in the water. Catch it, pull. Almost. Don't lose your footing, further out. A little further. There she is. But then a wave, sudden as a slap, shoving and rolling, liquid sandpaper all over her body and icy water up her nose, in her ears in her mouth, green-grey all around. Which way is up? Don't panic. Hold your breath, don't scream. Mangled and trampled and kneaded. A pause. Firm underfoot. Stand up, gasp down air, cough, breath, quick, before the next wave, Laura. There, a coat sleeve. Grab it, heave and pull. Come back to me. I am not letting you go. I am giving you a second chance. Come here and be alive. Tugging at cloth as slippery as weed and a body heavy as an anchor and lifting up, away from the greedy sea. Another wave comes, jaws snapping, but Laura has her feet this time, holds the body high and tight, cradling her safe. Now, she has her, how to get back to shore without slipping under again?

'Take it, Laura!' What's that? The hooked end of Harold's cane, Harold reaching out, tethered by a phalanx of boys. 'Take it!'

The wood, smooth-solid, something to cling to through the next wave-rush. She shoves the girl's body over her shoulder like a sandbag, begins the slow stagger up the shifting sands.

And the girl is struggling on her shoulder, coughing, vomiting. Alive – alive! People are running, shouting, hands like anemones sucking and pulling her up, away from the sea. And someone is tugging at the girl, trying to take her away. '*Thank you, oh dear God, thank you. Is she alive? She's breathing, oh thank God. Thank God.*' And the hands are pulling at the girl, and Laura won't let go, because the girl is safe with her. Who knows what will happen if she lets go? But they prise her away and Laura's arms are empty and the girl is gone.

She sinks to the sand and the tears come suddenly in a saltwater rush, and the sobs heave like the wind in the waves and it's all over. All over. '*Zelah, Zelah, Zelah.*' She chokes out the words, snot and tears running warm rivulets through her old, wrinkled cheeks.

A presence, next to her. An arm round her shoulders. A familiar voice. 'Dearest. You saved her, my brave, foolish wife.'

Laura spat out water, wiped a hand over her wet face. Looked at the dark beach, crowded as a summer's day, the sunset casting odd shadows, like a negative of a photographic print. Someone put a blanket round her shoulders, thrust a metal flask into her hands, guided it to her lips. A sip of fire. The last rays of sun piercing the grey skies. Heaving upwards. A guided shuffle up the beach. Colours all shadowy, jumping and spinning, or was it her dizzy mind making it so?

'Let's get you in the warm and out of these wet clothes. Where are we staying?'

'Ocean View. The yellow one.' She tried to point but found she could no longer lift her arm above waist height, and let it fall, trembling, to her sodden skirts. 'You're sure she'll be all right, the girl?'

'Yes, they're taking her up to the RAF medical centre now, but she's breathing, she'll be fine.'

'We saved her?'

'You saved her.' Her husband's arm was firm and strong at her back as they made their way towards the hotel. 'She's got a second chance, lucky thing.'

Laura gulped in the cold air, twitching like a netted herring. Her arms were empty without the little girl to hold. 'A second chance?' she said.

Chapter 29

Violet

Vi heard the sound of a lorry pulling up at the kerb behind her and turned to look. She was almost home now, the baby asleep in the brand-new Silver Cross pram, so big they'd had to travel down in the guard's van with all the bicycles, but Vi hadn't cared.

She was just on her way from the station, passing the King's Arms. Up ahead, on the opposite side of the street, she could see Mr Lavery behind the counter at the chippy, serving a knot of young women. She was thinking about maybe popping in and buying a load of chips for them all, as a surprise. It wouldn't be the only surprise, either, she thought, glancing down at the baby's scrunched-up apricot face nestled amongst the lace-edged covers.

She turned when she heard the lorry, saw a hatless man jump down from the cab, slouch-swagger towards the pub – something in his gait made her pause a moment. He hadn't noticed her, and if she kept on walking he probably wouldn't clock she was there at all.

'What a coincidence, meeting you here,' she called down the street, and watched as he looked in her direction, faltering, one hand already on the cracked black paint of the pub doors.

'Vi?'

'Hello, Frank.'

She waited for him to come to her, along the cracked kerbstones, treading on the lines. He looked smaller than she remembered, older, too, his dirty blond hair beginning to inch away from his creased forehead. He drew close. 'I thought you'd gone, Vi. I thought—' He stopped speaking and looked into the pram.

'You thought what, Frank?' Her hands gripped the smooth rubber on the pram handle as she watched him lean over and peer into the muddle of sheets.

He cleared his throat. 'Yours?' he muttered.

'Of course she's mine. Who else's would she be? Her name is Zelah, in case you were wondering.'

He cleared his throat again and straightened up. 'She's a little darling, Vi,' he said, and Vi thought she heard a catch in his voice. She knew what he was thinking: a whole year since she'd done a bunk after that night in the alley, and here she was, back in town, baby in tow.

'Yes, she's a pretty thing, ain't she? Blonde, like her dad.'

'Vi, I didn't know—' he began, but she cut in.

'How's Frank Junior, and how's your missus these days?'

She saw him start, pull into himself. 'What, you thought I didn't know?'

He shook his head, the sunset behind the gas works casting his face in partial shadow. 'We lost him, Frank Junior. Scarlet fever – Gloria hasn't been the same, since.' Frank's features disintegrated and then reformed themselves into position as he spoke. I used to kiss those lips, Vi thought. I used to kiss those lips and run my hands down inside his jacket, around his waist.

'I'm so sorry,' she said, and reached over to pat him on the sleeve with her left hand. The gold ring caught the lowering sunshine. 'I lost someone myself recently,' she said, leaving her hand on his sleeve. She saw him look down, knew he'd seen it. 'Zelah's dad was a Polish pilot,' she said.

The chippy doors flew open, letting out the hot-fat-vinegar smell, along with the knot of girls, talking nineteen-to-the-dozen through their chip-filled cheeks as they traipsed along the pavement opposite. She took her hand off his sleeve, looked up at his face. His eyes were grey, just like the pilot's had been, that night in the hostel.

Frank blinked. Was it relief or disappointment that washed over his face as he spoke? 'I'm sorry for your loss,' he said, running a hand through his hair and tousling it up, the way she remembered it. He took a packet of Woodbines from his pocket. 'Where did you go, anyway?' he said, beginning to sound and look more like the old Frank, the one who'd liked a joke over the bar in the King's Arms. He held open the packet: 'They said you'd been sent to Coventry, but I never believed them.'

'No, not Coventry. Somewhere up that way, though.' She smiled and waved away the offer of a fag. 'I did night shift – better paid.' In the pram Zelah shifted and made a sound like a small miaow. She'd be due a feed, soon, Vi thought. 'Anyway, don't let me keep you,' she said, starting to shift the pram forward.

'You back for good?' Frank said, flicking ash into the gutter. 'You might be able to get some shifts in the King's Arms, if your ma can help out with the little one?'

'Oh no, I'm only on leave,' Vi said. 'I'm back in work end of the week. They're opening a nursery in the factory, see – so many women on munitions these days – and I'm to be the manager.' Zelah was beginning to make gurgle-cough noises. She'd wake up hungry soon. 'Better go. She hasn't half got a set of pipes on her, this one,' Vi said, and she leant across to kiss Frank on his stubbled cheek, rough as brickwork against her lips. 'Goodbye, Frank.'

And she set off, not looking back to catch his expression, but sensing him watching her, as she walked up the street, past the chippy and the shelter, past the bombed-out house on the corner and the shuttered-up fishmonger's, all the way. Everything's just the same, Vi thought, pushing the pram over the broken kerbstones. Everything looked the same, smelled the same, nothing had changed at all, except her: the girl who'd got a second bite at the cherry.

Chapter 30

Laura

'Did you order fruit scones, or the plain?'

'Keep still, Harold. Your head dips when you speak.'

Harold closed his mouth and Laura placed her stick of charcoal back on the paper. She was using charcoal, chalk and watercolour, just as she'd used for the factory poster. If she could get a decent likeness then she'd work it up in oils afterwards. Harold was letting her paint him, after all these years.

There was the usual muted chatter and chink of china in the British Camp Hotel tea room. Outside, the sky was a slice of amber. Inside, the air was fragrant with the applewood log on the fire. Laura pulled the charcoal over the paper, tracing the line of her husband's jaw. Her watercolour tin lay beside her on the table. She'd move it, when the girl came with the tea things.

She put down the charcoal and picked up a piece of chalk, working at the highlights, where the firelight silver-plated the planes on his face. He kept very silent and still – an excellent model, as it turned out, even though it had taken him fifty years to allow her to discover that for herself. She pulled a forefinger across the paper, stroking his face and softening his features.

Laura paused and squinted at her work, her head on one side. Had she finally captured Harold: the heavy brows, the long nose, the dark eyes behind his spectacles? Had she finally captured Harold, after all these years?

She put down the chalk and Harold shifted in his chair. 'You can relax for a moment, if you'd like,' Laura said, still regarding his face on the paper, unsure of what she'd drawn. 'Do you think I have time to make a start on the watercolour before tea arrives? It does always seem to take an age, even when they're not busy. Sometimes one wonders what goes on in that kitchen.'

'I shouldn't. She'll be here any minute,' Harold said, taking out a packet of cigarettes. 'Might just have time for a smoke, though. Care for one?' He pushed the packet across the table towards her.

'Actually, I think I'd rather get on, before the light changes. Put that down and take up your position again, please.'

Why did she have to be so defiant, Laura thought, even now? He was probably right about the tea things, but she always had to stick out her chin and do the opposite. She lifted the lid on the watercolour tin and dipped her brush in the jam jar of water next to it on the table. The carmine would be too pink, wouldn't it? Even for the ruddy shadows on the fireside edge of his face. She mixed it with a little yellow, loaded her brush and looked across at her husband's face. From behind her she heard the thud of the kitchen doors and Kipper yapping at something. She swept the brush in an arc, describing the flush of firelight on Harold's features. She had the brush poised again, ready to run a wash round his jawline, when she was shoved from behind and there was a clatter-crash as a tea tray thudded to the floor.

'Oh, I'm terribly sorry, Missus Knight. I must have caught my shoe on the chair leg there. I do apologise – are you all right, Missus Knight?'

'I'm fine, dear. No harm done. It was only a sketch,' Laura said, to soothe the girl. But the brush had splodged against the paper, making a pinky-yellow welt on Harold's face, as if someone had slapped him, very hard. Harold was up and out of his chair, helping the girl with the dropped tea things. Laura tore off the spoiled sheet and took it over to the fire, kneeling down on the hearth. The flags were hard beneath her knees. The girl and Harold were fussing with the things. Someone had gone to get a dustpan and a damp cloth.

Laura reached into her pocket and took out the scrap of painting, still there, after all these months: the painted eye, soot-dark, with a heavy, arched brow. She held it next to the spoiled watercolour. Then she laid it over the top: the arch of the brow, the distance between the eye and the bridge of the nose. If you covered up the watercolour of Harold with the fragment of Zelah, it was an almost perfect match.

413

Laura could hear the palaver of the tea tray calamity continue behind her. She took the canvas and the watercolour and fed them both into the flames, watching as the features combined, blackened, curled up and disappeared into nothing but ash and smoke.

She felt Harold's hand on her shoulder. 'Here, let me help you up. They're going to get more tea things.' She let him help her to her feet. 'I'm sorry about all that,' he said, as she stood upright. And he bowed over and kissed her hand, in that gallant, theatrical way that had been the fashion when they were young. He kissed her left hand, in the place where her wedding ring should have been. 'I'm so sorry, Laura,' he said, again, straightening up and looking into her eyes. 'Shall we start afresh?'

George

The half moon was sliding westwards. Low clouds pulled sideways, alternately blotting and revealing a smattering of stars. The rooftops of the terraced houses in the Meadows were a dark scribble, and the River Trent uncoiled like the tail of one of the dolly knots they used to sling the gun barrels to the cranes. George imagined a giant hand reaching down from the skies and giving the river rope a tug, and watching as the tangled mess of slipknots gave way, and everything falling apart.

Everything falling apart.

One day it all would, he thought, looking out into the Nottingham night. Hitler was done for, the papers were full of it. It was only a matter of time before the war was over. And then what? Who needs anti-aircraft guns in peacetime? No more war effort. No more night shift. What then? What the hell would he do when it was all over?

George thought of the empty house on the Park Estate, the moored-up dinghy at Trent Lock, Lexi's grave in Attenborough churchyard. The peacetime years stretched ahead, dark, flat and empty as the farmland beyond the riverbank.

He rubbed his hands together and blew on them. Should have worn gloves up here. It was still chilly at night on fire watch duty, even though spring was on its way. He heard the door to the stairwell open behind him. 'You're back early. No need to hurry back on my account, though. Adolf's otherwise engaged this evening.' He took his pipe out of his pocket and tapped the remains of the old baccy out on the wall, hearing footsteps coming towards him across the factory roof. 'I'm quite all right, really, Alfie, you get back down to the canteen and have another cuppa in the warm.'

'Mr Handford?' He turned, then. Because it wasn't Alfie Perkins' voice.

'Violet?'

'I thought you might like this.' There she was, in the old beige coat of hers, holding two mugs of steaming tea. 'Mrs Whiley's minding the night nursery so's I can have a break. Alfie said I'd find you here. Thought you could use a hot drink.'

She walked over and put the mugs down on the parapet. He stuffed his pipe back in his pocket. 'Thank you. How thoughtful.' The mug was warm in his cold palms, and the tea ran hot-sweet down his throat. He saw her pick up her own mug and turn as if to go. And with a sudden rush he realised that that wasn't what he wanted. 'How are things going, down there?' He stalled her with a question.

'Very well, thank you for asking. We've got six at present on this shift, although Mrs Fry is due any day, so that'll take us to seven in a few weeks' time.'

'And how are you coping?'

'The babies are calm as anything. Strange, you'd think it'd bother them, all that noise, but they seem to like it – I manage to get the odd forty winks in myself, between feeds.'

'I should come down and take a look, do a report for the Board.'

'That would be – nice.'

He noticed how she hesitated when she replied. He looked at her, holding her mug like a prayer, steam blurring her features. She had always been just another factory girl to him, Zelah's mouthy colleague – a nuisance, at best. But she was making a real success of this workplace nursery – production was better than ever since the women could come back to work with their little ones.

'I should probably leave you to it,' she said, removing the mug from her lips. A faint breeze lifted her coat collar, and it flapped against her face like a wing. She began to turn away.

'Don't go,' he said, watching as she paused. 'Finish your tea, at least.'

She smiled, then, and he noticed how her left cheek dimpled. 'If you're sure?'

'I could use the company, to be honest.'

So she stood beside him, looking out across the ragged edges of the city, where railway tracks frayed farmland and waterways hemmed terraced rows, and the colliery belched smoke.

She lit two cigarettes and passed one to him, without asking if he wanted it. The smoke was a warm curl inside as he inhaled. Together they sipped tea and finished their cigarettes and George felt no need to say or do anything other than just be with her, looking out into the night.

It was Violet who flicked her fag away first and drained the dregs of her drink. He waited for her to take her leave. It had been a comfort to have someone to share the empty skies with, just this once, he thought. Then – 'I miss her,' Violet said, and he felt a hand reach for his, a warm contrast to the cool concrete beneath his fingertips.

'So do I,' he said, taking her hand in his – small and smooth. 'Every moment.'

And they stayed like that, hands clasped, looking out into the midnight skies: fire watching, together.

Author's Note

Although *The Night Raid* is entirely fictional, certain real-life characters provided a catalyst for the story, as did actual wartime locations.

Dame Laura Knight was a war artist in both the First and Second World Wars. Her husband, Harold Knight, was also a well-known painter from the 'Newlyn School'. (Anyone who has read Barbara Morden's excellent biography *Laura Knight – A Life* will know how much I am indebted to her. Janet Dunbar's biography *Laura Knight* also provided valuable insights, as well as Laura's own autobiographies *Oil Paint and Grease Paint* and *The Magic of a Line*). Director of the National Gallery Sir Kenneth Clark – known to friends as 'K' – chaired the War Artists' Advisory Committee, which commissioned and acquired work from more than 400 artists during WWII.

During WWII there was a Royal Ordnance Factory (ROF) in Nottingham on the site of what is now the NG2 business park. Around 14,000 (mostly women) workers put in 12-hour shifts, making anti-aircraft guns. After the war the factory made Centurion tanks, and finally closed in 2001. Nearby ROF Ruddington, a shell-filling factory and ammunition depot, was decommissioned in 1945 and the land converted into Rushcliffe Country Park in the early 1990s.

The Flying Horse Inn, Nottingham, was a popular drinking spot for the Polish pilots who trained at RAF Hucknall. The pub itself no longer exists, but the frontage remains, as the entrance to a shopping arcade. Other actual locations in and around Nottingham include Laura's childhood home opposite Forest Fields (there's a blue plaque above Ethel Villas), Angel Row (Bromley House Library still exists, but the Ritz Cinema closed a few years ago), The Park Estate, Wilford Village, Attenborough Village, and Trent Valley Sailing Club.

Laura and Harold Knight spent much of the war living in the British Camp Hotel (now the Malvern Hills Hotel) in the Malvern Hills.

Six army camps lay within three miles of Barnard Castle in County Durham in WWII, including a Battle School for training tank crews near Stainton Grove. The last army camp closed in the 1970s.

Scores of city children were evacuated to Sennen Cove on the Cornish coast in wartime. The fishing village also hosted RAF Sennen (otherwise known as Skewjack), which operated Chain Home – an early warning radar system. The RAF camp closed in the 1970s.

*

Laura Knight's famous painting 'Ruby Loftus Screwing a Breech Ring' provided the stepping-off point for the creation of *The Night Raid,* which inserts an entirely fictitious timeline and set of circumstances into the renowned war artist's life. Laura Knight fans will know that 'Ruby Loftus' was first exhibited on 30th April 1943 at the Royal Academy Summer Exhibition. For the purposes of this story, the date and location of the painting's unveiling have been altered – I hope readers and Laura Knight devotees won't mind a touch of artistic licence in this instance.

If you're interested in discovering more of the books and films that inspired *The Night Raid*, take a look at my website: http://clareharvey.net

Acknowledgements

Massive thanks go to *all* friends and family who have had to put up with me during the writing process.

Here are some who deserve a particular mention: Phill Brookes for explaining about capstan lathes and the workings of munitions factories; Alex Walker for providing useful information on WWII bombs; Rob Murphy for mentioning dolly knots; Tessa Carpenter for reminding me of boarding school, and Caroline Mullen, who suggested I iron out a plot wrinkle by having a scene with a giant eagle swooping down and carrying everyone off (sorry, that bit got edited out, Caroline . . .).

And special thanks to my fabulous agent, Teresa Chris, for her wise advice to 'lose the butcher's shop' (she will know what this means) – as usual, she was right.

Clare Harvey

The English Agent

How far will two women go to survive a war?

Having suffered a traumatic experience in the Blitz, Edie
feels utterly disillusioned with life in wartime London.
The chance to work with the Secret Operations Executive
(SOE) helping the resistance in Paris offers a fresh start.
Codenamed 'Yvette', she's parachuted into France and
met by the two other members of her SOE cell.
Who can she trust?

Back in London, Vera desperately needs to be made a
UK citizen to erase the secrets of her past. Working at the
foreign office in charge of agents presents an opportunity
for blackmail. But when she loses contact with one agent
in the field, codenamed Yvette, her loyalties are torn.

'Brimming with intrigue, heart-pounding
action . . . and a cast of dynamic characters'
Lancashire Evening Post

Paperback ISBN 978-1-4711-5057-9
eBook ISBN 978-1-4711-5058-6